LOVE, POLITICS AND POSSIBLY MURDER

LOVE, POLITICS AND POSSIBLY MURDER

by

Jane Ions

First published in 2022 by
Bluemoose Books Ltd
25 Sackville Street
Hebden Bridge
West Yorkshire
HX7 7DJ

www.bluemoosebooks.com

British Library Cataloguing-in-Publication data
A catalogue record for this book is available from the British Library

Paperback 978-1-910422-65-6

Printed and bound in the UK by Short Run Press

Chapter One: January

My close friend Jen has announced she is getting married for the second time. She says a second marriage is a wonderful thing because it offers the hope that you might actually get it right this time. Also, it gives you the chance to update your wedding photographs, which can be so embarrassing after thirty years that you can barely stand to look at them.

I never really got to know Frank, Jen's first husband, because she kept him under wraps. She said she didn't trust him in public. He was liable to say things that made her insides clench together in embarrassment, and he never understood the indelicacy of an audible fart. He was inclined to share too much of his own medical detail and was not above describing his sputum samples. He could not be persuaded that it is not always a good idea to speak your mind. He and Jen didn't socialise much, not after he told their hostess at a dinner party that she had male pattern baldness. Frank died two years ago, to Jen's enormous relief, and since then she has been looking for a man she could leave the house with.

Jen hasn't known Sam very long at all. She met him only just over a year ago and they have had a whirlwind romance. In fact, a whirlwind may be too sluggish a meteorological phenomenon to describe their romance: it would be more apt to liken it to a hurricane or a tornado, it has blown them both off their feet and into each other's arms with such force. They fell in love before each knew whether the other took milk with their tea. Jen says all those years of being with the wrong man have been the best preparation for knowing when she is with the right one.

She says she doesn't need to give the relationship time because her previous experience short-circuits the need to wait and see, and she and Sam feel that at nearly fifty years old they ought to know what they're doing. So she is planning the wedding she wished she had had first time around.

It has crossed my mind to caution Jen that there may be a whole other set of irritations associated with a new man and a new relationship. There are, after all, so many ways in which men can be irksome; she is unlikely to have seen them all in Frank. There may be many more irritations lying in wait for her in this new relationship. But although this is no doubt true, it would certainly put a downer on things for me to talk like this to Jen, and it does nothing to address the necessity to update her wedding photos. Jen is looking forward to expunging her mullet hairstyle from the record, and she is convinced that Sam is the man she has been waiting for all of her adult life thus far. So I've decided to keep quiet.

Sam is Chrissy's father, and Chrissy is our lodger, which means we are linked to him twice, and have got to know him a little over the last year. He seems a likeable, sensible man, quite charmed and even mesmerised by Jen, who is apparently nothing like his first wife. I can believe that, because Jen is nothing like anyone I've ever known

She has asked me if I would read something at her marriage ceremony. I said, yes, of course, and asked her what she would like me to read. She said she would leave it up to me, she knew I would choose just the right thing. I was an English teacher, after all. I asked her to give me a clue about where to start looking for an appropriate reading. Did she want something from the Bible or Shakespeare or Jane Austen or Winnie the Pooh, or what? She said nothing too heavy. Something short and snappy from Shakespeare might fit the bill.

I suggested sonnet number 116, *Let me not to the marriage of true minds Admit impediments*. But she said, 'God Sally, I said short and snappy,' so it's back to square one.

I asked Laura if she had any ideas for readings at wedding services when I saw her yesterday. She said there was a Marvin Gaye single called 'Baby Don't You Do It' which might have been appropriate at her own wedding. I looked shocked, and in response Laura laughed, so maybe she hadn't been serious. It's difficult to know sometimes, with Laura. I'm her mother, but that doesn't seem to help me understand her. I tell myself that Laura is very independent-minded, but really, sometimes I think she's just strange.

Anyway. After dinner this evening the phone rang, and it was Jen again. She said that on my advice she'd been flicking through *Winnie the Pooh* and had come across a passage which includes the words, 'A day without a friend is like a pot without a single drop of honey left inside,' and what did I think about reading that?

I advised against it. I said in my opinion it was both vacuous and pointless, it was sentimental drivel, unworthy of the occasion. She said on the contrary, she thought it was quite appropriate for the occasion. I said it would be appropriate for the occasion of a teddy bears' picnic where most of the teddy bears were absent because they had more interesting things to do. She said she thought it was rather sweet. I said I could read it, but I would retch. We've agreed to meet up in a week, and I'll bring some suggestions for readings with me. This is only January and the wedding isn't until April. Plenty of time.

***

Dear Ella,

You sounded so down in your last letter, I thought a bit of scandalous gossip might cheer you up and I have some for you – read on, you won't be disappointed, and neither will you think of our dear Mrs Prime Minister in the same way, ever again. Honestly, there are times when it is almost worth being married to a politician.

Bill told me last night that the PM is under tremendous strain and – now you mustn't tell anybody this – Bill is pretty sure she is having a relationship with the Foreign Secretary that goes way beyond the professional. Yes – a wonderful piece of gossip – I know you'll enjoy it – I'm loving it! I won't mention the name of the Other Party, but he's the FS, so you'll know who I mean. Bill says he saw the PM after she had been with the FS, and she was very flustered and dishevelled. And apparently, there have been Other Signs. I quizzed Bill on these Other Signs but he wasn't very forthcoming. He said there has been talk of irregular items in the PM's diplomatic box. Sex toys and, of all things, a parsnip.

I have to say, it cheered me up no end last night to see the PM and the FS on the News and imagine them in a threesome with a parsnip. They seem a very unlikely couple to have got the hots for each other. She is such a statuesque goddess in appearance, and bless him, he looks like an extra on the set of War of the Zombies. I think he only has two facial expressions, blank and very blank. For you or I that would make life difficult, but it's surprising how far you can get in the Foreign Office with just those expressions. And if a parsnip can turn our PM on, maybe the bar isn't set very high. If nothing else, it adds another dimension to Prime Minister's Questions. Mum's the word Ella, but I'll keep you posted, discreetly of course.

In answer to your questions, yes, we do still have our waifs and strays living with us, although they are all very robust of course, and they are all working, just not in the kind of jobs that will pay rent or a mortgage on properties around here. And yes, it is nice for Dan to have his friends around him while he's living at home, and sometimes it's nice for me too. I really like his girlfriend Chrissy, she lives with us more or less permanently now and her father, Sam, has proposed to my good friend Jen. So there is a wedding in the offing.

Yes, the taxidermy parlour is still doing well. Baz and Sophie are becoming quite expert at stuffing moles. Obviously, it's not ideal that it takes place at the back of our utility room, but again, if Baz had to pay for workshop premises the enterprise would not make any economic sense at all. Sophie is Baz's assistant and has really taken to taxidermy. She enjoys the work and says it's entirely different from her job as a carer in the nursing home, so that's good, isn't it?.

Bill is fine. You're his mother, so you know how philosophical he is. He took losing the leadership election in his stride, and that seems ages ago now, so we have moved on. Bill is just as busy as ever, and now, of course, there is this other Scandalous Thing to make his life interesting. And ours too!

I'm quite happy to continue to correspond by letter. I agree, letters have a substance and a permanence that emails will never have, but I think you're wrong about email being a passing fad. It's here to stay, Ella, even though letters can endure for centuries, and emails are puffs of electronic smoke by comparison. Just think, if the Bloomsbury Group had emailed each other rather than written letters, we would have no idea now who slept with who.

Laura sends her love, and little Harry. I think she may have settled down a bit, thank the Lord. She has been very unsettled since Harry was born. Motherhood is such a shock to the system, I'm sure you'll agree. My system is still in shock and it's 22 years since I last gave birth.

Well, Ella, I'm going to have to run. I've got to go to school this afternoon for a session with Lee, my mentee. You remember – I told you about him and you diagnosed him as 'very naughty'? Sadly, there's no such thing as 'naughty boys' now Ella. I don't know where they went. I miss them.

With love,

Sally xx

***

Re my role in Jen's wedding ceremony, I've spent a bit of time today thinking about what is important in a marriage. If I can identify some of the essential ingredients of a successful marriage, that might help me in my search for an appropriate reading for Jen's wedding. Obviously, there's mutual love and support and willingness to compromise, we know all about that until we're sick of hearing about it. But there are other things too, like whether it's okay for Saturday nights to be ruined by Match of the Day, less poetic things maybe, but important nevertheless.

I don't often look to Lee for inspiration. In all the time I have been mentoring him at the school where I used to teach he has inspired me to do very little other than wash my hair when he gave me head lice a year ago. But because it was on my mind, I asked him today about his thoughts on what makes a successful marriage. Personal relationships are not Lee's forte, but I thought it might do him some good to explore this field a little.

So I told Lee that I'd been thinking about marriage and the reasons why it sometimes works out fine and sometimes doesn't, and I asked him, 'What do you think is important in a good marriage, Lee?'

He thought about it. 'Marriage? What? Like, what makes people start yelling at each other?'

'I suppose what I'm saying is, what makes a marriage work? What things are essential for a good marriage? I just wondered whether you'd ever thought about it?'

'Fuck's sake Miss. It's not exactly important.'

'Well, I think I'd have to disagree there, Lee. Surely it's important to know what makes relationships work?'

He looked at me, frowning. 'Why're you asking me? Ain't you got none of your own friends to help you sort your marriage out?'

'I'm not thinking about my own marriage, Lee. I'm just thinking about marriage in general.'

'You're mental, Miss,' he said.

So we changed the subject to West Ham United, about which he has much more focused views.

When I got home, I asked Sophie the same question. Sophie lives with us now, along with her boyfriend Baz, who I have recently discovered is not called Baz at all, but Neil. I offered Sophie and Baz temporary accommodation until they were able to find viable alternatives, and I have now established that far from being viable, the alternatives are barely able to draw breath.

Our house has never been converted into flats, as many of the houses along this road have been over the years. We have accommodation over four floors, and since Dan came home from university just over a year ago, the house has acquired additional occupants by osmosis, rather than design. The first of these was Gentle Rain, a former girlfriend of Dan's, who lived with us for a while until Dan discovered she was an imposter. Her name is not Gentle Rain at all, but Victoria, and neither is she impoverished, as she professed to be. She is actually very wealthy. Her family is titled, they spent every summer on their ocean-going yacht visiting exotic places you can't know about unless you have lots of money in an off-shore account. Apparently she was rebelling against this massively irksome level of family privilege and went off radar for a while, and struck up a relationship with Dan, and managed to convince him she was borderline destitute. Once Dan discovered her true identity, he was unable to forgive her this deceit, and broke off their relationship. In similar circumstances I'd have been a lot more forgiving and would probably have thrown a party and, mindful of the yacht, bought a snorkel. But Dan is much more principled than I, unfortunately.

So Victoria left us, and then Dan and Sophie struck up a relationship which endured until they discovered they had nothing in common but a love of liquorice allsorts. Dan's current girlfriend, Chrissy, an amateur thespian, spends most of her time with us now. She is a lovely girl and just as authentically skint as she claims to be, which is wonderful.

Sophie is now in a relationship with Baz, our resident taxidermist.

'Sophie,' I said, once she was settled at the table with the pot noodle she has every afternoon, 'what qualities do you think make for a successful marriage?'

'Are you saying Baz and me should get married?'

'No. No I wasn't saying that, I was just wondering if you had any thoughts on what makes a successful marriage. Jen wants me to read something at her wedding, and I'm just looking around for ideas. That's all.'

'Oh right,' she said. 'Well, I think living in the same house helps. Baz and I wouldn't even know each other if we weren't both living here.'

This is undeniably true. Since Sophie and then Baz moved in here, a touching romance has blossomed between the two of them. Other things have blossomed too, like the small but productive taxidermy business which they are preparing to operate from the back of my utility room. Baz and Dan are employed by an 'elite-space' landscape gardening firm, but Baz operates a freelance mole eradication service in his spare time. He saw a business opportunity after discovering how receptive gardeners are to the idea of having their moles stuffed once they have been caught. Baz's taxidermy skills have improved in recent months, and his stuffed moles no longer look as if they have swallowed two kilos of Lego. As he says, it's amazing what you can learn to do on You Tube. Last week Sophie presented me with one of their best efforts so far, and it's now displayed on our kitchen window sill. The position of the mole's two front paws makes it look as if it's praying, which is entirely appropriate.

'Actually Mrs Forth, it's funny you asked that about marriage, because I was thinking Baz and I might get married,' said Sophie.

'But where would you live, Sophie? You don't have a house.'

'No,' she agreed, 'we'd just live here, with you and Mr Forth. Like now.'

'Sophie,' I said, 'I think it would be better to wait until you and Baz can get your own place, before you get married.'

'Mmm,' she looked doubtful. 'Not sure. It'll be ages before we get enough money for our own place. I've only got £383.34 in my savings account and I've been putting money in since last Christmas. We'll have to sell a lot of stuffed moles. But we could stuff other things as well, don't you think? Like people's dogs.' She considered the idea. 'We could offer to do that for people when they die, and stuff them. The dogs I mean, not the people. What do you think of that? D'you think it would work?'

I wished I hadn't asked her about what makes a successful marriage. I said, 'Sophie I'm not sure if I want you and Baz stuffing dogs at the back of my utility room.'

'I meant just small dogs,' she said. 'We'd be on for ages stuffing a labrador.'

***

Dear Ella,

I thought I would just follow up my phone call of last night with a letter. I know you don't hear so well on the phone these days.

Sorry for sounding so urgent and panicky on the phone to you last night. I didn't mean to alarm you. I think the confusion arose when I said 'the situation is dire' and you thought I'd said 'the sitting room's on fire.' Must have been a combination of your wonky hearing aid, and some dry crackling on the line, which didn't help. Anyway, good job we managed to clear that up before you rang 999.

I do hope by now you've managed to find my last letter and disposed of it! Really, I shouldn't have been so indiscreet about you-know-who having a you-know-what, and as I explained on the phone, if the letter were to fall into the wrong hands there would be all hell to pay! It would put my mind at rest enormously if you could just find my letter and burn the damn thing. Or put it through your shredder, the one you use for any piece of paper with your name or address on it. While you're at it, you'd better do the same to this letter. If someone finds this one they might start looking for the other one!

Of course, I trust you not to say anything, absolutely! But the crucial thing is, I should never have committed the information to paper. I'm an idiot Ella, I should have known better, but if you find the letter you can save the day!

Lots of Love,

Your foolish,

Sally xx

***

I vowed I would never agree to anything Judith suggested to me ever again, not since my charity-swim-turned-breakfast-TV debacle of last year that she was responsible for, but yet again she has persuaded me to get involved with something against my natural inclination. I met her for one of our combative M&S afternoon teas, and she told me about her local history class.

'You should come along,' she said. 'A very nice bunch of people go. You're too family-focused, you've said so yourself, you need things to change. Remember how upset you were after the election when everything went tits up for you and Bill?'

'Well thanks for thinking of me Judith,' I said, 'and for reminding me how I felt after everything went tits-up. But when I said my life was driving me mad and things had to change, I wasn't thinking in terms of solving it by joining a history evening class. I had more momentous changes in mind.'

'Well, you might have done,' she said, 'I don't know, do I? I'm just one of your oldest friends. From school days, for heaven's sake. But I do know you haven't made any changes at all yet, and you've had long enough. You're still sitting at home with Dan and his crazy pals, and trying to make some progress at school with that crackpot Lee who gives you infestations. Why don't you just start to make some changes in a small way? Get your hair done properly, join an evening class, meet some new people. Honestly, I do know what I'm talking about. I did a counselling course once, you know. To learn how to help people, and – what's that word? Where you pretend you care about how someone else is feeling?'

'Empathise.'

'That's it. Anyway, I managed to finish the course, even though it was a load of bollocks.'

'But why would I join a history evening class, Judith? I'm not particularly interested in history.'

'Who cares about that?' She snapped a shortbread biscuit in half to show how little she cared about that. 'Who cares what you think about history? It's not about that. You don't join a history evening class because you're interested in history. You join to see who else has joined.'

So. I'm going along to the history class tomorrow night. Judith just goes on and on and on until you either fall out with her, or avoid her for ever, or swallow arsenic, or do as she says. It's intensely annoying.

I told Dan when he came in from work that I was going to a history evening class with Judith tomorrow. He put a comforting hand on my shoulder and said he hadn't realised things were that bad. Sophie offered me some advice when she came home. She said whenever she wants to get out of doing something she doesn't want to do, she usually tells people she has terrible period pains, and I could try that, if I wasn't too old. Chrissy said a history class sounded like a great idea, she didn't know what the problem was, and Baz said there might be a pub to go to afterwards.

Bill said nothing, because Bill isn't home.

***

Dear Ella,

Well, it is frustrating that you haven't managed to find my letter. Keep looking for me, will you Ella? It would put my mind at rest if I knew that very indiscreet letter had been properly disposed of.

Actually no, I haven't told Bill about it. I thought we might just keep it to ourselves. No point in worrying him, do you agree? He's got a lot on his plate, and I don't want him panicking about scandalous leaks. I'm sure you'll turn that letter up in a day or two, then you can shred it and we can forget all about it.

We are all well, thank you. Don't worry about Laura, you know she's always been a bit of a drama queen. She hasn't said anything to me about this idea of hers to start a new political party, and I'm not planning to ask her about it. My advice would be not to encourage her by asking lots of questions. Like you, I don't think offering tax breaks for people who trade in their TV for a piano is likely to be much of a vote winner, and free prescriptions for vegans would be a difficult sell.

It's your birthday this Tuesday! Hope June is taking you somewhere nice to celebrate. Glad to hear she's not doing that thing with her teeth quite so much, and yes, very satisfactory that you didn't have to tackle her about it.

Just a thought. Have you looked in some very unlikely places for that letter? For example, in the vegetable compartment of your fridge? I sometimes find I absent-mindedly put things in the most peculiar places. When I lost my passport it turned up in the salad spinner. Have you tried looking in your linen basket? I found a pair of handcuffs in my dirty linen basket once. I threw them straight in the bin and said nothing about it.

Love as always,

Sally

***

Meeting Jen this afternoon about wedding plans, so must have some suggestions for readings. I might have to be prepared to be flexible about considering something from Winnie the Pooh. I mustn't do a 'Judith' and railroad Jen into something she's not comfortable with. I have a copy of W the P propping up a table leg somewhere – I'll take it with me just in case.

It occurred to me that I could suggest that Jen writes something herself, then she could read it, or if she wants me to, I could read it for her. It would be absolutely unique, and heartfelt of course. She might like that idea, and it would save me hours of digging around for a text that would match her mood and fit the requirements of 'short and snappy.' We are also going to discuss cake and flowers and dresses, so it will be a long afternoon, but not too long, because I have to be back for the history class.

I'm worried about the praying mole on my window ledge. I think it's attracting flies.

***

Dear Ella,

So glad you enjoyed your birthday, and you liked the cashmere shawl I sent from Bill and me.

I puzzled over the frightening little doll you said you'd received in the post. But I realised what it was when I discovered Sophie and Baz had sent you a birthday present. Apparently, it's a 'Mrs Thatcher' novelty stuffed mole from their proposed political series. I can imagine it does look quite gruesome, with its blonde wig, and the lipstick. Sophie said she thought you'd know straight away it was Mrs Thatcher because of the bag and the blue suit. I said I have a nice little blue suit and a handbag, but that doesn't make me Mrs Thatcher. Sophie said, 'Yes, but the thing is Mrs Forth, you're not a mole.'

If it starts to smell, don't hesitate, chuck it out.

Don't worry about that indiscreet letter any more, Ella. It must have slipped out of view somewhere. As you say, you didn't throw it out, and you haven't taken it out of the flat, so it must be safe. Maybe it has slipped down the back of a sofa, or something similar. In my experience, things that slip down the back of the sofa disappear for at least ten years, so we'll stop thinking about it.

I'm replying to your last letter from memory, because you repeated my revealing comments about you-know-who so clearly in your second paragraph I had to burn it as soon as I'd read it. Nothing wrong with your memory! You will be careful, won't you Ella, not to repeat what I told you about that person and the other person to anyone else? Sorry to be a bit cloak and dagger about things, but indiscretion could really land me, and Bill of course, in the soup.

Good job we're all friends!

Love,

Sally.

***

Well, I'm off the hook. Jen loved the idea of writing a little piece herself for me to read out at the wedding. I said, wouldn't you rather read it yourself, if you've written it? She said no, she thought she would be too nervous. Much better if I read it for her. Okay, I said, but give it to me to practise well in advance. She said she would.

In some respects it's not going to be a conventional wedding. She isn't planning to have wedding cake, as such, she's going to have two large ham and egg pies which will cut up into a hundred and twenty pieces and be served with a cherry tomato. The ham will symbolise nourishment, the egg will symbolise renewal, the pastry will symbolise the protection of good things, and in Jen's circumstances the cherry tomato will just be a cherry tomato.

Jen plans to wear a cream dress with a gauzy, pale lilac train falling from a tiara of contemporary design, and Sam will wear a cream suit with a pale lilac shirt. This will symbolise the fact that they complement each other. Very sweet. I asked her what I should wear. I've been a friend for so long I should fit into this carefully co-ordinated scheme somehow. I could get something to wear in the appropriate colour scheme from the end of season sales and symbolise being a bit of a cheapskate. Jen said I could wear whatever the hell I liked, but if it clashes with lilac, please don't stand anywhere near her on the day.

I asked about flowers for table decorations. But she's not having flowers, she's having twigs. Each table will have a sturdy twig as its centre piece, and hanging from the twig by silver threads will be a number of blank cards corresponding to the number of place settings around the table. Each place setting will include a pen. During the course of the meal, each guest around the table will take a card from the twig, write their own message to the happy couple on it, and hang it back on the twig.

'Why?' I said.

'Because,' she said, 'the twig symbolises strength, the silver thread symbolises precious human bonds, and the messages will symbolise the good will which will follow us throughout our lives together. And it will be so nice afterwards, to sit and read everyone's lovely comments.'

'Will it?'

'Of course it will. Try and be a bit more positive.'

'All right,' I said. 'So what about your bouquet? Surely you'll be having flowers in your bouquet? Tell me you won't be walking down the aisle with a twig?'

Jen said if she could find a small twig that was perfectly formed she might spray it gold and carry it to continue with the theme of strength and beauty.

'And the meal?' I asked her. 'Are you having goldfish to symbolise prosperity and bird of paradise to symbolise fantastic sex, and warm beer to symbolise great holidays on the Costa Brava?'

She said they were having a roast chicken dinner. I said that sounded very nice, and I asked about Chrissy.

'Are you going to ask Chrissy to be your bridesmaid?'

'Why?'

'She's Sam's daughter. After you're married Chrissy will be your step-daughter'

'Yes, but she's a bit young and pretty and fresh-faced to be standing so close to me on the day, don't you think?'

'Jen, you're starting to sound like Snow White's mother.'

'All right. I'll ask her. But I think Snow White's mother has never been properly understood.'

***

Everything about Jen's proposed wedding plans convinced me that a quick dash in and out of a registry office is a great way to get married, so it was a bit of a relief to get back home yesterday, even with the history class in prospect. I was getting ready to go out when Sophie asked why there were so many flies on the praying mole. Baz had a look at it and put it in a plastic bag and dropped it in the bin outside. They have promised to do me a better one. I said they should concentrate on their customer base. They said they hadn't sent any out to customers yet, they were still perfecting their technique. Ella and I were the only ones who had actually received a finished product, so far. Although of course, mine was in the bin.

The history group was actually a very pleasant way of spending an evening. I estimated the average age of the group membership to be a hundred and eight, so I felt ridiculously young at not quite fifty. I was a girl again, and for that reason alone it is worth the subscription. Arthur, an old gent who didn't give his age but said he wouldn't see eighty again, claimed to remember the execution of King Charles 1. The small group of us in our forties and fifties sat at the back of the class because our hearing was sharper, and because it wasn't cool to sit any further forward. We had tea and coconut macaroons at half-time, made by Marjorie, one of the older ladies. I got talking to Geoff who had quite a twinkle in his eye and was only in his seventies, and he said by golly, if he'd been twenty years younger... But then he choked on his macaroon and had to sit down and have a glass of water. Judith said later that she'd noticed me having a very long conversation during the break with Max, one of the younger men. I said I didn't think it had lasted that long. She said she thought he was quite attractive. I said I hadn't noticed. She asked me if I planned to go again next week, and I said, yes of course, why not?

Laura came round this afternoon. Harry was at Waddle Tots or Piddle Pots or whatever they go to these days. She didn't have long before she had to get back to pick Harry up, but she wanted to eat some cake and run something past me. She has that young mum, no-time-to-beat-about-the-bush manner of speaking, so she got straight into what she wanted to say.

'Mum,' she said, 'I'm going into politics like Dad. All the existing political parties are crap for one reason or another, so I'm starting my own. I've asked around at Tiny Tiddlers, and it'll get masses of support. It has one basic manifesto promise, to get rid of TV as we know it. Think about it Mum, it makes so much sense.'

I thought about it. It made no sense. 'People like TV, Laura. They want to watch it. I watch it.'

'Yes but, it's bad for us. Mentally and physically. And it's so bad for children. I'm never letting Harry watch TV. People would be so much happier if every television was smashed to bits and they had to go out of their houses and talk to someone.'

'Er, well, you might have a bit of a point, I suppose, I'm not sure ...'

'Anyway, I'm going to need your help.'

'Oh, well, I'm a bit pushed just at the moment, but ....'

'So I'll let you know what you can do. You can start by just talking about it, spreading the word, creating a groundswell. We'll be a pressure group at first, and then we'll feed into politics as our support grows.'

'I admire your energy, Laura.' I wanted to say something positive.

Then she said, 'Don't look at me like that Mum. As if I'm going mad or something. We can't just sit by and watch the world spiral downwards into the shit. We have a moral duty to act. Just because I'm a mother doesn't mean I have to resign myself to sitting on the side-lines for the next twenty years. I don't have to be impotent just because I change nappies. I know it wasn't right for you to get involved in politics, and motherhood squashed most of the life out of you. But it energises me, because it's Harry's future at stake. And I really believe that television sows envy and disrespect and disharmony and inactivity and resentment and bigotry and sloth. We have to cut down its influence. Can I take the rest of this cake? I've got to go.'

I thought I'd run Laura's conference speech past Sophie when she got home from work this afternoon. She was checking out tonight's TV, marvelling again at yet another opportunity to see *The Bourne Identity,* so it seemed a good time to get her views on Laura's manifesto.

'Laura was here earlier Sophie, and she was saying that she thinks television is bad for us and we should throw our TVs away,' I told her.

'Throw them away?' she said.

'Yes. Smash them to bits and throw them away.'

Sophie stood up unsteadily and clutched the TV listings to her chest. 'She's not here, is she? Laura?'

'No, she isn't here. She's at home.'

'What if she comes here, when we're out?'

'She won't throw our TV away Sophie.'

'But you said... '

'In principle, she doesn't like TV, but she's not going to throw ours out. She just thinks we shouldn't watch it.'

'I have to watch Eastenders tonight Mrs Forth.'

'Yes, I know. That's not a problem.'

'Good. She's funny your Laura, isn't she?'

'She has very strong opinions. That can be a good thing though, Sophie. Admirable.'

'Yeah. I think so too. Do you think it's because of her dad? Politicians have to have opinions don't they, otherwise there's no point in them.'

'Possibly,' I said. 'Although, I have opinions too, you know.'

'Do you?' she said, genuinely surprised. 'I thought you were just normal.'

***

Every few weeks, when I see Bill for long enough, I give him an update on what his children are doing and, if required, on their personalities, likes, dislikes, hopes, fears, relative ages, first names and so on. He's a busy man, and these details can slip his mind.

We had our periodic catch-up last night when he got home about 9.30pm. Bill had a brief chat with Dan, who was going out as he arrived. I heard them in the hallway.

'Dan! How's it hanging?'

'*How's it hanging*? Dad, have you any idea how ridiculous that makes you sound?'

'Oh, right. See you later then.'

Dan went out and Bill came into the kitchen and dropped his briefcase on the floor. He was looking in the fridge when Sophie spotted him from the living room and came through to say hello.

'Mr Forth! Hi! We haven't seen you for ages, have we Mrs Forth? I wanted to ask you, what do you think about moles stuffed in novelty poses?'

'I...' said Bill. 'I...'

'Because Baz and I are thinking,' she continued, 'if we can make them look as if they're knitting, or fishing, or writing with a pen, they'll be more desirable? And cute? So – hang on,' she paused and listened, 'is that my phone?' And she went back into the living room. A little later we heard her go upstairs.

Bill had already eaten, so we sat down with a small glass of wine. 'Are they all still here?' he said, looking around.

'Yes,' I said, 'where else would they be?'

'Apart from Dan, how many have we got now?'

'Just the same. Two permanent, and one frequent. Well, Chrissy's here most of the time now.'

He nodded. 'How's Laura? Any news?'

'She's fine. Lots of ideas, as always. She plans to start a political movement.'

He drained his glass and held it out for more. 'Without going into too much detail,' he said, 'what's that all about?'

'She's planning to start a campaign to restrict the amount of television we all watch. Thinks it's bad for us.'

Bill nodded thoughtfully. 'A complete non-starter then?'

'Well. It has its challenges. But anything can happen in politics.'

'Yup,' he said. 'Anything but that. Let's go to bed. Very early start tomorrow. How are you, by the way?'

'I'm fine by the way. Oh, and speaking of things that can happen in politics, any more news on dangerous liaisons between she who must be obeyed and you-know-who?'

'God, Sally, you haven't mentioned this to anyone, have you?'

'I, no, what? No! Mentioned? No, I—'

'Because it's absolutely essential that you don't say anything. Absolutely essential, Sally. I could be wrong about the whole thing.'

'D'you think you're wrong? About it happening?'

'I don't know what's going on for sure. I'm not in the room, obviously. I'm pretty sure something's going on but I'm trying not to know about it. I'm trying not to have suspicions about it. I'm trying to un-know what I might already know about it. The whole thing might have stopped. I'm assuming it has. If it ever started, which is something else I don't know. So that's my position. Total bloody ignorance.'

'Oh. I thought people knew.'

'Well there's knowing, and then there's people knowing you know. They're two different things. It's when people know you know that you actually do know something.'

'Right.'

'Either way Sally, it's absolutely essential that you don't breathe a suggestion of a hint about this. It's a disaster if this gets out.'

So then I didn't feel as if I could say, 'Actually I've just written to your mother telling her all about it, and she's lost my letter.' So instead I said, 'Right. Let's go to bed.'

***

Lee has become a school refuser. His mother rang school this morning while I was in the office, so I took the call. Mrs Watson said that Lee had got wind of the fact that one of the girls in his class was a school refuser, and that was why she'd had been off school for months. Now Lee's decided he's a school refuser, so he's refusing to go to school. Mrs Watson wants to know what we're going to do about it, because she doesn't want him hanging around the house all day pretending to be mental.

I told Mrs Watson that I would discuss this with Lee's Head of Year, Mrs Short, and she would get back to her today. I went to see Marie Short in the Maths department and she listened to my account of the phone call with Lee's mother and then she rolled her eyes and rolled them again and then suggested I go out to talk to Lee, seeing as we had a rapport, and we lived in the same general neck of the woods. With any luck, Marie said, I might be able to talk him out of being a school refuser before the idea becomes rooted in what counts as his brain, and bring him back into school with me in the afternoon. I said okay, I'll give it a try, and twenty minutes later I was on my way.

When I got to Lee's, his mother was not happy. 'It's my day off today,' she said, 'and I could have done without him deciding he's got a condition. It's the school's fault, so you'll have to talk to him. He's upstairs.'

She led the way, pushed open the door to Lee's room and stood in the doorway. 'I told you the school would be on to you didn't I?' she told him. 'They've only sent a teacher down to see what the fuck's going on with you. I'm surprised they can be bothered. Sit up and talk to her and watch your bleedin' language.'

'Lee!' I said, 'What's all this I hear about you being a school refuser?'

'I'm a school refuser now,' he said, 'like Lillian Sykes. I can't go to school no more. It's a condition.'

'But you haven't got this condition, Lee.'

'Yes I have. I'm refusing to go to school.'

'But Lee,' I sat down on a small red plastic stool next to his bed, 'just because you're refusing to go to school doesn't make you a school refuser.'

'Why not? 'Course it does. That's what a school refuser is. It's a person what refuses to go to school. Lillian Sykes isn't coming to school 'cos she's a school refuser. Why can't I be a school refuser?'

'Lee,' I said, 'the thing is, Lillian is poorly. She has an illness, a psychological condition.'

'Same as me,' Lee was indignant. 'Same as me. Look at the condition I'm in now!'

'Lee, it's time to stop being silly and get up and come into school where you should be today. Come on, up you get, and let's get going.'

'No,' he said. 'I got school refusal. I'm not coming.'

'But Lee, you were perfectly all right yesterday. Your teachers all say you were fine yesterday. You don't get school refusal overnight.'

'It's come on sudden. I'm really poorly with it now. Why don't you go and tell Lillian Sykes she's got to go to school? She should be getting over hers now. Mine's just started.'

I went back downstairs and found Lee's Mum, now back in the kitchen. 'I'm sorry Mrs Watson,' I said, 'I'm afraid I'm not able to persuade Lee to come back to school with me. He's convinced he's got a bad case of school refusal.' I smiled.

But she wasn't smiling. 'Well what do you expect? Telling kids about school refusal. There wasn't any school refusal in my day. There was going to school, and there was skiving. School refusal? Whose idea was that? I'm surprised you haven't got them all going down with school refusal! School refusal? Up my arse! What's next? Work refusal? What do you think would happen to me if I rang up work tomorrow and said I couldn't come in because I had work refusal? The sack! That's what'd happen, I'll tell you that for nothing. You put daft ideas into kids' heads and you're surprised when they do daft things. Who in god's name thought it'd be a good idea to allow kids to have school refusal? It's obvious they're all going to want to go down with it! Christ on a bike!'

We looked at each other in stunned silence for a few seconds after she'd stopped, and while I thought of some sort of response. I reflected on the fact that Lee was very like his mother. 'I take your point, Mrs Watson,' I said, 'and I do sympathise, but you know, it has to be said, some children quite enjoy school.'

'Yes but I'm talking about normal kids, aren't I?' she said. 'Normal kids is what I'm talking about.'

'Tell you what,' I said, 'let's see how he feels tomorrow. He's going to get bored, isn't he, sitting up there on his own all day?'

She considered this. 'I'll tell *you* what, Mrs Teacher. If he's still got school refusal tomorrow I'll give him some medicine to make him better. I expect you miss him. Do you? You'll all be wanting him to get better,' she said, arms folded and head on one side, enjoying putting me on the spot.

'Of course we'll miss him,' I said. 'Lee? He's a character!'

'Ain't he though.' She dismissed my response. 'Well, I'm off out, can't hang around here all day with you and his nibs.' We walked down the hallway to the front door, and outside. 'He'll be back in school tomorrow,' she promised me, 'whatever condition he's in.'

***

It's the history class again tonight. I'm actually looking forward to it. I enjoyed chatting to Max last week and the history part wasn't too bad. When I was getting ready to leave the house, Chrissy said, 'You look nice.'

'Thanks Chrissy,' I said, looking in the mirror. 'Actually, I'm thinking I might need to do something with my hair.'

'Mmm,' she said, 'because of all the grey, you mean?'

I peered at my reflection. 'Well yes, there is a bit of grey. I suppose.'

'I know what you need!' she said. 'You need to go blonde! Blonde highlights, that's what you need – it'd look great. Make you look so much younger.'

'Well,' I said. 'I might just do that. Thanks Chrissy.' And feeling slightly less buoyant, I left the house.

We discussed Tudor morality this evening. The Tudors had a simple moral code, but it was not open to interpretation. Essentially, if you agreed with the monarch you were in the right, and if you disagreed with the monarch you were in the shit. Nuancing was not their style.

During the break I had the beginnings of a fascinating little conversation with Max. Nothing historical. He told me he was a solicitor, but he had studied history at university and had always been interested in it. He asked about my interest in history, and when that had started. I spotted Judith heading in our direction with a plate of shortbread biscuits so I knew I wouldn't get away with pretending to have any interest in history at all. I confessed that I had just come along at the insistence of my friend Judith, who was by now standing next to me proffering biscuits.

'I told her to come and give this a try, Max,' said Judith, wearing her I'm-a-good-person-and-I'm-really-concerned face. 'Because she needs to get out of the house more. Sally needs a life, she's in too much of a rut. She needs some intellectual stimulation, you know? To stop her vegetating and becoming depressed. It can make you ill, being so house-bound.'

I protested. 'Judith, please! You're making my life sound very forlorn. Much more forlorn than it is. My life is great. And I'm fine. I'm absolutely fine!' I laughed, to show how absolutely fine I was.

'That's not how it looked to me a year ago,' said Judith. 'If you ask me you were on the verge of some sort of breakdown back then. All that fuss following your attack on the woman in her pyjamas in Tesco. It took its toll.'

Max was beginning to look quite concerned. 'Oh,' he said, 'I'm sorry to hear you've been under the weather.'

'I haven't,' I said. 'I haven't been under the weather at all, quite the opposite. I've been over the weather.'

'Over the weather?' said Judith. 'I don't think you can be over the weather. Not even you, Sally. You can be under it, but not over it. You never hear people say, I'm feeling over the weather, do you? I've never heard anyone say that.'

'Judith,' I said. 'Please go away.'

'Oh well,' she said. 'Suit yourself.' And she flounced off with the biscuits.

'Judith's an old friend,' I said to Max, by way of explanation.

He laughed, but he was slightly guarded, and our conversation lost its momentum.

After the class, when we were walking back across the car park to our cars, Judith caught me up. 'I've realised why you didn't want me to say all that to Max, earlier on. Sorry.'

'What do you mean?'

'I've just realised. You fancy him, don't you? Max. That was why you didn't want me to tell him you're a housebound depressive.'

'I didn't want you to tell him I'm a housebound depressive because I'm not a housebound depressive! And I don't fancy him, Judith. That's absolutely ridiculous.'

'Good night!' Max called from the car parked opposite mine.

'Good night!' We both called over to him, waving enthusiastically, as if his popping up was an absolute delight and not an extreme embarrassment.

'See you next week,' said Judith, getting into her car. 'If not sooner, if we decide to meet before then. Bye!'

As she fastened her seat belt, I slashed all four of her tyres. Or I would have done, if my eyebrow tweezers had been up to the job.

When I got home Baz and Sophie were trying to make a stuffed mole look as if it was playing a ukulele, so I didn't linger in the kitchen.

I'll make an appointment to get my hair done tomorrow.

***

Dear Ella,

I was interested to hear about the chat you had with June about our living arrangements here, and not too surprised to hear that she thinks they're a bit eccentric. But as you say, they do seem to work, most of the time.

The little lean-to annex made of recycled materials that Dan built on the side of our house and lived in for a while was called Aspire, not Aspirin. It was actually only in place for about six months, although it probably did feel like six years.

After Dan moved back into the house, Baz re-vamped it as studio accommodation for his day time use, but then we had to take it down when a complete stranger moved in while Baz was at work. Baz found him in there fast asleep on his sofa bed when he came home one evening. He was a man in his fifties or sixties, difficult to say for sure. We all stood around for a while like the Three Bears, watching him sleeping and wondering what to do. When he woke up, he asked for a cup of tea, and we tried to find out a bit about him while he sat up in bed and drank it. He wasn't very forthcoming, but he rambled on for a while and then he asked what time it was and when we said it was six thirty he wanted a gin and tonic. He said he would probably be bringing a few of his friends round for cocktails later. That's when I said that, unfortunately, we had to take the structure down because it didn't meet building regulations. He said he was happy to overlook any breaches of building regulations, so not to worry about them. But I said I did worry about them, I worried about them a lot. We said he could sleep in Aspire that night and we'd have a chat with him in the morning about alternative accommodation, but by the next day he'd gone, and by the same evening so had Aspire.

So Aspire has gone from the side of the house. It had been a big part of our lives for six months and then it was thrown into a skip. Quite sad in a way. Like saying goodbye to a shambolic but amiable stray dog. However, Baz has re-created it internally in the little attic room upstairs on the third floor. I don't know what happened to the gent who moved in and anticipated cocktail parties. I hope he's found somewhere else to have them.

Anyway! I've brought you up to speed now, and you can reassure June that we don't add cardboard extensions onto our house willy-nilly when we need a bit more room. We're all bricks and mortar now, and very respectable.

Glad to hear you've thrown the Mrs Thatcher mole out. Good move. I'll let them know you don't want a replacement. It's not my kind of thing either, but I suspect I'm going to be seeing a lot more of them. The novelty poses are getting ever more extreme. If you've ever wondered what a mole looks like playing the drums I can send you a photograph.

Getting my hair done tomorrow. Blonde highlights – exciting?!

With love,

Sally xx

***

Ashleigh did my hair this afternoon. She said was I thinking of ash blonde highlights or light copper blonde? I couldn't decide, they both looked nice on the chart. She said why didn't I have both? She said it would look lovely. I said, 'Are you sure?' She said yes, she was. 'Okay then,' I said, 'I'll have both.' And off she went to mix the brew.

After weaving the colours through my hair, Ashleigh left me to stew for half an hour, and to catch up on the latest copies of 'Hello!' magazine, which I always pore over at the hairdressers. I spent a pleasant half an hour gazing at the immaculately appointed houses and gardens of a variety of celebs, admiring the way they drape themselves provocatively over their furniture and nurse their infants in evening gowns, and set their dining tables elaborately for twelve when they appear to be all alone in the house. A rare glimpse of a dream kitchen confirms that celebs don't cook, they roll around the granite work surfaces in mini skirt and white knee-length boots, looking to the right or the left or straight ahead, and when that doesn't produce any food, they hop down and go out for a meal.

A trainee chatted to me while she washed my hair. She seemed obsessed with what I was doing after I left the hairdressers. I wished I had something interesting to tell her that I was proposing to do, like cleaning out the lion enclosure, or returning to Mars, but I had nothing to reward her enthusiasm for my day. I could only tell her I was planning to nip into Tesco's and then go home.

Ashleigh combed through my coloured and washed hair and said, now, what about the cut? Did I want a more sculpted look, chunky and squared off so that it would bounce up naturally, or was I going for a more feathery, elfin look? I said I might be getting a bit long in the tooth for elfin looks, because once they hit fifty, elves look like walnuts. Ashleigh said yes, definitely, she would advise chunky.

So, it's all done, and I'm really pleased with it. Surviving the process psychologically unscathed wasn't easy, but I'm very happy with the end result. I bounced home, tossing my head about and hoping the sun was catching my golden highlights.

Sophie was the first to see it when I got home. 'You've had your hair cut and coloured,' she said, as if it might have happened without my noticing.

'Yes, do you like it?'

'It's nice, yes.'

'Chrissy suggested it.'

'Oh, did she?' There are some tensions between Dan's current girlfriend Chrissy, and Sophie, who was his previous girlfriend. 'Well,' she said, 'I think next time I'd ask them to cut it a bit longer.'

'It's quite nice and bouncy though, don't you think?' I patted my new hair, looking at my reflection in the mirror.

'Yeah, it is nice and bouncy. Mrs Forth – you know how you can't get pregnant if you keep your fingers crossed while it's happening and drink cranberry juice straight away afterwards?'

I turned to look at her. 'What?' I said. 'What did you say?'

'I said – you know how you can't get pregnant if you keep your fingers crossed while it's happening and drink cranberry juice straight away afterwards?'

'Sophie, that's rubbish. Who told you that?'

'I must have heard it the first time at school. I thought everybody knew that.'

‘That’s complete rubbish. There’s no truth in that at all.’

‘Oh,’ she said.

‘You haven’t – you and Baz haven’t been relying on cranberry juice as a contraceptive, have you Sophie?’

‘Well, it’s worked up to now.’

‘Up to now?’

‘Yes, it’s worked up to now.’

‘Have you? Are you? Sophie, do you think you might be pregnant?’

‘No.’

‘Oh, that’s a relief. I thought you were going to tell me you were pregnant.’

‘No. I’m just a little bit overdue my period. I won’t know for a while yet.’

‘God.’

‘I’ll have some more cranberry juice. D’you want some?’

‘Cranberry juice isn’t a contraceptive Sophie. People say it’s good for cystitis, but it’s not a contraceptive.’

‘Ah, I knew it was good for something. Cystitis? Right. What’s cystitis again?’

‘It’s a urinary tract infection.’

‘Oh of course. I should have known that. Everyone’s got a urinary tract infection at Merry Dale. Well, I shouldn’t have cystitis, anyway.’

‘Sophie, if you and Baz are going to have sex, you should both go to the doctor’s and get some proper contraceptive advice.’

‘Do you think?’

‘Yes! Yes, I do Sophie. And while you’re waiting for an appointment you should be using a sheath, like Durex, for men.’

‘Right. Baz said he thought that’s what we should do, and he does sometimes. But I told him about the cranberry juice.’

‘Baz was right.’

‘Would I have to leave here if I was pregnant?’

‘Sophie, how overdue are you, with your period?’

‘Difficult to say, really.’

'Just a rough estimate.'

'Maybe two days?'

'Well, that's not long. Let's give it a week, and then we'll have another chat.'

'Right. Are you mad with me?'

'No. But I will be if you don't start using sensible contraception, straight away. Tonight.'

'Tonight? What if we don't do it tonight?'

'I mean, the very next time you do, and then every time afterwards. You have to be sensible about this Sophie.'

'I know,' she sighed. 'I should have asked you sooner, about the cranberry juice.'

'Well, you know now. Let's just wait and see, shall we?'

'Yes. We'll just have to wait and see. At least you've got a really great hair style, so that's good isn't it?'

***

Dear Ella,

We're fine, thanks. Just getting on with things here. No news, but that's how I like it these days. Bill is as busy as ever, and the kids continue to live their crazy lives, they constantly amaze me, but I won't go into details.

I haven't seen Laura for a few days, so I can't report on the progress of her anti-TV party. I certainly will suggest June's name when she gets to the point of selecting candidates. I didn't know that the only programme June approves of is 'Gardeners World.' I imagine that does make it a bit difficult for you to watch 'Disgusting Bodies,' especially when she keeps coming into your flat unannounced.

So you're getting a cleaner? Well, that should make life easier for you. No need to feel guilty Ella, you'll probably make friends with her and spend half the time just drinking coffee and chatting, although the lady June has in mind does sound very efficient.

Ella, it occurs to me that your cleaner might turn that letter up? You know the one I mean? If she's the efficient sort she'll be heaving the cushions off the sofa and chairs, and poking things down into their furthest recesses and coming up with all sorts of stuff you've forgotten you ever had. Trust me, it's astonishing what can hide among the cushions of a sofa. I knew a girl once who lost a boyfriend in her sofa.

I think the best thing to do, Ella, about the letter, is to arrange to be at home with your cleaning lady for the first few times she comes to you, so that you are around to scoop it up if it is found. Remove it from view until your cleaning lady leaves, then shred it as soon as she's gone. That's the best plan, I think. If she hasn't found it after about three or four visits, she isn't likely to. My experience of cleaners is that they go berserk the first few times to impress you with their energy and thoroughness, and then they settle down a bit.

Does this sound like a good plan to you? I hope so. Let me know in your next letter.

Life gets complicated sometimes, doesn't it?

Love as always,

Sally. XX

***

I went to see Laura this afternoon. I took a home-made quiche with me and we sat down for a late lunch while Harry had his nap.

'Laura, can I tell you something serious, and in confidence?'

Her eyes widened. 'What? Oh-oh. You and dad aren't getting a divorce, are you?'

'No, of course not! What on earth makes you say that?'

'Well, you hardly see each other, as far as I can make out. But, good. I'm glad you're not getting a divorce. So, what is it?'

'Sophie might be pregnant.'

'Oh right! Wow. Pregnant? Sophie? Oh god! Is Dan the father? Dan's still a bit of an idiot and Sophie's crazy. You'll have to bring the kid up, Mum, they'll never manage it.'

'No, not Dan. Sophie's with Baz now. Dan is with Chrissy. You knew that.'

'Oh yeah, of course. Difficult to keep up with it all. Well, Baz and Sophie are pretty much broke, aren't they? Are you thinking you might have them in residence for a bit longer than you thought?'

'Yes.'

'Like, twenty years.'

'Twenty years?'

'You've gone a bit pale, Mum. I thought you liked Sophie.'

'I do like Sophie. I just wasn't reckoning on a life-time commitment.'

'I was just joking. You won't have Sophie for twenty years, even if she is pregnant.'

'I'm not sure.'

'She's not going to want to live with you and Dad for twenty years, Mum. That's not what's on her mind. She'll want to move out and get her own place.'

'Sophie's mind,' I said, 'is a curious place. I think she wants us all to live together until your dad and I get old, and then she will become our carer and look after us.'

I could see Laura considering the advantages of this arrangement.

'And by the time we die,' I continued, 'she'll be such an expert taxidermist she'll stuff us both and prop us up on the landing.'

Laura looked up at me and laughed. She should laugh more often, laughter transforms her. 'That's hilarious,' she said. 'And actually, I think you're right, that would appeal to Sophie. She has that sort of quirky mind-set. I can see her thinking it would be a good idea. I wonder if there are laws against doing that sort of thing? It might be perfectly legal. It probably is, if it's done properly. Embalming is still practised, isn't it? People have their pets stuffed, don't they? And your landing is just about big enough for both you and Dad, and not too sunny which is good. Unless – maybe we could put Dad at the bottom of the stairs and just you on the landing? Although, it would seem a shame to split you up, you've spent so much time apart in life.'

I smiled. But really, I hadn't expected her to give the idea anything like this much consideration.

Laura helped herself to more quiche. 'I think you're maybe over-stressing about this Mum. Honestly, if Sophie's pregnant she's going to want her own place, trust me. She could still be your carer though, when you get old, that's a good idea. Do you want any more of this quiche? Before I eat it all?'

***

I decided to have a chat with Dan today. Every now and again I have to make a conscious effort to find out what he's thinking and feeling. I can't assume I'm up to speed simply because I'm his mother. Dan gives out his thoughts and feelings on a strictly need-to-know basis, which means if I want to know anything more, I have to ask.

We were in the kitchen together on Saturday morning, so I asked him how things were going.

'Fine,' he said. 'What happened to the shit mole we had on the window ledge?'

'Baz put it in the bin. It was attracting flies.'

'God, that's gross.'

'Pretty gross, yes. Does it bother you, the taxidermy in the utility room?'

'No, it doesn't bother me. Did you see the one last week? The mole playing the ukulele? It looked as if it had its head stuck in a cheese grater.'

'Is it a pain for you sometimes, Dan, having everyone living here?'

'Why would it be a pain? I've got my own room.'

'How are things with Chrissy?'

'Chrissy? Fine.'

'And work? How's work?'

'Work's fine.'

'All's well in the landscape gardening world?'

'Yeah, yeah.'

'I sometimes think it must be a bit frustrating for you, having to live at home with your Mum and Dad.'

'Well, I don't see much of Dad.'

'Me, then.'

'Oh, you're all right.'

'Good.'

'Anyway, I don't know anyone my age with their own place round here. And most people rent in groups. It's all right, being here. I suppose if I lived in the north I might be able to afford a thatched castle or something.'

'Not many thatched castles in the north. And if you found one it would cost a fortune. The countryside is beautiful up there.'

'Yeah but, you can't live in the countryside Mum.'

'People do. Some of your clients do.'

'I'm too young to live in the countryside.'

'So you're happy here, with things the way they are?'

'Yeah, yeah, I'm all right. I'm fine.' And then he said, 'Are you happy here?'

***

I don't see quite so much of Susan, my next-door neighbour, since the rubbish annex that was Aspire came down. I saw her frequently when it was still standing, because she wanted to update me regularly on how much she hated it and wanted rid of it. Now that she hasn't got anything much to complain about I see very little of her, so when she called this morning I knew something mustn't be right.

'Number 32 was burgled. Last night. They got in round the back. Gave old Mrs Winston a hell of a fright.'

'Is she all right?'

'She's all right. Staying with her daughter. They haven't got anybody for it. But the house is empty now so god knows who'll get in.'

I gave her a cup of coffee. 'Have you got any good news, Susan?'

'No,' she took a sip. 'Anyway. What I'm thinking is we need some sort of neighbourhood watch carry-on around here. Even if it's just for our two houses, for starters.'

'Sounds interesting. How would that work?'

'Pretty obvious isn't it? I'll watch yours if you watch mine.'

'Well, we do that anyway, don't we? Keep an eye out for each other?'

'We need to step it up a bit. I'm going to buy some binoculars and keep a close eye on your place. You need to do the same, I reckon, for us.'

I had a vision of Susan and I staring at each other through binoculars over the garden fence.

'All right. I'll look out our binoculars.' I've learned that it's useless to argue with Susan. It's best to just agree with what she says and then let things rest.

'Right.' She was a bit deflated. I think she was looking forward to an argument. 'So, you might see me looking across here through the binoculars, but I'm just keeping an eye on things, checking everything's okay.'

'That's fine.'

'We don't want a break-in, like at number 32. Can't be too careful.'

'No, you're right.'

'I'll only look through your windows in an emergency. Like if you're being attacked.'

'Bloody hell, Susan. Can we change the subject?'

'If you like.' She drank more of her coffee and helped herself to a biscuit. 'Heard on the radio this morning there's going to be a storm. Very high winds, likely to blow the slates off your roof. Better watch out. It could kill you, you know, a flying slate. I knew someone once who was decapitated by a flying slate. Cut his head clean off. Nasty piece of work he was, I wasn't sorry. Make sure your wheely bins are pushed under cover. I don't want them taking off and flying through my lounge window. So, what's been going on here since I was last over? Have you still got that motley crew living in?'

'Yes, yes. They're all still here. Three of them now, and Baz of course. One big happy family.'

'Don't know how you stand it.'

***

Dear Ella,

I was very pleased to hear you suffered no storm damage and no flooding. All well here too, although Sophie's bra was whipped off the washing line and ended up on the roof of next door's shed, it was caught by its strap to a little weather vane. It spun round and round merrily for almost an hour this morning until Susan next door spotted it, and rang to say she was going to cut it free with a pair of shears. Sophie went out to talk to her and I heard her asking if Susan would agree to the bra staying where it was until it dried. The answer was obviously no, because Sophie came back in seconds later with her bra, soaking wet, but in one piece.

So glad you like your cleaner. Maybe I should think about doing the same? I used to have a cleaner years ago when I was working full time and the kids were just little, but she bought a puppy and left to look after it, and since then we've all just muddled along. I think I'll look into it.

No need to feel guilty Ella, not if you pay well. Why shouldn't a talent for cleaning be able to earn good money? And it is a skilled job.

You're right, I think Bill would be surprised if he knew you hardly heard a word he said to you on the phone the other night. He thought you'd had a good long chat, and apparently you sounded very bright and on the ball. Have you ever thought of getting a new phone – one which would allow you to turn the sound up a bit? Although I agree, it can be quite useful sometimes not to hear people when they're speaking to you on the phone

I'll let you know how I get on with my search for a cleaner, and yes, I do like my hair. It looks really nice. All the kids like it, and Bill said I looked as if I had slept well, so he must have noticed something.

With love,

Sally.

***

'We're going to get a cleaner,' I told them all at the weekend. 'I should have done it ages ago. I've been in touch with an agency, and they're sending Mrs Krevice round on Tuesday morning.'

'Mrs Krevice?' said Dan.

'Yes,' I said, 'Tuesday morning. She'll be here for three hours, possibly four. I want everyone's bedroom really tidy so she can clean up easily. I'll inspect your rooms on Monday night.'

***

I was sitting at the kitchen table today reading a letter from Ella, when I heard a noise behind me.

'Hiya!'

'Sophie, how do you manage to open the back door without making any noise?'

'I did make a noise. You were just concentrating. Guess what? Guess what Mrs Forth!'

I stared at Sophie in what I hoped wasn't horror. 'What?'

'I'm not pregnant!'

'You're not pregnant?'

'No. I'm not pregnant. My period started at work. I'm unpregnant. Tad-ah!' she held her arms out sideways for me to admire her single self.

'Oh,' I said. 'Well. There you are then. That's a relief. Not pregnant. Right. And have you got some sensible contraception sorted out now, Sophie?'

'Yes. It's all sorted. I've told Baz he has to put two of those Durex things on. That should do it, don't you think?'

'Two? That should do it, yes.'

'Better than cranberry juice.'

'Much better than cranberry juice.'

'Phew, eh?'

'Yes,' I said. 'Phew. All the same, you might want to make an appointment with your GP though Sophie, to have a chat about contraception and discuss some sensible options.'

'Right,' she said. 'Is it not sensible for Baz to put two of those Durex things on?'

'There are better alternatives I think.'

'I could tell him to put three on.'

'Sophie, that's ridiculous.'

'Yeah,' she agreed. 'Too expensive.'

***

Lee is back in school. Hurrah. His attack of school refusal has abated, thanks to some medicine administered by his mother.

So I was able to test my latest suggestion for engaging Lee in the learning process, which is for him to be tasked with promoting the learning of a younger pupil, who could reasonably be expected to benefit from Lee's help.

My reasoning is that I have noticed in Lee, a love-hate relationship with learning. He has a grudging respect for people who can learn, but he has no confidence in his own ability to learn and would rather not put himself to the test.

So, I suggested to the Head that what Lee needs is to be responsible for teaching another pupil a skill which he is already reasonably proficient at, and then as he advises and coaches his pupil, he will see how his own attitude to learning has to change.

The Head listened patiently and remarked on the fact that I didn't give up easily, and said by all means, give it a try, but monitor the situation very closely. He didn't want to hear that Lee had been administering punishment beatings to his tutee.

So I explained to Lee what the plan was, and expected that he would be intrigued.

'Lee,' I said, 'we need your help.'

'Why?' he said. Instantly suspicious.

'We have a pupil in year seven who could do with some reading practice, and we think you might be just the person to give him some help.'

'Me?'

'Yes.'

'Bollocks.'

'No, it's not bollocks Lee. It's a very good idea.'

'Bollocks.' But I could see he was interested.

'You struggled a little bit with reading at first, didn't you? So, you will know how to help people with the same problem. It stands to reason.'

He thought about it. Looking for the catch. 'So I'd be like, a teacher?'

'Yes, a bit like a teacher.'

'Would I get paid?'

'No, you wouldn't get paid. You have to be properly qualified to get paid.'

'But I'd be doing the work without pay.'

'The pay isn't the important thing here, Lee. You'd be helping another pupil learn something. That's a good thing to do, even if you're not paid.'

'It's not a good thing to work without pay. I'd have to go on strike.'

'God, Lee. You haven't done anything yet, and already you're going on strike. Why don't you just give it a try? You might enjoy it.'

'Would I get breaks?'

'Of course you'd get breaks. You'd get the same breaks you get now.'

'Would I be able to go into the staff room?'

'No.'

'Why not? I'd be a teacher. I should be able to go into the staff room. Same as you.'

'God sakes, Lee! Are you interested in doing this or not?'

'Might be.'

So, if we can agree terms, we're going to give it a try next week.

***

Tuesday morning, and I was waiting for Mrs Krevice to arrive.

There was a knock on the door promptly at nine, and I went to open it.

A very attractive young man stood on the doorstep. He looked as if he was in his early twenties, and he was gorgeous. 'Hello,' he said. 'The agency sent me. Me name's Ivor Krevice, and I bet you were expecting me to be a woman. Ah'm a Geordie by the way.'

I invited Ivor in and we sat and had a chat. He was at pains to point out to me that although he is a man and a Geordie, he is an excellent cleaner. He said cleaning was his passion, he loved it, he lived for it, he would be doing it all the time if his friends didn't call to him and say, 'Ivor! Ivor! Give ower man. Stop cleaning now, Ivor! Yer makin' us dizzy.'

Ivor is a Geordie with so much energy for cleaning. He looked around and said I had a beautiful home, but he could see so many things to clean, and he couldn't wait to get started. He said some people didn't like male cleaners, and they told the agency – don't send us a man! I need a woman! And that was such a pity like, because he could have made their houses so clean, if he'd had the chance.

I said I was more than happy for him to clean my house. He could start just as soon as he had finished his coffee. He was delighted and so was I. There was no way I was going to pass up a drop-dead gorgeous Geordie with a passion for cleaning called Ivor Krevice.

So when he had drained his coffee mug and donned a no-nonsense apron, I gave him a brief tour of the house. Ivor was very taken with what he saw, and he saw lots of things he could clean. He admired Dan's bedroom, which has recently been fitted out as the interior of a Star Wars Death Star. Ivor looked around and said he knew a smashing range of products for cleaning Death Stars and he would bring something with him next week. Then he went downstairs and got to work, kitchen first. I drifted into the lounge and decided this would be an excellent opportunity to write the letter to the newspaper that I had been toying with writing for months now. So I fired up my laptop and began typing away.

> *Sir*, I began. *As a responsible member of society with serious concerns about climate change, I would like to raise the issue of excessive air conditioning in high street shops, and in particular, in Marks and Spencer's food hall. On an averagely warm day the shopper*

in that part of the store can expect to be frozen to the very marrow within five minutes of crossing the threshold. Anyone brave enough to venture into the food hall needs sealskins to maintain a comfortable body temperature.

After buying a bag of frozen peas in the food hall last summer I had to make a dash to Café Revive to buy a hot cup of coffee and thaw out, but my hope of resuscitation was crushed by a downdraft of cold air which washed over me wherever I chose to sit. I noticed many of my fellow coffee drinkers were blue around the lips. The friend I was having coffee with, who speaks very little sense anyway, made even less sense because her teeth were incessantly chattering.

Marks and Spencer's customers may be a little more mature than the average high street shopper, but we are still living, and we do not yet require deep freeze refrigeration to stop us decaying as we walk around the store. M&S is by no means the only culprit, but if it is possible to get frostbite anywhere on the high street in winter and summer alike, it is in the M&S food hall.

On my trips to the café in M&S last summer, my friend suggested that we bring warm sleeping bags to wrap around us and I must say, I thought that might be one of the most sensible suggestions I have ever heard her make. Although to be fair, she can make some pretty stupid suggestions, in fact -

Ivor came into the lounge wearing his Marigolds. 'Mrs Forth, I don't know whether you know like, but something bad is happening in your utility room. At the back. Ah'm pretty sure someone's been dismemberin' animals.'

Chapter Two: February

A good day. We all managed Sunday lunch together, Dan, Chrissy, Sophie, Baz, Bill and I. All sitting around the table like Christmas, although today we celebrate the beginning of February and the now noticeably longer days. It doesn't get dark now in the evenings until after five, and the sun is up in the mornings comfortably before eight. The world is turning us away from the dark.

Everyone helped with the meal. Sophie's Yorkshire puddings set the smoke alarms off, Baz's gravy had to be cut with a knife, and Chrissy peeled the potatoes so thoroughly they were the size of grapes. Dan sliced the turnip, cut his finger, and had to sit with his head between his knees for a few minutes. But eventually, we all sat around, raised our glasses in a toast, and tucked into our lunch.

I said, 'Isn't this nice? Good food and good company.'

'I bet you're quite pleased none of us can afford our own house?' said Sophie. 'It wouldn't be as much fun, if we were all living in different houses.'

Then, after what I hoped was a contented silence, Baz said, 'My Dad says, because we're not paying rent, you could chuck us out at any time, so I needn't think doing your garden is going to make any difference. But I said, you wouldn't just chuck us out like that. He doesn't know you like we do.'

'You should get a reward, for letting us stay here,' said Sophie. 'I know eventually I'm going to look after you when you're old, but that might be a long time to wait.' She glanced up at us, just to make sure.

'A reward from who?' said Baz.

'I don't know,' said Sophie. 'The Queen? Maybe the Queen could say you're excused paying any taxes?'

'A tax break,' said Dan. 'You should be able to fix that, Dad. You're in charge of housing.'

'Fantastic!' said Bill, looking around the table. 'Tax breaks for accommodating low paid workers in high rent areas. We'd be quids-in here. Know anyone else who wants to come and live here Sophie? Line 'em up. Maybe we won't have to pay any tax at all? I'll drink to that!' He raised his wine glass.

'Do you think it's a good idea? Really?' said Sophie. 'Cos I thought of it first.'

'It might be,' said Bill. 'It might be a good idea. Almost certainly is if it makes us rich.' Bill looked around the table. 'It would be good to make some money out of you lot, somehow.'

'Brilliant,' said Sophie. 'Are you going to pass a law saying so?'

'As soon as possible,' said Bill, reaching for the wine bottle. After a few glasses of wine Bill sees the funny side of politics. After a bottle he thinks it's hilarious.

When the meal was over, and the kids were upstairs somewhere watching a DVD they said we wouldn't like, Bill said, 'Remind me, what's wrong with Sophie's idea for tax breaks in exchange for giving free accommodation to a low paid worker in your home?'

'You mean, apart from its being Sophie's idea?'

'Yes, apart from that.'

'There has to be something wrong with it, Bill. Sophie thought of it. And until recently she thought cranberry juice was a contraceptive.'

'I must have had too much wine to figure it out. I'll see it straight away in the morning, the flaws in this plan.'

'Yes. They'll jump out at us in the morning,' I said.

'And you've put her right about the cranberry juice?'

'Yes. Yes I've done that. She's not relying on cranberry juice any more. I've suggested she goes to the docs to get some proper contraceptive advice. At the moment, she's got Baz wearing two sheaths.'

'Two?' said Bill. 'Where's he putting the other one?'

***

Last week's suggestion that Lee help with another pupil's reading did not go quite as well as I'd hoped because it brought out the shop steward in him, and resulted in a frustrating wrangle over pay and conditions which wasn't the object of the exercise. So I was hoping he had got all that out of his system and we'd make more progress when we had another chat about it this morning.

'Now then Lee, tomorrow you will be meeting David. David is a really nice young lad from year seven, who needs a bit of reading practice to help him get the hang of it, and you're going to help him do that.'

'He sounds a bit thick to me.'

'No Lee, he's not thick, he's just doing a little bit of catching up. And with your help, he should be reading well in no time.'

'Year seven? He should be able to read by now.'

'Yes, that's why we need your help.'

'I could read properly in year seven.'

'Yes, you could.'

He sighed. 'All right then. I'll help him.'

'Brilliant. That's great. I'll tell him, he'll be so pleased.'

'Mind, if he's thick, there won't be nothing I can do.'

'Lee, you mustn't tell him he's thick.'

'Why not? He probably is, if he can't read.'

'It will be very unhelpful to tell him he's thick. It won't help him to learn.'

'Well, it'll help him learn he's thick.'

'Lee, if someone told you that you were thick, how would you feel?'

'I'd feel like punching them in the neck.'

'Well, there you are then. It's not helpful.'

'Yes, but, thing is, I'm not thick. If this boy's thick, he'll know he's thick, and he won't mind somebody telling him that's why he can't read.'

'We should just concentrate on the teaching, and avoid any mention of whether or not David might be thick.'

Lee frowned and looked weary. 'Well, if you think it might work.' Which was much the same response I'd got from the Head.

***

Some very disturbing news from Jen today. Or maybe not news, but a revelation. She is staying with her cousin in Haringey for a week to progress her wedding plans, and we met for lunch.

We were talking innocently enough about how happy she is. About how lucky she is that things have turned out so well for her, after all those years of being married to the wrong man. She said sometimes she could hardly believe how generous Fate had been to her. She told me she was blessed, absolutely blessed beyond her wildest dreams. Actually, she was so pleased with her life that I began to nod off. I was slipping into a stupor. Other people's good fortune can be so tedious to listen to. But then she said, 'Sometimes I think I don't really deserve to be this happy, especially after what I did to poor old Frank.'

Obviously, my ears pricked up. 'What did you do to Frank?' I asked her. This was the first time I had heard her refer to her late husband as 'poor old Frank.' I was more used to her referring to him as an irritating sod.

'Well, you know,' she said, and then, 'have I not already told you this?'

'No, I don't think so. So, what did you do?' I asked her, and I made a few flippant suggestions. 'Did you refuse to cook for him? Did you make him do his own ironing? Did you have an affair? Did you do him in? What?'

And she said, 'Well, I wouldn't say *do him in,* exactly.'

I stared at her and my blood ran a little cold. 'You wouldn't say do him in *exactly*? So what would you say?'

Jen glanced over her shoulder, and leant a little closer to me. 'Don't tell anyone this, but you know Frank had a heart complaint? He had to take daily medication for his heart, and he was always losing his pills. He was forever asking me to help him find them. Anyway, he lost his pills a few days before he died, and I didn't tell him where they were.'

'Did you know where they were?'

'Yes.'

'So why? Why didn't you tell him where they were?'

'He was driving me nuts, Sally. I can't remember exactly what he was doing now, but it was probably something which reminded me of his mother. He had this way of turning into his mother. His mother was the most irritating woman who ever walked this Earth. I'm sorry, it pains me to say it, but she was. We lived in with her for a couple of years after we were married, remember? But then we had to move out when the atmosphere became outright dangerous and I started to lose my mind. I was staring at the cutlery drawer and fingering knives. I was imagining her head on the draining board and all the juices running into the sink. Okay, that's maybe a bit extreme. She wasn't all bad. I'm not saying she had no redeeming features. Her fruit scones were quite nice. But honestly, she'd try the patience of a saint.

'God, Jen. The juices running into the sink?'

'Yeah, well. That's all in the long distant past now. Anyway, a few days after Frank lost his pills, he wanted sex for the first time in years. Maybe some sort of gruesome side effect of coming off his medication. Or maybe he was just excited by Match of the Day? But whatever the cause, there was a ghastly awakening of something we both thought was dead. A bit like those nature programs on the telly, when it rains and some grotesque tentacle starts filling with fluid and moving around in the undergrowth. Once I'd got over the shock, it crossed my mind that it might not be good for him, you know – all that heaving about with a weak heart and no pills. But then I thought, knowing him he'll probably be all right. So, I agreed to the sex and hoped for the best. By which I probably mean I hoped for the worst. Anyway. You know the rest. That's when he died.'

'Oh my god,' I said.

'You have to put this in context, Sally,' she said.

I tried to think of what context might make any of this this all right.

'I wasn't to blame for his death.'

'Why not?'

'Well, it wasn't my fault he lost his pills.'

'But you knew where they were?'

'Oh yes, I knew where they were.'

Again, I wasn't sure how to respond.

'Don't look at me as if I'm a murderer,' she said. 'After all, when you think about it rationally, he might have died anyway, even if he had taken his pills.'

'So why did he need the pills?'

'For his heart, I told you. But we'll never know whether the lack of pills was actually the reason why he had the heart attack. It might have had nothing to do with that. Some might say that's a bit unlikely, but there's no actual proof. Anyway, it's not worth thinking about now. I don't know why I brought it up. I thought we'd discussed this before?'

'I'd have remembered,' I said.

'Look Sally, I do sometimes need to talk about this, and when I really think about it, I'm absolutely certain I'm not to blame for anything. Let's forget it for now, shall we?'

'It's going to take a bit of digesting,' I said.

'Don't go digesting it,' she said. 'Just leave it alone. You're lucky, you've never had to live with a man who drives you mad. It doesn't bring out the best in you.'

On the way home in the car, I fretted over our conversation. Really, I wish friends wouldn't confess to murdering their husbands out of the blue like that. It catches you off guard and gives rise to so many conflicting emotions. I've known Jen for years. I know she's not a bad person. They spoke very highly of her when she worked at the doctor's surgery just down the road from here. The patients loved her. Old Mrs Bentley, who was never away from the surgery with a succession of complaints, some real, most imagined, left her much-loved cat Bonzo to Jen in her will. Mrs Bentley doted on the cat, so leaving it to Jen was a measure of how highly she regarded her. Bonzo was fourteen years old when Jen inherited him and he suffered from arthritis, so Jen had him put down just days after Mrs Bentley died. Everyone agreed it was the right thing to do. As Jen said, it was nice to think of them both united in the afterlife, and also, cats made her sneeze, so a satisfactory outcome on two counts. Jen is a pragmatist, but I have never thought of her as in any way malicious or cruel. This revelation that she may have been in some way responsible for Frank's death is a shock, although it does seem to chime uncannily with the hasty dispatch of Mrs Bentley's cat.

Another thought occurred to me. Suppose I don't tell anyone, and Jen is found out, and it becomes apparent that I was told about this deliberate withholding of Frank's medication – am I an accessory after the fact if I've kept quiet about it? Am I culpable of obstructing the course of justice?

I probably am. I should probably turn her in to the police. The wedding would have to be postponed, even cancelled altogether. Jen might have to stand trial, suffer a prison sentence, and end up sewing the mailbags which would have contained her wedding invitations.

Or maybe I'm over-thinking this. Maybe I'm becoming melodramatic, getting carried away? There is, as Jen says, no proof now that Frank suffered a heart attack as a direct result of not taking his pills, he might have had a heart attack in any case, even if he had taken his pills. Or his heart attack may have been due to something else entirely, something not related to his heart condition. I tried to think of some other cause of his heart attack that would not be related to his heart condition, but it is difficult to pin this on anything else. Frank's heart was beating, and then it stopped. It was the transition from beating to not beating which caused his death, and if that's not something to do with a heart condition, I don't know what is.

I parked the car in our drive and sat for a minute, wondering what to do, or whether it was appropriate to do anything, and after a few minutes when I had come to no conclusion at all, I got out of the car and went into the house.

***

After dinner this evening Dan and Chrissy pulled out copies of *Uncle Vanya,* which they are rehearsing with the Highfield Amateur Dramatics Group. Sophie watched them highlighting text, underlining speeches and writing notes in the margin, and eventually she said, 'What are you reading?'

'It's a play by Chekhov,' said Chrissy, 'called *Uncle Vanya*.'

'Well, at least it's not Shakespeare,' said Sophie. '*Uncle Vanya*? What's it about? Is it a sit-com?'

'No,' said Dan. 'It's the exact opposite of a sit-com. It's seriously depressing. It's all about futility and emptiness and hopelessness.'

'That's really sad,' said Sophie.

'It is sad,' said Chrissy. 'It's very sad.'

'But,' said Sophie, 'no-one will want to see it.'

'You don't *want* to see *Uncle Vanya*,' said Chrissy. 'You *have* to see it.'

'Why?'

'Because it's *Uncle Vanya*.'

'So there's no laughs or anything?'

'God no,' said Dan. 'Well, there are hollow laughs maybe. But mostly after you've seen *Uncle Vanya* you want to slit your wrists.'

'Are you sure you're doing the right play?'

'Oh yes. It's the right play.'

'Well, don't expect me to go and see it.'

'No no. You'd hate it.'

'I think I would.'

'You definitely would,' said Chrissy.

'Will you go and see it Baz?' said Sophie.

'Fuck no.'

'Sounds worse than Shakespeare. Hope it goes well though. Is it even more sad if it goes well? Or not as sad?'

'I think,' said Dan, 'I think if it goes well, it's even more sad. And weirdly, more funny.'

Chrissy looked up from her copy. 'Do you notice something, Dan?'

'What?'

'This conversation we're having. It sounds like Chekhov. We sound like characters written by Chekhov.'

'Christ yes. You're right.'

'Oh no,' said Sophie. 'I'm going upstairs.'

***

I was driving up to school this morning, when another driver, a man, pulled alongside me and started hooting his horn, and waving 'V' signs, and mouthing something which I was pretty certain was not a lullaby.

My first thought was, I must have done something wrong. But what could I possibly have done to have caused this much rage? Had I accidentally deployed my vehicle-vaporising blasters in his direction? Did I leapfrog over his car back there and drop a ship's anchor on his bonnet?

We were on a section of dual carriageway, and he came to a stop alongside me at the next traffic lights. He was still mouthing and gesticulating, and I thought, this is ridiculous, we are both adults, we should be able to talk about this.

I rolled my window down, and he did likewise. 'What's the problem?' I said.

'What's the problem?' he yelled, incredulous. 'What's the fucking problem? Did you see what you did back there?'

I had no idea. 'What did I do?

'What did you do? Are you asking me what you *did*?'

'Yes.'

'I don't fucking believe this!' He thumped his steering wheel.

The lights changed, and we all drove on, until we came to the next set of lights, and he pulled up alongside me again.

'So what did I do?' I asked him. Genuinely puzzled.

'You were a fucking idiot back there!'

'Are you sure it was me?' I asked him.

'Am I sure it was you? Are you asking me whether I'm fucking sure it was you?'

'Yes.' The lights changed again, and we all drove on to the next set.

At the next set of lights he was slightly ahead of me, half a car's length, but he didn't let this put him off. 'You!' he shouted back at me. 'You must be some kind of moron!'

The woman in the car ahead of me rolled down her window and shouted across to the man, 'What the hell is the matter with you? Shut up!'

'What the fuck has it got to do with you?' he yelled at her.

'We're all using this bit of road!' she yelled back. 'Leave her alone!'

I thought she needed some encouragement for supporting me. 'Well said!' I shouted up to her. 'Thanks for that!'

'Not a problem!' she shouted back to me.

'Fucking unbelievable!' yelled our man, and thumped the steering wheel.

Then, in a surprise development, the man in the car in front of our angry man got out of his vehicle and walked back towards our man, and said to him very clearly, 'Shut the fuck up.' He pointed at me, 'Can't you see she's a woman? Are you some kind of idiot? Expecting her to know how to drive? Expecting her to understand a roundabout? Look at her, man! She's a nice lady. Now shut the fuck up. I'm getting seriously pissed off, listening to you.'

Now this new man was very big. About six foot six, substantial in every direction, looked as if he could carry an elephant upstairs, looked as if he could uproot trees. Made Desperate Dan look like a boy scout. He strode back to his car just ahead of the angry man, and got in, and his car bounced as the suspension took the strain.

That settled us all down. He was obviously going to have the last word.

As the lights changed my lane moved forward, so I set off. The angry man looked back at me sneering, and he set off too, at speed, but he hadn't noticed that his line of traffic was still stationary, so he crunched into the big man's car ahead of him.

I didn't hang about, I turned off at the next exit and took a slightly longer route into school.

I was a little shaken when I arrived. I took deep breaths and paced about a bit to calm down. It took me about ten minutes to relax enough to enjoy thinking about the fate of the angry man on the dual carriageway, his bonnet embedded in Mr Universe's car boot.

I was breathing normally again by the start of my half an hour with Lee, and his tutee David.

'Lee,' I began, 'this is David. David is going to read his book to you today.'

'You told me that yesterday,' said Lee.

'Right,' I said. 'David, would you like to show Lee your book?'

David was looking anxious. He fished a book out of his bag and showed it to Lee.

'Well no wonder he can't read!' said Lee. 'Who gave him this crap?'

'We'll chose another book for next time. Let's just go with this one for today, shall we? Sit down, David, so that Lee can see the book. I'm going to sit over here, and get on with something else while Lee helps you with your reading.'

Lee picked up the book which he had just tossed to one side, and opened it randomly and pointed to a word. 'What does this word say?' he asked David.

David looked at the word. 'And' he said.

'That's an important word to know,' said Lee. 'Pick out some more 'ands' and write them down on this piece of paper.'

David took the piece of paper and started looking through the book. Every now and again he wrote 'and' down on the paper in front of him. Lee stared out of the window.

After about ten minutes, when David had written 'and' about twenty times, I said, 'Lee, it might be a good idea to give David some practice at reading out whole sentences?'

'Well, he hasn't finished this yet,' said Lee.

'Right.' Obviously, it would not be a good idea to challenge Lee's authority in front of David. 'Okay,' I said, and went back to my paperwork.

When the bell went, David had written 'and' over a hundred times. Lee picked up David's piece of paper, looked at his work and gave him some feedback. 'Well, your writing's not very good, is it?' he said. 'I can't even read some of these 'ands.' What does that word say there?' He pointed to a word on the sheet.

'And,' said David.

'And this word here?' Lee pointed to another word.

David looked. 'And,' he said.

'Well, you could have fooled me,' said Lee, letting the paper drop onto the table. 'We'll have to do a lesson on writing next time. Now buzz off.'

David left the room, and I said, 'Lee, I wonder if we could just take a minute to reflect on that lesson?'

'What do you mean?' he said. 'I didn't do no swearing.'

'No you didn't, that was good, but did your lesson help David with his reading?'

He showed me the piece of paper, 'Look what he's done! He worked all lesson.'

'But did he learn anything?'

'He knows 'and.'

'It was a bit boring for him, don't you think?'

'Yes, but it was a proper lesson!' said Lee. 'That's what lessons are like.'

I couldn't immediately think of a reply.

'Can I have my break now?' he said.

***

I managed another little chat with Dan by himself today. It's quite rare now that we manage to sit down together, just the two of us. I don't think this is any sort of problem to him, in fact, I think from his perspective it probably has some advantages. But I miss our little chats about what he aims to do with his life in the longer term, and whether he has any career plans, and if he is aware that even at his young age he needs to be thinking about his pension provision, and whether or not he has been to the dentist recently, and if he thinks that little beard is really a good idea.

'Ah, Dan!' I said, pleased to see him in the kitchen by himself, leaning against the kitchen bench staring intently at his phone.

'Mum,' he said, glancing up.

I put the kettle on. 'It's been a while since we've had a chat. Sit down and we'll have a slice of cake.'

'Oh.' He stuffed his phone into his back pocket. 'Actually I'm a bit pushed for time.'

'Just a quick one then.'

'Right.' He sat down, but on the edge of his seat.

'I'm glad I've caught you Dan, because I've been wanting to ask you something.'

'Oh.'

I gave him a slice of cake and started to make coffee. Dan looked at the cake as if it might or might not be poisonous.

'Yes, I've been wanting to ask you whether you've been mulling over any plans for your future?'

'My future?'

'Yes.'

'My future what?'

'Career. Your future career. Are you going to make a career of what you're doing now, or is this just a stopgap while you think of something else?'

'I thought we were just having a piece of cake.'

I gave him a cup of coffee. 'We're having some cake and a chat. We hardly ever get the chance just to sit down and chat together, the two of us. And this is something you should be thinking about.'

'So this is a loaded chat.'

I laughed, determined to keep things light and easy. 'No, no. Just a chat. I'm just curious, that's all.'

'Well,' he said, very cautiously, 'I have been thinking about it, a bit.'

'Oh have you? Really? Good, that's good! Great!'

He looked startled.

I made a conscious effort to relax, and sound casual. 'I did wonder whether you might have been mulling it over. So, what thoughts have you had?' I took a big bite of cake, to show him that his answer wasn't the only thing that mattered.

'I was thinking about, maybe, architecture.'

I took a breath in and choked on cake and had to drink some coffee. 'You mean,' I said, 'you've been thinking about becoming an architect?'

'Well yes, maybe. I don't know. It's just an idea. I haven't thought about it much.'

'I think it's a brilliant idea! You love building things. You built Aspire and you do all the sets for the theatre productions. It's a wonderful idea, why didn't we think of this before?'

'Mum, honestly, it's just knocking around in my head a bit. It's not a definite career plan. Don't go buying me coloured pencils and protractors and stuff. Let's just mull it over like you said. It might be a terrible idea.'

'Okay,' I said. 'Okay. Let's just mull it over. Maybe we could each do some research, and compare notes. We could talk about it again in a day or two.'

'Maybe longer. A week or two. It's a big thing, I'll need to think about it properly. And I've got a job, for now, so that's all good.'

'Right.' I hesitated, and wondered if I could suggest work experience with Bill's cousin Robert who is an architect. That might be a good idea.

'Anyway,' said Dan. 'I think I might shave this beard off. Not sure if it suits me. What do you think, should I get rid of it?'

Another miracle, and so soon after the last. 'I think you should Dan, I really do. I've never liked it. I think you looked much better without it.'

'Okay,' he said. He stood up and took his cup and plate across to the sink. 'Right, I'd better go before you persuade me to go to the dentist.'

'Oh yes,' I looked across at the calendar pinned to the side of the 'fridge.

'Just joking,' he said. 'See you later Mum.' And then he patted me gently on the head, and went out.

***

Saturday. My birthday. I told Bill I'd like us just to go out for a quiet meal somewhere, maybe stay overnight in a nice pub a little way out of town, and have a relaxing twenty-four hours together. He said he would book something. I couldn't wait.

I went shopping in town for a new skirt to go with the top I can never wear because it doesn't go with any of my skirts. It's a lovely top, but when I wear it with one of my skirts I look as if my top and bottom halves should be running in opposite directions. I got back home much later than planned, just before six. There was barely enough time to grab a cup of coffee and then jump into the shower before Bill was due to pick me up. I badly needed to do something with my hair. It was completely the wrong shape after battling my way around the shops being buffeted by winds, and running my fingers through it absent-mindedly while trying to make difficult skirt-length decisions. My eyes felt itchy and dry, so I rubbed them vigorously while I was waiting for the kettle to boil. It didn't matter that I had mascara all over my cheeks. I ran my fingers through my hair again, making it stand on end. Who cares if it's standing on end, I thought. I'll be in the shower in ten minutes.

I put the coffee in the cup, and stared out of the window, and because I had eaten so many dried apricots to keep me going while I was marching up and down Oxford Street, I farted gently.

I thought I heard a noise, and listened.

Nothing.

I poured the hot water over the coffee, added some milk, picked up the cup and turned around.

'SURPRISE!' Sophie leapt up from behind the island in the kitchen, and blew a party whistle.

'Bloody hell! Sophie!' I said, and I spilled coffee down the front of my blouse.

'Happy birthday! I've got you a present!' said Sophie. 'Come and see!'

'I need a shower Sophie,' I said. 'Desperately. Look at the state of me. Can I see it after my shower?'

'No! It's *really important* you see it now! *Really, really important!* Come on, this way.'

She took hold of my hand and led me into the living room.

The room was as it always is. No sign of a present. I looked at Sophie, I didn't want to seem churlish, but I was in a hurry. 'Where is it?' I said. 'Where's my present?'

'It's coming!' she said.

'Come on then Sophie,' I said. 'I need my present now. I haven't got time to faff about here. Where's my present?'

'It's coming!' she said again, and then she started to count down from ten. 'Ten – nine – eight – seven – six –'

Suddenly terrified, I scanned the room.

'– five – four – three – two – one –'

'SURPRISE! SURPRISE! SURPRISE!' People leapt up from behind the sofas and the armchair, emerged from behind curtains, and came in from the hall. Bill came up to kiss me on the cheek and say 'Happy Birthday!' and hand me a glass of prosecco. Laura emerged from the throng and said, 'Mum you look an absolute mess! Happy Birthday!' Little Harry saw me and burst into tears.

Everyone had a present they wanted to give me. I opened them, and admired them, and thanked everyone. I was so busy. Too busy to do anything but apologise for my appearance. 'I'm sorry,' I said more than once, 'I was just going for a shower when the fun started. I must look a bit of a fright.'

'You look great!' said someone who clearly hates me.

'So many presents,' I said, 'everyone has been so generous, you really shouldn't have,' I said, as the presents kept coming.

'Just obeying instructions!' someone said.

'Instructions?' I said, holding my glass out for more prosecco. 'What instructions?'

But by then someone else was giving me a present. Judith tapped me on the shoulder just as I was finishing my thanks. I turned around and she said, 'Great party! God, your face! Sorry! It's not that bad, honestly. But normally when there's a surprise party they arrange it so that you're looking good.'

'I had absolutely no idea,' I said, 'about any of this.'

'No,' Judith agreed. 'That's obvious. Sophie wanted to surprise you and she did. I was hiding behind the curtain when you came into the room like a panda in a wind tunnel demanding presents.'

'Well,' I said, 'that must have been very amusing.'

'Look,' said Judith, 'everyone's chatting, why don't you just pop upstairs now and get yourself sorted out a bit? Honestly, I wouldn't go out in a foggy eclipse looking like that.'

'Right,' I said, and turned for the door without ceremony.

'Not so fast, birthday girl!' Sam, Jen's fiancé, stood between me and the door into the hall. He held up a beautifully wrapped box. 'Look what we've got for you!'

After midnight when everyone had gone, we sat around drinking milk to stave off hangovers. I looked around the room at the piles of wrapping paper. 'So many presents,' I said. 'You must have forgotten to tell them not to bring any?'

'I did the invitations,' said Sophie. She picked one up from a side table and studied it. 'Yeah, I did forget to tell them not to bring any presents.' The invitation read, *'From Sophie at the Forth's. Please come to our SURPRISE party for Sally Forth on Saturday 10th February at 38 The Chestnuts. Be here at 6.30 for the surprise!!'* And then, in place of the usual, 'Please, don't bring any presents, we would just love to see you,' Sophie's instruction was *'BRING PRESENTS EVERYBODY!!'*

I thanked them all for organising my surprise party for me. I said it had been a real surprise. More than that, it had been a shock. I made them promise never, ever, to do anything like that again. Next time, I said, I don't want a surprise or presents, but I do want plenty of time to make myself look good.

'Don't worry,' said Sophie. 'You'll be fifty next year, and by then you might be a bit old for surprise parties.'

I went upstairs and had a shower.

***

Ivor arrived on Monday, and looked around the lounge. 'Somebody's been havin' a knees-up in here I reckon.'

'Yes, they gave me a surprise birthday party at the weekend. Still clearing up in here I'm afraid.'

'No problem,' he said, 'I'll sharp sort this lot out. Don't you worry.'

'Thanks Ivor,' I said. 'That's great.'

'You go an' get yersel a cup of coffee, Ah'll deal with this.'

I made coffee, and sat down at the kitchen table, and started a letter to Ella.

Dear Ella,

I'd like to apologise for that surprise birthday party we threw for your eightieth. I understand now why you looked so cross when we came in with the fizz and the birthday cake and switched off your television and took over your kitchen. It must have been very annoying. I know now why you said you would much rather be given a surprise visit to the dentist -

.

Ivor came into the kitchen carrying a very skimpy pair of scarlet panties. 'Ah found these down the back of yer sofa cushions. Not yours, Ah'm guessin'? Ah'll just drop them in the washin' machine pet. Must have been a crackin' party?'

***

Bill and I went out for a quiet meal together last night. Not to celebrate my birthday, I've had enough of my birthday, I won't be ready to celebrate it again for at least another year. No, I was hoping that last night would help to expunge the memory of my recent birthday celebrations, not add to them.

Sophie called our evening out together last night a 'date night.' I told Bill, and I said I thought that was very sweet. Bill said it was, it was very sweet. Just wholly inaccurate.

We agreed in advance, Bill and I, that while we were out together we wouldn't talk about his job, or our children, or our lodgers or my annoying friends. We would just focus on each other. We would spend the whole evening just reconnecting, removed from the frustrations and irritations of our daily lives. The evening was to be exclusively ours.

I suppose it was inevitable that after ten minutes we were staring at each other glumly and had nothing to say to each other. So I suggested we relax the rules, and talk about anything at all, provided it was upbeat, and positive and worthy of celebration.

'Okay,' said Bill, 'good plan. Right, well,' he looked at me and smiled. 'Upbeat, did you say?'

'Yes,' I said, and smiled at him, in anticipation.

He glanced around. 'Nice place.'

'Very nice,' I agreed. 'Lovely.'

'Your hair looks nice.'

'Thanks, I had it cut a while back. It suits me better.'

'Tell you what,' said Bill. 'It seems a shame to hobble the evening. Let's just have a good old moan about stuff. Slag a few people off. Enjoy ourselves a little. What do you say?'

'Yes okay,' I said. And we chatted away quite happily after that.

Over coffee I told Bill that I had managed a five-minute chat with Dan about his future career plans, and he had mentioned the word 'architect'.

'Ah,' he said. 'Right. That's interesting.'

'It is interesting,' I said. 'But I don't think we should get too excited.'

'Oh, definitely not. No.' Bill agreed.

'He has to think about it in his own time. We'll just have to leave him to mull it over. It would have to be his choice. We should stay out of it and not interfere.'

'Yes, yes, of course.'

'But I was doing a bit of research on the internet earlier and I saw a book called *So You'd Like to be an Architect?* And I wondered whether I should get it? I could just leave it lying around, where he might see it. In his bedroom, maybe.'

'Slip it under his pillow, perhaps? Like an architect fairy.'

'Yes,' I said. 'I could do that, I could slip it under his pillow.'

Bill thought about it. 'That's an absolutely terrible idea,' he said.

'You're right,' I said. 'Too pushy.'

'Much too pushy. Very likely to be counterproductive.'

'Yes, of course. I see that now.'

'Definitely not a good idea. Don't buy the book.'

'No I won't. I'll take it out of his bedroom as soon as we get home.'

***

I hate to say it, but Judith was absolutely right about the history evening classes. I'm enjoying them far more than I ever thought I would. Meeting new people is just what I need, she was right when she told me that, and Max is becoming a good friend. It was the Tudors again in history class this evening. The reign of Henry VIII is everyone's favourite medieval soap, featuring love, longing, commitment, betrayal, despair, decapitation and a cast of unsmiling men and women upholstered like three-piece suites. The allure never fades. Are we going to continue to find the Tudors fascinating in a hundred, two hundred, three hundred years' time? Are we going to be sitting on Mars in our bio-pods mending tears in our spacesuits and debating the evidence for Anne Boleyn's adultery? Will we be mulling over whether Henry was a tyrant as we navigate the universe and sling our spaceships around black holes? And when we are sucked into a black hole, and the laws of physics make us infinitely long and infinitely heavy, and Time becomes as bendy as a rubber codpiece, will we see Henry himself, sitting on the event horizon? Will we sit down next to him and ask if he thought in retrospect that he would have benefited from a course in Anger Management? Might we ask him whether, after all this time, he and Anne are reconciled?

I'd like to answer 'yes' to all of the above, because I think other planets might be a bit short of interesting historical detail. Imagine trying to write a mini-series based on the history of Mars in the last thousand years. Mars needs the Tudors more than we do. Anyway, our class ended early this evening because our history tutor Terry had a domestic emergency and had to dash away. Apparently, his wife had accidentally locked herself out of their flat and there were eggs hard-boiling on the stove. So we stood around at only eight fifteen and wondered what to do, and it wasn't long before someone suggested popping around the corner to the appropriately named 'Executioner's Block' for a drink.

Once in the pub and each furnished with a drink, we continued to discuss things historical, and as the evening wore on, our curiosity about the Tudors deepened. Marjorie had a book of portraits of the Tudors, which we passed around among us all. Someone wondered why the Tudors' mouths were so small. Somebody else wondered why none of them had any eyelashes. Someone wondered what they wore in hot weather. I wondered if they had teeth. Judith wondered what they used to wash their hair. Did the women shave their legs? Is it time the garter made a come-back? Why do all portraits of historical figures look so serious? When was the smile invented? Did no-one smile until Kodak gave us the Box Brownie? So many important questions, all ignored by exam board specifications. No one ever turned over their A level history exam paper to see the question, *The Tudors all had very small mouths. Discuss.*

Max and I had quite a long chat over a few glasses of red wine. What a lovely man. He's divorced, still single, two children, one married, no grandchildren. I asked if he'd been divorced long, and he said ten years. I said, in the spirit of an enquiring student of medieval history, that I was surprised he hadn't re-married because he seemed like such a nice man and he looked very good in his smart, tight jeans which were much sexier than the baggy knee-breeches worn by the Tudors. He said he had tried wearing baggy knee-breeches and although they were very comfortable, they didn't make him a babe magnet. I asked if he was comfortable in his tight jeans. He said he was becoming less and less comfortable. I said he had extraordinarily blue eyes which would look good in a portrait by Holbein, and he said my eyelashes were much too long to be accepted in Tudor society.

Then Judith appeared out of nowhere and said if I wanted a lift home she was going now so I'd better get myself into gear.

On the way home in the car Judith came over quite Mother Superior-esque.

'What were you doing with that man?' she asked me.

'What do you mean, what was I doing? I was talking to him. That was perfectly obvious.'

'I could see you were talking to him,' she said. 'I could see that. It was the *way* you were talking to him. You were flirting outrageously.'

'Don't be ridiculous.'

'Come on Sally, you were flirting with him, he was flirting with you. Let's not pretend otherwise.'

'Oh, lighten up Judith. Even if there was a bit of flirting going on, what harm can it possibly do? I'm a sensible adult, I'm not going to do anything daft. Give me some credit!'

She looked at me sideways. 'Is he married?'

'Divorced.'

She was quiet for a minute, and then she said, 'Sally, you watch your step. That's my last word on the subject for now.'

'For heaven's sake Judith – where on Earth has all this come from? I only had a light-hearted conversation with the man.'

'And I only have your best interests at heart,' she said.

We drove the rest of the way in uncomfortable silence. I resented the suggestion that I had done something underhand, or was planning to.

When I got home, Bill was looking through a heap of papers in the lounge, and circling passages with a highlighting pen. He glanced up when I walked in. 'Good session?' he asked.

'Yes,' I said, 'good session.'

'Foul night, hope the place was warm enough.'

'Not bad,' I said, and I went back into the kitchen to pour us both a small glass of wine, so that he wouldn't know I'd been sitting next to a wood burning stove in the pub since just after eight.

***

Jen has made a touching request. But I will build up to it.

We met for lunch today and I managed quite successfully not to dwell on the possibility that she might have murdered her first husband. Somewhere at the back of my mind I was thinking it would be a shame to let that spoil a good friendship, so I didn't refer back to our rather awkward chat of a couple of weeks ago, and I sensed she wasn't keen to revisit it either. Maybe I had got some of the details wrong and over-reacted. I could have jumped to the wrong conclusions, but I wasn't going to ask her for any clarification.

Instead, we spoke of wedding favours. Jen said she would like to give the wedding guests a gift to take away with them, and to keep as a memento of the day, and as a thank-you for being present and celebrating with her and Sam.

'Lovely,' I said, and I asked her what gift she had in mind.

She said she would like to give everyone a universal travel plug.

I said, 'What is a universal travel plug?'

'A universal travel plug,' she said, 'is a plug that will fit any sink, anywhere in the world, so you need never be without a plug, and you will always be able to fill your sink with water.' She said it might not be very romantic, but it was very useful, and every time a guest used the plug in future, they would think fondly of her and Sam. She said she had just such a plug in her bag for me to look at, and she fished it out and handed it to me, and told me it was a quality product.

It was a soft rubber disc, much larger in diameter than an ordinary plug, and it looked a bit like a standard rubber plug which had been run over by a steamroller. I said it looked very useful, if not particularly decorative, and I asked her what it symbolised.

She said she hadn't thought much about its symbolic significance because she had been concentrating on its utility, but, off the top of her head, she thought it would symbolise all those good things in life that we wanted to hang on to and didn't want to run out of.

I couldn't fault its symbolic value and had to agree that it was significant and worthy, so I okayed the choice of a universal travel plug as a wedding favour for each guest. All that remained was to decide on how it should be presented, and I was mulling this over when Jen thought of the answer herself. She would suspend the plugs from a length of blue ribbon for the men, and a length of pink ribbon for the women.

'Marvellous idea,' I said. I couldn't think of a better way to present someone with a universal travel plug.

I thought then that we might move on from wedding plans and talk about me, but that was when Jen made her touching request. She asked if I would give her away at the wedding ceremony.

I said of course I would give her away, I would be very touched and honoured to give her away. I asked her if she was sure she wanted me to do it? Was there anyone else in the family she should ask first?

She said no, she had thought about it, and I was entirely the right person. However, she said, because I would be walking up the aisle with her, I would now have to be dressed to colour co-ordinate with the wedding party. So she would like me to wear cream, if that was okay.

I said cream it is. No problem. And then I asked if – as befitting my enhanced ceremonial status – I would now be in line for a deluxe version of the universal plug? But she said no, I'd be getting the same as everyone else. So I asked about Chrissy.

'Did you ask Chrissy if she'd be your bridesmaid?'

'I did, yeah. But she said no. She said her mother was very difficult to stay friends with, and there'd be problems if she agreed to be my bridesmaid.'

'Oh well,' I said, 'fair enough. At least you asked.'

I told Bill later that night that Jen had asked me to give her away, and I'd been really touched. Bill said, 'You've wanted to give her away a few times over the years, haven't you? Good to finally get the chance.'

***

Laura, my daughter, is apt to embrace causes.

When she was nine, she was given a nurse's uniform and became a nurse, and vowed to heal the sick and dedicate herself to the nursing profession. At ten years old she discovered religion, and began preparing herself to take holy orders. At eleven she was an artist and by twelve she was a tennis player and slept with her tennis racquet in her bed. At thirteen, she became a vegetarian, and by sixteen she was a vegan. At eighteen, she was a Quaker, and at nineteen she was fascinated by Buddhism. From twenty until she married, she devoted herself to Ben, now her husband. Since giving birth to her son, she has become very interested in psychological freedom through self-expression, but fortunately she moved on from this phase just before it threatened to end her marriage.

Now she is a campaigner, campaigning against the prevalence of television in our lives. She would like to see its influence curtailed. Personally, I think that particular horse has bolted, but she has the bit between her teeth, and I suspect we will all just have to ride this one out. We have never been successful at moving Laura on from an obsession before she is ready to do it herself.

When I got home from the dentist this afternoon, Sophie greeted me anxiously in the kitchen. 'She's here,' Sophie said, 'in the bathroom.'

'Who?' I said. 'Who's here?'

'Laura. Not Little Harry though, he's at Titchy Tikes.'

'Hi!' In came Laura. 'Just passing through on my way to pick Harry up.'

'Good to see you,' I said. 'Have you got time for coffee?'

The three of us sat down and had coffee together, but Sophie was on edge.

'I've just been telling Sophie,' said Laura, 'that if you watch just two hours of television a day for a year, that amounts to one whole month a year watching TV for twenty-four hours a day, continuously. Just two hours a day, and one twelfth of the year is gone, entirely, to watching a glass box in the corner of the room. You might as well just have eleven months in your year. You're wasting an entire month every year, damaging your health and shortening your life in the process.'

I understood Sophie's unease.

'Just two hours of TV a night? That can't be right, Laura,' I said. 'Surely your sums are wrong?' But it was just a delaying tactic, because I knew she'd be right.

'It's right,' she said. 'Two times three hundred and sixty-five divided by twenty-four equals just over thirty days a year watching television twenty-four hours a day. One whole month a year. Shocking, isn't it? That's two whole months of watching telly for twelve hours a day. And then when you consider that most people watch more than two hours a night, it's even worse than that for them.'

'Oh no,' said Sophie. 'How much do you watch Laura?'

'I don't watch any. I got rid of our telly when I realised it was corroding my life.'

'Did Ben mind?'

'No, he didn't mind, not after I explained it to him.'

Sophie looked depressed.

'Statistics always sound a bit drastic when you express them like this though, Laura,' I said. 'It's like saying, if you add up all the time the average person spends blowing their nose, they spend three years of their entire life just blowing their nose.'

'Three years just blowing your nose? Oh no,' said Sophie.

'That would mean,' I did a quick calculation, 'we spend about ten years of our lives doing nothing but watching television and blowing our nose.'

'I heard that we swallow twenty spiders in our sleep,' said Sophie.

'A night?' said Laura.

'No,' said Sophie. 'Not a night. In your whole life. If it was a night you wouldn't want any breakfast.'

'Oh god Sophie' said Laura. 'That's revolting.'

'Well,' said Sophie, 'we don't know we're swallowing them, because we're asleep. So it's not that bad. But if you add all those spiders up together, like you just did with the watching telly, we'd have to swallow twenty spiders a night.'

Laura looked blank, and then she said, 'Here's a really interesting statistic. If you estimate that on average during the course of her life a woman has sex four times a week for forty years, and each episode lasts fifteen minutes, that's an hour a week for fifty-two weeks of the year times forty, that's about eighty-six days of continuous sex in a lifetime.'

'Eighty-six days?' said Sophie.

'Yes,' said Laura. 'That's about three months.'

Sophie weighed this up. 'I wonder if it would be better just to get it all over with at one go? It would give us more time to do other things.'

'Anyway,' said Laura, recognising that the conversation was going seriously off-piste, 'must be off. Harry's at Wobble Bots so I'll have to dash.'

'Are you going to take our telly with you?' said Sophie.

'No of course not! It's entirely up to you how much telly you watch. If you want to ruin your life with it, that's your business. You're grown-ups, you can make your own decisions. I'm just making you aware of what's at stake. Watch telly and be a passive moron, or live your own life. Simple as that really. Over to you!'

Laura breezed out, taking her reforming zeal with her, and the house sagged slightly in her wake.

Sophie was subdued. 'I like a bit of telly,' she said. 'I don't think I want to give it up. I hope that doesn't make me a bad person.'

***

Bill came in very late last night, just as I was going to bed. Sophie and I had been watching a late-night showing of *The Graduate*, and she had just gone upstairs. She said it was the best film she had ever seen, and I enjoyed seeing it again. Sophie particularly liked the bit where Ben was in the swimming pool wearing his diving kit. Neither of us felt we had wasted a single minute of our lives watching it.

Bill took his jacket off and threw it over the back of the sofa and then sat in an armchair with his feet up on the footstool.

'You look tired,' I said.

'I am tired. How are things here, at Open House Central?'

'Good,' I said, 'Dan and Chrissy went upstairs about ten, Baz had a very early night because he has a very early start. Sophie and I have been watching *The Graduate*, she's just gone up. All present and correct.'

'You know that idea of Sophie's, the other Sunday, when we were having lunch? Tax breaks in exchange for provision of accommodation for low paid workers in expensive inner cities? Incredibly, we're looking into it. I've put a team on it. I said to them Look, here's an idea, there's got to be something wrong with it. Run with it for a while, explore the implications, and let me know why it won't work.'

'So, why won't it work?'

'Don't know yet. They're still working on it. So far, they like it.'

'Sophie's thinking,' I said, 'is formulating government policy?'

'Extraordinary, isn't it? She just casually came up with it over lunch, and now there's a whole team of Oxbridge graduates working on her idea.'

'That's incredible,' I said, thinking back to that Sunday. 'She couldn't even get the Yorkshire puddings right.'

***

This time, Judith and I took ourselves to the history class separately. I have had quite enough of her breathing disapproval down my neck. I sometimes think she is entirely lacking in the sympathy or empathy or good humour or understanding or something, to know how to cement a good friendship. She seems to specialise in raising the anxiety level of her companions. I wonder sometimes if she's got some kind of syndrome. Not autism but something similar. Fraughtism. Well, she overstepped the mark last week, thinking she could tick me off for having a lively conversation with a friend. By mutual agreement, we got ourselves to the history class under our own steam, and met up in the car park.

She left her car as I was leaving mine, and we walked into the building together. 'I didn't offer you a lift because I have to leave prompt at nine, and after last week I thought you might not want to be dragged away,' she said. It was a simple enough explanation, but her tone was accusatory. She might as well have said, 'I didn't offer you a lift because I have to leave prompt at nine, and after last week I thought you might like to stay longer and eat human flesh.'

Anyway, I'm glad she could leave under her own steam, because she would never have been happy to stay so late after the class.

***

I'm enjoying having a cleaner. Turns out I don't suffer from tight-lipped middle class angst about someone else cleaning up after me. I haven't cleaned a loo for weeks now, and that suits me just fine. Neither do I have to worry about Ivor being judgmental. He's implacable, takes everything in his stride. He doesn't mind a bit of taxidermy in the utility room, he's cheerful about exotic underwear behind the sofa cushions, he's efficient and not remotely censorious. He brought a bottle of sink un-bunger with him this morning and asked if I would mind if he used it in the little bathroom on the top floor. 'There's been a Yeti or sommat sheddin' its hairs in the bath,' he explained, 'but this'll sharp shift it.'

When he leaves, the house looks lovely, and I sometimes walk from room to room, smiling.

'Thanks Ivor,' I said when he'd finished this morning. 'The house looks great. See you next week.'

He hesitated. 'Sorry to say this petal, but this week might be me last week.'

'Oh no! Why? Have you got another job?'

'Not another job, like, no. See – rents round here, they're astronomical! Astronomical like! Ah've used up all me savin's, an' I just can't afford it, livin' here, even with me little evenin' job. I'll probably have to gan back up to the Toon, and get something up there. It's a shame like, 'cos I like it down here. Folks is friendly. People say they aren't in the south, but I think you're a friendly enough bunch of folks. But if you can't afford it, you can't afford it. No use blubbing.'

'Oh dear. That's an awful shame.'

'Aye. Ah've been hangin' on like, but reely, Ah can't afford it down here. Ah've given it a go like, but it's too dear. Sorry, petal.'

'Listen Ivor,' I said, 'why don't you sit down for a minute and we'll have a cup of tea and a chat.'

'No bother,' he said. 'Ah'm sorry to leave youse in the lurch, but you'll sharp get another cleaner. Not as good as me, like. Three sugars, petal. Thanks.'

***

I told them all together in the kitchen the following night. I said I'd offered Ivor free accommodation if they were agreeable; it would just be for a trial period of one month, and then if we felt the arrangement was working, we would continue for another five months or until either side wanted a change. In the meantime, Ivor would have some time to make himself more economically viable to live in the south, if that was where he decided he wanted to be. I was very aware that none of them had met him yet, so I'd asked him round this evening to introduce him.

'What's he like?' said Sophie.

'He's very nice. Very good-looking, as it happens. A Geordie. Very pleasant, straightforward. I think you'll like him. He's going to call in at eight, so you can meet him, and then we'll decide whether we think it would work.'

'If he moves in, would he be roving around cleaning the house all the time, like one of those robotic hoovers?' said Dan.

'No, he'll clean for four hours on an agreed day of the week, but apart from that he won't do any cleaning or go into anyone's room.'

'Does he look like Robson Green?' said Chrissy.

'A bit,' I said. 'A bit like a young Robson Green in a blue stripy apron.'

He arrived promptly at eight. Sophie went to the front door to let him in. 'Hiya!' I heard her say.

'Hiya!' said Ivor.

Sophie brought him into the kitchen. 'Everybody,' she said, 'this is Ivor. Sit down Ivor. I really like your accent, by the way.'

'He hasn't said anything yet,' said Baz.

'He said *Hiya*,' said Sophie, 'so I can tell.'

'Anyway, Ivor,' I said when he was seated at the table with the rest of us, 'would you like to just tell us a little bit about yourself? I'm the only one who's met you yet.'

'Would you like some tea, Ivor?' said Sophie. 'We've all got some.'

'Yes please,' said Ivor. 'Milk and three sugars, petal. Champion.'

'Right,' I said, 'Ivor, the floor is yours. What can you tell us about yourself?'

'Okay,' he said, folding his arms and leaning in to rest them on the table. 'Me name's Ivor Krevice. Ah'm twenty-one, a Geordie, but Ah only said one word and you worked that one out.' He looked at Sophie, and smiled a very charming Robson Green smile.

She handed him his tea, coquettishly.

'Anyway,' he continued, 'what can Ah say? Ah left school at sixteen, coulda stayed on an' done some 'A' levels, but Ah couldn't sit still like, that was always me problem at school. Ah worked in a bottling factory for a while—'

'What were you bottling?' said Sophie.

'Drinks.'

'What kind of drinks?'

Dan looked at his watch. 'Tell you what. Let's go out. Have a few beers.'

'Champion!' said Sophie. 'I'll just get my coat.'

***

I was in bed when they came back, so Dan told me today what they thought of Ivor.

'I think it could work,' he said. 'He seems a really nice guy. I don't think it matters too much that we can't understand what he's saying. Chrissy says we'll get tuned in to the accent quite quickly, and when we've learned the vocabulary we'll probably be able to speak a bit of Geordie ourselves, and it's useful to have another language. He said he couldn't come unless he could bring his board, and he wasn't sure how we would feel about that. I said it would be no problem he could put his board in the shed. I thought it was a skateboard or something, or a surfboard. But it turns out he's got a parrot.'

'A parrot?'

'An African grey parrot. He got it from a friend who was sick of looking after it and wanted to throw it out the window. Ivor said he would take it. It's called Marra. That's Geordie for

Mate. He said it likes a bit of company. They're very intelligent birds, they get lonely if they're on their own.'

'A parrot?'

'He'd look after it. We wouldn't have to do anything with it. He said there'll be no mess anywhere. He'd keep it in his room, apart from when it needed some company. He says it's house-trained.'

'House-trained?'

'Yeah, and it doesn't bite. And it talks, apparently. So that's good.'

'Is it?'

'Yeah. What do you think? Do you mind the parrot?'

'I don't know. I might hate it. I don't know anything about parrots.'

'Sophie and Chrissy like the idea. Baz says if the bird's a pain he'll wring its neck and stuff it. I'm okay with a parrot.'

'I'm going to be very strict about this Dan. I'll agree to a four-week trial period, but if at the end of that time I don't think it's working, then we're all agreed it comes to an end. No argument. My decision is final.'

'Yeah, yeah. But this was your idea, wasn't it?'

'I wasn't reckoning on a parrot.'

'He says it's very intelligent. And it talks. Sophie thinks it will be like Alexa with feathers.'

***

Jen has been down here staying with her cousin again in Haringey. She came over for lunch today and I told her about Ivor, and introduced her to the parrot, which was sitting in its cage in the corner of the kitchen delicately nibbling its feet. Jen said she didn't like birds, they gave her the creeps, and judging by Marra's expression when he looked up, he didn't like her either.

We discussed the wedding, which is getting closer now. I haven't yet bought my dress, the one I will wear to give Jen away in. We talked about the exact shade of cream required of the dress for longer than I would have believed it possible to discuss a shade of off-white. The cream in question has to be a grey-cream rather than a pink-cream and definitely not a yellow-cream or a buff-cream. I asked her if she was sure the human eye could detect these fine distinctions, and she suggested we went shopping together for the dress, to avoid any ghastly mistakes.

As we were finishing off our quiche and salad she asked me what I'm planning for her hen-do. She said I needn't spill the beans with all the details if I was intending to surprise her, but she wondered if I could give her a hint, at very least she'd like to put the date in her diary.

I was momentarily stunned, but recovered quickly. 'Hen-do? God, Jen, we're much too old for that kind of nonsense, aren't we? You're nearly fifty for Christ's sake. You can't be a proper hen anyway, you've been married before.'

'Of course I'm a proper hen!' She put down her forkful of rocket leaves and toasted seeds. 'What do you mean, I'm not a proper hen? I might be an older hen, but I'm definitely a hen. A hen is any female person who is about to be married. Not a proper hen? Look at me I'm eating seeds for god's sake. And anyway, it would be fun to have a do, wouldn't it?'

'Can't we just nip into Marks and Spencer for a chicken sandwich?'

'No! We have to have a proper venue and dress up and drink cocktails. And we need to be wearing sashes with 'Jen's Hens' printed on them. It'll be great! Loads of fun!'

I looked at her in disbelief, and the parrot looked up from his feet and said, 'Fuck!'

'Don't tell me I have to organise my own hen-do,' said Jen. 'That would be the pits.'

So I had no choice. I've agreed to organise a hen-do. But I have beaten her down from a weekend away for twenty with sashes, activities and speeches, to a night out in London for ten, a bride-to-be-only sash, and speeches only if someone is moved by the spirit, which in this case will probably be gin.

'Speaking of speeches,' I said, 'have you thought any more of the speech you want me to give on the day itself? The wedding day? Have you written it yet? I'll need to practise it.'

'I haven't written it yet,' she said. 'But I know roughly what I'm going to say. Actually, it might be best if you didn't see it first.'

'I have to see it first, Jen, if I'm going to read it. I have to practise it.'

'I think it would be best if you came to it fresh. Trust me.'

I was about to protest, but Sophie arrived.

'Hiya!'

'Hello Sophie.'

'Hiya!' said Marra.

Sophie dropped her bag on the floor. 'Did you hear that? Marra said hello to me! Did you hear him say Hiya when I came in?' Sophie turned towards his cage. 'You said hello to me, didn't you Marra?'

'Hiya!' said Marra.

'He's done it again! He's dead intelligent.'

'We were just talking about Jen's hen-do, Sophie,' I said, to distract her from the dead intelligent parrot.

'A hen-do! Brilliant! Is Chrissy going? Can I come? You need to wear a sash with Bride-to-Be printed on it, and we'll all need sashes, and probably those headbands with something pink and fluffy bouncing around on it. Hearts maybe. I can get the sashes done, if you like. Oh! And you'll have to have a stripper. A man of course, not a woman – that would be stupid. When is it? I'll make sure I'm not working.'

'Er, well, it's date to be arranged at the moment Sophie, but we'll let you know.'

'Right,' she said, 'but don't fix it for a Tuesday. I can never get a swap on Tuesdays. Any other day is fine. It's ages since I've been to a hen-do. Actually I've only been to one and the bride was sick all down her sash. It was a great night though. Fantastic! Anyway, I'm going upstairs to get out of my tunic. See you later Marra!'

'Hiya!' said Marra.

'God,' said Jen, when Sophie was on her way upstairs. 'How do you stand it? What with the girl and the parrot, it's not exactly restful around here is it? You may as well go back to teaching.'

'It's a lot more restful than teaching. No comparison. And I've noticed that the parrot only swears when he hears excitable, raised voices.'

'Does it? Well that's something. Anyway, on reflection, I think you might be right about a more low-key hen-do. Something about Sophie's enthusiasm brings you to your senses. She's welcome to come, but better warn her there'll be no male strippers.'

Marra put his head on one side, but made no comment.

***

Dan was kneeling down putting his boots on beside the back door when I came downstairs this morning. It wasn't the best time to quiz him about his highly speculative plans to become an architect, but a lemming-like instinct drove me forward.

'Morning Dan,' I said, 'I'm glad I've caught you. Just wondered if you'd had a chance to consider whether or not you're still interested in becoming an architect?'

He stood up. 'Becoming a what?' he said, puzzled.

'An architect,' I said. 'You were thinking about architecture. As a possible career?'

'Was I? When was that?'

'Just a few weeks ago. Don't you remember?'

A car horn sounded.

'Gotta go, Mum. Getting picked up. See you later.'

Chapter Three: March

There's been a leak. Bill seems irritated rather than annoyed or alarmed, so I'm assuming as leaks go, it could be worse. The headlines this morning are variously: *Tax Breaks for Wealthy Landlords, Help to House Low Paid, Lots of Lolly in Exchange for Live-in Lodgers.*

I said I hadn't realised these plans were so far advanced. Bill said they aren't, they're still just looking into it, and there are significant problems to overcome, but the Press have got hold of it and have decided to run with it because their readers are getting tired of the current crop of disasters. Sophie saw the headlines and read them while she was eating her toast at breakfast.

'Wasn't this my idea?' she said.

'I think you did suggest it first, yes,' I said.

'Will I get a reward or something?'

'Probably not a reward, no.'

'Will I just be famous again, like the last time?'

'You might. Difficult to say, really.'

'It's dead easy being famous living with you.'

***

Lee, too, was fully briefed when I saw him in school this afternoon. He is amazingly well informed on current affairs for a special needs student. I blame his father.

We were in an art lesson, looking at a virginal sheet of A1 paper onto which he was supposed to be sketching a design for a stained glass window.

Lee held his pencil above the paper, ready to bespoil it. 'My dad says your Bill's onto a good thing.'

'What?'

'You'll be coining it if you don't have to pay any council tax, with all them weirdos living in your house.'

'I beg your pardon?'

'Just sayin.'

'I don't have weirdos living in my house, thank you Lee. Now then, what shape will this window be? Circular maybe? Or square?'

'I'm doing a house-shaped window. An' I'll put some rooms in it.'

'Why?'

''Cos.'

'Normally you put a window in a house, not a house in a window.'

'Yeah, well. It's modern art, innit.'

Lee outlined the shape of a house and divided it into six room shapes.

'This looks all wrong for a stained glass window, Lee,' I told him.

'Lee!' Sarah Simms, the art teacher, swooped by and looked over my shoulder at Lee's page, 'What have you got for us Lee?'

'It's a house.'

'A house! Brilliant! Great idea. That will work really well. You can emphasise the room shapes with heavy black lines to make them look like leaded panes. Will you put some figures in those rooms?'

'Numbers?'

'People.'

'Oh yeah. There'll be people in all the rooms. All the spare rooms'll have people in them.'

'Great. Carry on then Lee.'

There was a little silence after she moved on, during which, magnanimously, Lee decided not to gloat.

'Anyway,' he said, going over the pencilled room outlines with heavy black paint, 'my dad wants to know, is this just for people with big poncey houses like yours, or can we cash in too? If Harrison and me share a room, someone could have my room. It might need cleaning up a bit. There's some stuff on the carpet could do with coming off. And they'd have to stay out of Mum's way when she's going apeshit. But if we don't have to pay any council tax, Dad says we could go to Tenerife twice a year.'

'Lee, as I understand it, this idea is just being discussed at the moment, nothing has been decided yet. It might not happen at all.'

'But it's in the papers!'

'That doesn't mean it's definitely going to happen.'

'Ah fuck,' he said. 'So we might not be able to go to Tenerife twice a year?'

'I wouldn't count on it, no.'

'Bloody politicians,' he said. And he spilled his water pot over his painting.

***

Bill was late home this evening. I was in the living room, Dan and Chrissy were out, Baz was doing something to a stoat in the utility room, and Ivor and Sophie were making a fruit salad for the parrot. I heard the front door open and shut.

'That'll be Mr Forth,' Sophie said. She put her head around the living room door off the kitchen and said, 'Mrs Forth, Mr Forth's home!' She turned back, 'Hiya!' I heard her greet Bill as he walked into the kitchen.

'Hiya!' said the parrot.

'That wasn't me saying 'Hiya!' to you twice, Mr Forth, that was Marra saying it the second time.'

'Hiya!' said the parrot.

'That wasn't me saying 'Hiya!' another time Mr Forth, that was Marra again.'

'Hiya!' said the bird.

Ivor stepped in. 'Eee lad,' he said to Bill, 'you look knackered. Sit yersel doon an Ah'll mek you a cuppa.'

'Thank you, er?'

'Ivor, Ivor Krevice. We met the other night, remember? An' Ah introduced you to me bord.'

'Oh yes. The bird. Well, I, -'

'You gan next door an Ah'll bring youse a cup a tea.'

'Thank you, Ivor.'

Bill came through to the living room and sat next to me on the sofa. 'Ivor Krevice?' he said quietly. 'Can that be right?'

'I don't know whether I'm hearing it correctly. He might be saying something else. It seems an odd name for a Geordie.'

'It's an odd name for anybody. Surely to god if you were called Krevice you wouldn't call your kid Ivor? What were they thinking?'

'I'm sympathetic to people with odd names. Remember I'm Sally Forth.'

'Yes, but, Ivor Krevice? Christ.'

Ivor swept in from the kitchen with a cup of tea for both of us, and a plate of biscuits. 'Here y'are. Wrap yersels aroond this.'

'Thank you, Ivor,' I said.

'Champion. Ah'm off to me bed now,' Ivor said. 'Sophie's staying up a bit to talk to Marra. She's taken a real shine to me bord. Baz'll have to watch oot! Just joking like.'

'Is Baz here too?' Bill looked around.

'Aye. He's in the utility room, stuffin' a stoat.'

'Oh right,' said Bill. 'Good.'

'Ah'll say night-night then. See yus later!'

'Night!' We called after him. 'Goodnight, Ivor.'

Bill turned to me after the door had closed behind Ivor. 'We're at capacity now Sally. No more.'

***

I really enjoyed our history class this evening. I was looking forward to it because it was billed as an in-depth study of Henry

VIII's medical history. It sounded fascinating, Holby City in a codpiece. And if anyone needed a dose of antibiotics in his codpiece, Henry VIII did.

I learnt that Henry probably had diabetes, but fortunately he never had any treatment for it. Generally speaking in medieval times, the less treatment you had for your illnesses, the more likely you were to survive them. He had smallpox and other poxes of different sizes, along with migraines and regular bouts of malaria. He had a permanently discharging ulcer on one leg and painful varicose veins in the other. He would have had housemaid's knee, but he ran out of legs. He might have had Cushings syndrome which would cause him to gain weight and suffer mood swings. He was constipated for the whole of his reign. He was so fat in later life he had to be hoisted with ropes up and down stairs, and on and off the toilet, and on and off his wife. The only thing he seemed not to have suffered from was a prolapsed womb. Although if he had possessed a womb, it would certainly have wanted to escape.

Judith, Max and I sat at the back of the class and marvelled at the illnesses Henry had to put up with. He beheaded two wives out of a possible six but, considering how his ailments must have added to his frustrations, we were amazed at his restraint.

I regret to say, on reflection, now that the evening class has finished and I'm back home, that Judith, Max and I might have been the cause of some low-level disruption at the back of the class this evening. We had to be told by Terry Forbes, our history tutor, to settle down. Once or twice, when we were giggling, Terry invited us to share the joke with the rest of the class. I wasn't blameless, but Max was definitely the ringleader. He was very funny on the subject of Tudor medicine. He had Judith and I in stitches. Quite an achievement, as far as Judith is concerned. She does not give way to laughter if she can possibly help it. If I'd been the teacher in the class this evening, I'd have separated Judith and me, and sent Max out of the lesson until he'd calmed down a bit.

We took Terry out for a drink to the pub around the corner by way of an apology after the session. It's a nice pub, The Executioner's Block, always has a cheerful stove lit in the snug. Judith and Terry started talking about medieval treatments for haemorrhoids, which I stopped listening to after Judith mentioned the cauterising prod. Instead, I told Max about the parrot, and our new lodger, Ivor. We each had a large glass of red wine, and I found myself being very entertaining on the subject of our lodgers and the parrot. It was easy, I was enjoying myself, and Max was so quick to amuse. I told him that Bill had declared, in the manner of a Victorian patriarch, that we were 'at capacity', and he had warned, 'No more!', as if I was Jane Eyre and he was Mr Rochester getting his side whiskers in a twist.

Then Max said, referring to our lodgers, 'Bill does well, doesn't he, to cope with all this? Surely he needs some peace and quiet when he comes home?'

I thought about it and stared at the firelight through my red wine. 'Well,' I said, 'he's not home that often. And I'm home most of the time. There are weeks when I hardly see Bill. Essentially, we live separate lives, and I can't surround myself with peace and quiet just because he needs to dip into it occasionally. I'd be very lonely in an empty house.'

We looked at each other, and Max said, 'I see.'

Judith had sobered up and reverted to type after her Britvic Orange. She started to bustle about, wanting to go home. Maybe it was the serious chat she'd had with Terry about treating haemorrhoids at the Tudor Court, or maybe she thought I was having too much fun. Probably the latter. She can cope with red hot pokers up the backside, but it upsets her to see me enjoying myself too much. So we had to drink up and collect our things and set off for home. The next session is on Elizabeth I. I can't wait.

I'm amazed at how my interest in history has blossomed.

***

I was getting ready to write a letter to Ella this afternoon when Sophie came into the kitchen with a sheaf of papers and sat down next to me at the table. 'Mrs Forth, right,' she began, 'at work they say I should apply for a promotion to deputy supervisor since Carole left. They said I'm good enough. What do you think?'

'Of course you should.'

'It's a bit more money, and I would get to wear a dark blue uniform instead of a pale blue one and be a bit more important around the nursing home. So that's good.'

'And more responsibility?'

'Yes. I'm very responsible at work. I have to be. People can get into a mess and need lots of kitchen roll. Anyway. So I've filled in this form. Can I read you the bit where I have to explain why I fit into the person specification for the person who should have the job?'

'Yes, go ahead.'

'Okay,' she cleared her throat and patted her chest in readiness, and began. *'I am cheerful and very patient and I love carrying heavy loads in small spaces. I am very capable of prioritising my tasks when I get round to it, and being a team player is what I do better than most people. People are always saying to me that I respond sympathetically to people's needs even when they are driving me mad and my back is very strong with no historical problems. I'm very willing to do courses, even though I know they will probably not tell me anything I don't know already. Even if I'm pretty sure the courses will be useless, I would be very willing to go on them. It's an afternoon off after all, so obviously I wouldn't complain. I'm very punctual when I remember to set the alarm on my phone. Oh yes, and even though this not on your list of what the right person needs to be, it is very important. Not much makes me puke.'* She looked up. 'Why are you smiling?'

'I think it might need some tweaking.'

'Was it no good?'

'It was brilliant,' I said. 'But it might need a few changes.'

'Well we can't change it too much because I have to fit into the Person Specification to get the job.' She studied it. 'And I've missed out saying I can resolve disputes.' She wrote something hastily, then after a minute she said, 'How about this for resolving disputes? *Resolving disputes is very difficult because everybody always thinks they are right and the other person is wrong. There's not much you can do about it. The best way is to put the hoover on and start hoovering so they can't hear the other person talking. Usually they just give up and walk away.*' She looked up. 'What do you think?'

'Sophie, I'd give you the job in an instant, but if you want my advice, I think we should do some re-phrasing.'

'Apostrophes and stuff?'

'I was thinking more about the Person Spec.' I glanced down the long list of requirements for the job. 'Well,' I said, 'at least it doesn't ask you to turn water into wine.'

'They wouldn't ask that. You can't drink wine on the premises.'

We worked on the application for forty minutes or so, until I was satisfied that Sophie had the best chance of getting an interview for the job she was born to do.

***

Dear Ella,

Your last was such a very intriguing letter!

Of course, I do understand your dilemma. You say Laura has told you a secret and made you promise not to tell me. And you gave that promise, and now you don't know what to do. I understand that you don't want to betray her confidence, but I'm guessing you are a little uneasy about keeping her secret, otherwise you wouldn't have mentioned it to me at all. Am I right?

Do you think this is a secret I really ought to know about? Can you tell me, without going into detail – is she in any sort of trouble? I don't think that would be betraying her confidence. I'd give you a ring to talk to you about it, but we always get into such a muddle on the phone. I promise I won't mention anything to her at the moment. And I won't say anything to Bill. (This adds another thing we mustn't mention to Bill. I used to tell him everything. He seems to be under our protection now.)

As for our news, the addition of Ivor the Geordie cleaner to our menage is working well. Our house is immaculate, and Ivor fits in well with the general zaniness of the household. The only slight anxiety I have is that he and Sophie seem to be hitting it off very well, and I fear for Baz if they become seriously attracted to each other. Baz is spending hours in the utility room honing his taxidermy skills. He has just finished a beautiful piece depicting a stoat pushing a supermarket trolley.

Write soon Ella, and reassure me that Laura does not plan to be the first woman to breastfeed a baby at the summit of Mount Everest.

Love again,

Sally xx

***

We had a proper Sunday lunch again today. Such a treat, when we all eat a large roast beef together. It was, quite literally, a joint effort. Chrissy prepared all the vegetables. Dan and Baz cooked the meal. Sophie made Yorkshire puddings again from a recipe her grandmother gave her, which I suspect is actually a recipe for omelette. I set the table. Ivor promised to do all the clearing away. Marra the parrot had a cover put over his cage because of excessive use of bad language. Bill is at home, which these days, is all that is required of him.

'Mr Forth,' began Sophie, 'Mrs Forth said I'm going to be famous again for having that idea about people being let off paying taxes for giving carers a room in their house.'

'No Sophie, I didn't say that.'

'Well, something like that.'

I remembered the exchange with Lee on the same subject. 'Which reminds me Bill,' I said, 'Lee was asking me about this council tax relief for renting spare rooms idea.'

'Lee?'

'Yes, Lee. He's the special needs pupil I mentor at school.'

'Oh yes. Didn't he give you head lice?'

'He did, yes. Anyway, he wanted to know whether his family would get council tax relief if he and his brother bunked up together and they freed up a bedroom.'

'I hope you told him that the papers have jumped the gun and this proposal is still just under consideration.'

'I did, but I was thinking about his query afterwards. He asked me if this scheme was just for people with big poncey houses like ours, or whether anyone could be included.'

Bill put down his wine glass, he doesn't drink much these days, but he allows himself two glasses of red wine if he's home for Sunday lunch, and the occasional glass in the evenings. Most evenings, when I come to think about it. 'Oh no,' he said, 'I reckon this scheme's just for the likes of us in our big poncey houses.'

I've noticed that when Bill has more than one glass of wine at home with us, he starts to enjoy talking rubbish. At work his job is to choose his words very carefully, picking his way cautiously across a minefield of verbiage. When he feels relaxed at home and among family he speaks much more freely and seems to positively enjoy spouting outrageous nonsense. He says he can't be on his guard all the time, and talking bollocks is a great way to unwind.

Sophie nodded, 'That's right. That's how it should be. I wouldn't want to have a room in Lee's house and get head lice. It's much nicer being in a house like this. He won't have a washbasin in his bedroom. Or stained glass. I didn't even know you could get bedrooms with washbasins till I came here. I was really surprised when I saw it.'

'She's right,' said Bill, topping up his second glass, 'we can't be giving tax breaks to people without washbasins in their bedrooms. Especially if they have a history of head lice. It wouldn't be right. Cheers everyone.'

'Good,' said Sophie.

'He's teasing you Sophie,' I said. 'Don't take any notice.'

'I'm serious!' said Bill. 'I'm going to call this the Poncey House Tax Dividend. And you'll have to prove you haven't got head lice before you can claim it, and have at least a square yard of stained glass in your front door and some surprising washbasins to qualify.'

'Enough!' I said. 'Let's change the subject before everyone gets completely the wrong idea.'

'These Yorkshires,' said Ivor, 'are the best Ah've ever tasted. Normally they're just puff-balls like, but these is like scrambled egg with a crust.'

'Champion!' said Sophie.

So we left it at that.

***

Baz is jubilant. He has sold his stuffed stoat for one hundred pounds. One hundred pounds! Astonishing. Who would have thought there would be anyone out there willing to pay so much for a stoat pushing a tiny supermarket trolley full of stoaty groceries? Naturally, I'm very pleased for Baz. I asked him when they all came in this evening, who had bought it, and he told me he'd sold it to 'Home Collectables,' who plan to sell it in one of their other London stores. They said it was a conceptual piece. We all looked at Baz, admiring his cleverness.

'What's a conceptual piece?' said Baz.

'It's a work of art,' said Chrissy, 'that makes some deep and meaningful comment on Life and the Human Condition.'

'Bloody hell,' said Baz, in awe of himself.

'How did you do that?' said Sophie. 'It's just a stuffed stoat.'

'It's not the stoat,' said Dan, 'it's the trolley. All the stoat food was wrapped in plastic. All the eggs and birds and voles in the trolley were wrapped in tiny plastic bags.'

'Ah,' said Chrissy, 'that'll be it.'

'I wondered why you'd bothered doing that like,' said Ivor. 'Stoats don't need their food wrapped in plastic.'

'Neither do we,' said Dan. 'That's the point. You're a genius Baz. You need to do a whole range of conceptual taxidermy and sell the next one for two hundred.'

'Right,' said Baz. 'Conceptual art? I'd better google it.'

'Beyond me like,' said Ivor. 'As long as you keep your hands off me parrot.'

***

Jen and I went shopping this afternoon, and I bought my dress for the wedding. It is exactly the right shade of cream, which is cream, as far as I'm concerned. We've had a very fraught afternoon. We fell out in John Lewis. I tried two dresses on, and one was clearly much nicer than the other.

'Well, I think you should get the other one,' said Jen.

'Why?' I said. 'It's horrible. This one's much nicer. I look good in this one.'

'It's my wedding,' said Jen, 'and I think you should get the other one.'

'But the other one makes me look frumpy.'

'It's not frumpy, it's classic.'

'It's not classic, it's frumpy.'

'Well, you have to get that one.'

'No I don't.'

'Yes you do.'

'Well I'm not buying it.'

'It's my wedding, and I say you have to.'

'What the hell? Do you want me to look frumpy at your wedding?'

'Yes.'

There was clearly some underlying psychology at work here, so we went for a cup of tea to thrash things out. Two cups of tea and a little square table in M&S later, we got down to business.

'Why do you want me to look like a matronly frump at your wedding when I could be looking my best?'

Jen sighed. 'The frumpier you look, the better I'll look. We'll be standing right next to each other in the aisle, remember. I need you to look frumpy. Surely you understand that? If you buy that other dress, you'll look better than me, and it's my wedding. I'd do the same for you.'

'I wouldn't ask you to!'

'You wouldn't need to ask!'

'For god's sake Jen, give me a break. It's got a shirt collar, shoulder pads and a pleated skirt. I'll look like a tennis umpire.'

'It's not that bad.'

We sipped our tea; the atmosphere was cool. After a pause, I said, 'We should calm down.'

'We should.'

'All right. I'll get the frumpy dress.'

'Thanks Sally.'

So I'm looking at it now. It really is awful, I hate it. I tried it on to show Bill. He glanced up from a pile of papers and said, 'Very fetching.'

***

No letter from Ella this morning. I was hoping she would have written to let me know whether Laura was in danger of falling victim to one of her own inspired projects. I had asked Ella in jest whether she thought Laura might be planning to be the first woman to breastfeed a baby on the summit of Mount Everest. Ella's lack of response was making me nervous. So I decided to go and see Laura. She might open up to me and tell me what she told her grandmother. The suspense is more than I can cope with. I love my daughter beyond my power to express it, but she is not easy. She is inclined to champion causes and acquire principles which she is passionate about, and which I almost always think are bollocks. I used to come straight out with it and tell her when I thought her ideas were nuts, but I have learnt better than that now. Now I pretend there is something in her ideas and I am giving them serious consideration prior to coming around to her way of thinking. Although what I am actually doing is wondering how to dislodge the latest ridiculous notion from her lovely head.

I thought I was doing the right thing by bringing her up to be a thoughtful, caring, unselfish person, but actually I was just storing up trouble for us both. These thoughtful, caring, unselfish moves of hers are so stressful for me. Now I want to say to her, 'Fuck everyone else Laura, just do what's best for you and Ben and Harry.' If I had my time again I would tell my children to put themselves first and trample over anyone who gets in their way. It would be so much easier for them and for me.

When I arrived at Laura's, Harry was in his highchair making large swirls of green and red arcs on the tray in front of him. I thought he was painting, but he was actually eating his lunch. Nothing seemed to be going into his mouth, so maybe he was absorbing it through his hands. Baby-led weaning is what it's all about these days apparently, and it's very difficult to distinguish that from painting. We took him for a walk in his pram after lunch, and had a chat while he napped.

'So!' I said brightly. 'How are things?'

'Well, you know.'

'No, I don't know. That's why I'm asking you.'

'Fine. Things are fine.'

'Any new developments?'

'What developments?'

'I don't know what developments. I'm asking you if there are any. The last time I spoke to you, you were planning to start an uprising against watching television. How's that going?'

'Well, obviously I'm still very committed to that, but something else has come up.'

Here it comes, I thought. Brace yourself. 'What?' I said. 'What has come up?'

'Actually Mum, I'd rather not say at this stage, if you don't mind.'

'Oh? Why? It might help to talk it over.'

'Well, I just don't want you to panic.'

'Panic? Laura!'

'Okay then. Ben and I are thinking about adopting.'

'Adopting what?'

'Twins.'

'Twins!'

'Yes twins. But not twin babies.'

'Not babies? What then? Twin elephants?'

'Twin boys, about six or seven years old.'

I tried unsuccessfully to speak.

'I thought you might be a bit surprised at first. But then I thought you'd understand because you've done mentoring for ages. With Lee at school. You love Lee, don't you?'

'What? No!'

'Of course you do!'

'No I don't!'

'You do! You've told me you do. You told me there were times you wanted to take him home with you – you definitely said that.'

'I didn't mean it!'

'Yes you did, you meant it, I know you did. Anyway, this will be like having two Lees to take home with you and look after.'

I put a hand out to steady myself on the pram.

'You've gone pale, Mum,' said Laura. 'I knew you'd worry if I told you beforehand. I should just have waited and surprised you.'

***

The phone rang after lunch today and a very refined voice said, 'Hello, this is Meredith Cope-Harding. Would it be possible to speak to Neil Jones?'

'Who?' I said.

'Meredith Cope-Harding for Neil Jones. This is the GoForth Studios?'

'Yes, of course!' I said brightly. Possibly too brightly. 'Mr Jones is working at the moment. I couldn't disturb him while he's busy, I'm afraid.'

'No of course!' said Meredith Cope-Harding.

'Could I take a message, and if necessary he could get back to you?'

'Absolutely. Tell him it's good news. We're looking for more of his work. There was a lot of interest in his last piece, *Stoatally Mad*. It's sold now of course. We'd like ten more pieces, at least, when they become available. But obviously we need to speak to him to discuss terms.'

'Yes of course,' I said. 'I'll speak to him and to our business manager, and we'll get back to you in the next few days.'

'Wonderful! I look forward to that!'

'Marvellous!' I said.

'Splendid!' said Meredith.

'Great!' I said.

'Fuck!' said Marra.

'I'm sorry?' said Meredith Cope-Harding.

'If you give me your contact details,' I said, 'Neil will get back to you.'

She gave me her mobile number, and said she was contactable most days in the Knightsbridge store. We said goodbye.

So when Baz came back later this evening I told him that Meredith Cope-Harding rang to speak to him this afternoon, and she wants more stuffed stoats.

Baz shook his head, 'Can't guarantee stoats.'

'She seems to be under the impression that you are working full-time from a studio, Baz? She mentioned GoForth Studios.'

'Oh yeah. Well I didn't think she'd pay that much if she thought I was stuffing animals in a corner of your utility room. She assumed I was a proper artist and she asked for the address of my studio. I didn't know what to say, so I just gave her this address. Is that okay?'

'Probably not,' I said, 'but it's done now. Anyway, she wants at least another ten of your conceptual pieces, and I think she's prepared to pay more than she gave you last time. The last one was a big success, they'll have sold it for a lot more than they paid you.'

'Really? Ten more? That's fantastic! Bloody hell, I only paid a fiver for the stoat!'

'Fuck! Fuck!' said Marra.

We looked at the cage. Baz contemplated Marra for a second or two and said, 'I've never stuffed a bird.'

***

I shouldn't have told Judith about my conversation with Laura the other day. I don't know why I did, I can't have been thinking straight. It would have been a bad idea, whatever had happened as a result.

We were on our way to history evening class, chatting in the car. Judith was driving and I said, 'I'm a bit concerned about Laura.'

'Oh? Why?'

'She's thinking of adopting twins.'

'What!' she said, and she turned and looked at me, and ran into the car in front.

It was only a little bump, she really only made contact with the tow bar of the car in front, so actually it was her car that suffered the damage and even that was very slight. But the man in the car ahead of her made such a song and dance about it. He got out of his car and told Judith she was a stupid woman who wasn't looking where she was going.

That did about sum things up, but we took him on. We pointed out to the man that he hadn't suffered any damage, so why was he making such a fuss? He said, how did we know he hadn't suffered any damage, we might have knocked his tow bar out of alignment. I said we might have knocked his tow bar into alignment. Judith said she had done far more damage to her car than she'd done to his. He said he didn't give a monkey's bollock what damage she'd done to her car. I said it was odd, but this was the second time I had witnessed a driver going into the car in front on this stretch of road in the last month. Judith rounded on me and accused me of causing the bump. I told her she was the one not looking where she was going. She said I had dropped a bombshell in the car, so of course she wasn't looking where she was going. She invited me to share with Mr Furious what I had just told her in the car, to demonstrate why she had taken her eyes off the road. I said I would do no such thing. Meanwhile Mr Steaming-Mad took a photo of the back of his car and the front of Judith's, and asked Judith for the name of her insurance company and her address. Judith said why did he want her address? They weren't going to be pen pals.

I got back into Judith's car to let them sort things out.

So we were late for the evening class, and when we got there Judith was in a foul mood and wasn't speaking to me and wouldn't sit next to me. She went and sat at the front of the class where she knew I wouldn't follow, and I sat at the back, next to Max.

Elizabeth I was our topic this evening. Her portrait was projected onto a screen at the front of the class. Funnily enough, she looked a bit like Judith. Put Judith into an orange wig and a heavily embroidered dress made of 200 yards of raw silk and you wouldn't be able to tell the difference. They both looked particularly stern today, although of course, Elizabeth had looked stern for almost five hundred years. I wondered how Queen Elizabeth I had looked when she smiled. Despite its trials, she must have smiled occasionally during her long reign, bearing in mind that the codpiece was a fashion accessory. But sadly, there are no portraits of that queen smiling, so we will never know her face at its most engaging. Unless we dress Judith up as Elizabeth I and ask her to smile. Although, given her present mood, it could be another five hundred years before Judith feels ready to smile.

After the session I looked for Judith to suggest that we went around the corner to the Block with Max and Terry to discuss the possibility that she might be able to demonstrate for us how Elizabeth I had looked when she smiled. But when I found her she said she was going straight home, and I could either go back with her now, or go to the pub to get tipsy with Max and Terry and make a fool of myself. The choice was mine.

So I thought about it for a split second and decided to go to the pub to get tipsy with Max and Terry and make a fool of myself. Judith said, very pointedly, 'You are playing with fire. If this was the Elizabethan court, you would be risking your head.' And then she narrowed her eyes and looked at me, and I saw that she would be quite capable of passing that sentence.

Anyway, she left and we had a great time in the pub. Stayed until closing time and got a taxi home. Great fun. Can't say I missed Judith particularly, but it was a shame Terry couldn't come.

***

Bill got home a little earlier this evening. Everyone was still up when he arrived. We were sitting around the table drinking our various nightcaps, cocoa, camomile tea, ordinary tea, when Ivor heard the front door open and said, 'Here's the boss.'

Bill came in and looked at us all around the table. 'I hope this isn't another meeting,' he said. 'I've had enough of meetings today.'

Ivor got up, 'Sit yersel doon,' he said, pulling out his chair for Bill, 'an' Ah'll put the kettle on again. What's yer fancy? Tea? Cocoa? Weird tea?'

Bill sat down. 'I'll have a glass of red wine.'

I poured Bill a glass of wine, and he took a sip and looked around at us all. 'So,' he said, 'how is everybody?'

'Champion,' said Ivor. 'Speakin' fer meself like.'

'And I'm champion,' said Sophie.

'We're all good,' said Dan. 'Tell us what you've been doing.'

'Meetings,' said Bill, 'discussions, plans, conversations, phone calls, emails, disagreements, compromises. All the usual stuff. Very boring. Much more interesting to hear about what you've all been up to.'

'Well,' said Chrissy, 'The Highfield Players are doing *Uncle Vanya*, and Dan is playing Uncle Vanya. As well as doing the set. I'm playing Sonya, Dan's niece.'

'We're going to set it in a nursing home,' said Dan.

'Oh god,' said Bill. 'That's... Are you expecting much of an audience?'

'I'm not going,' said Sophie. 'I work in an actual nursing home, I don't need to see a play about one.'

'*Uncle Vanya*?' Bill tried to recollect. 'Isn't that the one where they all die of boredom in the end? Or are they all dead of boredom at the beginning?'

'It's not exactly action-packed,' said Chrissy, 'but there's a shooting in Act Three.'

'Yeah,' said Dan. 'I get to run on stage with a loaded gun and shoot someone.'

'Well that sounds more like it,' said Bill.

'But I miss, and then I can't be bothered to try again.'

'So not exactly *Die Hard*?' said Ivor.

'No.'

Nobody said anything else so Ivor stepped in. 'Well, on a different note entirely like, Ah was cleanin' a house today, and this woman said to me, are you any relation to Robson Green? That's the second time somebody's asked me that.'

'Well, I've got some news,' said Sophie, looking at me coyly, and then at everyone else. 'Guess what, everybody?'

Dan shook his head, 'What?'

'When Mrs Forth came in last night, she was drunk.'

'What?' I said. 'Drunk? Don't be ridiculous Sophie! I was not drunk!'

'Well,' she said, 'maybe not drunk, but you know, pretty drunk.'

Bill looked at me, 'Where had you been?'

'I'd been to a history class, and I had a glass of wine afterwards. Really, Sophie, I was not drunk.'

'Well, you were going on about pieces of cod and laughing. And you put your handbag in the dishwasher. It's all right though. I didn't mind. It was nice to see you laughing.'

'Really Sophie, just because I was laughing didn't mean I was drunk.'

'You don't normally laugh that much.'

Ivor looked at his watch. 'Eee lad, is that the time?'

'Tell you what,' said Dan, 'it's late, and we have to be up early. I'm going to bed.'

'It's not that late,' said Sophie.

'Yes it is,' said Baz. 'Bedtime guys.'

They stood up and cleared things away and stacked them in the dishwasher. Then they wandered around the kitchen collecting up phones and phone chargers, and pouring glasses of water to take upstairs with them, before saying goodnight.

And then there was only Bill and me left in the kitchen.

'So you enjoyed your evening class?'

'Yes, it was good fun.'

'I thought you were going with Judith?' said Bill, puzzled, because he knew these two things were not compatible.

'Well, she's not the only one there.'

'No, of course,' he said, 'so—'

'Bill,' I said, 'there's News.'

'Oh god,' he said. 'What?'

'Laura is thinking of adopting twins.'

'Twins? Jesus. Are you sure?'

'That's what she told me.'

'Could she cope?'

'I don't think so.'

'Could we cope?'

'No.'

'What did you say when she told you?'

'I was speechless.'

Bill nodded. 'How far on is this plan do you think?'

'Early stages.'

'Wait and see then.'

'Yes, wait and see.'

And there was no more talk of the evening class.

***

Sophie apologised to me this morning. She was quite upset.

'Mrs Forth,' she said, as soon as I came downstairs, 'I feel terrible.'

'Why?'

'Because I told Mr Forth you were drunk and you probably didn't want him to know.'

'Don't worry about it, Sophie. I don't think I was drunk.'

'Right. I won't say anything if you get drunk again at the hen-do.'

'I won't get drunk at the hen-do.'

'You might.'

'I won't.'

'It's at Luigi's, isn't it?'

'Yes.'

'The new one, just opened?'

'Yes.'

'On New Bank street?'

'Yes.'

'This Friday?'

'Yes.'

'Good,' she said. 'Not long now.'

***

We gathered in the bar at Luigi's at six thirty for drinks. There were only eleven of us. Two of Jen's friends from the surgery weren't able to come. One was in Ibiza and the other was in labour.

Jen wore a sash which said *BRIDE TO BE,* and Sophie wore a sash which she had made herself and which said, *FORJENSHENNIGHT,* which somebody thought at first might be German for *Hen-Night,* or some other word ending in shite. Sophie had to explain that the letters were iron-on, and they were quite expensive, so she didn't want to waste any. She had made a sash for Chrissy too, which said, *MYDADSTHEGROON* which drew a few puzzled glances, but Chrissy was happy to wear it.

We all looked appropriately glamorous, mostly wearing little black dresses, some more skimpy than others. Jen's dress was very smart, stretchy and figure-hugging in black and white chevrons, I was wearing a black sheath dress with lace sleeves, and Sophie's dress was an off-the-shoulder number with a frill at the neck which she kept pulling down to show off her cleavage and possibly even her nipples before it snapped back into place.

We drank cocktails. I sipped mine very slowly, mindful of being accused so recently of being a drunk. Jen was pacing herself, but Sophie, my accuser, was showing no restraint. She obviously thought that we weren't being sufficiently rowdy for a bunch of proper hens, and it was up to her to liven things up a bit, for Jen's sake. She asked us all who would like to try a cocktail especially for hen-nights called a Virgin Gobbler, and there were eight takers. She ran out of money attempting to pay for them and I lent her fifty pounds.

The Virgin Gobblers did seem to have an effect. The talk became louder and more animated, and Sophie – who didn't really know anyone but Chrissy and me – drifted off and appeared to be propositioning one of the waiters.

The meal began, and the party moved unsteadily towards a table by the window laid for eleven, set back from the main room.

Oysters to start. Two dozen between us. They went well with the Virgin Gobblers. I swallowed mine down whole and enjoyed the garlicky, buttery aftertaste. Jen had two, she tried chewing the first, but swallowed the second whole. Sophie was so excited at trying her first oyster that she accidentally tipped it down the front of her dress. She stood up and tried to reach it, wriggling and plucking at her clothing, and after a while pronounced the oyster in her knickers. She turned her back to us and fished it out, and turned around again and ate it. She said it was too expensive to waste, and it was all right because she'd had a bath before she came out.

The conversation over dinner focused appropriately on Jen. Pam, a friend of Jen's from her doctors' surgery receptionist days, told us all a story. Apparently, a patient with a late appointment at the surgery, a middle-aged man, nodded off on a sofa in the waiting room. He fell back against the sofa and his head lolled to one side, Jen saw him and assumed the worst. She ran across the room and leapt astride the slumbering gent ready to thump him in the chest and resuscitate him. He woke to find Jen straddling him with her skirt hitched around her waist, and once he had recovered from the shock, he thanked Jen and said it was his lucky day.

In her defence Jen said she knew this patient had a heart condition because she had been talking to him about it the day before, and she had just done her annual CPR certification course, so all the necessary resuscitation moves were fresh in her mind. Any misunderstandings about Jen's dramatic interruption of this man's nap were quickly cleared up, and she was commended on her prompt action, but advised in future to assess whether or not a patient had died before she tried to bring them back to life.

I laughed along with the others, but I made a mental note to ask Jen whether she had done anything to restart her husband Frank's heart, when it stopped beating. She was obviously more than capable.

Towards the end of the meal, Sophie leant towards me and asked me what time it was. I told her and she said, 'Are you ready?'

'Ready?' I said. 'What for?'

'Nothing,' she said. 'But Chrissy and me organised something.' She looked towards the bar and smiled. 'You know, 'cos this is a hen night,' she said. 'We rang *Butlers For Babes*, it's just a bit of fun. Jen'll love it.'

So obviously, I knew what to expect.

Jen was sitting on my other side. I leant over and told her Sophie and Chrissy had organised something, and it probably wouldn't be wearing much apart from testosterone. Jen took her sash off and turned around to hook it over the back of her chair. 'Just a precaution,' she said. 'As of now, Sophie is the bride. That sash of hers could be saying anything.'

Sophie's excited anticipation at my other elbow was driving me nuts, so I engaged Anita who was sitting opposite me. 'I bet you miss Jen at the surgery,' I said. 'How long did you say you'd known her?'

She looked up and said, 'I've known Jen since – oh shit.' I turned to follow her gaze across the room. A very nearly naked young man was approaching. He was wearing a bow tie, and a pair of tight and tiny shorts. He had a napkin over his arm, and he carried a glass of champagne on a little silver tray. He was young and sexy and very attractive and heading straight for us.

Sophie leapt to her feet. 'Ivor!' she screamed.

Ivor saw me and held his napkin in front of his shorts. 'Shit,' he said, 'it's youse! Did I tell you I had a little job in the evenings?'

I nodded and looked into his eyes and nowhere else. 'I think you did mention something, yes.'

'Well, I can't do this now,' he said, tucking his napkin into his shorts to fashion a modesty bib, 'it'll be too embarrassing like. I'll give you your money back.'

'Actually Ivor,' I said, 'Sophie organised this.' I turned to look at Sophie. She was still standing with her mouth open in shock, and a hand flat on each side of her face like Edvard Munch's *Scream*, unable to take in that she had ordered Ivor for this evening's entertainment. 'What do you want to do, Sophie?'

'I don't want my money back,' she said. 'He's here now. What are you going to do, Ivor?'

'Well, stuff I can't do now. With youse here. And Mrs Forth.'

'No, go on,' she said. 'We don't mind, do we, Mrs Forth?'

'But I think Ivor might be embarrassed,' I said.

I hoped.

A consensus was building around the table that Ivor should just man-up and get on with it. The table was being thumped. Ivor's name was being chanted. Anita leant over to me and said, 'He's gorgeous, how do you know him?'

'He does my cleaning,' I said.

She looked at me wide-eyed. 'What part of you does he clean?' she said.

'My house,' I said.

'Oh right! Yes. Your house. Amazing.'

'Tell you what girls!' said Jen, 'Sal and I are going to run to the loo. You get started on the warm-up, Ivor, we'll be back.'

So we picked up our bags and headed over to the ladies' toilets. When we got there Jen said, 'Right, you call a taxi and I'll send Anita a text to say we're off home, love to Ivor and have fun. They'll manage fine without us now.'

'You can't walk out of your own hen-do,' I said.

'I'm principal Hen,' she said, 'I can do anything I like. You can go back in and sit on Ivor's knee if you want, but it's eleven thirty, it's been fun but I'm knackered, I'm going home. It'll be midnight before they miss us.'

We looked back towards our table, and it was true, a lot of elastic and a few other things would have to be twanged before anyone realised we'd gone. Ivor was now looking very relaxed and pouring drinks. The modesty bib was a napkin again.

'You want to call it a night?' I said. 'Certain?'

'Positive. I'm sure Ivor's a nice boy, bless him, but Scott wasn't much older than Ivor. I'm into more mature men now.' Jen's last boyfriend was at least twenty-five years her junior, and he had been tricky to manage at first, then later on he was difficult to manage, and finally he became impossible to manage. They split up over a ball of kapok and, shortly after that, Jen met Sam.

So we caught a taxi, and each of us was home before midnight.

I was in bed when Sophie and Ivor came back. As I was drifting off I thought I heard raised voices in the kitchen, but was much too tired to investigate.

***

We have a problem. A love triangle. Sophie, Baz and Ivor. Or rather Sophie, Baz, Ivor and Marra. So a love rectangle. Baz loves Sophie, and dislikes Ivor and Marra. Sophie loves Baz, Marra and Ivor. Ivor is very fond of Marra and Sophie, and wants to be friends with Baz. Marra couldn't give a shit about anybody.

I was glad to be going into school this afternoon to spend time with Lee in his art lesson. His cheery indifference to just about everything would be a welcome relief, I thought, to tensions at home.

But there was something very wrong with Lee. He was not himself, and I became more and more alarmed as the lesson progressed. Seconds after first seeing him, I knew things weren't right.

'Hello, Miss,' he said.

'Hello, Lee. How are you today?'

'Fine,' he said. 'How are you?'

I was instantly alerted to something being amiss, and I looked at him more closely. 'I'm good thanks, Lee. Have you had a good morning?'

'Very good,' he said, and nodded. 'Had geography. Quite interesting.'

'Are you okay, Lee?'

He sighed. 'I'm okay.'

So we got stuck into our art project, but before long I was seriously worried. He didn't contradict me once. He followed all my suggestions. He was careful not to spill his water, and worse than that, he allowed me to pin up his drawing of an orchid on the display board and agreed that it looked good. Something had gone very wrong, and Lee's behaviour was a cry for help.

'Lee,' I said at the end of the lesson, 'you're not yourself today, I'm a bit worried about you. Is anything up? What's the problem?'

The classroom had emptied, and Sarah Simms was pottering around in the prep room out of earshot.

Lee appeared to be thinking, which was an alarming sign in itself. He picked up a pencil and pressed it against the end of the desk until the point broke, and then he said, 'You were probably a girl once.'

'Yes,' I said. 'I was a girl once.'

'Might have been a long time ago.'

'It was a little while ago. Why?'

'So you know about girls?'

'Yes, I know a bit about girls. Is there something you want to know?'

'Not really.'

'Is there a girl in particular you're thinking about?'

'Might be.'

Ah! Could Lee be in love? I would have to tread carefully. 'So,' I said, 'have you spoken to this girl?'

He shrugged. 'I asked for a bite of her Snickers bar.'

'What did she say?'

'She said I could piss off.'

'Right.'

'Not sure what to say to girls. Girls are mental. Probably their monthlies.'

'Not necessarily,' I said. 'Why don't you buy a Snickers bar, and before you have any, ask her if she would like a bite?'

'She has first bite?'

'Yes.'

He looked tormented, as if I had underestimated his emotional angst. 'First bite?' he said, 'but, the ends of a Snickers bar are the best bits.'

'Yes,' I said, 'but you like this girl, don't you Lee? And you want her to know you like her? So, you offer her the best bit of your Snickers bar. Then she'll know you like her, because you've offered her first bite. Or better still, why don't you buy her a Snickers bar, as a present?'

'Buy her a Snickers bar?'

'Yes. Why not?'

'Fuck!' he said. 'I don't like her that much!'

'Oh. I thought you did. I thought you really liked her.'

'I never said that.'

'Sorry Lee, I must have picked that up wrong.'

'And don't go saying stuff.'

'I won't say anything.'

'Cos if you do, I'll... '

'You'll what?'

He squared his shoulders and sat up straighter.

'I won't say anything, Lee. I don't know who this girl is, anyway, do I? And even if I did, I wouldn't say anything.'

He relaxed a little. 'Right,' he said, 'I'm going now.' He picked up his biro and slotted it into the pocket of his shirt, making a little black line on the white fabric to join the three others already there. 'So you think the Snickers bar might work?'

'Worth a try.'

He shook his head. 'Women,' he said wearily. 'Costin' me a fortune.'

***

Dear Ella,

No, I haven't said any more to Laura about her plan to adopt twin boys. I thought it was very brave of you to 'tackle' her about it. I usually think twice about 'tackling' Laura on any subject so I take my hat off to you. As you know, Laura and I fell out last Christmas over her open marriage adventure, so I'm not too keen to take her on again so soon after the last show-down. My view of her recent plan to adopt twin boys is that if she was an entirely different person it might be a very good idea. But she's not, so it isn't.

Anyway Ella, if you could keep me in the loop re any other plans Laura has to save the world, I'd be very grateful.

In answer to your query about how we are all getting along in our boarding house, I have to say it's not as harmonious here as it was. Sophie can't resist flirting with Ivor, and given his looks and his talents I can understand why. Baz is jealous, and is closeting himself away in the utility room furiously stuffing vermin. Dan says not to worry about it, they'll all sort themselves out in time, and in the meantime a bit of stress will probably be good for Baz's art. Chrissy agrees, and says artists do their best work when they are being tormented by fickle women, and this period will definitely enhance the artistic merit of Baz's taxidermy.

To be honest, I'm not sure how much I care about the artistic merit of Baz's taxidermy, so if we aren't all on pleasant speaking terms in a day or two, I'm going to have a conversation with them about how they see this emotional difficulty playing out. I don't like having an atmosphere in my own kitchen. Even the parrot is subdued. It sat with its head under its seed pot for over half an hour yesterday.

Thank goodness for my history evening class. There's nothing like learning about the troubles of medieval monarchs to put your own problems in perspective.

With love as always,

Sally Xx

***

But young people are mercurial, and for a spell this evening their mood changed. Bill was not at home, and I was in the kitchen by myself at nine thirtyish contemplating a mug of cocoa as a substitute for a husband. In sharp contrast with my mood, there were general sounds of merriment coming from all over the house. Baz and Sophie were trying to coax a stuffed mouse into a pose which was truly hysterical, judging by the sounds coming from the utility room. Ivor was running through his hen-night routine to Tina Turner's *Simply the Best* for Dan and Chrissy upstairs. Everyone was having a whale of a time, peals of laughter coming from everywhere.

I had wanted the recent tense atmosphere in the house to lift, so it was perverse of me to find all this hilarity annoying. I had an urge to put a stop to it. When the snorts of laughter from the utility room became too irritating, I went out into the hall and listened at the bottom of the stairs. Something was thrown over the bannister and landed at my feet. I picked it up. It was a bow tie.

I waited for a lull in the music and then I shouted up the stairs. 'Daniel! Daniel, can you spare me a minute please? I'd like a word.'

I heard someone say, 'Ooops. Better get down there.'

I went into the lounge and waited for Dan to arrive.

He put his head around the door.

'Hi,' he said. 'What's up?'

'You seem to be enjoying yourselves up there.'

'Ivor's teaching me to do a hen-night routine. Turns out I'm a natural. Do you know how much he makes for doing a hen-night?'

'No. And I'm not particularly interested.'

'A hundred quid! A hundred! If I did just one a week I'd make five hundred quid in five weeks. Fantastic! I knew that Performing Arts degree could earn me a living.'

'Daniel,' I said. 'I thought – well – you gave me to understand some weeks ago, that you were thinking in terms of becoming... Look, Daniel, what happened to your plan to be an architect?'

'What plan? I don't think I had any actual plan to be an architect. It was just an idea I was kicking around.'

'Daniel, I'm sure you told me you were considering a career in architecture.'

'Yeah. But that was before I knew about this. Now I'm considering a career in hen-night entertainment.'

'Just a minute, Daniel. I don't think you've thought this through properly.'

'No, Mum, I've been thinking about it for at least half an hour. It's a brilliant idea. Why do you keep calling me Daniel? Are you pissed off?'

Sophie opened the door from the kitchen to the lounge. 'Hey you two,' she said. 'Come and look at this. We've managed to get a mouse to sit on the loo and read the paper.'

Dan went through to look. I went upstairs to run a bath.

***

Despite all the hilarity last night, Baz still isn't happy. I've been around young people long enough to know when they're not happy, I have a nose for it, I can sense it, and it helped that when I asked Baz outright this morning whether he was happy, he said no.

'What's up?' I asked him.

'Everything was great until he arrived – Ivor.' He shrugged. 'I'll get used to him, I suppose. Sophie likes him. Do you know how long he's staying?'

'Not exactly.' I could have added that I didn't know how long any of them were staying.

'Maybe he'll go soon,' Baz glanced over at the parrot, now resident permanently in the kitchen. 'He said he would keep that bird in his room, but now it's living in the kitchen. You can get diseases from birds, you know. I keep telling Sophie.'

'Sophie!' said Marra. 'Sophie! Hiya!'

'Anyway, gotta go,' Baz pulled on his beanie hat and gave me a wave at the door, 'See you later. Bye.'

'Hiya! Hiya! Hiya!' said Marra.

***

I rang Jen at lunchtime about the address she wants me to give on her behalf in the church during her wedding service. She told me she was still working on it, and I got the feeling she isn't keen for me to see it too far ahead of time. I am beginning to feel uneasy. I suspect that when I see this address, I will want to make some major edits, and that will take time.

'Jen,' I said 'I can't stand up in church and read something you've written without looking over it first, and thinking about it and practising it. I might make a mess of it. The wedding is only a couple of weeks away. You must finish it and let me see it, so I can rehearse it. You've written it, haven't you?'

'Yes. But it might need refining.'

'Email it to me, so I can look over it.'

'I'll do that as soon as I get a minute.'

'You're stalling. What have you said in this address?'

'I thought I might say something about Frank.'

'Frank? Who's Frank?'

'My first husband. The one that died.'

'Oh, Frank! Why? Why talk about Frank when you're marrying someone else? Surely the timing is all wrong.'

'I thought I might mention the fact that I might possibly have killed Frank, without fully meaning to. And sort of confess to that, before I marry Sam. The timing would be perfect for that.'

What? What did she say?

'You can't be serious,' I said. 'Tell me you're not serious.'

'I'm not going to say I actually killed Frank, I'm just going to say that shortly after I didn't tell him where his heart pills were, he died. Of a heart attack. And it's possible that the two things were connected somehow. But they might not have been. He might have died anyway. We'll never know – that's the thing. I'd like to make a clean breast of the whole thing before I marry Sam. I want to make my peace with everyone, including God, before I embark on married life for the second time. It seems more honest, and I think it might be bad luck not to say anything. It might jinx things for me and Sam.'

'It might jinx things for you and Sam? Have you taken leave of your senses, Jennifer? You can't stand up in church and confess to possibly murdering your first husband, and then expect your marriage to your second husband to go ahead as if you'd just read a verse from the Bible. Surely you can see that?'

'Well, obviously, I realise it's a bit unconventional.'

'Unconventional! Does Sam know about any of this?'

'Yes, he knows about it. Well, he knows Frank died of a heart attack, and I might have hinted that I was a bit slow in, you know, fetching his pills. I don't know, I can't remember exactly what I told him. To be honest Sally, I haven't over-burdened Sam with the details. Obviously he doesn't know about the plan to make a clean breast of it during the marriage ceremony, because he doesn't know yet that there's anything wrong with my breast. He quite likes my breasts actually, but that's a different thing entirely. I don't know, Sally, the whole thing's just preying on my mind. I'd just like to say my piece, to get it all out in the open, and move on. I think the moment in the ceremony – just before the actual marriage – would be a good time to do it. It would be before God and all my friends and family, it would feel honest. So then everyone would know and understand, and I'd be sort of purged, before I make my commitment to my relationship with Sam. I think God would appreciate it.'

'You think God would appreciate it?'

'I do, yes.'

'Has God told you that?'

'No. Not in so many words. But He moves in mysterious ways.'

'Take it from me, Jen, God does not move in ways as mysterious as this. This is way too mysterious a movement, even for God. You have to re-think this.'

'So, does that mean you won't read out my speech?'

'No. I can't stand up in the middle of the ceremony and say, *Ladies and Gents we all love Jennifer and we wish her well on this wonderful day, shame about her last husband, she didn't mean to kill him but she'd like us all to move on.* For goodness' sake, Jen!'

There was a pause on the end of the line, and I wondered whether she'd hang up. But I heard her sigh, and then she said, 'I just want to be straight with everyone, and get rid of this whole, nagging Frank thing. I want to draw a line under it, before I go into my next marriage. I want absolution. I hate feeling I'm hiding things.

'Jen,' I said, 'how accidental was your contribution to Frank's death? Honestly?'

'Well, I didn't expect him to die. I really didn't think he would die. He was a real drama queen, you know Sally. I thought all that gasping and clawing at the sofa and mouthing 'Pills' was just him making a fuss. You could have knocked me down with a feather when he flopped over and I saw that he was actually dead. He was usually so predictable, it was the first time he'd done anything to surprise me in years. I'd have congratulated him if he could have heard a word I was saying. Anyway, I have this strong sense that God would want me just to say, in church, *Listen folks, this is what happened, not my finest hour, but that was then and this is now, what's done is done, let's all move on and try to do better*.'

'I don't think God would want that,' I said. 'I really don't. He knows all about the Frank thing anyway, doesn't He? He's like that, God knows everything. I think God would think it very self-indulgent of you to make a big deal of this on your wedding day. He hates self-indulgence.'

'Does He?'

'Yes.'

'God hates self-indulgence?'

'Yes.'

'I didn't know that,' she said.

'Shouldn't you discuss all this with Sam in private, before the wedding? So that you understand each other?'

'I'll ask him.'

'Ask Sam?'

'No,' she said. 'Not Sam.'

***

When I got in from the dentist this afternoon, Sophie and Ivor were teaching Marra to shake hands, undeterred by the fact that Marra has no hands. Sophie's hen-night sash was draped over the clothes airer to dry, but after she washed it most of the middle letters came off and now it says 'FRIGHT'.

'Ah!' I said, 'I'm glad you're both here. I'd like a word with you together, before the others get back.'

Sophie said, 'Is this going to be a telling-off, or a nice surprise?'

'Well, neither. It's just a chat, a chat we could do with having, I think.'

'It's a telling-off,' said Sophie, giving Ivor the heads-up.

'You might have noticed,' I said, once all three of us were sitting around the kitchen table, 'that Baz isn't very happy these days.'

'It's because he's jealous of Ivor,' said Sophie.

'No,' said Ivor. 'What? Jealous of me? No.'

'He is,' said Sophie, 'he's jealous of you. Because of me.'

'He needn't be jealous of me, like,' said Ivor. 'I can't hold a candle to Baz. Ah'm in awe of him reely. What with all the stuff he stuffs. And making good money too. Ah haven't got talents like that.'

'You've got other talents,' said Sophie.

'What? Like the cleaning? Anybody could do that man.'

'No, I meant your other job.'

'Oh, you mean the entertainment side of things? That's just me makin' some cash and havin' a bit of fun, like. That's not what you'd call a talent.'

'Some people might think it was a talent,' said Sophie.

'Eee lad.' Ivor rubbed his chin. 'I didn't know Baz was jealous, like. That's not good. Poor lad. D'you think it would help if Ah said Ah was gay?'

'Are you gay?' said Sophie, shocked.

'Why no.'

'I thought you weren't,' she said.

'No, Baz doesn't need to be jealous of me. Ah mean, you an' me Sophie, we're just pals, nothing more than that.' He nudged Sophie with his elbow. 'Isn't that right, petal?'

'Yeah,' said Sophie.

He turned to me. 'It's like, Sophie's the sister Ah never had, y'know what Ah mean?'

'But you've got two sisters.'

'Oh aye. Well apart from them two. No, you'll have to reassure him, Sophie. Tell him the truth, that there's nowt going on between us two. Put the poor lad's mind at rest. Ah'd do it meself, but it'd be better coming from you, and Ah've got a gig tonight.' He glanced at the kitchen clock. 'Ah'll better get meself organised before Ah have to piss off. '

'Right,' said Sophie.

Ivor stood up. 'If Baz is still up when Ah get back, Ah'll tell him you an' me are friends and nothing more, so he doesn't have to worry. Eee, the poor lad. Ah didn't know he was upset like, or Ah'd have said something already. Anyways! Gotta run. There's twenty young lasses wanting to see me strut my stuff on the other side of London tonight. It's good money so Ah'm not complaining. Nice work if you can get it, some might say. But don't worry,' he assured me, 'Ah'll take Baz out for a drink tomorra, and we'll have a laugh about it.'

He left the kitchen in high spirits.

And Sophie burst into tears.

***

It was a late night last night, what with Sophie so upset and Bill coming in after eleven thirty wanting egg and chips. We were all in bed before one, but around two in the morning a shelving unit in Dan's bedroom collapsed and made a god-awful noise when it hit the floor, and Chrissy screamed. Everyone woke up and it took a while for us all to calm down afterwards. Dan thought a bracket must have worked loose behind the shelving attached to his bed, somehow, and caused the collapse. Chrissy, who was staying the night, sat on the floor on the landing wrapped in a duvet like an earthquake victim. She refused to go back to bed until Dan and Bill had checked the other shelves to make sure they were going to stay in place until morning.

Sophie said Chrissy could sleep in with her and Baz if she liked, but the offer wasn't taken up.

***

I was glad to escape to school this afternoon to the relatively relaxing ambience of an afternoon with Lee. He was finishing some geography work which he had been too idiotic to get finished in his lesson. We were in a quiet corner of the library and I think I might have been nodding off after a night with very little sleep, when Lee glanced over his shoulder to check he wouldn't be overheard and hissed, 'You owe me a Snickers bar.'

'I beg your pardon?'

'You owe me a Snickers bar.'

'Why?'

'Because it didn't work, did it? And you said it would.'

'I didn't say it would work, Lee. I said it might be a nice way to show this girl you like her. If you give her a Snickers bar.'

'Well it didn't work.'

'What happened?'

'She told me to piss off.'

'Right. So she didn't take the Snickers bar?'

'No. She took the Snickers bar, then she told me to piss off.'

'Lee, are you sure you like this girl? She doesn't sound very nice.'

'She's very nice. She likes other people.'

'But does she like you?'

'No. She hates me.'

'Well, are you barking up the wrong tree perhaps?'

'Trees? What trees? There ain't no trees.'

'I'm just thinking, there might be another girl you could like, a girl who would like you back, maybe? Do you know any girls who might like you?'

'I can't go round givin' out Snickers bars to half the class!'

'No, I know that. I just meant—'

'It was a stupid idea, anyway.'

He looked upset, so I put the geography on hold. 'Lee,' I said, 'sometimes you can like someone, and they just don't like you back in the same way. It doesn't mean there's anything wrong with you, it just means they don't feel the same way you do. The best thing to do is to forget about that person and find someone who can like you back.'

'But she's the only girl in the class with any boobs.'

'Right,' I said, 'let's get back to question 4.'

***

'Bill,' I said last night when he came to bed, 'I know you're tired, but there's something I'd like to mull over with you, if you can manage to stay awake?'

'Right,' he said, and he rolled over and switched the bedside light on. 'What's up? Is it the kids?'

'No, it's not the kids. It's Jen.'

'Jen? God, Sally, it's nearly ten to one. I've got to be up at five. We should have talked about this earlier.'

'You only came in at twelve thirty. When am I supposed to discuss things with you?'

'Yes, but Jen? I've never been able to understand Jen. I hardly know her.' He rolled over towards the light again and switched it off. 'I can't help you with Jen, Sally,' he said in the dark, 'she's a mystery to me. Normal rules don't apply. Sorry. You're much better with Jen than I am. You'll sort her out just fine. Without my help.'

'Actually Bill, there is some news on Dan's career plans, if you feel strong enough. Although, you might want to wait 'til morning.'

'Ah. I take it architecture's off?'

'It's been brushed aside by another career opportunity.'

'So, what other career opportunity?'

'He's considering going in for hen-night entertainment.'

'I see. Is that providing entertainment for women on hen-night outings?'

'Yes. Well, it's being the entertainment at hen-night outings. I think he'd be moving about provocatively to music while bare-chested. Apparently, it's very lucrative.'

'Well,' he said. 'Moving about provocatively to music while bare-chested. That's marvellous news, isn't it?'

'Yes, isn't it?' I said.

'Knocks spots off architecture.'

'That's what I thought.'

'I'm going to sleep now Sally.'

'Me too,' I said. And I lay awake for about an hour.

***

Sophie is feeling a little better. She is getting over the shock of Ivor's cheerful indifference to the idea of her as a potential partner. She's calm enough now to consider how she feels about Baz and Ivor, the men in her life at the moment. We had a heart-to-heart after she got home this evening.

Sophie said the problem is that she loves Baz, but she fancies Ivor like crazy. She said she isn't sure whether she loves Ivor, or just fancies him until she can't think straight. She said, the fact that she has the serious hots for Ivor is making things difficult between her and Baz, because when she is with Baz, she wants to be with Ivor. To really be with Ivor, if I knew what she meant.

I gave her a cup of filter coffee, because the situation required it, and we sat at the kitchen table for a no-holds-barred, woman-to-woman talk.

'I don't think you do love Ivor, Sophie,' I said. 'You've only known him a few weeks. I think you really love Baz, and Ivor is just a distraction.'

'But, Mrs Forth. He's gorgeous. Ivor, I mean.'

'I know, he's very good-looking. But—'

'And when I was watching him at Jen's hen-night, dancing and getting all the girls going, you know? You weren't there, but he did this thing with his hips and it was—' she flushed, and fanned herself with a flutter of her hands, 'well, it wasn't a bit like watching Baz stuff a stoat.'

'No,' I said, 'I can see that, but what you have to remember, Sophie, is...' I paused to think what it was she had to remember, because I was getting a little warm myself. 'What you really have to remember is that Baz loves you, but Ivor, well, he's fond of you, but he doesn't love you the way Baz does.'

'Yeah right,' she said. 'So what do I have to remember?'

'You have to remember that Baz loves you, and Ivor doesn't.'

'Yes I know,' she said. 'But the problem is that when I look at Baz, I think he's a really nice man, and I want to give him a cuddle. But when I look at Ivor, I think *Oh My God How Gorgeous Are You?* And my insides go all funny, and I just want to sort of, jump on him. That's the problem. If Ivor did love me, I wouldn't stay with Baz, I'd be with Ivor.'

'But you do love Baz, don't you?'

'Yes, and I would really miss Baz, if I wasn't with him. But if I could jump into a jacuzzi with Ivor I'd probably forget Baz existed. Like, probably, before I hit the water. What should I do? Should I finish with Baz, even if I can't be with Ivor? But that would be so sad! I'd be so sad to finish with Baz. It would break my heart. Oh no,' she put her head in her hands, 'my life is ruined!'

'Shit!' said Marra.

'I don't think you should finish with Baz, Sophie. I think this thing with Ivor is an infatuation that will probably die down quite quickly, and then you'll feel more normal again.'

'I just want to feel normal again.' She blew her nose as if sounding a lament. 'I don't want to be thinking of Ivor all the time in his little shorts and that cute bow tie, doing that hip-wiggling thing. I don't. I wish I hadn't seen him do it.'

I had an idea. 'Maybe Baz could wear some little shorts and a cute bow tie, and do the hip thing? What about that?'

'Baz?' she said. 'Baz! Do the hip thing? What? No!'

'What the fuck?' said Marra. 'Fuck! Fuck!'

I grabbed a tea towel and flicked it in the direction of Marra's cage. He said, 'Hiya!' and attacked a slice of apple wedged between the bars.

'Baz is a really lovely man,' said Sophie. 'I don't think he'd want to do all that stuff Ivor does. I think he'd be embarrassed. I think he's too nice to be that naughty. That's the trouble. Baz is so nice, and Ivor is so, gorgeous and naughty. Have you ever fancied anyone more than you fancy Mr Forth, Mrs Forth?'

I laughed. Not sure why. 'No, of course not.'

'Really? In your whole life?'

'Not that I can remember.'

'Oh no! That makes me think I should break it off with Baz! I haven't been with Baz very long and I'm already fancying other people. You've been with Mr Forth since forever and you've never fancied anyone else. And it would be dead easy to fancy someone else more than Mr Forth. I don't think I properly love Baz.' She started to cry.

'No, Sophie, you're picking this up all wrong. When I said I have never fancied anyone but Mr Forth, I meant, I've never done anything about the other people I might have fancied. I just fancied them for a bit, and then forgot about them, because they turned out to be not very important. In the end. I think that's what will happen with you and the way you feel about Ivor.'

'Do you?' I had given her a straw and she clutched it. 'Honestly? I hope so. Are you telling the truth about fancying other people? And them turning out to be not important? Is that the truth?'

'Yes, but I'd appreciate it if you didn't tell anyone else, Sophie. I'm just telling you this because I think it might help you with this problem you've got at the moment. I do think in the end Ivor won't be important to you, and Baz will.'

She nodded, 'Because that's how it is for you when you start really fancying other men and wanting to jump into jacuzzis with them?'

'Well I —'

'Thanks Mrs Forth. I feel a bit better now.'

'Good, I'm glad that helped.'

'I won't finish with Baz.'

'No, I don't think you should.'

'It would be terrible if you'd finished with Mr Forth all those times when you got the serious hots for other people.'

'It would yes. Feeling better?'

'Yes, much better.' She blew her nose again. 'Baz and me might go out for a pizza tonight.'

'Good idea. I'm going out tonight too, to my history evening class. So it's a good night for you and Baz to get a meal out.'

'Yes okay. I'm going to the shop. I might meet Baz coming home.'

'He'll be very pleased to see you.'

Sophie put her hand on my arm. 'Thanks Mrs Forth. I feel much better now I know this has happened to you lots of times, and things turned out okay.'

I smiled, glad that I'd been able to help. I don't mind concocting a bit of a story if it's going to make someone happy. Then I glanced at the cooker clock and remembered with a shock that it was an hour later than the clock was saying, because we haven't adjusted the time since the hour went forward last Sunday. I'd have to be quick if I was going to wash my hair and iron my new blouse, and get to the history class early enough to be sure of sitting next to Max.

Chapter Four: April

High-born Elizabethan women did not have vulgar suntans. They bleached their faces white with a mixture of lead powder and vinegar. They used cosmetic preparations made with tin, ash, and sulphur, and applied them to their faces. The toxic mix poisoned their skin, making it grey and shrivelled, and requiring thicker and thicker subsequent applications, which were made without removing any of the underlying layers. They painted over their make-up with a glaze of uncooked egg white to hide wrinkles, even though this made their faces stiff and hard and difficult to move. As a finishing touch they painted blue veins onto this thick white face-mask to give the impression of translucent skin, and stalked around the Court like heavily upholstered milk lollipops.

They would apply layer after layer of this foundation over days, only cleansing very occasionally with urine, mercury and donkey's milk. Rouge was applied to the cheeks, eyeshadow made from ground mother-of-pearl was applied to the eyelids, and fake eyelashes were fashioned from mouse fur.

Elizabethan ladies must have wandered around Court like the undead. To give one of these women a peck on the cheek would be to risk your front teeth. Their make-up was so metallic, that if one woman lent close to whisper into the ear of another, their heads would clash together like cymbals.

Is this why Elizabeth never married? How alluring can you be, caked in lead, vinegar and egg white and smelling of urine, sulphur and donkey's milk? It's not exactly a come-hither combination, particularly on a hot day.

Just imagine, if you could go back in time to the court of Elizabeth I with a large supply of Ivory Rose Pressed Powder, mascara, eye shadow, lip gloss, Chanel Number Five and some good facial cleansers? You could give them to Elizabeth along with a quick make-up demo, and she'd be so grateful she'd chuck the Percys out of Northumberland and hand it over to you and your heirs. So when you came back to the present you'd be wearing plus fours and living in Alnwick Castle.

There was a little group of us in the pub after the history class. Everyone had observations to make on Elizabethan cosmetics. Judith pointed out that we needn't be so smug about our cosmetics, because a common ingredient in lipsticks today is cochineal dye, which is made from insects which live on cacti.

Trust Judith to know that. I nipped to the loo to reapply my lipstick and smacked my lips to demonstrate that I didn't give a fig about the squashed insects, and then I went back into the snug and found Max talking to Terry, so I elbowed Terry out of the way.

'Max,' I said, 'I have a little dilemma I need to talk to a sensible adult about, and there seems to be a bit of a shortage of sensible adults in my life at the moment. Have you got half an hour or so to spare?'

'Yes, of course,' he said. 'Let's grab a seat.'

We sat down, and I told him the story. 'I have a friend, a good friend of long-standing, who is getting married for the second time, and she's asked me to give her away.'

He nodded, and smiled, enjoying my pleasant tale.

'But the thing is, she has confessed to me that she may have murdered her first husband, and —'

'What?' he said. 'Confessed what?'

'She's not sure, but she thinks she may have slightly murdered her first husband, by accident, by not telling him where his medication was when he was having a heart attack. After which he died.'

'Bloody hell.'

'All very unfortunate.'

'Well, yes.'

'The thing is, she wants to confess to all this, in church, at her wedding, to make a clean breast of it all.'

'At the wedding? To her second husband?'

'Yes. Just before the vows. I've told her that her timing might be off.'

He laughed.

'I know,' I said. 'It has its funny side – but if you could bear with me.'

'There's more?'

'What I want to know is, if my friend has to face the music over this at any stage, could I be considered an accessory after the fact?'

'Right.' Max frowned, preparing to bring his legal training into play. 'So, what facts do we have here, exactly? I think the problem is we're a bit light on facts for you to be an accessory after. That's my gut feeling. There was no intention to commit murder. We don't have a definitive cause of death. Your friend might have irritated her husband seconds before he died by not fetching his pills, but was it lack of pills that caused his death? Or did he die of irritation? Or something else? Difficult to give any firm view without being entirely sober and having all the facts. We have suppositions, but no hard facts. As far as I know, you can't be an accessory after a supposition.'

I nodded. 'That's a relief. I suppose.'

'However,' he said, 'I'd probably discourage the confession at the altar idea, on the basis that it would be a bit of a downer, just before they tie the knot. It's depressing to discover someone's a murderer seconds before you marry them. And it must make the honeymoon a bit edgy.'

I like this man.

***

Laura and I met in John Lewis while little Harry was at Wobbly Weaners. She told me while we were walking through the cosmetics department that she has spoken to a very nice lady from the Adoption Service about her interest in adopting twin boys. They had a long chat. Laura gave the nice lady some background on herself, telling her about her leanings towards an open marriage, and her campaign for the abolition of television. She also mentioned her enthusiasm for a spiritual life, and the fact that she had committed to five different religions in the last ten years, although sadly she is now an atheist. Laura told this lady about her views on the colour green, which she thinks should be the only colour permitted for children younger than ten years old to wear, because it is soothing, calming, and it has a real and significant connection to the natural world. Red over-excites children, blue and pink colour-codes them, beige makes them look like lumps of putty, black makes it impossible to know how dirty they are, and you'd be insane to dress a child in white. Green, Laura says, is the only sensible colour for young children's clothing and it should be made mandatory.

The lady from the Adoption Service told Laura that she might not be quite ready for the commitment of adoption, and she should think about it again in a few years' time. No rush.

Laura was disgruntled, she wanted to take issue with this judgement and use me as a sounding board, so I played my trump card. I said I had two John Lewis vouchers for free coffee and cake which were about to run out, and we should make our way to the café through the homeware department. By the time Laura had admired some table mats and had chosen and eaten her cake she was gruntled again, and she went off to collect Harry from Wibbly Tiddlies feeling relatively happy. To celebrate, on my way out of the shop I bought Harry a T-shirt and leggings in Lincoln green.

***

Dear Ella,

You know, it always makes me a bit nervous to say things seem to be on more of an even keel. It feels like tempting fate. But yes, the household has settled down a little here, Baz and Sophie are back on track, Dan and Chrissy seem quite happy with each other, Ivor keeps the house clean and tidy without seeming to get in anyone's way, we don't see a lot of him really, (although we saw a lot of him at Jen's hen-do, but that's another story.) And Laura is in one of her quiescent periods, long may that last.

Your refurbishment plans sound great to me. What does it matter if your old three piece suite is perfectly serviceable? If you're sick of looking at it after thirty years, get rid of it and buy yourself something you like better. It seems all wrong that you should have to put up with it for ever just because you have looked after it so well. I know June gnashed her teeth when you told her about your plan to upgrade, but you might be wrong about that indicating her disapproval. She might have gnashed in surprise, or she might be gnashing for pure joy. Who knows? Go for it, I say, and buy yourself a new three piece suite. And if Mrs Rob who does your cleaning wants the old sofa and chairs and can arrange to have them taken away, then you don't have to worry about disposing of them, so that's great.

I'm fine thank you Ella, still really enjoying my history class. We had an interesting session on Elizabethan make-up a few weeks ago which made me appreciate L'Oreal anew. And there's a plan to have a history trip away, which is very exciting. We're going to Stratford, and staying for a couple of nights. Not all the class can make it, but about eight of us have signed up for it, and everyone is arranging their own accommodation. Should be fun!

I'm rushing today, The Wedding is only two weeks away, and Jen wants a rehearsal in the church this afternoon.

Crack on with the sofa plan, and let me know how it's progressing!

With love,

Sally Xx

***

The wedding rehearsal didn't take long. Jen and I have stopped discussing the proposed address in the church on the problematic last few minutes of her first husband Frank's life. To be frank, and I'm glad I'm not, I think the less I know about this distressing, sofa-clawing scenario, the better. I'm very worried in case Jen reveals to me that the lack of those pills she didn't fetch for Frank when he was having a heart attack were almost certainly the direct cause of his death. I would have to get my head around the fact that my closest friend is a murderer. It's better that I remain in ignorance as much as possible. I already know more than I'm comfortable with. I'm a little hazy now on the details, but I have a slight suspicion that Jen might have said some time ago that Frank had been without his medication for several days before his death, and although she knew where his pills were, she didn't tell him. I can't remember now how accurate this is, and I'm not planning to ask for clarification, or rifle back through these pages to check. Anyway, I've told Jen that I'm not prepared to read out in church anything which I haven't seen first, and I have strongly advised her to stick to the script during the marriage service. During the last conversation we had on this subject, I told her that in the case of her and

Frank and the missing pills, least said, soonest mended. And some.

She has listened to my advice without comment, so I don't know what she's planning to do, and I don't want to. I shall turn up, walk with her up the aisle, carry her twig while she gets married, and forever hold my peace.

Regarding the walk up the aisle, Jen wants to walk to Julie Andrews singing *Climb Every Mountain,* so we will have to pace our progress up the aisle so we don't arrive at the altar too early in the song, and then have to stand with our backs to the congregation while Julie sings her way right through to the end. There are six short verses to the song, which are repeated several times. I suggested that we don't set off until after the first chorus, which comes at the end of verse two, and then walk slowly up the aisle, so as not to arrive at the altar too early. Jen wanted us to take an extra-long step at the words *Ford every stream,* as if stepping over a stream, but I said no, please God, absolutely not.

Anyway. We played *Climb Every Mountain* on Jen's phone, and paced it out until we had our timings about right. Then Jen told me where I would be sitting throughout the service.

So. I know where I will be if any shit hits the fan.

***

Baz unveiled another mole this evening. He brought it into the kitchen after dinner with a cloth draped over it and whisked it off with a flourish to show us all. An adult mole sits on a three-legged stool lifting a very tiny golden worm out of a large box. The mole is surrounded by piles of packaging which have been removed from the box. A baby mole sits to the side, with its mouth full of plastic packaging, arms flung wide, eyes staring in moley alarm, unnoticed by its parent.

'What do you think?' said Baz.

Before anyone could say anything, Sophie explained what it all meant.

'You're meant to think – too much packaging is a really bad thing. That's what it's supposed to make you think. I keep wanting to take that plastic out of the baby mole's mouth, but Baz says that's the whole point so leave it in.'

'I'm taking it down to Meredith Copenhagen tomorrow. What do you think? Is it conceptual enough? It's called *Packs a Punch*.'

'Well done Baz,' said Chrissy. 'That really gets me here, you know?' She put her hand over her heart. 'And I really want to pull that plastic out of the baby's mouth too. It's very moving Baz. It's saying, our children are choking on our waste. So emotional, and- '

'I told Baz he should charge two hundred quid this time,' said Sophie.

'Or more,' said Dan. 'Say you want fifty percent of what they get for it.'

'But Baz, it's not the money that's important here, surely?' said Chrissy. 'It's the message isn't it, that matters most? The message is more important than the money, isn't it? Everyone?'

'No,' said Sophie. 'The money's more important than the message. Baz doesn't just want to sit here sending messages. He's saving up for a Vespa.'

'But we know what you mean, Chrissy,' said Dan. 'We know the message is most important.'

'Just not as important as the money.'

'I think,' insisted Chrissy, 'what this is saying, is that the quality of our children's lives is the most important thing, more important than stuff we might buy, or money. The whole point of this, surely, is that money is never the most important thing.'

'The whole point of this is to get money to buy a Vespa.'

'No Sophie! You don't understand what I'm saying, you're getting things all mixed up!'

'Up!' said Marra. 'Up yours!'

'Tell you what, ladies and gents,' said Ivor, pulling two bottles of red wine out of his bag and putting them on the table, 'let's chill out with a glass of something. Them moles is terrific, whatever the hell they mean. I got some really good tips last night, so this is good stuff. Let's have a drink.' He put six glasses on the table. 'We'll toast the moles, and the Vespa, and the money, and the message. How's that, eh?'

And he poured the wine.

***

I don't like it when Bill takes his computer to bed. In fact, I hate it. He always says he just has a couple of things to finish off, and it won't take long. He sat up in bed last night, tapping away with a fixed expression. I was reading a book. Five, ten, fifteen irritating minutes went by, then I looked across at him and said, 'I have a new friend at my history class.'

He glanced at me. 'Oh yes? That's good. Who is she?'

'It's a he.'

'A he? So who is he?'

'He's called Max. He's a solicitor. He's very nice.'

Bill smiled, but at the screen, not at me. 'Good. That's nice. I'm glad you've got a new friend. A solicitor?'

'Yes.'

Bill focused again on the screen.

'Do you mind?' I said.

'About your new friend?' Bill turned to look at me. 'Of course not. Of course I don't mind. I'm glad you've got a new friend. Why wouldn't I be?' He picked up my hand and kissed it, and said, 'Silly.' Then he went back to the screen.

'There's a history trip planned, to Stratford. Two nights away. I thought I'd go.'

Bill shut the lid of the computer and put it down on the bedside table. 'That sounds interesting. Stratford? I don't think I've ever been.'

'We're all staying in different places in Stratford. There's about eight of us going.'

'I hope you've booked yourself somewhere nice.'

'Not yet. But I will.'

'Great. I hope you have a lovely couple of days.' He smiled, and tried to stifle a yawn, and put the light off. He made himself comfortable in the dark and said, 'I'm glad you're having a few days away, Sally, you deserve it.'

He's absolutely sure of me, I thought. Absolutely certain he has nothing to worry about.

***

Interesting art lesson with Lee this afternoon. A very pretty sixth form girl was posing for the class, sitting in a deck chair reading a book. She was wearing jeans and a T-shirt, and her long hair was fetchingly tousled, and pulled to the side so it fell over just one shoulder. The class was arranged around her in a semi-circle. Sarah Simms, Lee's art teacher, wasn't sure Lee would be able to cope with this kind of lesson, but I said I thought he would be okay. I said he had matured in the last six months, and I thought he would be fine in a figure drawing class.

So Lee set up his pencils and paper on his desk and looked up. 'Oi!' he shouted across to the sixth form model. 'You'll have to get your arse off that deck chair, or we're not going to see what we're drawing.' The beautiful sixth form girl looked up at Lee, as if he was a moist turd stuck to the desk.

'Lee,' I explained, 'you'll be drawing this girl sitting on the deck chair.'

'What?' he said. 'Drawing the girl?'

'That's the idea, yes.'

'Not just the chair?'

'No.'

'Well she might have brushed her hair.'

'Her hair looks lovely. Let's get started.'

Lee sighed, and began to draw. The class worked quietly, the presence of a model focusing their attention. 'You know,' observed Lee, into the silence, 'from where I'm sitting, this girl looks as if she's just got one arm.' He turned to Tom, who was sitting next to him, 'Do you think she's just got one arm?'

Tom squinted at the girl. 'It must be under her hair, the other arm.'

Sarah, the art teacher, weighed in. 'Ah! This is what is so interesting about figure drawing. It makes you really observe the person you are looking at very closely, and notice things you may otherwise have missed.'

'Well, I'd have missed her only having one arm,' said Lee. 'I'd have totally missed that.'

Sarah came and stood behind Lee and said quietly, 'Lee, this girl does have two arms. You can't see one of her arms from here, because it's under her hair.'

'Well, don't blame me if she just has one arm in my drawing.'

'Just draw her as you see her, Lee. That's what figure drawing is all about.' Sarah moved off, and Lee continued drawing. I moved over to help Tom, who had rubbed a hole in his paper and was wondering what to do about it.

Lee made another announcement, so I turned back to him. 'The way this girl is sitting,' he said, 'I don't know where her legs start.' Again he leant across to Tom, 'Do you know where this girl's legs start? Cos I'm buggered if I do.'

'Language Lee!' Sarah called over to him.

'Sorry!' said Lee. 'Sorry Miss!' And he looked at me and rolled his eyes. He turned his attention back to his page, and whispered to me, 'I'd start her legs somewhere near the bottom of her arm, but she ain't got no arm on that side, so I don't know where the fuck to start them from.'

'Shh!' I said. 'Start her legs from here.' I indicated a spot on his drawing that looked about right.

'From there? That's way up her other arm. She'll look like a bleeding frog.'

'Start her legs from here,' I said, jabbing at the paper, 'just here. Go on, before I lose patience.'

He sighed again. 'All right.' He started drawing a leg, and then he looked at it. 'That don't look like her leg. It looks like some other person's leg.'

The leg he had drawn looked chunky and more angular than the model's leg, more masculine.

'It just needs a little re-shaping,' I said, and I gestured to Sarah to come and advise, she was doing her rounds nearby.

Sarah came over. She looked and said, 'That leg is a little heavier than you would want it to be Lee, but just draw it in again, until it looks right, don't worry too much about those other lines for now, okay?'

'No,' he said, considering his drawing. 'She just needs a different head.'

'A different head?' Sarah was alarmed.

'Yeah. A different head. Then it won't matter if the legs belong to someone else.'

Sarah drew breath to protest, but it would be futile, so I caught her eye and she hesitated. Then she turned to speak to Tom, who was distressed about another hole which had opened up in his drawing, and she left the model to whatever grotesque transformation Lee had in mind for her.

He started to draw, and all was quiet in the art room for two glorious minutes. I didn't comment on Lee's artistic interpretation because I knew better, but his neighbour, Tom, began to take an interest. He looked from Lee's drawing, to the model, and back to Lee's drawing. He studied the figure reclining in the deck chair on Lee's page. 'Who's that?' he said.

'Well it's her,' said Lee. 'Innit.'

'Don't look like her to me.'

'Shutup. Nobody asked you anyway.'

Tom shrugged, 'Don't look like her to me,' he said again, making some adjustments to his own drawing. 'She don't have a beard, for a start.'

Sarah heard the word 'beard,' and came to investigate. She looked at Lee's drawing. 'Lee! You silly boy! What have you done? This is nothing like the model, it's a completely different person. You've drawn a man with a beard! Didn't you hear me say to draw the model exactly as you see her?'

Sarah is an excellent art teacher, enthusiastic, energetic, helpful. If I have any criticism of her classroom management, it is that she can sometimes fail to see when she is driving her lesson over a cliff.

'I think the problem was—' I tried to remedy the situation, but it was too late.

'The problem *is*,' said Sarah, 'Lee has not been paying attention to anything I've said. That's the problem, pure and simple. Instead of drawing our lovely model here, Lee has drawn a man with a beard.'

There was a ripple of laughter from the artists in residence around the room, and the model shook her lovely head in disdainful disbelief. Somebody in the room muttered, 'What a loser.'

Lee stood up and knocked his chair over backwards. 'Well fuckit,' he said. He picked up his drawing and began to tear it up. 'I wasn't drawing her anyway, I was drawing some other bloke. I never wanted to draw her. Her legs ain't normal. An' she's ugly if you ask me.'

'How dare you, Lee!' said Sarah. 'Chloe has given up her free period to come and sit for us, and you have insulted her. That is so rude, Lee. So rude! Apologise – right now.'

And so, in under a minute, we had the equivalent of a perfect storm in a classroom. The teacher can't lose face, Lee can't lose face, the class were all now facing Lee and not the work they were supposed to be engaged in. My face, incidentally, was bright red and the lovely Chloe's face staring up from Lee's page was wearing a dense beard.

I had to demonstrate my fitness for the role of trouble-shooter where Lee is concerned, so I spoke up. 'I am so sorry that your lesson has been interrupted, Miss Simms. And of course we apologise to Chloe who has been a superb model for our class in every way. Now, Lee and I are going along to the Chill-Out Room for some quiet reflection after which we—'

'Reflect?' said Lee, who knows this word well. 'I'll tell you something I've reflected. Her over there, her legs ain't on right. And my drawing is better than his.' He looked at Tom's paper. 'His is full of fucking holes.'

'Well at least Tom has drawn the model, Lee!' said Sarah. 'I don't know who you've drawn. And I'm still waiting for an apology for your foul and insulting language.'

Lee drew breath. He had some utterance in mind, but it would not be an apology, so I intercepted with a remark of my own. 'So sorry to have disrupted your lesson Miss—'

'But I don't want an apology from you!' said Sarah, continuing to herd us all doggedly towards the cliff edge, 'I want an apology from him, from Lee, for Chloe and Tom, and I want it right now. Quick as you like, Lee.'

The class had put down their pencils and were settling down for a humdinger of a showdown. Chloe had abandoned her pose and was sitting forward with her elbows now resting on her knees, anticipating Lee's response.

Lee didn't disappoint. 'I'm not fucking apologising. I ain't done nothing wrong. I drawed my best. I can't help it if she's deformed.'

Chloe's jaw dropped. She stood up, hands on hips. 'Deformed? Did he say deformed?' She turned to Lee, 'Have you taken a look at yourself recently?'

'Time we were going,' I said. 'Come on Lee. Get your stuff together. Where's my bag? Here's your bag. Let me take my jacket off the back of this chair. Shame about your drawing, I rather liked it. Right! We're ready now I think. Excuse us folks. Lead on Lee, thank you. Thank you everyone. Goodbye. Bye.' We were safely in the corridor before Lee realised he had been insulted by the lovely Chloe.

Once in the Chill-Out Room Lee snapped his drawing pencil in half. 'I hate art,' he said, 'I'm not doing it no more.' He tried to snap the half pencil in two, but he couldn't do it. He was frustrated, angry, humiliated, outcast and uncomfortably close to tears.

'Let's forget about art for the moment Lee,' I said. 'Let's talk about something else. Tell me what you want to do when you leave school. What plans have you got for when you're finished here?'

***

It has been a frustrating day. I turned up at The Queen's Head Hotel at ten-thirty this morning and presented myself ready to help set up the function room for Jen's wedding the day after tomorrow. There were a few women there already, helping Jen set tables, tying bows onto the backs of chairs, and setting champagne glasses out on little silver trays. They looked as if they had everything pretty much in hand, so I was hoping to be dismissed as superfluous to requirements, but no such luck.

'Ah,' said Jen, 'there you are! What I would like you to do, Sally, is to secure these twigs in these vases so that they don't fall over or flop about. There's ten twigs and ten vases of varying sizes, one for each table. Then when you've done that, I'd like you to tie ten silver threads around ten branches of each of the twigs, so that people can write their good-will messages in these little note pads, and then tear out the pages and roll them up and fasten them to the silver threads. So you'll have to put a note pad beside each of the ten vases, and if you can get hold of ten sweet little pens, you could put them beside the notepads, in case people don't have a pen on them.'

'Would you like me to fashion ten little nests each containing ten little eggs for ten little birds to sit on, and secure them to the tenth largest branch of each tree?'

'Ever the joker. No, that won't be necessary. But you can manage that, can't you? I saved this job for you because I thought you'd like it. But I could give it to, er... ' She looked around the room.

'That's all right,' I said. 'I should be able to manage. Leave it to me. You carry on tying ribbons around bits of furniture and let me get on. I want to get this done before ten o'clock tonight.'

'Excellent!' said Jen. 'It should be a walk in the park for a woman of your talents.'

Well, it wasn't a walk in the park. It was a descent into hell. The twigs were too large, the vases were too small, the twigs were top-heavy, and the vases fell over. I tried weighting the vases with gravel from the drive outside, but the twigs leant over at crazy angles until the vases tipped and spilt gravel over the tablecloth. I went out to buy pens, and bought double-sided sticky tape. I stuck the base of the vase down to the tablecloth, but the vase lifted up, pulling the tablecloth with it, and even though the vase didn't actually tip, the effect was all wrong. I took my socks off, and stuffed them into the vase around the base of the twig to try and wedge it into place so that it would stand upright. This almost worked, but the twig was dangerously unstable to one side, and the sight of my socks through the glass vase was not celebratory.

I was ready to smash the vases underfoot and make a bonfire of the twigs, when I hit on a solution. I cut the twigs in half, so that they lost almost all of the main upright stalk and became low-lying bushes. Then they didn't need a vase, because they sat on the table quite nicely on their own. It was a different effect to the one Jen was after, the twigs looked like tumbleweed which had rolled into the room, mounted the tables and lodged in the middle of each one. I trimmed off some of the longer branches that were straggling too far over the table, because they might find their way into the guests' food. Then I stood back to admire my work. Jen might be a bit surprised at first, but I thought I could bring her round. I went to find her, to show her what I'd done.

Jen was standing in the bar across the hall, chatting to a group of her friends from the surgery. I joined the circle.

'Of course,' Anita was saying while looking earnestly at Jen, 'it's not long since your first husband died. Poor Frank, it was very sudden, wasn't it? I remember you coped really well at the time. I felt so sorry for you. You hardly gave yourself any time off work.'

'I didn't grieve properly for Frank,' said Jen.

The group became very serious. Anita put her hand on Jen's arm. 'Were you in shock?' she said.

'No,' said Jen. 'I didn't like him.'

'Sorry to interrupt,' I said, 'but I'm wondering if you could just come and have a look at the table decorations Jen, if you've got a minute?'

She excused herself and we walked out of the bar and back into the function room.

'Do you think it's a good idea to tell people you didn't like Frank?' I said, as we walked across the hallway. 'I think you should keep that quiet. He's dead now anyway so I don't see what purpose it serves, and given that you think you might have —'

Once inside the function room Jen abruptly stopped walking. 'What the hell have you done with my twigs?'

I looked around the room at the tables. 'Jen, they just wouldn't stand upright in those vases. I had to make modifications.'

'They're ruined! They look like enormous squatting spiders.'

That was actually a very accurate description of how they looked.

'They don't look anything like that,' I said. 'They look fine, and they won't fall over. They're much more stable as bushes than twigs.'

'Bushes? But I don't want bushes as table decorations. They remind me of something. Oh God.' She put her hand to her mouth. 'They remind me of Jesus' crown of thorns. They look like the crown of thorns! That's awful. I can't have crowns of thorns for my wedding breakfast table decorations – what would people think? What would God think? I've pissed him off enough already. And they might be under copyright. No, I can't have these. I need you to stick the stalks back on and turn them back into twigs.'

'Jen,' I said, 'with the best will in the world—'

We were interrupted by Jen's nephew, who was drifting around with earplugs in both ears. He pulled his earplugs out and looked at the crown of thorns in the centre of the table. 'Hey,' he said, 'cool table decorations.'

'I don't like them Damien,' said Jen. 'They remind me of Jesus' crown of thorns.'

'Oh yeah?' he said. 'Never heard of them. Do they do like, Gospel stuff?'

Jen introduced me to Damien, who she said would be taking some photos tomorrow. Apparently he's doing a photography A level, and knows how to work a camera.

Damien was inspecting the tangle of twigs in the centre of the table. 'This stuff looks a bit, sort of... ' He struggled for the right word and then found it. 'Dead. Are you going to spray it with like, sparkly gold paint?'

'No,' I said.

'Yes,' said Jen. 'Great idea. They need to be sprayed gold. Sparkly gold paint, that's what we need, it will lift them and make them look more festive and less sacrificial. That's the best we can do.' She looked at me. 'You'll need a few tins, at least four, and spray them outside. For god's sake don't spray them in here on the tablecloth.'

So it was late when I got home.

***

I stayed with Jen on the night before the wedding at the hotel across the road from the church. Sam and Chrissy stayed in Greenwich with Sam's sister.

Jen and I didn't stay up late. We painted our nails. We ate a small celebratory box of chocolates. We drank a little wine and reminisced, then I retired to my room across the corridor to have a hot soak in the bath before bed.

We were up early on Saturday morning.

Once Jen was ready, her hair curled with curling tongs, her make-up applied, her something blue in place, wearing a pretty robe before putting on her dress, she and I had a glass of champagne sitting at the window of the hotel room overlooking the street below. We couldn't see the entrance to the church, it was just out of sight, but we could see the whole of B&M's shop frontage, so we watched people going in and out of the shop, and sipped our champagne.

Jen was in reflective mood. She looked at her watch and said, 'It's two and a half years since Frank died.'

'Is it?' I said. 'Not that long ago.'

'Some people think I'm remarrying too hastily.'

'I haven't heard anyone say that.'

'Oh yes. Some people are saying I'm marrying Sam on the rebound. Funny, isn't it, how people can get completely the wrong idea about a situation?' She shook her head in disbelief. 'Marrying Sam on the rebound? I couldn't bound away from Frank soon enough.'

'Why didn't you just divorce him?'

'He died before I got the chance.'

I looked away from the front of B&M and across at Jen. 'This is not the right mood music for a wedding, Jen,' I said. 'We should be looking forward, not back. This kind of talk doesn't go with the champagne.'

'Yes,' she agreed, and then, 'No. You're right. I need to exorcise the whole of my first marriage, and move on. I feel he's sitting on my shoulder sometimes, Frank. I should just shrug him off and get free of him.'

'Jen,' I said, with a little trepidation, 'do you remember the story Pam told at your hen-night? The one about the man you thought had had a heart attack in the surgery? The man you thought had died? The one you leapt across the room to resuscitate?'

'The man who had just fallen asleep? The man who couldn't believe his luck when he woke up and found me sitting on him?'

'Did you do the same for Frank? When he had his heart attack, did you try to resuscitate him?'

Jen looked blank. After a second or two she said, 'Well. Not as such.'

We looked at each other steadily from our positions on either side of the bay window, and we agreed without saying anything, not to go any further. But I wanted some air.

'Shall I go and see if Sam's here yet?' I said.

'Yes please. Go and see if he's here. I'll put my dress on when you come back. It's the only thing left to do. Don't be long. Tell him not to text.'

'I won't be long.' I drained my glass, and stood up to go. As I left Jen was re-filling her glass. 'No more after that one,' I said. 'Long day ahead.'

'But it's champagne,' she said. 'It won't keep.'

I wagged a finger, and left to find the wedding party.

I enjoy weddings, even when I have to attend them on my own. I love the air of anticipation before the ceremony, the buzz of conversation, the feathers in the ladies' hats, the flowers in the men's buttonholes, recognising people you haven't seen for a while, wondering how much weight they've gained. And then as the time approaches, everyone waiting for the bride to arrive with her retinue, craning their necks to catch a glimpse before she sets off down the aisle ... She's here! She's here! She looks lovely! Doesn't she look lovely? Doesn't she look just gorgeous?

Sam and his brother and sister stood together at the entrance to the church, which boasted a spacious lobby where everyone was gathering prior to the service beginning. They each had a lovely white rose in the buttonhole of their lapels, the blooms just the right side of being overblown. Sam saw me crossing the road and waved.

'How's she doing, my bride?'

'She's fine Sam. She looks lovely, and she's nearly ready. She just wanted to know you were here. But you mustn't text her, she says no contact before she walks down the aisle.'

'I'm here,' he said, 'all present and correct. Ready and waiting.'

Sam's brother John looked at his watch. 'Just another fifteen minutes till half past,' he said.

'I'm going to say hello to a few people,' I said, looking beyond them to the lobby, 'then I'll go back and bring Jen over, once everyone is in the church.'

There was a small crowd inside the lobby, gently jostling and making an excited hubbub. Dan and Chrissy, Baz and Sophie, stood in a group just inside the door.

'Do you like my hat?' said Sophie. 'It's fascinating.'

Chrissy frowned. 'It's called a fascinator.'

'That's what I said,' said Sophie. 'It's fascinating. Do you like it?'

'I love it,' I said.

'I look as if there are bees buzzing round my head, don't you think?' Sophie shook her head from side to side, and the fronds on her fascinator bounced jauntily in front of her face.

Dan and Baz both looked very smart, and I saw how they would look if they were trainee accountants.

'I bought this suit for my grandma's funeral,' said Baz. 'But it's the same dress code, isn't it?'

'I think men look really sexy in suits,' said Sophie. 'Probably even better at funerals because they have to wear a tie.' She looked at Baz and Dan's open-necked shirts and seemed disappointed she wasn't at a funeral.

'Your dress is a bit crap Mum,' said Dan. 'You look like a milk bottle that's decided to play tennis.'

Baz turned to him, 'Fuck off and be nice to your Mum.'

'Mum's all right,' said Dan. 'It's the dress that's crap.'

'Your dad looks very happy Chrissy,' I said, and we looked across at Sam laughing together with John and some friends on the steps just outside.

'Yeah,' Chrissy smiled. 'That's nice.'

'See you all later then. You all look great. Have fun.' I moved away, and said hello to little groups of people, and stopped to talk to Jen's mum Dorothy, and Jen's daughter Emily. Dorothy was wearing a pale pink satin coat and a hat like a marshmallow of the same colour. Emily wore a very pale pink shift dress and a lace jacket with a pretty stand-up collar.

'You look lovely, both of you,' I said. 'Your hat looks good enough to eat, Dorothy.'

'Thank you dear,' said Dorothy, 'I don't suppose I'll wear it again. You can eat it after the photos if you like. Your dress is charming, did Jennifer help you choose it?'

'I'm so nervous,' said Emily. 'I'm not sure why. I'll be glad when this is safely over. Mum is so, she's so bonkers sometimes.' She glanced at her grandmother and then looked back at me. 'It's all right, gran knows what I mean. I couldn't believe it when mum told me she was buying universal plugs for wedding favours.'

'Is she?' said Dorothy. 'What the heck is a universal plug? It's not something to do with feminine hygiene, is it?'

'No, no Dorothy,' I said. 'It's a plug that will fit any sink. Quite useful really.'

'Oh well.' She looked resigned and tucked her clutch bag further under her arm. 'If you say so.'

'And the ham and egg wedding cake,' said Emily. 'It's bizarre really, isn't it?'

Anita from the surgery drifted past, carrying a present wrapped in silver paper and a blue bow. 'Hi!' she said. 'I'm Anita from the surgery,' she said to Dorothy. 'Emily and Sally know me. You must be Jen's mum?'

'That's right Anita,' I said, 'this is Dorothy, Jen's mum, and—'

'Hi Dorothy!' said Anita. 'She's a cracker isn't she, your Jen? We had such a laugh at the surgery, you know. We really miss her. I expect she's told you all about the prosthetic leg?'

'No, I don't think I heard that one,' said Dorothy. 'Emily might have heard it.'

Emily looked blank.

'Oh, you must get her to tell you about the prosthetic leg,' said Anita. 'I laugh now every time I see fishnet tights. Anyway, I'm looking for somewhere to put this and I can see a pile of pressies over there, so I'll drop this off with those others. See you later!'

'I'm going to let Sam's brother know it's time for people to file through and take their seats,' I told Dorothy and Emily. 'Then I'll pop back over the road to the hotel, and bring Jen over. It's nearly time. She's nearly ready, she just wanted me to make sure everyone would be in position when she arrives. And that Sam would be here, of course.'

'That's good,' said Dorothy. 'Time to get the show on the road then.'

'I'll feel more relaxed once this bit's over,' said Emily. 'Like I said, it's making me nervous. I don't know why.'

'Don't worry Emily,' I said, 'your mum is a free spirit, but she's not daft. Everything will be fine.'

'Well,' said Dorothy, who obviously knows Jen pretty well. 'Let's not speak too soon.'

I moved towards the entrance again, telling everyone the bride would just be a few minutes. When I reached Sam and John, I told them I was going over to collect Jen and escort her across the road to the church, and I suggested that they usher everyone into their seats and take up their positions. People were already filing through the big oak doors into the church beyond to sit and wait. Sam and John moved off to bring up the rear.

I crossed the road back to the hotel, and went back upstairs to Jen's room.

'Is he here?'

'Yes, of course he's here. Of course he's here! And he looks gorgeous in his cream suit and lilac shirt.'

'How do I look?' She had put her dress on, and it did look good.

'You look absolutely lovely. Absolutely lovely Jen.'

'You're such a good friend Sally. And you agreed to wear that dress for me. It's not great, is it?'

'It's not bad. It's fine. Dan says I look like a milk bottle playing tennis."

Jen started to cry.

'Don't cry, you daft thing.' I gave her a tissue. 'The dress isn't that bad. You'll smudge your eye make-up.'

'I'm so lucky Sally. So lucky to have you as my friend, and to be marrying Sam.'

'I know,' I said. 'You're very lucky to have me as a friend. You're really lucky there. And Sam of course. Now let me just arrange this little train at the back, it's catching a little bit.'

'I want to say to you, Sally, before we leave here,' Jen dabbed her eyes with the tissue, 'you've been so good to me over the years, and what I particularly love about you is that you—' she caught sight of my watch. 'Shit! Is that the time? We'll have to go. I'm going to be late. It's after half past already. I'll tell you later.'

'Slow down,' I said, 'they'll wait for you. You're the main event. Take your time. Let's do this properly.'

So I opened the door to let her come through. I arranged her dress and little train, and then very sedately we walked down the stairs towards the door onto the street. A small group of hotel staff were manoeuvring a trolley through a swing door on the landing. They stopped to watch us pass, and gave us a round of applause.

And so, the day began.

Once outside, all we had to do was walk across the crossing to the church on the other side of the road. Jen's nephew,

Damien, met us outside the hotel and suggested he take some photographs while we were using the crossing, Abbey Road-style. He said we should look straight ahead, rather than turning to smile at the camera, because that would make the echo of the Beatles album cover unmistakeable. So we did. Cars stopped and bipped their horns in celebration, a few pedestrians broke into a straggled applause. Someone whistled and shouted 'Nice one!' It occurred to me that they might have thought Jen and I were going to marry each other.

Once in the lobby just outside the church, Jen put her arms around me. 'Thanks Sally,' she said. 'Thanks for everything. This is going to be such a good day, nothing can go wrong, I feel it. Everyone loves me. I feel so strong, I feel invincible, as if I'm on some sort of wave of good fortune. Sam and I will have a wonderful life together, I know it. We're starting late, but it was meant to be this way.'

Damien wasn't listening, he had spotted a painting on the wall of the lobby depicting the Angel Gabriel appearing to Mary. Gabriel had a hand on Mary's head, and Mary was kneeling before him with her hands pressed together in prayer. Both were in white. 'Fantastic!' said Damien. 'Listen guys, I want you both to stand underneath this painting. Sally, you should be kneeling down, and Jen, put your hand on her head. Or maybe the other way around? Guys? Just had a thought. Are either of you pregnant?'

Jen kissed him on the cheek. 'Maybe a photo when we come out Damien,' she said. 'But this is my wedding and I can't wait for it to start.' She glanced up at the painting. 'You've got a point though. See? See what this means? It's a sign. I'm blessed. That's what it means. I'm blessed. Let's go.'

And so we moved into position. Damien slipped into a seat at the back of the church. 'Climb Every Mountain' struck up, and Jen and I waited to begin our walk up the aisle.

The service started unremarkably enough. There was a hymn, 'Love Divine All Loves Excelling,' and then Anita from the surgery stood up to give a reading. She stood at the pulpit and put on her reading glasses, then opened a book and solemnly smoothed down the pages as if she was about to read from a sacred text. She drew breath and looked up over her reading glasses and said into the expectant void, 'Good morning everyone. As the first reader, I would like to welcome you to the joyous occasion of Jen and Sam's wedding, and to begin the ceremony with a reading taken from chapter eight of Winnie the Pooh, by a milne. Sorry. By A A Milne. Jen asked me to choose something from Winnie the Pooh, because she feels there are some valuable lessons to be learned from its pages, and I agree with her. So after studying it carefully, I can't think of a more appropriate few lines than these I am going to read to you now.'

I glanced at the vicar. He looked tired.

Anita looked at her flock over her reading glasses, and began. *'Sing Ho! For the life of a Bear! Sing Ho! For the life of a Bear! I don't much mind if it rains or snows, 'Cos I've got a lot of honey on my nice new nose! I don't much care if it snows or thaws, 'Cos I've got a lot of honey on my nice clean paws!'*

She lifted her head and looked at us, and we looked at her.

'Honey,' she said. 'Honey is what Pooh Bear is talking about here.'

She scanned our faces, and nodded.

'And I want us all to think about honey for a minute. What do we think about when we think about honey? What thoughts do we have? When we think about honey? I know what you're thinking. You're thinking about sweetness, and goodness, and maybe too,' she smiled, 'you're thinking about how sticky honey is.' She nodded. 'Because it is, very sticky. Sometimes, this stickiness is a bad thing. Irritating, even. But sometimes it is a wonderful thing – and today, today my friends, it is a wonderful thing, because today, the honey in Jen and Sam's life is sticking them together! Because yes! Jen and Sam have honey in their lives now, after a long period when they had none at all. And this honey will stick to them, and see them through the bad times when there is not so much honey around. So stick your noses in the honey! Smear it on your paws, Jen and Sam! Because you deserve it. You will, like the rest of us, have rain and snow in your life, but as long as your nose is in the honey, you will always be happy. So let us all sing Ho! For the life of Jen and Sam! Ho! Ho! Ho! Amen.'

Anita picked up her copy of *Winnie the Pooh* and walked sedately back to her seat with all the serious composure of someone who had not spoken utter bollocks.

The vicar roused himself from the swoon he had fallen into to avoid listening to the moronic musings of Winnie the Pooh, and stood up.

'And now,' he said, 'perhaps we could—'

Jen stepped forward and put her hand on his arm. 'Just a second vicar,' I heard her say, 'may I have a word with everyone first?'

He was startled, but recovered quickly. 'Yes of course you may.'

Jen turned around and faced us all, flushed and excited and anxious to engage. St Joan, about to light her own blue touch paper.

'Ladies and gentlemen,' she began, 'friends and family, welcome! And thank you so much for being here to celebrate our wedding. It's great, it's absolutely great to see so many friendly, familiar faces to support Sam and me on our wedding day. I'm overwhelmed. And overjoyed.'

'Yay!' shouted Sophie from her pew halfway down the church.

'Thank you Sophie!' said Jen. 'Now, I want to say a few words, before we do the deed,' she glanced at Sam, who was smiling and looking bemused, 'because there is something I want to share with you all. And Sam.'

The vicar glanced down at his order of service, obviously wondering if he had overlooked this item, or whether it was in fact, impromptu and unscheduled. I looked at Jen, and managed to catch her eye, and slowly shook my head.

Jen carried on. 'My very good friend Sally has told me not to do this, but I'll leave you to judge whether I've done the right thing or not.'

Sam looked at me and gave a little what's-going-on shrug. I shrugged back. Then all eyes were on Jen, waiting to hear what she had to say.

'The truth is,' she said, 'I want to get something off my chest, and I want to be among friends when that happens, and also, in a place like this, where we might all expect to be forgiven, and blessed.'

The congregation began to look a little concerned, they seemed to sit forward as if to catch every word. The vicar put his head on one side and frowned slightly.

'Friends, as you all know, my first husband Frank died a few years ago. Some of you may remember Frank. He wasn't a nice man. I'm sorry,' Jen turned to the vicar, 'but he wasn't.'

The congregation tensed; faces were now frozen with fixed expressions of concern. I was sitting very close to where Jen was standing, so I said quietly, 'Jen, I wonder if we should leave this for another time? I think everyone is wanting to see you and Sam get married.'

'Sally knows what I'm going to say,' said Jen, 'that's why she's getting anxious. She's such a good friend, but on this occasion I'm not going to take her advice. I've thought long and hard about this, and to be honest, until now I wasn't actually planning to say anything. But I've just changed my mind. Just as I was walking into the church, just now. As if I'd had a sign, or something, from the Lord. I'm sure it's the right thing to do. And what I'm going to tell you is – and some of you might be a little shocked by this – it's just possible that I had something to do with Frank's death.'

There was a collective, audible gasp. The vicar's jaw dropped open. One of Sam's knees buckled and he put out a hand to steady himself.

'Jen—' I began again.

'No, Sally,' she said, 'I know you think I should keep quiet about this, but these are my friends and I know they'll understand. You see,' she turned to the congregation, 'what happened was, Frank mislaid the pills he took for his heart condition. He was always losing those pills and I was always having to find them for him.' She smiled, and rolled her eyes, 'What was he like?' It was a rhetorical question; no-one replied. 'Anyway, just to sort of make the point that he should take better care of his pills, and – I have to be honest – because he was such a very *annoying* man, I didn't tell him where his pills were when he was looking for them that last time. And for a few days before that. If I remember correctly. So by the time he eventually had the heart attack, it was a while since he'd had any of his heart pills. Because he couldn't find them, even though I sort of knew where they were. Unfortunately.'

Jen's audience was now horrified. There was no sign of the supportive response she was expecting. 'So er,' she hesitated, looking out over the sea of wide-eyed and tense faces, 'so er, anyway, it occurred to me that I might possibly have contributed in some way, to er, to Frank's actual er, death. I'm not saying I killed him. Obviously! I never meant him to die. Of course not! That would be... Well. That would be awful.' She shook her head. 'Gosh.'

She looked around, hoping for a sympathetic expression somewhere among her listeners, trying to engage and elicit some warmth, but she couldn't thaw their frozen faces. So right there at the altar she continued digging down into her large and gaping, jagged and perilous, hole.

'No, I'm just saying... Well, I suppose I'm saying that if he'd had them, his pills, he might not have died and been so very dead now.' She stopped, and left an agonising pause. 'Of course,' she set off again at a trot, 'there's probably no way of knowing. No way of knowing what would have happened if he'd had his pills. Now that he's been cremated. I don't suppose his heart's in very good shape now. For any sort of investigation. Even supposing – you know – even supposing you could actually find it. To look at it. Which you won't now, of course, it'll just be – well, it'll just be ash, I suppose. Like the rest of him. After the er, after the er, cremation. You see, I can't be sure now, how much difference it would have made to Frank, if he'd had his pills. This is the awkward thing for me. But obviously,' she rushed headlong, 'this whole thing is much more awkward for Frank. I understand that of course, far more awkward for him than for me. He's actually dead now, and I'm, as you can see, right as rain. Anyway. I just thought I might make a clean breast of it, in church, before God, while we're all here, and then Sam and I could, you know, move on, with your blessing, and er.' She glanced at the vicar, now rigid with shock. 'So.' She looked out across the congregation. A number of people now had hands over their mouths. 'Oh dear. Maybe we should just carry on with the ceremony now? Vicar? I think that might be best.'

The vicar took a few seconds to react. Then he said, quietly and just to the wedding party, 'I wonder if... Perhaps, you both might like...' He looked at Sam, 'Perhaps you both might like to take a minute, maybe in the vestry, just to have a quiet chat, so we can gather our thoughts, after your little speech, Jennifer?'

'No, I don't think so,' said Jen.

'Yes,' said Sam. 'Yes please.'

The vicar gave me a reassuring smile and bent down to speak as he brushed past, 'Maybe you should have a word with everyone, make a little announcement, just to let them know the plan? I'll ask the organist to play something soothing while we're in the vestry. Back in a tick,' and he led Jen and Sam off to the side, and through the vestry door.

I stood up and turned to the congregation, who looked now as if they were watching a performance of Macbeth. 'Well folks,' I said, 'there will be a short break now while Sam and Jen have a chat with the vestry in the vicar. I'm sure they'll be back with us very soon, and in the meantime we can look forward to being soothed by an organ. By some organ music. Thank you everyone.' I sat down again.

The congregation abandoned their shocked silence and began to whisper urgently among themselves, and the whispering rose to a muted hubbub, enervated and intense, barely subdued. Dorothy on my right leant towards me and said, 'Did she just say she killed Frank?'

'No, no she didn't say that. She's just feeling a bit guilty about the way he died.'

'Because she killed him?'

'No, no, she didn't kill him.'

Emily, who was sitting on the other side of her grandmother sat forward and hissed at me, 'Sally! Did you know she was going to do this?'

'She said she was thinking about it.'

'For Christ's sake! Why didn't you stop her?'

'I thought I had! I told her it was a very bad idea. I thought she'd changed her mind. I was sure she had.'

Anita was sitting in the pew behind me. She tapped me on the shoulder and when I turned around she said, 'God Almighty. What just happened? What's going on in the vestry?'

'The vicar said they should have a chat.'

'Someone needs to go in there and find out what's going on,' said Emily.

We all looked at the vestry door, which was impressively large and firmly shut.

'How long do we wait?' said Anita.

'You know,' said Dorothy, 'Frank was one of the most irritating men I have ever come across. I'd have been tempted to hide his pills, I don't mind telling you.'

'Don't say that Granny,' said Emily. 'He was very annoying, but he was my dad. I could cheerfully have strangled him myself sometimes, but we don't want people thinking we're a coven of witches.'

The vestry door opened, and the vicar came out. He walked over to us and put his hand on my arm. 'Sally, is it? I wonder if you'd mind stepping into the vestry for a minute, Sally? Jennifer has asked for you.' I stood up and followed him into the vestry.

Jen was sitting on a small wooden chair in the middle of the room, and Sam stood a little apart from her. Jen had the end of her gauze train balled up in her fist and was using it to dab her eyes.

'Sally,' she said. 'Help. I'm just trying to explain. I didn't actually want to murder Frank. I just wanted him to take responsibility for his pills.'

'But,' said Sam, 'you hid his pills. And he died because he hadn't taken them.'

'No,' said Jen, 'I didn't hide his pills. He put his pills in the key drawer, and then he couldn't find them because they were in such a stupid place. I just didn't tell him that's where they were because he was always so careless with them. I thought it would teach him a lesson.'

'Well,' said Sam, 'it certainly did that. Shame he didn't live long enough to learn anything. And you might as well have hidden the pills. You knew where they were, and he didn't. It amounts to the same thing.'

'It's also a pity that you haven't had this conversation before now,' said the vicar. 'This is a difficult stage to thrash this one out. Halfway through your marriage ceremony is cutting it a bit fine.'

'I didn't know we needed this conversation,' said Sam. 'I wasn't expecting to hear my fiancé was capable of murder when I was standing next to her at the altar.'

'Murder?' said Jen. 'That's ridiculous! I didn't murder Frank. That's so hurtful. How can you think that of me?'

'Where are Frank's pills now?' said Sam.

'I told you,' said Jen, 'they're in the key drawer, where he put them.'

'Still in the key drawer? Fuck. You didn't even get them out when the poor bloke was having his heart attack? Christ.'

'Sam,' I said, 'you must know Jen well enough by now to know she's not capable of murder, surely?'

'Do I though? Do I know that? Look at what she's just hit me with! And seconds, literally seconds before she expects me to marry her. What the hell am I supposed to do? I need some time to get to grips with this. Can any of us say she isn't capable of murder after this?'

'I didn't murder Frank. I never intended to murder Frank,' said Jen. 'That was never my intention. I was really surprised when he died. He was always exaggerating his symptoms.'

'*Always exaggerating his symptoms?* Did you really just say that? The poor bloke had symptoms – then he died. He didn't have time to exaggerate his symptoms. Look,' said Sam, striving to stay calm, 'you told me you didn't like Frank. You said you weren't upset when he died. Okay. I could deal with that. I know what it's like to be in an unhappy relationship. But now I discover you withheld his medication and didn't let him have it when he was dying for lack of it.' He began pacing back and forth across the room. 'This isn't looking good, Jen. It's looking really bad. It's not something an averagely nice person would do. I don't expect you to be a saint, but – bloody hell.' He wiped his brow with the white rose. 'I don't think I can go through with this whole thing today. It's killed the mood. I'm – well to be honest – I'm spooked, if you want to know the truth.'

'But,' said Jen, gesturing weakly towards the interior of the church, 'everyone's here. Everything's ready.'

'I'm not ready,' said Sam. 'I'm really sorry Jen, I don't feel I can go through with this today.'

The vicar nodded, and said gently to Jen, 'You have rather put him on the spot dear. He probably does need some time to reflect.'

Jen bent forward and sobbed, and blew her nose.

'Here's a hanky Jen,' I said. 'Don't blow your nose on your train.'

Sam tried again, gesturing now with the rose which was shedding petals like tears. 'Why Jen? Why didn't you tell me this before? I needed to know this before now. I really did. I don't want to be hearing this kind of stuff now. God's sakes! Talk about timing!' Sam turned to the vicar and addressed him directly. 'Help me out here, vicar. You know what I'm trying to say.'

And the vicar was decisive. 'I don't think this ceremony can continue today,' he said. 'I'm very sorry, for both of you, but I really don't think we can continue. Not today. I think that's obvious. We must look for another way forward.' He turned to Jen. 'I'm very sorry my dear. It was brave of you to make that confession in church, but it has altered the course of events. Sadly.'

There was a stunned silence, while we took this in.

'So what happens now?' said Sam. 'Do I just go out through the back door?'

Jen stood up. 'You're leaving?' she said. 'No! No Sam! Please don't go. What am I going to do with all these people? Please Sam, stay with me. We don't have to get married, we can just have a party, but don't walk out on me, please. Honestly Sam, if you'd known Frank, you'd understand. You'd stay.'

'That's not the point, Jen. It's not about what kind of man Frank was.' He looked at the vicar and me. 'It's not about the kind of man Frank was. I understand he wasn't a nice man. Okay, he might have been an awkward sod, but, to bring about his death by hiding his pills? I can't live with that. You shouldn't be able to live with that, Jen. How can you live comfortably with that?' He shook his head and said, 'I have to go.'

'No, please don't go Sam.' Jen was desperate now. 'We can get married and then I can explain everything. Or no. No, we needn't get married today. We don't have to get married today, we can just go straight to the reception now and call it something else. I'll get changed. I'll take the dress off. But don't walk out on me Sam. Let's just stay together, married or not. I know I can make you understand. You've got hold of completely the wrong end of the stick.'

'But the problem is Jen, I don't want to be holding this stick. At all. Not now. I'm sorry. I have to go. Seriously, there are things I need to think about before I go through with this. I'm sorry. But this isn't just your wedding day. It's mine too. And I can't do it.'

'Look,' I said. 'I'm groping around for solutions here, clutching at straws, but I can't bear to see you both so upset. How does this sound? How about getting married here, today, as planned, and if Jen can't convince you she's not a murderess, well, just get a divorce!'

'Yes!' said Jen. 'Let's do that.'

'Absolutely not!' said the vicar. 'Absolutely not. I couldn't in all conscience conduct a marriage ceremony in those circumstances. We don't just dispense marriage certificates here you know. We aren't a glorified slot machine. I can't perform the ceremony as a holding operation until you work out if one of you is capable of murder.'

'I'm sorry vicar,' said Sam. 'I have to leave.'

'No,' said Jen. 'No. Please no.'

'Of course,' said the vicar. 'I do understand. Do you want me to say a few words to the congregation?'

'I could do that, if you like,' I said.

They looked at me, and then Sam turned to the vicar, 'Yes please vicar, if you wouldn't mind. I don't feel able to myself.'

Jen was sobbing now into her train, which was covered in mascara and snot.

'You'd better go Sam,' I said, 'if you're determined to go.'

He handed me the rose and left, and Jen and I sat down together on a pew pushed against the wall. I put my arm around her while she cried, and gave her paper hankies. The vicar pulled up a chair, and quietly and sympathetically he began to suggest what he might say to the congregation, and he asked us what we would like to do about the reception.

The vestry door opened, and Chrissy stepped inside. She looked around at the sorry scene. 'What's going on?' she said. Then, realising one of the key players was missing, 'Where's Dad?'

'He's just left, Chrissy,' I said. 'He didn't feel he could get married. Not today.'

'Oh shit,' she said. 'Wow. He's gone? Wow. Why didn't you wait until after the wedding, Jen? You didn't need to fess up now. So, what are we going to do?'

'We're just discussing that,' said the vicar. 'Come and sit down with us while we talk it over.'

'Yeah right,' said Chrissy, pulling up a seat. 'We'll have to get a shift on, though. They're getting restless out there. They're going to need some more entertainment if we want to keep hold of them. One or two at the back have already left. They aren't the sort of crowd to slow hand clap, but they're getting fidgety.'

Emily pushed open the vestry door and took in the scene at a glance. She half turned, and said to someone standing behind her, 'You're right Gran, it's all off.'

Chrissy found another two chairs, and everyone sat in a semi-circle around Jen and I, still sitting uncomfortably on the pew against the wall.

Dorothy took her daughter's hand.

***

I was very impressed with the vicar. He did a really good job. He told the congregation that the bride and groom had decided to take time out to talk some things over, and that personally he thought they had made a sensible decision to postpone the ceremony until a time when things between them were more settled. He said if more couples did that there would perhaps be fewer divorces, and although it was unfortunate that a potential difficulty had cropped up so late in the proceedings, he hoped we would all bear with them, and give them our support while they worked things out. He said the bride wanted the reception to go ahead for the guests, and she might join them later in the day, if she felt able.

I shook hands with the vicar while we were waiting for a taxi and Jen was in the loo. I thanked him for dealing so tactfully with everything.

He smiled. 'Well, it's all part of the service, of course. But if I may just mention – while Jennifer is in the bathroom – the circumstances surrounding the death of Jennifer's first husband do seem to be problematic.' He drew me aside a little and lowered his voice. 'It occurs to me that this may be of interest to the authorities. There may be some questions to answer. Jennifer seems a little, how should I put this? A little disconnected to the potentially serious implications of whatever part she played in the death of her husband. It's concerning. She rather gives the impression that because he wasn't a nice man, we needn't worry too much about the manner of his death. And unless I'm very much mistaken, that's not how this works. She seems almost, not flippant, but oddly unable to understand the potential seriousness of her predicament.'

The toilet chain flushed and Jen came out of the toilet cubicle. She looked a mess, so soon after looking lovely. There is something shocking about looking a mess in a wedding dress. I helped her into the taxi and took her home with me.

***

Naturally, we have all been thinking a lot about Jen and Sam and their abortive wedding ceremony over the last few days. We talked endlessly about what had happened in the hours and days immediately after the non-wedding. (There should be a name for a wedding which is planned but doesn't take place. A shredding, maybe.) Jen was heartbroken, but she insisted that she would be able to talk Sam around when she saw him again, and they could discuss the whole thing without being in the pressure cooker of circumstance and emotion that they were in on the day itself. She's still hoping that she and Sam will be able to reach an understanding and have a very quiet ceremony, at a future date, to seal their union. There would be absolutely no fuss, no tumbleweed, no universal travel plugs, and very few guests. Once she had calmed down, Jen didn't blame Sam for walking away.

Emily wanted to know what had made Jen think the speech she gave at the altar was a good idea. Jen said she hadn't intended to say anything at all when the day began, but just before the ceremony she felt moved by the spirit. She got to the point in the service when she had once thought she might say something and found herself saying it. At the time, she felt sure it was the right thing to do, although of course, that certainty fell away rapidly as her address progressed. She said she should just have stopped talking, instead of trying to justify herself to the congregation. I was expecting Emily to be less sympathetic to her mother, but she seemed prepared to give Jen the benefit of all doubt.

Before they left to go home I said to Emily that I was impressed with how supportive she had been of her Mum, considering -

'Considering she didn't exactly rush to save Dad when he was having a heart attack?'

'Well, something like that.'

'Dad could be very difficult,' she said, 'he drove her mad. And you know, if you insist on driving someone mad, you can't be surprised if they start to do mad things. People should think twice before they drive the person they live with mad. Particularly when they need medication to keep them alive. That's the way I see it, anyway.'

There is a pragmatic streak running right through the womenfolk in that family.

***

Sam rang me the day after Jen and Emily left, to make a proposal which I thought was sensible. He said he thought there should be a period when he and Jen didn't contact each other, say four weeks, during which time they would allow their emotions to settle down, and get things into some sort of perspective. After four weeks he suggested they should meet up and talk freely, with no expectations made of either of them, nor any preconceptions about how things should progress from that date. He said he would pay all the outstanding wedding expenses. I put this proposal to Jen, and she agreed, although she asked me to tell Sam she would pay her share of the expenses. She sounded better for having had some indirect contact with Sam.

I rang Sam to tell him Jen accepted his proposal, and we had a little chat. I told him that Jen was hopeful there might be a reconciliation, once the dust had settled. Sam said it was a bit early for him to think in terms of a reconciliation, he was still thinking he might have had a lucky escape.

Obviously, I didn't tell Jen that.

Jen is back in the north now with her daughter Emily, for some rest and recuperation. Emily thought that Jen might best achieve this through close contact with her grandchildren, because young children drive all the negative thoughts out of your head. Young children also drive all the wits out of your head, but I'm sure it will do Jen good to have a complete change of scene.

Chrissy says her dad is lying low at home for the moment, but has made arrangements to go on a birdwatching trip to Norway with a friend at the end of next week. I said I didn't know Sam was a birdwatcher. Chrissy said he isn't, but this came up and as things stand, he's at a loose end.

Dan said he hasn't been to many weddings, but if they are anything like Sam and Jen's he hopes theirs is the first of many he could attend. He said he particularly enjoyed Jen's speech, especially the part when she was speculating on the state of her former husband's cremated heart, which he thought was surreal and possibly hilarious. Sophie wondered what Jen planned to do with her wedding dress, seeing as it didn't look as if she would be needing it anytime soon. She asked me whether I thought Jen would want to throw it away. I said I didn't think she would throw it away; a wedding dress isn't something you stuff into a wheely bin, however disappointing the day had turned out to be. I said she might sell it on eBay. (I remember occasionally seeing small ads in newspapers years ago, 'Wedding dress. Immaculate condition. Size 14. Never worn. £500 ono for quick sale.' Was that a small ad? Or a short verse to a broken heart?)

Bill of course had missed the whole thing, although I did get a chance to tell him about it last night when he got home. He had eaten, so he just wanted a cup of tea, and while I made it he cut a generous slice of apple to wedge between the bars of Marra's cage. Bill had a budgie when he was a boy and he has a fondness for caged birds. He watched as Marra delicately nibbled the apple, and then he came to sit down with me at the kitchen table.

When he heard that the wedding hadn't gone ahead, he assumed that either Jen or Sam hadn't turned up on the day, but I said no, they were both there, it was the speech Jen made when she was standing at the altar that had led to the ceremony being cancelled.

Bill was intrigued, and I got his full attention while I described the distinctly un-festive revelation Jen made in her speech. Typically though, Bill focused on one aspect of the speech and wouldn't move on.

'So, let me get this right. Jen said in church that you knew she had withheld Frank's pills?'

'Yes, that's right.'

'Is it right that she said this in church, or is it right that you did in fact know before the ceremony that she had withheld Frank's pills?'

'Both.'

'How long have you known that Jen withheld Frank's pills?'

'Weeks. She told me weeks ago.'

'And you advised her not to say anything?'

'I advised her not to say anything at the wedding. I didn't think it would be a good idea. And I was right.'

'Was this made clear at the wedding? The fact that you advised Jen not to say anything?'

'Indirectly.'

'How indirectly?'

'Jen said I knew what she was going to say and I didn't want her to say it.'

'That sounds pretty direct. And if Jen is found guilty of an offence, in connection with Frank's death, where do you stand?'

'I did think about that. I asked Max about it actually.'

'Max?'

'My history group friend, a semi-retired solicitor.

'Oh yes, Max. So what did he say?'

'He said – let me try and remember correctly. It's a while ago, and bearing in mind that we'd drunk a glass of wine and spent the evening discussing cosmetics at the court of Queen Elizabeth I, I don't know how focused he was, but I think he said that you can't be an accessory after the fact if the facts associated with the offence aren't clear. Something like that.'

'Well, there do seem to be some clear facts here, on the face of it. One, Frank needed medication to stop him having a heart attack. Two, Jen prevented him from taking that medication. Three, Frank had a heart attack. Four, Frank died. Five, you knew about all of this and advised Jen to keep quiet.'

'Yes, but we don't know whether the missing heart pills caused the heart attack.'

'Don't we?'

'No.'

'Why not? Are we stupid?'

'The heart attack might have been caused by something else.'

'Something other than not taking the pills which would prevent the heart attack?'

'Yes.'

'Well. I think we're on a sticky wicket there.'

'He might have had a heart attack even if he had taken his pills,' I said.

'Surely that's not likely?'

'It's possible.'

'It's not impossible.'

'But you're right,' I said, 'it's not likely.'

'I think if push comes to shove here, I'd rather be working for the prosecution than the defence.'

'The prosecution! God, Bill. What are you saying? Do you think there'll be a court case? Should I go to the police? What should we do?'

'Fuck!' said Marra. 'Fuck! Fuck!'

So I switched off the lights and we went upstairs.

Chapter Five: May

Judith rang me this morning.

'Sally,' she said, 'I'm just ringing to tell you I've booked us a twin-bedded room on the outskirts of Stratford for the history trip. So no need for you to do anything. The room is very reasonable, you can settle up with me next time we see each other.'

'Oh,' I said.

'What do you mean, oh? We have to get something booked Sally, it's getting close now, we can't leave it too long.'

'No. Actually Judith, I've already booked somewhere.'

'You've already booked us somewhere? Why didn't you say?'

'Sorry. I didn't think. But -'

'Well that was stupid. What am I going to do with my room now? I suppose I could cancel it, if yours is better. How much did you pay for the one you booked? Did you go for the cheapest room? Or the nicest room? My preference would be for the cheapest, personally, no point in splashing out on a pricey room just for us. What do you think? The one I booked was just eighty pounds a night, including breakfast, for two people. Not bad. Place is a dump, mind.'

'Actually Judith, the room I booked was just for me.'

'Just for you? A single room? Did you book a room for me too?'

'No. I – sorry Judith. I just assumed we'd be booking independently.'

'Oh, right,' she said. 'Not very friendly. Didn't we say we'd book together?'

'Did we? I don't remember. Sorry Judith, I honestly don't remember.'

'Well, you could always cancel yours.'

'I don't think I can.'

'Why not?'

'I had to pay up front. It's non-refundable.'

'Well I wish you'd told me. I've got this twin-bedded room now. Where are you staying?'

'It's just a small place in the centre of Stratford. Very few rooms.'

'What's it called?'

'Oh, *The Bard's Beak*. Something like that.'

'*The Bard's Beak*? That's a very strange name for a hotel.'

'Something like that. I can't remember exactly.'

'*The Bard's Beak*? Are you sure you've got that right? I suppose I could cancel my room, and see if I could get a room in the same place. What's the number of this place? I'll give them a ring.'

'Honestly Judith, I don't think they'll have another room. It's a small place, very few rooms. Quite expensive too.'

'You sound as if you're trying to put me off.'

'No, of course not.'

'Wait a minute,' she said. 'Wait a minute. I know what's going on.'

'What? What's going on?'

'I know what you're doing.'

'I'm not doing anything. I just booked a room.'

'Is anybody else staying in the same hotel? From our group?'

'Possibly. Maybe. I don't know. I didn't ask for the guest list.'

'You and Max have booked into the same hotel, haven't you? My god – are you sharing a room?'

'Of course not!'

'But you've booked into the same hotel?'

'Judith, what does it matter whether Max is staying there or not? Can we stop this now before it becomes any more ridiculous?'

'I see. Right, well, far be it from me to interfere with your arrangements for whatever orgy you're planning.'

'Orgy? What? That's a vile suggestion Judith. Anyway, you can't have an orgy for two. You need at least five people.'

There was a pause on the line, and then she said, 'I don't like this at all. I worry about you. You've obviously been researching orgies. How else would you know you need five people? I don't think you have things in perspective. I think you could get in over your head.'

'Don't worry Judith. There is absolutely nothing to worry about.'

Again there was a pregnant pause on the line, then she said, 'I'll keep my double room. In case you change your mind.'

Judith rang off without saying goodbye, so I listened to the dial tone for a few seconds, and then I hung up.

***

I had an interesting chat with Baz this afternoon. He was rained off work and came home to consider his next piece of conceptual taxidermy. I asked him what he had in mind. He told me he wants to source a polar bear and depict it skating on thin ice, and underneath the ice to show a monstrous man-trap, with gaping human jaws, ready to snap up the bear if the ice breaks.

I said I thought that was a great idea, conceptually, but in practical terms, it wouldn't be easy getting hold of a polar bear this close to the centre of London. Nor would his contacts outside London be likely to spot a polar bear among the road kill items they regularly came across. Baz agreed that sourcing a polar bear would not be easy, and he asked me if I had any ideas.

This is what I love about living with young people. One is constantly being presented with new and exciting challenges. If not for Baz and his taxidermy enterprise, I daresay I would never have been required to consider the logistics of how to acquire a recently deceased polar bear in central London. It's like being a contestant in a reality show, with no audience and no prizes.

Baz wondered whether London Zoo would sell him a polar bear if it were to die of natural causes any time soon, and as an afterthought he asked me if I had any idea how big polar bears are when they are fully grown.

I said I was pretty sure London Zoo no longer have polar bears, and I thought a fully grown polar bear might be about the size of a small car.

'A what? A small car? Shit. Are you sure?'

'Pretty sure. It's a big animal, a polar bear.'

'I thought they were the same size as a sheep.'

'Oh no. Much bigger than that, Baz.'

'Difficult to tell the size from these wildlife programs,' he said. 'They're just a white shape against a white background. You get no idea of scale. They should show them standing just a meter away from a person.'

'They should, yes,' I said. And he could be right. A film of a polar bear standing a meter away from a person would make exciting viewing. I don't think they would stand that far apart for long. I think the polar bear would want to stand much closer to the person and the person would want to stand much further away.

'Anyway,' said Baz, 'I can't stuff something the size of a small car at the back of the utility room, we wouldn't be able to get at the dishwasher. I'll have to scrap that idea.'

The back door opened. 'Hiya!' said Sophie, dropping her bag on the floor and shrugging off her coat. 'I'm desperate for coffee. Anybody else want one?'

'Hiya!' said Marra. 'Hiya! Hiya!'

'We've got coffee, thanks Sophie,' I said. 'Make one for yourself and sit down. We're talking about Baz's next taxidermy project.'

'The polar bear?' said Sophie.

'We can't do a polar bear, Soph,' said Baz. 'They're too big. And we couldn't get hold of one anyway. What I'm thinking now is, instead of a polar bear skating on thin ice, we could have a little man skating on thin ice, and underneath the ice you can see the Earth like a round ball, opening its jaws, ready to swallow him if he falls through.'

'Wow, Baz,' I said, 'that's a powerful image.'

'Yeah,' said Baz. 'I'm getting the hang of this conceptual stuff.'

Sophie frowned. 'I don't know, Baz. It would be a bit gross stuffing a little man at the back of the utility room.'

'I'll make a model of the man, Soph,' said Baz.

'Oh right! Yeah. But then it's just a model, if nothing's stuffed,' said Sophie. 'The whole point of your stuff is that you stuff stuff.'

Baz then frowned. 'You're right.' He took off his beanie hat and ran his fingers through his hair. 'You're right. Something has to be stuffed. Otherwise it's not taxidermy. It's just a model.'

We puzzled over this collectively for a few minutes, and then, 'What about,' said Sophie, 'what about if you stuffed the Earth? With actual earth. Like, soil. Under the ice.'

We both looked at Sophie in frank amazement. 'Sophie, that's a brilliant idea,' I said.

'Brilliant Soph,' said Baz. 'Because what I'm saying is – basically – the Earth is stuffed. Fantastic!'

'Brill!' said Sophie.

'Fuck!' said Marra.

'Well,' I said, smiling at them both, 'I think you make a great team.'

It was difficult to imagine three people and a bird happier with the Earth's sorry predicament than we four, just at that moment.

***

It's two weeks today since the wedding that never was. So far, there has been no come-back on the potentially problematic revelations in Jen's speech. So far, so good. Jen is still with her daughter Emily. I haven't had any contact with either of them since two days after the event, when they headed north.

I rang her this evening, to see how she was. Nine o'clock is the best time to catch her. The twins are in bed and asleep by eight, and Jen will have had time to eat her meal. She will be trying to find something to watch on TV, and will be pleased to hear the phone ring.

'Hello?'

'Jen! It's me.'

'Well, you took your time. I thought you'd have rung before now. How do you know I'm not suicidal?'

'Are you?'

'No, I'm knackered to be honest. Emily thinks it's good for me to be occupied so she's got me taking the twins to all their clubs and groups. Their social life is crazy, Sally, and they've only just learnt to walk. God, when I was a kid no-one thought it was worth talking to me until I was six and I didn't see another kid until I started school. I played by myself with a ball of string and a Barbie doll with a missing leg. She's lovely, I've still got her. Anyway. Emily obviously thinks if I'm frenetically busy through the day and exhausted at night, I'll recover from being heart-broken quicker.'

'So how are the twins, Tiffany and Sammy?'

'They're adorable. Adorable. I have to get out quick, Sally, or I'll never be able to leave. I'm starting to feel a tiny bit guilty for wanting a life of my own, for wanting to get married for heaven's sake. Some little apple cheeked grandma inside my head is whispering at me, trying to persuade me that I don't need a life. She gets the twins to smile at me and put their little chubby arms around me and, oh God! Another six months of this and I'd be their devoted servant for life! I have to get out before I start thinking I'm not the most important person in my life, and the door slams shut.'

'Didn't you see this coming?'

'I thought I could control it. But I'm not sure I can. If I'm not very careful, I'm going to be consumed by my grandchildren before I've had a chance to get my own life back on track. I wish I'd suggested to Sam that we get in touch in three weeks, rather than four. Every week that goes by strengthens my inner granny. She's flexing her muscles Sally, she's gnawing at my insides and wrapping me up in her silken, sticky, geriatric, fucking, threads.'

***

'Fantastic news!' said Sophie when she got home from work this evening. She dropped her shoulder bag on the floor and spread her arms wide. 'Guess what?'

'You've got an interview for that job you applied for?' I said. I hoped.

'Yes! Yes, I've got an interview!'

'Brilliant Sophie!'

'Well done Soph!' said Baz.

'Yeah that's great,' said Chrissy.

'Nice one Sophie, well done,' said Dan.

'When?' I said. 'When is it?'

'Week after next.'

'Good,' said Chrissy, 'so you've got a bit of time to prepare.'

'Prepare what?' said Sophie.

'Prepare for your interview,' said Chrissy. 'To think about what questions they might ask you, and what you might say. I'll coach you if you like. It's like drama. I can show you how to project yourself so that you come across really well and make the best impression.'

Sophie was hesitant, 'I don't know.' She looked at the rest of us. 'What do you think?' she said. 'I was just thinking I'd wear my denim skirt and my best red top.'

I made a suggestion, thinking this might be a way of cementing a deeper friendship between Chrissy and Sophie. 'I think you should take Chrissy up on that offer Sophie. You want the job and I think a bit of interview coaching is an excellent idea. I'd go for it if I had an interview coming up.'

Sophie considered this for two whole seconds. 'Yeah okay,' she said. 'Thanks Chrissy.'

'My pleasure!' said Chrissy. 'That's great. And I bet there are a few things you could teach me in return?'

'I could teach you how to get someone off a bedpan.'

'There you go! Fantastic. Come on, let's get started.'

'Now?'

'First lesson just takes a minute. I'm going to teach you how to sit.'

'I know how to sit.'

'Ah! But do you know how to sit in an interview?'

'What?'

'We need a hard chair.' Chrissy pulled out one of the kitchen chairs and sat down. 'See? You need to sit with your knees together, and your legs to one side, and your hands resting in your lap. Like so.'

We all stood in a semi-circle and admired Chrissy's sitting.

'Good sitting, Chrissy,' said Dan.

'Yep,' said Baz.

'Right, I think I've got that,' said Sophie, and she turned to me and rolled her eyes. 'I'll just get changed and we can have another lesson tomorrow.' She picked up her bag and went upstairs to get out of her uniform.

'That's a really kind gesture Chrissy,' I said. 'I'm sure it will be very helpful.'

'Thanks,' said Chrissy pushing the chair back under the table. 'I'll make sure she gets the job.'

***

It's Laura's birthday tomorrow, and she called in today while little Harry was at Tottering Tottlebots to collect her cards and presents. Fortunately, Dan and Baz were both here because they have to work late tonight, and they had this afternoon off in lieu.

'Sis!' said Dan. 'Happy thirtieth.'

'I'm twenty-eight,' said Laura.

'Oh shit,' said Dan.

'You told me she was thirty,' said Baz. 'My card's a bit inappropriate now.'

'Anyway,' said Laura, 'never mind. Hand over your cards. I'll overlook anything that says *Thirty Today*.'

'I got you a box of chocolates Sis,' said Dan. 'Haven't wrapped them, but it's a nice box. Didn't think I could do any better if I'd wrapped it. Happy birthday.'

'Thank you Dan.' She gave him a kiss on the cheek. 'That's very kind of you. I won't eat the chocolates, but I love the box! I'll definitely be using the box. It's beautiful.'

'So, why won't you be eating the chocolates?'

'I'm a non-placentarian.'

'You're a what?'

'A non-placentarian.'

Dan looked vague. 'A planetarium?'

'No, a non-*placentarian*. I don't eat anything which had a placenta.'

'Chocolates don't have a placenta, Laura.'

No, but chocolates contain milk, and milk comes from cows, and cows have a placenta in the womb.'

'You're nuts,' said Dan.

'So!' I said. 'Sit down everybody, I'm making coffee and I've got cake. What are you doing for your birthday Laura? Do you want me to come over and baby-sit while you and Ben go out somewhere? Would you like to go out for dinner?'

'How can she go out for dinner?' said Dan. 'Everything worth eating had a placenta.'

'It's just like being a vegan, Dan. But I can eat eggs and honey.'

'Oh, well, said Dan. 'Congratulations.'

Laura turned to me. 'Thanks mum, but Ben and I are going to eat in. Ben's cooking.'

'What's he cooking?' said Dan. 'Scrambled honey?'

'I don't know why my diet should be such a problem for you, Dan,' said Laura. 'Why should it bother you if I'm a non-placentarian?'

'Because I've just bought you an expensive box of chocolates and you're not going to eat them because cows have a placenta.'

'Look, why don't I give you these chocolates back, and you can give them to Mum for her birthday.'

'That's a good idea,' I said. 'You can look for something else for Laura, Dan. A house plant, maybe.'

'Are you a non-houseplantarian?' Dan asked her.

'No, I'm not. I'd like a house plant. Providing it's not poisonous.'

'Why? Are you going to eat it?'

I set a tray down on the table and gave them all a mug of coffee.

'Oh Mum,' said Laura. 'You've put milk in mine.'

We all looked at the offending mug.

'Would it kill you,' said Dan, 'to drink that coffee?'

'Dan, there's no point in doing something on principle if you sometimes do it and sometimes don't. Is there Mum?'

'But Mum's just made you that coffee,' said Dan, 'and now you're going to make her pour it down the sink.'

'Well Mum doesn't mind. Do you Mum?'

'How do you know Mum doesn't mind? She might mind.'

'Er,' I said. 'I think I can speak for myself here. I'll drink this coffee of yours later today, Laura, if you make yourself another one now, without milk.'

There was an uneasy truce for a minute while Laura boiled the kettle again. Baz seized the moment and tried to move us on. 'Orchids make a nice house plant, if you've got a warm place to put them.'

'Fish!' said Dan. 'You can eat fish. And duck-billed platypus.'

'Yes, I can eat fish and duck-billed platypus, no problem,' said Laura. 'In fact, I think Ben's got platypus steaks for tomorrow night.'

'Excellent,' said Dan.

'Yes,' said Laura. 'My favourite.'

And disaster averted, we drank our coffee.

***

Judith and I arrived separately at the history class this evening. Our topic tonight was Shakespeare, in anticipation of our trip to Stratford. I knew very little about Shakespeare at the beginning of the evening, apart from his bad hair-do and the business of the second best bed which he left to his wife Anne in his will. And of course, I knew that he died on his birthday, which is the temporal equivalent of disappearing up your own backside.

So it was interesting to learn this evening that Shakespeare had married Anne Hathaway when he was eighteen years old and she was twenty-six, and six months after the wedding they had a daughter, Susanna. He probably spent most of his working life in London. In retirement, he wrote a will and signed it, and in it he said he was in excellent health. Then one month later he died, aged fifty-two.

He may or may not be the sombre-looking man in the portrait we all know, with the bald head and the incongruously bushy bob. This portrait, although of a successful man of this period, is not an authenticated likeness of the playwright we all know as William Shakespeare. Shakespeare might have had a full head of hair and a mischievous grin, while the serious man in the portrait might be someone else entirely, maybe a fishmonger, maybe an ironmonger. No-one knows for sure who the bushy-bobbed man was. If the man in the portrait did simply mong iron or fish, and couldn't in fact string a sentence together, he must be astonished in the afterlife to find himself credited with the entire works of William Shakespeare.

Judith was much intrigued by Shakespeare's insistence that his bones must not be disturbed after his death. She is convinced he was buried with evidence of a guilty secret. Maybe a confession that his plays were written by his landlady, or perhaps an admission that he deleted every other word from his plays and sonnets to make students of his work suffer and do badly in their English A levels.

We will never know, because Shakespeare's bones never have been disturbed. Shakespeare claimed he would curse anyone who attempted it, and no-one has. The author of Macbeth knew a thing or two about curses, and no-one has been brave enough to tempt Fate, for fear of three witches turning up on their doorstep chewing on newts and outrage and spitting out revenge.

So we are primed now and ready for our trip to Stratford. Eight of us are going, including Terry. There was talk in the pub afterwards about whether Judith was planning to take a trowel and do some exploratory digging when we visit the Holy Trinity Church in Stratford where Shakespeare is buried. Judith said she would bring a selection of trowels and we could all help, we'd have him up in a jiffy. We laughed, but testament to the curse, not entirely comfortably.

During a lull in the conversation I asked if anyone thought Shakespeare's work was over-rated, but no-one did, so that line of enquiry didn't go anywhere.

When people were beginning to disperse, I had a brief chat with Max. I thanked him for giving me the details of the hotel, which I said looked very nice. He said he thought there would just be the two of us staying there from the group. I said Judith had wanted to book in, but I had told her it was full and a bit expensive. He said that was almost certainly true. He said he was looking forward to the performance of *Love's Labour's Lost* planned for the first night, but he didn't have anything planned for the second night. I said I didn't have anything planned for the second night either. We both said we were looking forward to the trip and expecting to enjoy it.

I'm home and in bed now, writing my diary. Bill rang earlier and said he'll be away an extra day so won't be back until the weekend. I'll put the light off soon.

To take my mind off things and unwind, I've been thinking about William Shakespeare and whether it would be easy for him to get his work published today. He would have to find a literary agent to take him on and approach a publishing house on his behalf. That might be difficult. I thought of the replies he might get from a literary agent, after submitting his plays for their consideration.

Dear Mr Shakespeare,

Thank you so much for submitting a selection of your plays for my consideration three years ago, and for the short and to-the-point email of yesterday requesting a reply and outlining what you would do to me if I ignored your request.

I did enjoy reading some of your plays, sadly however, they are not right for my list at present.

Although I am unable to give detailed feedback, I might perhaps suggest that each play is much too long, and should be edited to a maximum of no more than an hour in length, preferably less. Forty minutes would be ideal. The Merchant of Venice is totally unacceptable as a character lead, and would be better portrayed as a transgender female employee with HMRC. Romeo and Juliet will have to be re-written as a musical with a happy ending to have any chance of success. The plot of Twelfth Night is ludicrously complicated and would never be accepted by a sophisticated theatre-going audience. Macbeth though, has promise. I loved the witches, but there are stereotyping issues here which need to be addressed.

And Wills – (if I may?) – I'd really like to see Lady Macbeth 'come good' in the end, and it would be **such** *a nice touch if King Duncan isn't really dead, as* *everyone thinks, but turns up at the end fit and well, and of course,* ***looking for answers!***

Also, I must point out after reading your text that you appear to have missed out every other word, and sadly this makes it almost impossible for the reader to understand what you are saying. There is really no need for this unless you intend to confuse A level English students, and I venture to suggest, we aren't in that ball park quite yet!!

Good luck with your next play Wills, and your continuing search for representation! Personally, I think you're more of a novelist. So if you ever try your hand at prose please don't hesitate to contact us again, but until then, please don't contact us again.

Yours, etc...

***

Sophie came in from work this afternoon, and took her coat off. She and Marra exchanged 'Hiyas' for a while, and then Sophie said to me, 'Guess what?'

My heart always sinks when she says 'Guess what?'

'What?' I said, clutching the bag of flour I had just taken down from my cake-making cupboard. I was making a fruit cake.

'Well... ' said Sophie, and then she put her finger to her lips, went across to the kitchen bench and unplugged the kettle and the toaster.

'Why have you done that?' I asked her.

'Because,' she said, 'these days you never know who's listening to what you're saying. People can hear you talking through kettles and toasters, if they're wired up properly.'

'Oh, right,' I said. 'Are you sure? It seems a bit unlikely.'

'No, it's true. Baz and I saw it in a film. Anyway, it's better to be on the safe side. And I don't want us to be overheard.'

'Why not? What's up?'

'I think I might have been chatted up by a reporter.'

'When?'

'Today. I went across the road for a sandwich during my break, and someone came in and got talking to me and asked if I was still living with you and Mr Forth.'

'What did you say?'

'I said I might be, and I asked him who wanted to know.'

'And he said?'

'And he said his name was Colin, and he thought I looked like the Sophie who had been on the telly a while ago. He said you must be a really interesting family to live with.'

'Hmm. It does sound as if he might have been fishing. Did you tell him anything?'

'I didn't say anything about you and Mr Forth. I just told him about Marra and Ivor and Baz.'

'Right. Oh well. Not that we have anything to hide. It's just slightly uncomfortable to know that people are asking questions.'

'That's what I thought. That's why I switched the kettle and the toaster off.'

'I see. Well, I wouldn't worry too much Sophie. Like I said, we aren't doing anything wrong here. But you should use your judgement, and if you think people are getting too nosey, just tell them to back off.'

'Yes, I will. I just thought I'd let you know. In case anything happens.'

'Anything like what?'

'Well, you know. Stuff happens around here, doesn't it? We're not exactly normal here, are we?'

'Er, well, fairly normal, I think. On the whole.'

'Not really,' she said. 'Anyway. I thought I should tell you.'

'Thanks Sophie, I appreciate that.'

'Right, I'm going to put the toaster and the kettle back on now. So...' she put her finger to her lips again, to warn me not to say anything more on the subject.

I nodded.

'Right Mrs Forth!' she said once both appliances were plugged in again. 'I've had a lovely nap, so I'm going to go upstairs now to get changed! See you later!' She winked, gave me two thumbs up, and went upstairs.

'Up!' said Marra. 'Up! Up yours!'

Actually she's right, as always. We're not exactly normal around here.

***

A letter from Ella this morning.

Dear Sally,

Such an odd thing dear, I had to put pen to paper straight away.

Well, someone rang me about half an hour ago and said they had something of mine which I might have lost, it was something that might have fallen down behind a sofa cushion. If I was interested in paying them to have it back, they would bring it round for me later today and say no more about it.

I asked them what it was. They said they thought I might know what it was. I said I had no idea. They said they would hand it over to me for the sum of one thousand pounds. I said I hadn't lost anything remotely worth that amount, and they could go and take a running jump. They apologised, and said maybe it wasn't mine. They would take it elsewhere, and I wouldn't hear from them again.

I rang Mrs Rob as soon as that person rang off, and asked her if she knew anything about this. You remember I gave her my old sofa and chairs? She said it sounded a bit dodgy, but she hadn't got a clue what, if anything, was going on. As far as she knew, there wasn't anything unusual found among the cushions of the sofa I'd just given her, and the people who had re-upholstered it in the material to match her curtains hadn't said anything to her about any interesting finds either.

So I am at a loss, although something rings a bell. Wasn't there a letter that went astray a while back, and we thought it might have slipped down behind a sofa cushion? I know you were anxious for me to find it and shred it. It was a letter from you to me. I can't remember the content in much detail, but I think it was the one where you told me the Prime Minister was having an affair with our Foreign Secretary. You remember the one?

Do you think we are in any sort of pickle? Write and let me know if I did the right thing by refusing to pay. Write soon dear, I'm too old for any cloak and dagger stuff. Miss Marple, I ain't.

Love,

Ella.

I panicked. Oh no. Oh no, oh no. Someone has that letter. Should I come clean to Bill? He'll have a fit. I can't even remember now how I worded that letter. Did I make everything explicit? Did I use names, or initials? I can't remember now whether I just dropped hints, or whether I came out with it on paper and said that Bill thought the PM might be having a fling with the FS, in Downing Street, between meetings. Surely I wasn't that indiscreet? Or maybe I was? Could the letter be traced to me? Was the letter lost with its envelope? What would happen if this person took it to a newspaper? How deep was the shit I was in? How much do I stink?

I took some deep breaths, and wrote Ella a reply.

Dear Ella,

You did absolutely the right thing by sending this person packing. I have written you many letters over the last few months, and I'm sure there will have been some we would both agree needed shredding! Don't give it another thought, I doubt you will hear from this person again, but if you do, you must ring the police and tell them they are making a nuisance of themselves. It really is quite wrong to contact you with that sort of extortionate proposal. Honestly though, I don't think you will hear anything more from them, they said as much and I believe they will be as good as their word. My advice would be to forget all about it.

Now then, I have a favour to ask. Would you ask June to take a photo of your new sofas and send it to me on WhatsApp? June will know what to do, and seconds after she's taken the photograph, I'll be able to see them on my phone. Marvellous, eh? I'll send a photo of all of us to June's phone, and one of the parrot, Marra. I'd send you a little video clip of him, he's quite a character, but he swears like a trooper, so a photo would be best!

With love,

Sally

Writing the letter had a calming effect. Surely, a newspaper would need more authentication than a stray letter which purported to come from me? It could have been forged, it could be staged, it could be a pack of lies to extract money from a vulnerable party, or a newspaper. Anyone can write a letter to anyone else, suggesting all manner of poppycock, it doesn't make any of those suggestions true. By itself, surely, a letter won't be taken seriously? And whoever has it, they could now be accused of trying to extort money from Bill's mother, so they might feel they have to keep quiet. I'll just have to try and forget about it, and hope for the best, and think of other things.

Lee. I'll think of Lee.

I saw Lee this afternoon, because I wanted to be there when he saw Sue Timpson, our careers guidance officer. We had a meeting about Lee at school after his spectacularly unsuccessful figure-drawing class, and we agreed that it might help his focus and his self-esteem if he started thinking about what career path he would like to follow after school. Ideally, we could link his progress at school with his progress towards an apprenticeship, so that he could start to see the relevance of his education. There was the possibility, too, of tailoring his timetable more towards what might benefit him when he leaves school. So we arranged a meeting with Lee and Sue to talk about careers, and I was keen to sit in.

So Sue and I settled down for a careers talk with Lee this lunch time. I put her in the picture a little, about Lee, before he arrived. I said he was one of our more exotic pupils; he had been at odds with school for a number of years and had put so much energy into hating school and what it had to offer that he had neglected his school work and his grades until they had ceased to exist. I said we were trying to motivate him through his last few years at school, by showing him how we could help with his future plans, and we might need some advice about whatever apprenticeships he might be interested in. His dad is a joiner, so that might be a way forward. Sue said, that's fine, she could do that, she had all the information to hand.

At ten to one, there was a knock on the door and Lee opened it, and stepped inside.

'Hello Lee!' I said. 'Good to see you! Come in, come in! Sit down, make yourself comfortable.'

He looked over his shoulder. 'What's wrong?'

'Nothing. Nothing Lee. Everything's fine. Just come in and sit down.' Obviously my joyous greeting had thrown him into some confusion, he isn't accustomed to being greeted with such enthusiasm in any area of his life, least of all school. 'Lee,' I said, 'this is Miss Timpson. She is here to advise us about apprenticeships and so on, because I'm not really up to speed on that kind of thing.'

'Right,' he said, and he glanced in her direction.

'Hello Lee, good to meet you,' said Miss Timpson.

'Yeah,' he said.

'Well Lee, you've had a few weeks to mull this over and chat to your mum and dad about it, so tell us, what do you want to be when you leave school?'

'A solicitor.'

'A solicitor?'

'Yes. My dad was nearly a solicitor but he changed his mind at the last minute.'

'At the last minute?'

'Yeah. That's why he's a joiner.' Lee gave a resigned sigh. 'Looks like I'll have to be one now.'

'A joiner?'

'No, a solicitor.'

'Right. I see.'

Sue Timpson looked at me and raised an eyebrow.

'This is a surprise Lee,' I said. 'I was expecting you to say you'd like to be a joiner, like your dad.'

'No,' he said. 'I've decided to be a solicitor.'

Sue shuffled some papers and appeared to be looking for something.

'Ain't you got nothing on being a solicitor?' Lee asked Sue. 'My dad says all you do is argue the toss an' you get paid a packet.'

'I don't seem to have anything with me about a career in law,' said Sue. 'You'd need good A levels.' She looked doubtful.

'What's them?' Lee asked me.

'Exams. Exams people take in the sixth form.'

'Oh well, if they want exams, I'll do some exams. That's no problem.' Lee seemed satisfied.

'And then you'd have to go to university,' said Sue.

'Yeah yeah,' said Lee. 'I don't mind going places.'

'Ah!' said Sue, looking in her briefcase, 'I do have something here about careers in law if you're interested, Lee.' She handed him a leaflet.

Lee took it and glanced at the photo of a barrister on the front. 'Well, I'm not wearing one of those poncey hats.'

'Not all lawyers have to wear wigs,' said Sue.

'I'd look mental in one of those.'

'You probably wouldn't have to wear one.'

'Good.' Lee sat back, relieved that the only obstacle to his career in law had been overcome.

'Well,' said Sue. 'Is law the only option you're considering Lee? Or is there anything else I can help you with?'

Lee inspected his nails and looked shifty. 'Might be something I could help you with,' he said, glancing at me. 'I could do you mates rates. Once I get started. If you wanted a divorce or something like that. Or if you were up for nicking something. Not you,' he said, looking over at Sue Timpson. 'Just her. For now.'

'Actually Lee,' I said, 'I'm not sure whether being a solicitor will suit your particular skills set.'

'Yeah it will. It's about disputes and stuff. Arguments. I could do that.'

'Yes, but..'

'And they make shed-loads of money, Dad says.'

'Are you sure about this Lee? Have you considered being a joiner like your dad? He's done well, hasn't he?'

'No. I've already decided, I'll be a solicitor.'

'Right. Thing is Lee, I think you might find being a solicitor a bit boring.'

'That's no problem. I'm used to that. School's boring as hell, doesn't bother me. I've been bored since I came here.'

'And also, Lee, it would be very hard work to become a solicitor. Lots of hard school work, and exams to pass, and loads of books to read.'

'Yes, I know about that. Dad said I'd have to read stuff. That's okay. I read a book once.'

The bell rang.

'See you then,' he said, and stood up. 'Got English next. And I remembered a pen today. Good start, eh? For being a solicitor? See you later, Miss.'

I watched him go.

'Bye Lee,' said Sue Timpson. She looked at me and said, 'Mates rates? Lucky you.'

***

I was home a little earlier than I expected, and decided to do something useful before starting on an evening meal. So I pulled out the drawer in the kitchen which is full of old keys and defunct pens and broken hair slides, and is the first place everyone looks when they've lost something, but is never the place where the lost item is found, although everyone remembers seeing it in there. The drawer is so full it is difficult to open, and once open it is even more difficult to shut. It is an abomination of a drawer, everyone hates it. I hate it. I've been thinking for a while that I must do something about it before someone manages to get the drawer open, and it becomes jammed, and is impossible to shut. It would be stuck half in, and half out of its housing. We would have to jemmy up the worktop to release it, and then we might as well replace the whole kitchen.

So I wrestled with the drawer and managed to pull it right out, and carried it over to the table, and up-ended it, and shook it, and emptied it completely. And then immediately regretted it.

Once the contents escaped the confines of the drawer, they obviously had no intention of ever going back in. They hit the surface of the table and doubled in size, and assumed angular, awkward shapes and scattered in all directions, glad to be free. There was no possibility of just scooping the whole lot up again and cramming it back into the drawer, because now I would need two or three or kitchen drawers to accommodate it all.

So I began to pick things up and consider whether to keep them, or throw them out. It took me almost five minutes to decide whether to keep or throw away the first item I picked up. I did a rough calculation in my head, multiplying the estimated number of items by five minutes each, then dividing by the approximate number of minutes in a year and adding my age minus my height and the number of days until the next full moon and then multiplying by infinity. The answer came to sixty one years, five feet eight inches and a full lunar eclipse, which was even worse than I thought.

I was picking over the surface layer of this monstrous detritus toad squatting on the kitchen table, taking care not to get swallowed whole, when:

'Hiya!' said Sophie from somewhere behind me. Then she saw the heap of stuff on the table and said, 'Oh shit, what's all that?'

'It's the stuff that was in the kitchen drawer.'

'Oh no! It's not, is it? You'll never get it all back in. Not now you've let it out.'

'I know, I was planning to sort through it. But I don't think I'll live long enough.'

Sophie took a closer look. 'What's in there?' she said. 'What is all that stuff?'

'It's rubbish. It's all stuff that either doesn't work, or no-body wants. I just can't face inspecting it all.'

'Why don't you just put it all in a bin bag and give it to me?'

'What will you do with it?'

'I'll hide it, and then when I think you've forgotten about it, I'll throw it out, without telling you.'

So that's what we did. Afterwards Sophie opened and closed the empty kitchen drawer a few times just to see how easy it was. 'You know,' she said, 'this is much better, because it just takes a second now to see that what you're looking for isn't in this drawer. But before it took ages.'

And that's why I've included this episode and recorded it here. It's a metaphor for Life. And if there weren't so many superficial, half-formed, unnecessary and inaccurate thoughts in my head, I'd be able to think clearly and tell you what it means.

***

Three weeks today since the wedding that wasn't, and I heard from Jen this afternoon, she rang while I was slicing apple for Marra. Or rather, I heard from Jennifer this afternoon, not Jen, because she has decided to make some changes.

She says she never wants to be known as 'Jen' again. She doesn't like the abbreviation of her name, she's never liked it, and looking back, she thinks everything started to take a wrong turning in her life since people started to call her 'Jen.' She thinks she should have put a stop to it sooner, but she is doing it now, because she wants her life to get back on track, and this seems like a good way to start. She wants to bury 'Jen,' along with all the mistakes 'Jen' has made, and resurrect Jennifer, and put her in charge of her life's direction from now on.

I said that was fine with me. I asked her just to let me know what she'd like me to call her and she could consider it done. I'd call her Eustachian Tube if she thought that would help her to sort her life out. She said Jennifer would be fine. So I said okay, Jennifer it is.

Then she asked me if she could do the same for me, and she wondered whether Sally was short for anything.

I said no, Sally was just Sally, it couldn't really be short for anything. Jennifer disagreed, she said it could be short for Salamander, and I should check to make sure. I said I was pretty certain I wasn't called Salamander, but I would have a look next time I came across my birth certificate.

Then I said, 'You sound a lot better, Jennifer? Last time we spoke you were worrying about being possessed by your inner granny. It's good to hear you sounding more positive and upbeat, even if you're talking bollocks.'

'I do feel much better,' she said. 'I've been an idiot, I've made mistakes, but I do have a real sense of re-birth, of starting again. I'm still worried about my inner granny, but there's just another week before the four week deadline is up and I can make contact with Sam, and I think I can hold out. The twins were both sick over me this morning and that helped. I've decided, I want everything to be different this time, with Sam. I'm going to let him organise the next wedding, it's only fair, we'll do whatever he wants. I'll get married wearing jeans and riding a bicycle, if that's how he wants it. That's why I'm ringing, actually, because that's what I want you to say.'

'Say to...?'

'Sam. When you contact him in a week's time.'

'Oh right, I didn't realise I was contacting Sam. I thought you were getting in touch with each other directly.'

'I'd like you to make the initial approach for me, if you don't mind, then I can take over. Like in the olden days, you know, when people had seconds.'

'That was for people planning to have a duel.'

'Was it? Oh well, not a perfect analogy, but you know what I mean.'

'Yes, okay, I'll make the initial approach, on your behalf.'

'Thanks Sally. And – a bit awkward this – but if he mentions Frank at all, just tell him not to worry about the Frank thing. I can explain everything.'

'Actually Jennifer, I might not say anything at all about the Frank thing, I might just leave that to you.'

'Okay,' she said, 'no problem. I can deal with that. Also, my preferred place to meet would be the Natural History Museum, because we were underneath the dinosaur when Sam proposed, so it would set the right tone. I don't mind getting the train up to London. I'm going to take him his share of the universal plugs, it seems unfair for me to keep them all, and he might want them for Christmas presents. Or some other kind of present.'

I thought about it. 'You know what Jennifer?' I said. 'I'm not sure I'd take sixty universal plugs along to your first meeting. I think I'd wait a bit.'

'Oh? Why?'

'It's unusual, isn't it, to present someone with sixty universal plugs? He might think it odd.'

'Do you think so?'

'I'd wait a while. Honestly, Jennifer. I would.'

She chuckled. 'You are funny, sometimes. The things you think. But okay, I'll wait a while. I'll take your advice. There, do you see how different I am, now that I'm Jennifer?'

'I do, yes,' I said. But I lied, because she's exactly the same.

***

Chrissy was so excited when she heard I was going to Stratford. We were all in the kitchen eating beans on toast at supper time when I told her I was going.

'Wow!' she said. 'Wow. That's amazing. What's really amazing about going to Stratford is that you will be walking around on the very stones, the very stones that the Bard walked on. Imagine! Your feet will actually touch the exact same stones which his feet touched. And if you touch a door knob in his house, you will be touching the exact same door knob in his house that he touched. The exact same one! It's incredible, when you think about it, isn't it? You'd want to just keep holding it, wouldn't you? To sort of, channel him somehow through his doorknob.'

'Sorry?' said Ivor.

Sophie lowered a forkful of beans. 'They've probably changed the door knobs in his house in the last four hundred years, Chrissy. My Aunty Fran was always changing her doorknobs.'

Chrissy carried on, 'Imagine, being in the same space which Shakespeare inhabited, all those years ago. Breathing the same air!'

'You definitely won't be breathing the same air,' said Sophie. 'Definitely not. The air will have changed every time anyone opened the door.'

Chrissy turned to Sophie. 'What I'm trying to say, Sophie, is that it brings you closer to the man himself, just being in Stratford.'

'Oh right,' said Sophie. 'He's been dead ages of course. He must be a pile of dust by now.'

'But we know what you mean, Chrissy,' said Dan.

'You mean,' said Ivor, 'you'll be in the same place what Shakespeare lived in.' He shook his head in wonder. 'Quite a thing, eh?'

'I think so, Ivor,' said Chrissy. 'Thank you.'

Sophie continued, 'But in London, we're in the same place Elizabeth I lived in, but we don't think we see her in Primark.'

'I heard an interesting thing about Shakespeare at my evening class,' I said, before anyone had a chance to process Sophie's last remark, 'apparently, he'll curse anyone who makes any attempt to disturb his grave.'

'Ah!' said Chrissy, *'Good friend for Jesus sake forebear, To dig the dust enclosed here, Blessed be the man who spares these stones, And cursed be he who moves my bones.'*

'That's exactly right Chrissy,' I said. 'People think he may have had a secret that he took to the grave with him.'

'Like he was a woman,' said Sophie.

'Well, that would probably count as one of the best kept secrets of all time,' I said. 'No, I was thinking more that he found all his plays in a box in the attic, and didn't actually write any of them.'

Sophie was shocked. 'Did he? Did he really find all those plays in a box in the attic?'

'No,' I said.

'Why don't they just dig him up and find out?' said Baz. 'I wouldn't mind doing that. I dig up all sorts of stuff at work. The stuff I dig up could be cursed and I wouldn't know. You can't go worrying about what you dig up being cursed. You'd never get any work done.'

'Anyway folks,' I said, looking around the table, 'I'm off to Stratford at the end of next week, so you'll be on your own.'

'Will Mr Forth be around?' said Sophie.

'He'll be around as much as he usually is,' I said.

'So no, Sophie,' said Dan. 'He won't.

***

I was holding up a pretty, pale pink bra in M&S and wondering whether it would suit my skin tones when I heard someone behind me say, 'If I were you, I'd go for padded.'

I turned around, 'Judith!' I said. 'What are you doing here?'

'What am I doing here? It's Marks and Spencer's Sally. I'm buying knickers. I see you're buying a new bra.'

'I am, yes. What do you think?' I held it up for her.

'Honestly. I'd go for padded. It's more defining.'

'Do you like the colour?'

'Well, it's a bit insipid. But, you know, if you like that kind of thing. I bought a nice lemon bra recently.' She looked around. 'It might suit you better. I'll show you.'

'I can't wear lemon.'

'Don't be daft, anyone can wear lemon.'

'Honestly, it doesn't suit me.'

'Have you ever in your life bought a lemon bra?'

'No.'

'Well how do you know it doesn't suit you?'

'It's just not my colour.'

'Look, put that one back and come and look at the one I bought.'

'Honestly, I —'

'I'm just asking you to look. No harm in looking.'

Judith marched me up and down the serried rows of bras. 'Ah! Here it is! Look at this.' She held up a lemon bra embroidered with a white bow. 'See how nice this one is? Look, it's got some light padding to give you a better shape. And feel it. Feel how soft it is.'

I felt it. 'It's beautifully soft, yes. But it's not my size.'

'What's your size? What are you? 36D?

'No. 36C.'

'Really? 36C? I'd have said 36D.'

'36C.'

'Oh well, if you say so. Look, here's a 36C!'

'Yes, but, as I said, lemon's not my colour.'

'You'll look gorgeous in this! Go on, treat yourself. See – there's little embossed flower sprigs on the cups. You don't notice them unless you look carefully.'

'Sorry Judith. I prefer the pink one.'

'But I bet you've got dozens of pink ones at home. Haven't you?'

'I've got a few, yes.'

'Go on then, have a change!'

'I don't want a change.'

'Yes you do.'

'No I don't.'

'Oh well,' Judith appeared to lose interest. 'Suit yourself.'

'I think you have to suit yourself over what bra you wear. It's a very personal thing.'

'If you say so.'

'I don't want to fall out about it, Judith. I'd just like to choose my own bra.'

'Up to you.'

'Right. Well, I'll go and buy my bra and then —'

'I don't suppose you've got time for a coffee?'

I hesitated. 'Actually, I —' I glanced at my watch to indicate that I might have other things to do.

'That's okay. If you're too busy.'

'No – let's have a coffee. Come on.'

'Well, if you're sure you've got time.'

'Yes of course. I'd love a coffee.'

So, in two shakes of a pink bra strap, we were sitting at a little table for two, cradling coffee cups, and looking at each other over the rim.

'This new bra,' said Judith. 'It doesn't have anything to do with our trip to Stratford, does it?'

'Sorry?'

'Are you buying a new bra to wear in Stratford?'

'Well I bought it to wear it. I might wear it in Stratford. Why?'

She sipped her coffee. 'I see.'

'What do you see? It's not very mysterious. I bought a new bra, I might wear it sometime soon. Can we change the subject? I think we've said enough about my underwear.'

'How's Bill?' said Judith. 'I expect he needs a lot of support from home, being in such a stressful job and so much in the public eye. I saw him on television the other night and thought he looked a bit worn down.'

'Bill's fine,' I said. 'He thrives on stress. Sometimes I think the more stressful things get, the more he likes it. He's out a lot, of course.'

'You probably don't see much of him just now?'

'Not an awful lot, no.'

'Are you lonely?'

'Lonely? Of course not! I'm hardly ever alone.'

Judith frowned and took another sip of coffee. 'Oh well,' she said. 'That's all right then.'

Later, when I was on a bus on my way home, I thought about Judith's suggestion that I could be lonely. And I wondered whether it might contain a groan of truth.

***

Chrissy was in the kitchen when I got home. She was making toast, and she asked me if I'd like a slice. I said yes please.

'Did Dan tell you,' she said, 'I told him I didn't want him to do the hen-night entertainment thing?'

'No, he didn't tell me. Last I heard he was considering it as a career choice.'

'I think he wanted to do it because Ivor says it pays really well. But I don't want him to do it. He's really good at it, it's not that I think he couldn't do it. I just don't want him to.'

'I understand that perfectly, Chrissy. What did he say?'

'When I said I didn't want him to do it? He just said he wouldn't do it if I wasn't happy with it, it wasn't a problem. He understood why.'

'Good,' I said. 'It's a bit of a relief to me to be honest. Apart from anything else, I wasn't sure there'd be a proper career management structure. I preferred the architecture idea.'

'Yes, he keeps thinking about that. I've been trying to encourage him a bit, but I don't want to push it. I don't want him to think I'm too keen on the idea, or he will start thinking it might not be a good idea. He's not deliberately awkward, it's just the way his mind works.'

Sounded like a good definition of awkward to me.

'You know,' she said, while she very carefully and deliberately put butter on my toast, 'I sometimes wonder about Gentle Rain.'

'Gentle Rain?'

'Yes, you know, Gentle Rain, Dan's girlfriend before Sophie. What was she like?'

'Well,' I said, 'she wasn't Gentle Rain, for a start. She was Victoria. She came from a very wealthy background, but she told Dan she was from simple peasant stock and had been suckled by llamas and educated by hermits and god knows what else. She was trying to escape her family for some reason, and pitched up here for a while. Personally I thought it was up to her what she chose to tell us about her family. She was actually very rich but she told Dan she was very poor. Dan thought that was a problem, and he felt badly let down.'

'Right,' said Chrissy, handing me a plate. 'Was she, you know, fantastically pretty?'

Ah. 'She had a nice smile,' I said. 'But no nicer than your smile. You have a lovely smile.'

'Dan says they were only together a few months.'

'Yes, it was just a few months.'

'But it got quite intense at one point?'

'Did it?' I took a bite of toast. 'You know, I don't really think they were on the same wavelength. You and Dan have a lot more in common.'

'Yes, I think so too. Did you like her?'

'Did I like Gentle Rain?'

'Yes.'

'Yes I liked her. I like all Dan's friends. It's my friends I can't stand.'

'Hiya!'

'Ah, Sophie,' said Chrissy, 'I was hoping you'd be back soon. We have to do some interview coaching.'

'Right,' said Sophie, dropping her bag on the floor and pushing it under the table so no-one would trip over it. 'What am I learning this time? I know how to sit. You told me that last time.'

'This time we're going to learn how to deal with tricky questions without panicking. It's an important lesson.'

'Yeah right,' said Sophie, putting the kettle on. 'What sort of questions?'

'Well, you must have an answer prepared to questions like, why do you want this job? What would you say if they asked you that?'

'Well that's a daft question, isn't it?'

'So, there's some work to be done there. And what if they ask you – where do you see yourself in five years' time?'

'I'd say on a beach in Malaga, I might just have saved up enough money for a holiday by then.'

'Okay.' Chrissy rubbed her hands together in anticipation of a job to tackle. 'I'll make you some toast, then we can go next door and get started.'

***

When Bill came in around nine thirty, I sat on our bed and gave him the good news while he was changing out of his suit.

'There's news,' I said.

'Oh shit no,' he said.

'Good news.'

He looked wary. 'Go on then.'

'Dan has decided against a career as a hen-night entertainer.'

'Oh,' said Bill. 'I was just coming round to the idea.'

'Too bad,' I said. 'He's moved on.'

'Right,' he said. 'So what's he considering now?'

'I haven't asked.'

'Good,' said Bill. 'That's good.'

***

My phone woke me up this morning at 6.30. It was a message from Jen, or rather Jennifer. *Sally, today is the day!! I need you to get in touch with Sam for me. Are you still in bed? I'm sending you an email to tell you what I want you to say. So you can look at it when you are talking to him on the phone. Have a look. Let me know what you think. Get up Sally this is important. Jennifer. xx*

I messaged back. *God sakes Jennifer it's only 6.30. Will get back to you asap. Xx*

Once I was up and showered and had a strong cup of coffee in my hand, I looked at her email.

The strap line was, READ THIS CAREFULLY!!

Dear Sally,

Today is the day you phone Sam for me and it is the most important phone call of my life so it is very important you get it right!! This is what I want you to do. You have to tell Sam that I love him and have been heartbroken since he left me. I have been unable to eat hardly anything and have lost weight. (Nearly 3 pounds). I want you to tell him that I would like us to meet up again at The Natural History Museum just for a chat, to start reconnecting again, under the dinosaur. As soon as possible please. Then, after that, I'd like you to say that I'm sorry I sprung that unfortunate piece of information on him in the church, but that there is Other Information he must have before he Judges me.

And finally I'd like you to get a date fixed for our meeting. I can manage any day at any time. I probably won't stay with you Sally when I come down, if that's okay? There's too many people at yours and I'll need some peace and quiet to think straight and get myself properly prepared. If you look at this email when you are talking to Sam you won't forget any of the points above.

What time do you think you should ring? Don't ring before 7.

Jennifer xx

I rang her and we agreed that I should ring at nine thirty a.m. Jennifer suggested eight thirty at first, but I said that smacked of desperation. So I waited until nine thirty and then I rang Sam's phone.

There was no reply. It went to answerphone. I hadn't been given any instructions about how to deal with an answerphone message so I just had to wing it. 'Hi Sam,' I said. 'It's Sally. Sally Forth. Can we talk Sam? I'll try you again later this morning. Bye. Bye Sam.'

And then I rang Jennifer to tell her I'd had to leave a message.

'Oh God, what did you say?'

'I just said I'd try later this morning.'

'Nothing more than that?'

'No, that was it.'

'You didn't mention that I loved him and I had lost three pounds?'

'Not in an answerphone message, no.'

'Try him again in ten minutes.'

'I thought I'd wait an hour.'

'An hour? That would make it nearly eleven o'clock!'

'That's okay. Eleven o'clock is fine.'

'I'll get off the phone then in case he rings back.'

'Good idea. I'll ring you as soon as I've spoken to him.'

I tried again at ten thirty-five. This time Sam answered.

'Hi Sally. I got your message.'

'Hi Sam. I don't know whether you've remembered, but the four week deadline is up today?'

'The four week deadline? Oh yes! Since the wedding, or rather, since that day. I hadn't realised actually, I wasn't keeping track. But I'm sure you're right.'

'Jen asked me to ring you, just to clarify a few things and make a suggestion.'

'Oh yes? Right. Okay. How are you doing, anyway?'

'Me?'

'Yes. How're you doing?'

'I'm fine thanks Sam. And you?'

'Yeah. I'm okay. Not bad.'

'The thing is Sam, Jennifer has asked me to communicate a few important things to you, before you and she meet up.'

'Are we meeting up? I don't think we made any plans.'

'Sam, what she would like me to say to you is that she loves you, and she's been heartbroken since you left. In fact, poor thing, she's lost a lot of weight: three pounds.'

'Three pounds? That doesn't sound like much.'

'Well, it's, you know, it's nearly half a stone.'

'I don't think so.'

'Near enough.'

'Seven pounds is half a stone.'

'Anyway, she would really like to meet with you, soon, at The Natural History Museum.'

'Why?'

'Why? Well, just for a chat.'

'A chat?'

'A chat, and to reconnect.'

I heard him sigh on the line. 'I don't know about that Sally. I don't know whether I want to reconnect.'

'Look Sam, I think you could give her a chance to talk to you. You did leave her standing at the altar, among the ruins of her own wedding ceremony.'

'Our wedding ceremony. Hers and mine. And the reason I left was because she confessed to killing her first husband at the altar.'

'I don't think she said she killed him on the altar. Oh yes – sorry – she made the confession at the altar. But, she didn't kill him, Sam. It wasn't as cut and dried as that.'

'The way I heard it, it was pretty cut and dried. Pretty damning. I'm surprised there hasn't been any come-back.'

'Come-back? What sort of come-back?'

'I'm surprised no-one has asked questions about how Frank died. Or maybe they have?'

'Not as far as I know. Sam – that aside – are you prepared to meet up with Jen?'

'*That aside?* This is the problem Sally. The murder of her first husband isn't something I can casually put aside.'

'Yes, I know it's a tricky one Sam, but—'

'A tricky one? Did you say a tricky one?'

'— but, Sam, Jen did not murder her first husband.'

'Just because she didn't wield a knife, Sally, doesn't mean she didn't kill him.'

'Well, if you want to be a pedant about it...'

'A pedant? Is that what you said? You think I'm being a pedant?'

'Sorry. Sorry Sam, I didn't mean that. Of course you're not being a pedant. And I understand there's more than one way of murdering someone. Obviously. We haven't watched all those episodes of Poirot for nothing, have we? No, we haven't. So. Where were we? Are you saying you'd rather not meet her?'

'I'm not keen on a meeting, to be honest. Since all this came to light, thoughts keep coming into my head. Difficult thoughts. You're a sensible woman, Sally, at least, I think you are. Look at this from my perspective. Supposing I married Jen, and sometime in the future I start getting on her nerves for whatever reason. I might feel a bit uncomfortable, a bit vulnerable, thinking about what happened to Frank.'

'That's appalling Sam.'

'It is appalling, yes.'

'She'd be utterly devastated to know you think that.'

'Well, don't say that. Don't tell her that. Maybe you could just tell her I've found someone else?'

'No. I can't see that helping.'

'I don't want her to come all the way down here to talk to me if it's not going to end the way she wants it to.'

'I think she wants the chance to see you again, and to talk about it, even if it doesn't end well. You did suggest a meeting, originally.'

He thought about it. 'All right then. If it's what she wants and she needs some sort of closure. We'll talk. Tell her to name some days that work for her. And ring me to let me know. It's a good idea to go through you at the moment, I think.'

'Okay, I will. Thanks Sam. I'll be in touch. So – have you found someone else?'

'No. It's just been four weeks since I was standing at the altar with Jen. That would be indecent haste. I just thought it might be easier for Jen to deal with, that's all. But, I could easily have got that wrong. Almost certainly have. A bit crass. Not thinking. Sorry.'

I waited until after eleven before I rang Jennifer back.

'What did he say?' she said. 'Tell me quick.'

'He's agreed to meet, but he's not very happy, Jennifer, I'm afraid. I don't think you should be thinking in terms of a reconciliation just yet. I think you'll have to take this very slowly.'

'Why? What did he say?'

'He's not happy about what happened to Frank. That's the problem Jen. And it's a very difficult one.'

'Well I'm not happy about what happened to Frank either. The way he died, it looks as if I killed him. It's the pits. Why doesn't anyone understand this and start feeling just a bit sorry for me?'

'The awkward thing is, Jennifer, Sam might think that if you stay together, and he starts to irritate you some time in the future, the way Frank did, you might be tempted to hide his medication, like, you know, the way you did with Frank.'

'What? Hide Sam's medication? That's outrageous!'

'I know.'

'And I didn't hide Frank's medication.'

'I know, but -'

'That's outrageous! It's horrendous, him thinking that. I'm really shocked. Sally, I have to do something. I have to put this right. I should go to the police, and ask them how I can prove my innocence. I should do that.'

'Oh,' I said, suddenly cautious. 'Hang about. I'd mull that one over Jen, Jennifer, if I were you. There might be a 'sleeping dogs' imperative here.'

'I don't think I have any choice. I have to go to the police and tell them everything and ask them what to do to show I'm completely innocent. I should have thought of this before. I confided in you when I should have gone straight to the police, I'm surprised you just didn't tell me to do that straight away.'

'But—' I said.

'But what? No ifs or buts Sally. This has to be done. I see it now. I'll wait till I hear from you about when I can meet Sam, and I'll tell him this is what I'm going to do. No buts.'

After she rang off, I thought – but what if she's not completely innocent?

***

We had a celebration in the kitchen tonight. Baz cooked. The meat was already in the oven when I came downstairs, and there were two bottles of red wine on the table. Meredith Cope-Harding loved Baz's conceptual piece *Stuffed*. He was given five hundred pounds for it. And once we were all sitting around the table enjoying our meal, Baz unveiled his latest idea.

'I'm going to do another Earth, right? With a man standing over it stuffing it with rubbish using a machine with a handle, like they do with those French geese they make pâté out of. So the Earth will be all bulging and lumpy and ugly-looking, and it will be crying tears made of plastic.'

'Oh my God, that's really sad,' said Chrissy. 'Isn't that sad?'

'Not if it makes another five hundred pounds,' said Sophie.

'You should give some of that money to Mrs Forth,' said Chrissy, 'for using her utility room.'

There was a slightly awkward pause, and then Baz said, 'Yeah, right. We should. I should have thought of that.' He turned to me. 'How does ten percent sound?'

'Hang on,' said Chrissy. 'Mrs Forth sets the rent for the utility room, not you.'

'Yeah, yeah,' said Baz, 'of course. Name your price, Mrs Forth. We couldn't do this without you. Ten percent, twenty percent, or more?'

'More?' said Sophie, dismayed.

'We'll have a chat about it later Baz,' I said. 'Let's eat first.'

Chrissy had made her point, and then she wanted to make sure we were all still friends. 'Anyway,' she said, 'I think you're very talented Baz. And Sophie. That last piece, *Stuffed,* was really good. Have you always been good with your hands, Baz?'

'That's funny,' he said. 'Meredith what's-it asked me if I'd always been good with my hands the last time I was talking to her.'

'Did she?' said Chrissy. 'What did you say?'

Baz shrugged. 'I think I just told her I hadn't had any complaints.'

***

I was driving along the M40 up to Stratford, listening to a phone-in programme on the radio. One of the topics for discussion was the new proposal from the housing minister, Bill of course, to give council tax rebates to householders willing to offer a room to young people working in high rent inner cities, who could not afford existing accommodation.

I was a little flustered at first, anxious in case Bill's plan was going to be rubbished by the callers, ready to switch off quickly if I didn't like the sound of what they were saying. But the discussion was sensible and measured, so I continued to listen.

A number of views were expressed. One caller was concerned about the possibility of older householders being taken advantage of by younger tenants, and wanted to know how householders would be protected from the risk of theft or intimidation. Another caller said they understood tenants were to be vetted and subject to enhanced DBS police checks. A caller rang in and said if the tenant offended in any way against the householder they should lose their job, and that should keep them in line. A very enthusiastic caller rang to say she thought it was a marvellous idea because it could help solve the problem of some owner-occupier houses being under-used, and also, loneliness among older retired people. I smiled as I drove. Everything was going well. Bill would be pleased.

And then the radio show host asked for the next caller.

'Hiya!'

I swerved over onto the hard shoulder and back out again.

'Hello!' said the talk show host. 'Thanks for calling in. Now, tell us a bit about yourself first.'

'My name's Sophie. And I live with Mr Forth. And his wife.'

'Ah! Sophie! We saw you on TV a while back, when you were running your little campaign to support Bill Forth's bid for the party leadership.'

'Yeah,' said Sophie. 'I was pretty famous for a while.'

'Indeed! So what have you got for us this time, Sophie? Fire away! I expect you like Bill Forth's proposal?'

'Yeah. Only it's not Mr Forth's. It's mine!'

'Sorry?'

'This whole idea. It's mine. It was my idea. But I don't mind Mr Forth pinching it. I'm very pleased about that.'

'So... Right. Tell us how this came about Sophie?'

I gripped the steering wheel hard and took a deep breath.

'Yeah okay. We were having Sunday dinner, and I said people should get a reward for letting young people live in their house with them if they have plenty of space. And Mr Forth said that's a good idea, because he and Mrs Forth have three young people living in with them right now, so if there was a reward they would be like, rich. I said it should really only be for nice posh houses like the Forth's and he said yes, it should only be for houses that have washbasins in the bedrooms and stained glass in the front door. And definitely not for anyone who has nits.'

'Really? Really Sophie?' said the broadcaster.

'Yeah. And he called it something. Hang on. I'll remember.'

I glanced down at the speedometer and saw I was doing ninety-five miles an hour.

'Oh yeah. He called it the Poncey House Tax Dividend.'

'Are you saying Mr Forth called it that Sophie?'

'Yeah. He said you would have to prove you didn't have nits before you could get it. The reward.'

There was the sound of supressed laughter in the studio. I indicated and pulled into a service station.

'Well,' said the broadcaster, 'I wonder if Mr Forth was joking a little bit there Sophie?'

'Might have been,' said Sophie, 'he was drinking wine, so yeah, he might have been.'

'Sometimes people say things they don't mean when they've had some wine.'

'Oh I think he meant it. Mrs Forth thought he was joking but Mr Forth said he was serious. He does drink a lot of wine though. He loves wine.'

'Did he? Does he? So, that must have been a very interesting lunchtime you had there, Sophie?'

'Yeah. We have lots of interesting meal times. Mrs Forth is interesting too. She's a very sensible woman and she does have a few opinions of her own. She's always giving me good advice.'

'Oh yes? Anything you can share?'

I put my hand to my mouth.

'Well,' said Sophie. 'She was my English teacher you know. We used to have such a laugh in her lessons. What's that thing called again? That little thing at the top? The apostrophe! She never knew where to put that. Anyway. When I was upset about something recently, Mrs Forth said even if you really, really fancy someone who isn't your husband and you want to jump into a Jacuzzi with them – you should remember that you'll probably just go off them eventually. Even if they can dance and do exciting things with their hips. So even if your partner is a bit boring and can't do that thing with his hips, she thinks it's best just to stick with them. In the end.'

'That...' More supressed laughter. 'That sounds really sensible advice Sophie.'

'Yeah, and—'

'Actually Sophie, we'd love to keep talking but we have to go now. Thanks for that Sophie. Thanks for calling in. It's been a great pleasure talking to you. Thank you Sophie. We love you. Bye. Bye bye.'

'Yeah bye,' said Sophie. 'Bye. Nice talking to you too.'

I switched off and sat in the car, with my hands over my mouth, presumably to stop myself shrieking. Should I ring Sophie, and tell her I heard her interview and warn her not to say anything more? Should I ring Bill and warn him that his political career might be coming to an end? Should I try and get in touch with God, and ask if I can start my life all over again?

And then my phone rang. Not God, but Dan. I answered and he said, 'Mum? I just heard Sophie on the radio.'

'I heard it.'

'You heard it? Fuck! It was hilarious.'

'I'm in shock here Dan.'

'Did you really say that stuff about getting the hots for someone and wanting to jump into a Jacuzzi?'

'Oh God, I can't remember what I said. Is Sophie with you?'

'No, I'm at work.'

'Listen Dan, can you get hold of Sophie and tell her not to say anything more about us, or anything at all. Tell her not to quote me, or your dad, or you, or anyone else, and to say nothing about any aspect of living with us, to anyone at all. Not even, what we have for breakfast.'

'That's a bit heavy, isn't it?'

'No. Get that message across Dan, I'm relying on you. I can't understand why she rang in, she told me she thought reporters were trying to get information out of her and she knew she had to keep schtum. She wouldn't even say anything standing next to the toaster, in case it was bugged. Then she rings up a radio programme and broadcasts to the nation.'

'It's just Sophie Mum, don't worry about it.'

'But I am worried, Dan. It's serious.'

'Honestly Mum, it's not. It's just Sophie. Don't get so worked up about it. You take stuff too seriously. Nobody's going to take this seriously. You have to see the funny side. You've got to admit, that was a pretty funny phone-in. Everyone was pooping their pants here.'

'I'm pooping my pants here Dan, but not because I thought it was funny.'

'Look, you're doing it again! I wish I hadn't rung. Chill out Mum. It'll be fine. Stop worrying. Something that funny isn't going to do any harm. Forget about it and enjoy your time in – where are you going?'

'Stratford.'

'Stratford.'

'You'll remember to tell Sophie not to say anything more?'

'Yeah. I'll tell her. I'll tell her not to say anything to anyone about anything ever again, ever. That was it, wasn't it?'

'Yes, that was it.'

'Lighten up Mum. Nobody died.'

'Okay,' I said. 'Okay. I'll see you in a couple of days.'

'Yeah, see you later. Just relax, and have some fun in Streatham.' And he rang off.

Strangely, I felt better after his call. I decided not to contact Bill. They would be dealing with it, if it needed to be dealt with. I probably wouldn't be able to add anything to the mix, anyway. If they needed to speak to me they would get in touch. I might as well calm down, and get back on the road.

I turned the key in the ignition and my phone rang again. It was Bill.

'Sophie's given some sort of interview,' he said. 'Have you heard?'

'Yes, I heard it on the radio.'

'I haven't quite got to grips with it yet. Somebody's looking at it. I gather it paints a picture of us in some sort of Bacchus-worshipping household on heat.'

'Yes. Dan rang me. He thinks no-one will take it seriously.'

'Does he? Well, that's reassuring. Anyway, I thought I'd give you a heads-up.'

'Right. Do you want me to come home?'

'Come home? Where are you?'

'I'm on my way up to Stratford.'

'Are you? Why?'

'It's the history group outing Bill, I told you about it.'

'Oh right, yes. No, no need for you to come home. Oh, and there's something else. Incredibly, someone found some compromising information down the back of my mother's sofa. Can you believe it?'

'Oh.'

'Don't worry about that one. I haven't seen it yet but I've got absolutely no intention of being held to ransom by my mother's sofa.'

'Maybe I should come home?'

'Why? What could you do to help? What difference would it make to anything whether you're home or not? You may as well stay where you are.'

'Oh, well. If that's what you think.'

'Got to go, Sally. Have a good time in Fleetwood.'

I looked at my phone and decided to switch it off. I pressed the button and held it, and the phone said 'Goodbye', and I said 'Goodbye', and I carried on up the M40 on my own.

Chapter Six: June

The hotel is wonderful. It's right in the middle of the town, and it looks and feels medieval, but without any of the annoying inconveniences of being that old, like fleas or open sewers or itchy bedclothes, or being mistaken for a witch in the lobby and taken outside and burnt at the stake. When I looked around I saw ancient brick fireplaces, beautiful carved oak surrounds, interesting paintings, leather upholstery, everything was warm and comfortable and lovely to look at. Not a plague victim in sight. The house boast is that Shakespeare might well have drunk mead here, and in truth, it's easy to feel that it's not long since he drank up and left. From the corner of my eye when I was standing at Reception, I fancied I saw him buttoning up his doublet. I felt the draught as he opened the door to leave, and I could see his empty tankard on the bar. I expected to see him again, I sense he is a regular.

I thought I'd share this piece of whimsy with the young man at the reception desk who was checking me in. He gave me my room key and I said, 'I think I just saw him leave. The man himself. I expect he's a regular at the bar here?'

'Sorry?' he said, and I got a sinking feeling, but I was committed.

'Shakespeare,' I said, indicating the portrait on the wall above his head, 'I expect he's always popping in?'

'Actually, er... '

'It's all right,' I said. 'I was just being fanciful.'

'Oh right yeah!' He was relieved. 'Cos he's been dead, oh, for ages now.'

'Yes of course,' I said. 'But do you ever think you see him? Out of the corner of your eye?'

He laughed, to humour me. 'No,' he said.

I pronounced the horse dead, and went up to my room.

The floor creaked and sloped as I walked along the corridor upstairs. There were wooden beams everywhere. I might have been on a ship, a Tudor galleon in full sail on choppy seas. My room was similarly decked in wood, and the bed was billowing with extra pillows and smaller cushions. I threw some of the cushions overboard to make room and lay down. I felt far from home, and comfortably removed from the here and now. I stowed my silent phone in the little wooden locker by the side of the bed. It doesn't belong to this world.

There was a very polite knock on the door of my room, and when I opened it Max was standing in the corridor. 'Nice hotel,' he said.

'It's lovely. How's your room?'

'Wonderful. I have a four-poster bed.'

'Wow. And is there a plaque, to say Shakespeare slept there?'

'I haven't looked. Maybe there is. I hope they've changed the sheets.'

'They charge you extra to sleep on Shakespeare's sheets,' I said. 'Give me ten minutes to get changed, and I'll meet you downstairs.'

I went into the bathroom and brushed my hair and touched up my make-up and generally fussed around like a teenager before putting on my dress. I was pleased with the result and gazed at my reflection in the mirror, and fell into a reverie and asked myself, 'Shall I compare thee to a summer's day?' But I got no answer, so I switched off the lights and left my room.

It was only five thirty, an hour before we were due to meet the others in the bar at the theatre. Max asked if I was hungry, and I said I was very hungry for a glass of mead, or failing that, white wine, so we sat in the lounge, each with a generous glass of white wine, and talked.

I was still talking at quarter to seven when I caught sight of Max's watch. We refused to hurry, and strolled along to the theatre as if we were fifteen minutes early, not fifteen minutes late. When we arrived and found the right bar, everyone was assembled and waiting for us at a table in the corner, waving programmes and beckoning us over.

Judith made room for me on her bench seat and indicated I should sit down. 'I thought you weren't coming,' she said, 'seeing as there seems to be all sorts of shit hitting the fan in your neck of the woods. I thought you'd decided to stay at home. But obviously not. You didn't answer any of my texts. What's your hotel like?'

'Very nice. How about yours?'

'Basic.'

Max asked me if I'd like another glass of wine. I said I might have one in the interval.

'So you've been drinking?' said Judith. 'At the hotel?'

'Well you've been drinking here,' I said.

'You look very relaxed, considering. Aren't you worried about what's happening with Bill?'

'Look Judith,' I said. 'I've spoken to Bill and he says he can handle it. Whatever it is. I offered to come home and he said it wouldn't make any difference to anything if I did. So I'm having a break. I'll have to go back to it all soon enough, but I'm going to enjoy my break. I hope that's all right with you?'

And then she said, 'Okay. Not so relaxed then. Never mind, you might be right. Forget about what's happening at home and enjoy the next few days.' She put her hand on my arm and squeezed it sympathetically and tried to smile, and I wondered briefly how bad things were.

But I didn't ask because Terry called us all to attention. 'Right gang,' he said, 'now that we're all here, I'm going to suggest Judith gives us a quick summary of the plot of *Love's Labour's Lost,* because it's a bit complicated and I think it helps to have an overview in your head before you start watching, so there's less to get to grips with. So if anyone doesn't want to know the plot before you see the play, can you talk among yourselves or wander off somewhere while Judith gives the rest of us the low-down.'

'All right everybody,' said Judith before anyone could decide to move off, 'I'll make this quick because we haven't got a lot of time. This is a play I know well because I've seen it before and I did it for A level. Here's the score. Basically, there's a king, three lords and a fool, and they decide to give up women and go on a diet and study in a castle for three years. God knows why. Anyway, the princess of France arrives with some of her women and they all meet up and the next thing is, everybody falls in love with everybody else, but there's a massive amount of confusion about who's in love with who. The men write to the women to declare their love, but the letters are intercepted and swapped and torn up and nobody knows what the heck is going on. Then, to clarify things, the men decide to dress up as Muscovites and go and see the women, and the women dress up as each other. And what the hell that's supposed to clarify God alone knows. So! Eventually they start to sort things out. But then, the French princess hears that her father has died, so she has to go home, but they all agree to meet up in a year's time for more fun and games because it beats watching telly. That's it.'

'Bloody hell,' said Max. 'What happened to boy meets girl boy loses girl boy finds girl?'

And ten minutes later, we were filing into our seats.

***

Love's Labour's Lost is in fact a joyous play, a two-hour advertisement for falling in love. We romped our way through all five acts and felt such good will towards our fellow men at the final curtain that we cheered and whistled and applauded and wanted Shakespeare himself to step out onto the stage and take a bow. We went straight to the bar afterwards to bask in the afterglow of the performance and, if possible, because it had been so highly recommended, to fall in love with someone. We sat around two tables pushed together, and raised our glasses to the Bard himself. And then, before my very eyes, I saw Judith start to fall in love with Terry. Terry was delighted because he soon realised that he too was in love with Judith. Arthur, our elderly historian who claims to be as old as Shakespeare, fell in love with the waitress who brought our bar meal. Marjorie, who bakes cakes for us, was delighted to discover that Geoff was in love with her, when she had previously thought he was in love with Judith. Arthur went to the loo, and when he came back he said while he'd been away, he had fallen in love with the girl who had been selling the programmes. The waitress came back to our table with condiments and on the spot fell in love with Arthur. There was consternation because Arthur was now in love with the girl who had been selling programmes. But then Arthur realised that in fact, he was in love with the waitress, and he had been all along! What a relief! Max fell in love with me and I fell in love with Max. Everything was working out splendidly.

I was surprised to find that when we got back to our hotel, I was still in love with Max. I thought it might have worn off during the walk back to the hotel, but no, such is the power of the iambic pentameter. So I accepted Max's invitation for a night-cap in his room with the four-poster bed because, as it turned out, he was still in love with me.

I made myself comfortable on the four-poster bed in Max's room, while he investigated the mini-bar and poured two glasses of wine. I wondered whether the very comfortable bed I was now languishing on was in anyway similar to the second-best bed mentioned in Shakespeare's will. Max said he had seen a plaque somewhere saying that this bed was in fact, an exact and contemporaneous copy of Shakespeare's second-best bed. This bed, and that bed, apparently, were sister beds.

I said that was extraordinary.

Then Max gave me a glass of wine and said that what was even more extraordinary was that it was on his second best bed that Shakespeare had fallen in love with Anne Hathaway, and to demonstrate how this might have happened, he lay down next to me.

I was amazed to think that we were both now lying on the sister bed of the bed that had played such a significant role in Shakespeare's life. And then Max rolled towards me, playfully, and a significant night passed...

***

A radio alarm woke me up in the morning, and I heard voices.

'Oh God,' said Max, 'another politician trying to wriggle off the hook. I'll make us both a cup of tea.'

He got out of the four-poster bed and went to fill the kettle, and I sat up, and listened to Bill being interviewed on the radio.

'– irrespective of whoever wrote this letter, my wife should be entitled to carry out private correspondence by letter to trusted individuals, if she so wishes. Letters are sent by post under the protection of the Royal Mail and shouldn't be read by anyone but the addressee, without permission.'

'You're up to your neck in it, aren't you?' the interviewer said. 'You've been instrumental in covering up a relationship between the prime minister and another minister which could adversely influence government policy, you've brought your housing initiative into disrepute by admitting you personally stand to make a considerable financial gain from it, your household is conducting a business enterprise on the premises in contravention of local bylaws and health and safety advice. There are rumours that you may have an alcohol problem. You're in trouble, aren't you?'

'The housing initiative should stand or fall on its own merits, and it has as much merit now as it ever had. Of course, I'll look into the reports of a business being run from our house, and if bylaws have been broken, I'll make sure that stops.'

'And then, of course, your wife may also be in trouble. I'm not talking now about the letter she wrote to your mother.'

'I'm sorry?'

'There are disturbing reports circulating in some quarters that your wife may be involved, incredibly, in some kind of nefarious cover-up of an act of manslaughter?'

Bill's tone changed. 'My wife?' he said, 'Let me just say a few words about my wife, if I may. My wife is as loyal, honest and honourable as the day is long. She could not lie about something, or cover something up if she tried. She has been my best friend and staunchest ally, and my most sincere and constructive critic since we were barely into adulthood. And I will defend her reputation to the death.' He laughed a little at the passion in his reply. 'Do I make myself clear?'

I switched the radio off, and looked across the room at Max, standing naked with the kettle held in his hand.

'That was Bill,' I told Max.

He looked down at his naked torso. 'Maybe I should get dressed,' he said.

'I have to go Max. I have to go home.'

He put the kettle down and came across to sit on the bed next to me. 'Of course,' he said. 'You must go home. For Bill. It's a good thing,' he said, 'that nothing happened last night. Between us. Otherwise you might have felt you had betrayed him. But you haven't. Not in the least.'

'Haven't I?'

'No, not in the slightest. Nothing happened of any consequence. Absolutely nothing. That's how it is. That's how it always will be.'

'Is that possible Max?'

'Yes. Yes it is. It has to be. Because of what you just heard on the radio.'

I got out of bed and he watched me get dressed.

'It's good to be friends though,' he said. 'Friends, I hope. Not just friends.'

'Yes, it's good to be friends.' I kissed him on the cheek, as a friend, collected my bag and my coat and my room key, and left.

When I got back to my room I took my phone out of the wooden cabinet beside the bed and switched it on. There were thirty-seven messages waiting to be read. I didn't look at any of them. I just had a shower, collected my things, checked out of the hotel and drove home.

***

I saw Sophie's face at the window when I pulled onto our drive. I parked the car and switched off the ignition and she came outside and opened the car door.

'Mrs Forth. Thank God you're back. The police have been here wanting to speak to you. It was so scary. I think you might be going to prison.'

'What?'

'I'm so worried Mrs Forth. Everything's going wrong. I wish I'd never rung that radio programme.'

'Just let me get out of the car Sophie.'

'I'll get your bag.'

'Are you the only one in? Where is everybody?'

Sophie pulled my bag off the back seat of the car and carried it into the house and down the hall to the kitchen.

'Mr Forth was here but he had to go out. Everyone else is at work. I'm on a day off. I was really lonely on my own. I'm so glad you've come back. Did you have your phone switched off? I texted you a hundred times to say come back because since you left everything has been going wrong. I think it's my fault for ringing the radio programme. Mr Forth says not to worry about it and I was right about the housing thing. It was actually my idea. Oh, and Marra's escaped.'

I looked at the empty cage. 'Where is he?'

'I don't know. Somebody left the cage door open.'

'Have you searched the house?'

'No, I've been too worried.'

'Let's sit down, and you can tell me what's been happening.'

'Well, after I spoke on the radio, Dan rang me and said, 'Nice one Soph, but don't say anything more about anything ever again.' So I thought I might have made a mistake. Then last night when everybody got back, Mr Forth came home and said to us all that he might be in a bit of bother for a while, but that we shouldn't get upset or angry because it was just politics. I said was it all my fault? And he said no. It was just politics and not to worry about it. But Chrissy said it would probably be best not to do any more phone-ins. Then Dan said that you had said I shouldn't talk to anyone ever again. But Mr Forth said I could talk to whoever I liked, it was up to me.' She paused. 'I've forgotten what I was saying now.'

'So, what happened this morning?'

'Oh god! The police came this morning! There was just me in. There was two of them, and they said they were police officers and they wanted to speak to you. I said you weren't in, you were on a history trip breathing the same air as Shakespeare. They said when would you be back and I said I would text you and tell you to come back straight away. They said no problem they would call back. I said, she isn't going to be arrested, is she? And they laughed, but you just never know. They could be being ironic. Then I came back into the kitchen and saw Marra had escaped.' She put her head in her hands. 'Oh god. Everything's gone wrong and I've lost the parrot.'

'Let's have a cup of tea and see if we can find Marra. He might be upstairs in one of the bedrooms. We'll have to search for him, he might be stuck somewhere.' I put the kettle on and went across to the fridge for some milk. 'We're out of milk,' I said.

'I'll go down to the Co-op and get some. And some biscuits, that might help.'

After she left I went upstairs to look for the parrot, anxious in case I found him head down in a toilet bowl, or chewing through an electrical cable with his feathers standing on end. I went from room to room expecting the worst. Then I heard a key turning in the front door lock, and thought it might be Bill, so I ran back downstairs.

It was Laura.

'Mum! I wasn't expecting to see you.'

'No, I thought I'd come home early.'

'I spoke to Dad last night, and things sounded a bit, you know, serious. Thought I'd call round while little Harry is at Teeny Teasers.'

'Oh, is he teasing himself?'

'No, Maz has taken him. We take it in turns to go to Teeny Teasers. Her turn this week. You remember Maz? She was a bit of an idiot at school. She ate that stick insect in year ten and ended up in Casualty. Anyway, she's settled down a bit. I trust her absolutely with Harry.'

'Oh,' I said. 'Do you?'

'I thought Sophie was going to be in and she might be able to tell me what's been happening.' She followed me down the hall to the kitchen, dropped her big pouchy bag on the floor and sat at the table. 'Mum, they're saying there's some sort of illegal business being run from this house. What is it? It's not drugs, is it?'

'Drugs? No of course not. It's taxidermy.' I sat opposite her. 'Would you like coffee?'

'Yes please. Small one. Black. Taxidermy? You mean, Baz's stuffed animals?'

'Yes, he's been doing very well. He stuffs them in the utility room, and sells them to a gallery in the city somewhere.'

'So, you're running an illegal taxidermy business?'

'Looks like it, yes.' I gave her a mug of coffee.

Laura frowned. 'Better than drugs I suppose. Although, it sounds a bit, macabre.'

'No,' I said, 'it's not macabre.'

'It's not exactly vegan-friendly though, is it?'

'Well it's not vegan anything, it's taxidermy. It's a different thing altogether.'

'Mum, I don't know how you can bear to have someone doing this kind of thing in your utility room. It's weird. And there's got to be health and safety issues.'

'Well it did feel weird at first, but we've got used to it by degrees. I hadn't thought about health and safety issues.'

'Mum, it's got to be a health and safety hazard, surely? I mean, there'll be entrails and stuff to dispose of. What does Baz do with all the innards?'

'God, Laura, I don't know. I don't want to know. He only stuffs very small animals, their innards will be tiny, not enough to fill a sausage. He's decided against stuffing a polar bear.'

'A polar bear? What? Shit Mum! There'd be truck-loads of innards.'

'He's decided against it. He didn't realise they're so big. He thought they were the size of a sheep.'

'He's mad. You need to keep an eye on him, Mum. You know how he likes to cook. He'll have access to all sorts of meaty bits and pieces in that utility room. For God's sake don't let him make gravy. He's a nice person, but don't encourage him to make casseroles. He has no idea about what's edible. I remember him at school. He always had something weird in his sandwiches.'

I was going to explain to her the eco-friendly theme of Baz's latest taxidermy series, which I knew she would be in sympathy with, but then she said, 'I feel so sorry for Dad. Do you think he'll have to resign?'

'It's possible.'

'Because of that stupid radio interview? I couldn't believe what Sophie said when I heard it. She's an idiot.'

'Hiya,' Sophie stood in the back doorway, holding two large containers of milk.

'Oh, hi Sophie.'

'Hi Laura. How's little Harry?'

'He's fine thanks Sophie. Actually,' Laura glanced at her phone, 'I'll have to go and pick him up.' She stood up and took a last sip of coffee. Her gaze settled on the empty bird cage in the corner of the kitchen.

'Is there meant to be something in that cage?'

'We've lost the parrot.'

'Oh.' Laura looked from the empty cage to the utility room. 'I don't suppose Baz knows where it is?'

***

We looked everywhere for the parrot once everyone got back from work, and Bill joined the search when he got back in at nine. I wanted to talk to him about more serious things, but he said he'd been talking about serious things all day, and he just wanted to think about the parrot and nothing else. So we concentrated on the parrot and we looked on top of wardrobes and under beds. We looked on window ledges and on chair backs and on bed headboards. We kept looking at his cage, although we could see he wasn't in there. We called his name. He didn't answer. We shouted 'Hiya!' There was no response. Sophie chopped some apple and distributed pieces around the house, to tempt Marra out of hiding. Bill looked in the garden, in between answering calls on his mobile.

Ivor was despondent. 'I think I've lost me bord,' he said. 'I think he's gone.'

'Will you get another one?' said Sophie.

'Why no, I could never replace Marra. He was a one-off.' Ivor became emotional and started looking through his phone at pictures of Marra. One shot in particular of Marra sitting on someone's bare bum was considered particularly poignant.

I was glad when Bill's phone rang again. Even if it was bad news it seemed preferable to grieving over a lost parrot, so I wasn't too concerned when I heard Bill say, 'Okay. What now?'

I still haven't told him I am wanted for questioning by the police and of course I haven't yet hinted that I might have slept with another man last night. There's only so much flesh and blood can stand.

We had to give up on finding Marra. Sadly he was gone, along with Bill's reputation and my integrity. We had a very subdued supper together in the kitchen, just soup, bread and cheese. Sophie put the cover over the bird cage, Chrissy took an apple from the fruit bowl, and placed it on the top, and Ivor shook his head.

We went to bed, and I asked Bill how bad he thought all this political stuff was going to get. Bill said it was going to be a mess for a while, and we'd just have to fasten our seat belts and ride it out for a few days before the caravan moves on, and then see how things were. 'Anyway,' he said, 'let's think about something else. You haven't told me about your trip to, where was it?'

'Stratford. I went to Stratford.'

'Oh yes. The history trip. So did you see a play? Did you stay somewhere nice? Sorry you had to cut it short.'

'Actually, I was ready to come home.'

'You should have stayed away as long as you could. But I'm glad you're back. I missed you. What a night I had last night. It was hell at work, of course, and then I got home and Sophie started to cry as soon as she saw me. Burst into tears as soon as I walked through the door. Then Laura rang wanting to know if I was going to get the sack. Baz turned up and started cooking some god-awful thing which, I kid you not, had spines. And Dan, Dan was ordering T-shirts from the internet which would have '*Do that thing with your hips*' written across the front. I told him to cancel the order and he accused me of having no sense of humour. God, by then I had no sense of humour and no appetite. Nightmare. Let's go to sleep. You can tell me all about your night away later. I might have a lot more time on my hands soon.'

'It would be nice to spend more time together. Or even some time together.'

'Be careful what you wish for. I could be all yours before much longer.'

'Actually Bill,' I said, 'about last night—'

'Listen,' said Bill, 'there's a cat. Don't they sound weird? Eerie.'

We listened to a cat howling in the garden outside, the anguished cry rising and falling in tone like a lost soul.

'They do sound strange,' I said. 'Very strange. They sound tormented.'

We lay close together listening to the howling lament, keening louder then softer in drawn-out, tortured wails, making it even more difficult for me to gather the strength I needed to confess. Bill had said, after all, that I could never cover anything up.

But then there was another sound.

'Fuck! Fuck-fuck-fuck! Hiya! Fuck! Fuck!'

'It's Marra,' said Bill. 'He's out there with the cat.' He got out of bed and crossed to the window. 'I'll see if I can spot him.'

'Marra? You'll never see him,' I said. 'It's pitch black outside. We'll have to wait 'till morning.'

'Fuck!' said Marra.

Someone was on the move inside the house. We heard tapping on a bedroom door, not ours, and Sophie whispering to Ivor. Then more tapping, and Sophie whispering to Dan and Chrissy. In less than a minute, there were several sets of feet on the stairs and the back door was unlocked and opened. We heard Ivor's voice, 'Marra! Marra! Get down here you stupid bird. It's half past one in the fucking morning.'

'Marra!' that was Sophie, 'Marra! Come here Marra!'

'Hiya!'

'Was that you?' said Baz.

'No it was Marra. It was Marra saying Hiya!'

'Hiya! Hiya!'

'There he is again. That wasn't me, it was him.'

'We need a torch,' said Dan.

'I've got a torch. We need a fishing net. To catch him in.' That was Baz.

'Fuck! Fuck!'

'Did you just say fuck?'

'No I didn't say fuck.'

'It must be him. Shine the light up there Baz.'

'Up! Up! Up yours! Fuck!'

And then there was another voice.

'Who's there? What the hell is going on out here?' Susan, from next door. Bill started to laugh.

'Oh, hello Susan,' said Dan.

'What's going on? I'm warning you, I'm a fully trained neighbourhood watch officer and my brother's a policeman.'

'Susan it's us,' said Dan.

'Susan? Susan! Over here! It's me! Sophie! Have you got a fishing net?'

'No I haven't got a bloody fishing net. What the hell are you doing?'

'We're trying to catch our parrot.'

'You must think I was born yesterday.'

'Look!' said Sophie. 'Look! He's in the tree, I saw him! Shine the torch up there again Baz.'

'Hiya,' said Marra. 'Fuck.'

'You tell that bird to watch its language,' said Susan.

'Susan, you haven't got a ladder handy, have you?'

'Of course I haven't got a bloody ladder handy. It's two o'clock in the morning.'

'It's okay. I think there's a ladder in the shed. I'll get it.'

'And keep the noise down. Decent folk are asleep.'

'I'll get the ladder.'

'Who's going up?'

'Me! I'll go. Marra knows me. I taught him to shake hands.'

'Will you be okay, Soph?'

'Of course I'll be okay.'

'Careful.'

'You'll break your neck going up that ladder in the pitch black young lady,' said Susan.

'Hold the ladder steady.'

'Take it slowly.'

'Steady Soph.'

'Where is she?'

'She's in the foliage.'

'Can you see her?'

'No.'

'Told you,' Susan again. 'I said this would end in tears.'

'It's okay. I'm here! I'm nearly at the top. Hiya!'

'Hiya! Hiya! Up yours!'

'She's with Marra.'

'I've got him!'

'She's got him!'

'Well done Sophie!'

'Are you coming down?'

'Yeah.'

'So, are you coming down?'

'Yeah.'

'Are you stuck Sophie?'

'She'll be stuck. Mark my words, she's stuck up the ladder.'

'I'm not stuck. It's just a bit tricky coming down a ladder holding a parrot. He's biting my finger.'

'Shove him up your jumper Soph.'

'Can't. I'm not wearing a bra.'

'God Almighty! It's a mad house.'

'She's coming down.'

'Ah, fantastic. Fantastic. He's a bloody nuisance like, sometimes, that bird. But I don't want him eaten by a fucking cat. Sorry Susan. Excuse my French.'

'French?'

'I'm down. Here's your bird, Ivor.'

'I've got him. Thanks Sophie. Thanks guys.'

'Don't mention it.'

'No, I mean it. Thanks guys.'

'You're okay. Sophie did it.'

'Thanks Sophie.'

'Did you see me up the ladder?'

'Yeah. You were brilliant. Thanks.'

'That's okay.'

'Right! I'm going to bed and I don't want to hear any more noise from you or the foul-mouthed bird. It's nearly three o'clock in the morning. French? I'll give you French at this time of night.'

'Goodnight Susan!'

'It's like living next door to a bloody circus.'

'Goodnight, Susan pet. Poor Marra. He was shitting himself when he heard that cat. Did you hear him?'

Laughter.

'Your folks slept through the whole thing.'

'Yeah. Shame they missed it really. They could do with a bit of excitement.'

The kitchen door closed behind them.

Bill and I, still smiling, fell asleep.

Chapter Seven: July

A policeman is coming to see me tomorrow. Someone rang and asked if I would be at home around two in the afternoon. They said he wouldn't keep me long, but they were hoping to shed light on an enquiry. I said yes, absolutely, I would do my very best to assist in whatever way I could. I tried to sound relaxed and unflustered, but actually I was alarmed to think that I would be helping the police with their enquiries. Whenever I hear that someone is helping the police with their enquiries I assume they are just filling in some paperwork prior to being thrown in gaol. I had to stop myself protesting on the phone that I had nothing to hide and was innocent of all charges. I thought it might give the wrong impression if I started pleading for my life before they had even knocked on the door. I must stay calm, and not give the impression that I think I'm guilty of something.

I was so pleased to be going into school this morning. Once in a school, the outside world fades away and is replaced by something essentially worthy and good, in the best sense of that word. Schools are a healing microcosm of well-intentioned initiatives designed to bring out the best in young people. Sometimes these initiatives are miraculously successful, more often they fail, but always they keep coming. Every new school year brings a new crop of initiatives with new terminology and a shiny new folder for everyone involved, with colour-coded stationery clipped inside. The aim is always redemption. I never fully understood the parable of the prodigal son until I started my teaching career. I know now why the father in the parable killed the fatted calf for the wastrel son who returned to the fold. I have felt a similar urge to shower Lee with commendations for compliance which, in another more well-behaved child, I would take for granted. I once gave Lee a *Gold Star Merit Certificate,* and Gold Star Merit Certificates are hardly ever awarded. They are reserved for instances of outstandingly meritorious behaviour, like rescuing teachers from packs of rabid dogs, but I gave one to Lee for not farting loudly in assembly.

I called at the school office to collect my ID lanyard. Deborah, the office manager, was surprised to see me. She said she thought I might have other things to attend to.

I told her I couldn't disappoint Lee, he would be looking forward to telling me that my life was in ruins.

Deborah said that was a fact. She said she had heard this morning on the radio that Bill might resign.

I said I hadn't been listening to the radio.

She said she had seen something on TV last night about how the Prime Minister and the Foreign Secretary had been having a torrid affair, and that was the reason why she couldn't sack him, even though he was a dip-stick.

I said I hadn't been watching any news on TV.

She said that was a shame, because apparently the Prime Minister and the Foreign Secretary had done things on the PM's desk in Downing Street that would make your hair stand on end.

I said I was trying to stop my hair standing on end, it didn't need any encouragement.

She said, honestly, the News was better than EastEnders at the moment.

I said oh god. And then I asked her how Lee had been this week.

She said she had heard no complaints about Lee this week, not a peep out of anyone, and she was beginning to wonder if someone had locked him in a stationery cupboard and forgotten to mention it.

But Lee was not in a stationery cupboard, he was waiting for me in D12, a small teaching room with a view of the school car park and a fan heater rattling away behind a metal grille blowing warm air into the room.

'Can we have that heater off?' he said to me in greeting when I came in. 'It's hot in here and that fucking flippin' thing makes too much noise.'

'Language, Lee. Let's get off to a good start.'

'I said flippin'.'

I inspected the heater. 'Sorry Lee, it's one of these heaters that you can't switch off,' I said. 'I think we'll just have to put up with it.'

Lee thumped it hard with his fist turned sideways. I jumped. The heater rumbled on for a few short seconds and then stopped. 'That's how you switch it off,' he said.

'Right.' I doubted it would switch on again without calling someone from maintenance, but still. 'I've got a book here that you might like Lee, and I'd like us to take a look at your report card.'

He sat down opposite me and glanced at his report card. 'My dad says your Bill's done for.'

'Never say die, Lee.'

'I never said die.'

'No, I mean '*Never say die*'. It's a saying.'

'Who's saying it?'

'People say it, when they mean don't give up.'

'Why don't they just say don't give up?'

'Because it's a more interesting way of saying it.'

'No it's not. It's saying something completely different.'

'The whole saying is, '*Never say die, until you're dead*'.'

'You can't say nothing when you're dead.'

'Right Lee. Let's move on. Let's talk about your report card this week. It's good. It's very good. I think you've been doing much better at school since you decided to become a solicitor.'

'Yes but, Mr Robinson says I'll never be a solicitor because I'm not that clever.'

'Oh.'

'So is that right?'

'I don't know why Mr Robinson said that.'

'No, but is it true?'

'If you want my honest opinion Lee, I think you are clever. I think you're a clever boy. But, you have neglected your schoolwork, and that is a problem. It means you're behind with certain things, and you will have to work hard to catch up.'

'How hard?'

'Very hard.'

'Been working hard all week. I'm worn out.'

'Don't you feel pleased with yourself? For working hard?'

'No. I'll feel like a dickhead if it's all been a waste of time.'

'It's never a waste of time to do some hard work, Lee.'

'Yes it is. 'Course it is. If you do some hard work and it turns out you needn't have bothered – what a waste of time! You could've been doing something different. Are you sayin' it's worth working hard just for nothing?'

'What I'm saying is, I think you might have to like hard work more than you seem to, if you want to be a solicitor.'

He thought about it. 'There must be some solicitors who don't work very hard. And still make shed-loads of money. I could be one of those.'

We agreed to look into it. I had to admit, he did seem to be developing an understanding of the legal profession.

***

In anticipation of helping the police with their enquiries tomorrow, I wondered whether to ring Jennifer once I got home. It would be useful to know what she had said to the police that had prompted their decision to speak to me. The most difficult question the police could ask me would be whether I had advised Jennifer to say nothing about the way Frank died, while at the same time knowing her to be guilty of some offence associated with his death.

What would I say, if they asked me that question?

'Yes officer, I did advise her to keep quiet about possibly murdering her husband because I didn't want her to ruin her wedding to another unsuspecting man.'

I started to feel anxious. The palms of my hands felt clammy. I was aware of my heart beating. I felt annoyed with Jennifer for dropping me into this mess. It's one thing to murder your excessively irritating husband but it's quite another to drag an innocent party into the mire with you. I was about to ring her and tell her as much, but then thought better of it. The police might be monitoring our calls and think we have been conferring to get our stories straight. It's better that I don't contact her before tomorrow.

So instead, I went into the utility room and dragged the vacuum cleaner out of the upright cupboard behind the door, and started to do some vigorous vacuuming. The advantage of being full of adrenalin is that you can use it to clean your house. I vacuumed every inch of the ground floor and was halfway up the stairs on the landing when the power was switched off.

'Oi Missus!' Ivor called up the stairs. 'That's my job. Give it here an I'll tek ower.'

'That's all right Ivor,' I said. 'I was just working off a head of steam. The carpets don't need cleaning really, I was just a bit anxious about something and it helps to be busy.'

'Ah pet,' he said. 'Am sorry to hear that. Are you worried about Mr Forth losing his job like?'

'No,' I said, 'it's not that.'

'So, are you worried about the taxidermy business being illegal like?'

'No, not that either.'

'Ah. So are you worried about what they're saying about that letter you sent to Mr Forth's mam?'

'No, not that.'

'Not that? How many worries have you got pet?'

I sat down on the stairs. 'I've done something really stupid.'

Ivor sat down on the stair below me. 'I can't believe it's that bad. You can't have done something that bad, surely?'

'It's pretty bad. A friend of mine – Jen, you remember? You were at her hen-night? Well, you were her hen-night. She might possibly have murdered her husband, and I told her not to say anything about it.'

'What?'

'And now the police want to talk to me. It's my own stupid fault, I should have told her to go to the police instead of telling her to keep quiet until after she married someone else.'

'Fuck! It does sound as if you might be in a bit of bother like,' said Ivor. 'But – you didn't actually kill anybody yourself?'

'No, no. No, I wasn't there when it happened. I just heard about it afterwards.'

'And you didn't tell her to do it?'

'No, no. I just knew what she'd done, or might have done, because she told me. And I told her not to say anything.'

'Right,' Ivor frowned and rubbed his chin in concentration. 'I think your best plan is to sound a bit confused when you're talking to the police. As if you might be a bit – not exactly doolally – but y'know – dopey. So you can't remember who said what an' when they said it an' when you knew about it, an' all that kind of stuff. When yer talking to them, sound a bit mental. So that they think, we'll never get nowt out of her, she's mental. A good tip – me mam's done this – is to put yer clothes on backwards, so they think, she's crackers, we'll never get no sense out of her, no point in asking her anything, she's got up all arse over tit.'

I looked at him and considered his advice. 'Thanks Ivor,' I said. 'That's very helpful.'

'If you was any younger, you might not get away with it, but you're the right age for starting to go a bit, you know, senile. I'm not saying you are! I'm not saying you're senile nor nowt like that. I'm saying you might be able to look as if you are. Temporarily like. To get yerself out of bother.'

'Right,' I said. 'Okay. Put my clothes on backwards and sound a bit mental. I'll remember that.'

'Champion. Mind you. If you don't mind me saying. She's probably not much of a friend, if she's going round killing folk.'

'Yes. You're right.'

'I knew a murderer once. He was a fucking idiot.'

'Was he?'

'He was. A fucking idiot. Get yerself some better friends who haven't killed nobody. And give us that hoover, pet.'

I gave him the vacuum cleaner, and went down into the kitchen, and felt so much better.

***

Around five-ish, there was a knock on the front door. An imperious, assertive rapping. Not a desperate pounding, and certainly not a polite 'coo-ee come-find-me' tapping, but a no-nonsense, impatient, authoritative, knocking. It wasn't the sort of knocking which goes away, and after a few seconds it started again. It was an aggressive knock. It made me want to hide under the kitchen table with a tea towel over my head, but that style of knock was a demand, a summons, so I walked down the hall to the front door as if I was walking the plank.

But it was Susan standing on the doorstep. 'Well what the hell was all that about last night Sally?'

There aren't many occasions on which I am genuinely pleased to see Susan from next door, but this was one of them. 'God Susan, I thought that was someone coming to arrest me.'

Her eyes narrowed, 'Why's that then?'

I invited her in and sat her down and listened, and listened, to her complaint.

'... cavorting around in the dark chasing after parrots and the language at that time of night and demanding ladders and fishing nets at two o'clock in the morning I deserve an explanation someone should have come round to talk to me so I waited and I waited and I thought surely someone'll come round and tell me what all that was about surely they'll have the common decency to do that and then when no-one came I thought no-one's coming so I thought bugger me I'll just have to go round myself and demand an explanation and an apology and—'

'Fuck!' said Marra. 'Fuck fuck fuck fuck fuck *fuck*. Fucking *fuck*!'

Susan stopped dead, and turned to look at Marra. 'That's him. That's the foul-mouthed bird I heard last night.'

'Hiya!' said Marra.

Susan stared. 'Hello,' she said.

'Susan this is Marra,' I said. 'He escaped, and we were worried about him last night when we heard a cat, so Dan and the others went out to rescue him. I'm very sorry they woke you up.'

'Hiya,' said Marra.

Susan turned again towards the cage. 'Hello,' she said.

'Hiya. Hiya.'

'Is that bird talking to me?' Susan looked at Marra more closely, peering at him through the bars of his cage. 'It's as if it's talking to me.'

'Fuck off,' said Marra.

'It is talking to me, the little devil. I'd just throw it out of the window Sally, and get rid of it.'

'Oh fuck!' said Marra.

'That bird's uncanny,' said Susan. 'Honestly. I'd get rid of it. How do you put up with it?'

'Up!' said Marra. 'Up up! Up! Up! Up yours! Up!'

Susan stood up. 'I'm going,' she said. 'Things to do. Better things than sitting around here talking to a bird with no manners.'

I saw her to the door. 'It's not talking to you, Susan. It has no idea what it's saying. It's just imitating what it's heard.'

'Doesn't say much for the tone of discourse around here. That bird's uncanny,' said Susan on the doorstep. 'I'd get rid of it Sally.'

When I went back into the kitchen I gave Marra a piece of apple. 'There you go Marra,' I said. 'A treat.'

'Fuck,' he said sweetly. 'Up yours.'

***

I decided not to ring Jennifer until after the policeman had been this afternoon, but at ten this morning she rang me. I explained that I didn't think we should talk and I was going to ring off.

'Why?' she said. 'What's the matter with you?'

'Jennifer,' I said, 'the police are coming to see me this afternoon. They want me to help them with their enquiries.'

'God,' she said. 'What have you done?'

'What have I done?'

'Is it about the letter you wrote to Ella? That's all over the papers this morning. Apparently, those two, the PM and what's-his-name, the foreign secretary, have had the hots for each other for ages. It was an open secret, apparently, it wasn't just Bill who knew. Honestly Sally, the things those two got up to. You just can't imagine it, looking at them sitting next to each other on the front bench in the House of Commons as if butter wouldn't melt. I'll never think of a parsnip in the same way again. They're saying Bill shouldn't have discussed the rumours with you, but I'm not surprised he did! You must have been in hysterics the pair of you. What with all that stuff about rubber gloves – and didn't they use a brillo pad for something? Honestly – never mind a parsnip – what those two couldn't do with a diplomatic box! I'm amazed the box could stand up to it, they're pretty ancient. And the PM's quite generously proportioned, isn't she? I'm surprised she had the balance for it. One of the papers had a photograph of the box and it did look as if it's had a rough time. Of course, it depends what papers you read. There's a lot of speculation and unconfirmed reports. And some papers are saying the parsnip has been over-egged. But everyone thinks you were an idiot for putting it all in a letter to Bill's mother. They all agree on that.'

'Right. Actually I haven't been reading the papers.'

'It's all over the BBC website.'

'I haven't looked since this started.'

'I wonder if the police want to see you about your letter?'

'It's not a criminal offence to write a letter.'

'Come off it, Sally. There's letters and there's letters. Oh, and speaking of criminal offences, I went to the police myself the other day, funnily enough. I said I would, didn't I? I decided to go before I meet up with Sam. That's why I'm ringing, actually. I went to tell them about the Frank thing. I told them everything and asked them what I should do. I've been trying to ring you to tell you but I haven't been able to get through to you.'

'I think that's why the police want to speak to me.'

'Really? Because of the Frank thing? Well, I don't know what more you can add. I've already told them everything. Okay. Give me a ring after they've been and let me know what the crack is. They said they would be back in touch with me in a day or two, and asked me if I was planning a holiday or anything. But I said I'd be here. They were very friendly. I felt much better after I'd spoken to them. Have you really not been listening to the news or anything?'

'No. Not for a while.'

'You should Sally. Bill was on this morning. He's sticking up for you. He said you can't be blamed for writing that letter, and it's all his fault for saying too much. He said he'll resign if the PM asks him to.'

'I've got to go, Jennifer,' I said. 'Something's boiling over in the kitchen.'

And I put the phone down, because there was something boiling over.

It was me.

***

The policeman arrived promptly at three, and I was ready for him. I didn't have my clothes on backwards because I'd decided that wasn't the way forwards. I wasn't going to dissemble or try to give the impression that I was totally innocent, or senile, or indeed ignorant of any of the implications of what I had advised Jennifer to do. I was going to be honest and up front and take any consequences on the chin. I was in trouble anyway, I thought I may as well get all the opprobrium over with at once now, rather than it creeping up on me in ghastly instalments. I couldn't deny what I had said to Jennifer, and I had been wrong to say it. I don't know the law, obviously, but I thought I might have assisted in perverting the course of justice.

The most important thing, as far as I could see, was to make sure that whoever interviewed me understood that I am solely responsible for what I might have done wrong, and there is no attempt made now or later to blame Bill for any of it. I don't want him to be involved, I haven't told him about this interview so that he can say truthfully that he knew absolutely nothing about it and gave me no advice about what to say, or what not to say. So that was what I was focused on when a very polite and respectful policeman called to see me this afternoon.

I showed him in and sat him down. I had set out mugs and saucers on a tea tray with a few biscuits. I took his order and made one tea, and one coffee, and then I sat opposite him on the smaller sofa and asked how I could help.

He said his visit was concerning an interview they had held with a friend of mine, and of course, it was Jennifer.

I said I thought this might be why he wanted to see me, and I went on to say that my good friend Jennifer had confessed to me that she thought she might have been responsible in some way for her husband's death by withholding the pills he needed to prevent him having a heart attack. I said that understandably, Jennifer felt very guilty about the whole thing. She was about to be married for the second time, and told me she planned to make a confession in church, in front of her wedding guests, and I told her I thought this was a bad idea. Indeed, I had advised her against saying anything at all about the part she might or might not have played in her husband's death, given that the matter seemed to be closed, and there did not seem to be much to be gained by opening it up again. I said looking back, I realised this was wrong of me, and I should have encouraged her to go to the police sooner, or gone to the police myself. Obviously, I understood that if her husband Frank had been able to take his medication, there would be every chance that he would still be alive today, and he would not have suffered the heart attack which killed him.

'Heart attack?' said the policeman.

'Yes,' I said. 'Frank died of a heart attack.'

The policeman hesitated. 'I don't think so,' he said. 'Your friend Jennifer's husband died of a pulmonary embolus. Nothing to do with a heart attack.'

'Nothing to do with his heart?'

'No, nothing. He had a clot on his lung. That's what killed him.'

'Oh,' I said. 'A clot on his lung? How marvellous! But that's wonderful!'

'I'm sorry?'

'I'm so pleased to hear that. That's such good news! '

'Well, hardly, Mrs Forth.'

'No. No, no of course not,' I said. 'That must have sounded terrible. No of course it's not good news.'

'Hardly anything to smile about.'

'No, no of course not.' I stopped smiling. 'Absolutely, nothing to smile about. No. Gosh. It's just, withholding the pills probably didn't make any difference in the end. To Frank.'

'No. Almost certainly not. He would have died anyway. Poor chap. So, you advised your friend not to divulge to anyone that she had withheld her husband's pills?'

'Well. I – yes. I did.'

'She didn't tell us that.'

'Oh.'

'She said she had confided in you, and you had both been upset by Frank's assumed heart attack, but she didn't give any details. She just said she had been slow in giving her husband the pills he needed for his heart, and he died of what she assumed to be a heart attack. We looked into this and the death certificate says cause of death was a 'pulmonary embolus', which is a different thing altogether, so the heart pills wouldn't have helped. We've had confirmation of the cause of death. There's no doubt about what killed him.'

'Oh. Right. I see.'

'Rather an unfortunate incident all round.'

'Yes. Sadly.'

'No-one covers themselves in glory.'

'No. Sorry.'

'Although you've been very honest.'

'Yes. Thanks. I have.'

'Actually Mrs Forth, we just had confirmation this morning that there had been no heart attack, but I thought I would still pop in just to clarify things for you. Because we know Jennifer confided in you, and she said she would be happy for us to speak to you.'

'Thank you. That's very kind.'

'Not a popular chap, Frank Spencer, by all accounts?'

'No. Poor Frank.'

'Poor Frank. Let's hope someone was genuinely sorry when he died. Well...' He stood up and lightly brushed some biscuit crumbs onto the carpet. 'I shan't keep you Mrs Forth. You'll have a lot to attend to, I expect.'

After he had gone I couldn't make up my mind whether the interview had gone well or not. I felt as if I had managed to escape from something, but then I had to walk home naked.

About an hour later Jennifer rang me.

'Sally, the police have been and guess what? Well, you probably know already, they said they would speak to you too. Turns out I had nothing to do with the way Frank died. He didn't have a heart attack! He had a pullman's bus or something. What a relief Sally. I'm in the clear. I wish I'd known that sooner. I'd have been married to Sam by now.'

'What on Earth made you think Frank had had a heart attack?'

'I just assumed. His heart stopped suddenly. I thought that was a heart attack. I didn't look at the death certificate, they gave it to me in an envelope and I don't know where my copy is now. I'm not very good with paperwork. I never open my electricity bills.'

'I thought you knew for a fact Frank had died of a heart attack?'

'Well I thought he had! You assume, don't you, that if the heart stops working, something must have attacked it.'

'But Jennifer, that would mean everyone dies of a heart attack. And they don't.'

'Well, let's not get too morbid. We can put all that behind us now. I'm going down to London to see Sam next week, did I tell you? He texted me directly in the end, and suggested a date. When I see him, I'll tell him I had nothing whatsoever to do with Frank's death. He died of something I haven't even heard of. Thank god.'

'Or thank Frank,' I said.

'Yes,' she said. 'Or thank Frank. I like him better now I know he died of some other thing. I don't think he died like that just to annoy me. I've been too hard on him.'

***

I've decided to go to history evening class tomorrow night. It seems silly to stay away because of what happened with Max on the Stratford trip. It feels immature, to just stop going. If I stop going, I'm acknowledging that something very serious happened in Stratford, and I want to feel the opposite. I want it to be so insignificant as to slip my mind. I'm hoping to forget all about it for now, before guilt impels me to tell Bill. Which it will, in the end.

And it's James I tomorrow. A whole new monarch to get our teeth into. I did some research on James this afternoon. James I was already King of Scotland when Elizabeth I named him as her successor. James suspected Elizabeth might favour him to succeed her on the English throne, which was why he didn't make too much fuss when Elizabeth executed his mother, Mary Queen of Scots. He was a thoughtful man, and he thought he wouldn't get too worked up about his mother's decapitation when his own head was in line for Elizabeth's crown. On hearing the news of his mother's execution he reflected that it was 'strange', but what's done is done, he couldn't plug her head back in, and although things might be a bit sticky for a while he should pipe down and take the long view. It doesn't sound as if James and his mother were particularly close.

Bill and I had the house to ourselves for a while tonight. Sophie was working a late shift, Dan and Chrissy were rehearsing for a performance of Uncle Vanya, Baz and Ivor were looking at Vespa scooters. Marra, as far as we could tell, was asleep.

'Well this is nice,' said Bill. 'The house is all ours. I can't remember the last time.'

'It's eerily quiet,' I said. 'No-one wants to know why the water isn't running hot, or where their phone is, or who ate all the mayonnaise. We go through about three jars of mayonnaise a week.'

'Just you and me,' said Bill. He glanced around the kitchen, 'Not even a stuffed fucking mole, or whatever. What's Baz doing at the moment? Taxidermy-wise? I never go into the utility room now.'

'I don't remember ever seeing you in the utility room. I'm surprised you know where it is.'

'I was in there just six months ago. It's off the kitchen I think. So what's Baz stuffing now?'

'A cat.'

'A cat? Oh shit.'

'Found it on the road at the top. Not a mark on it, apparently. Too good to miss.'

'Has he changed his business address?'

'Yes, officially he's doing all his taxidermy at work now.'

'Why doesn't he just do it at work? Why do any of it here?'

'To be honest, I think he just likes working here. I think he just likes chatting to us all about his plans. What to stuff. How to stuff it. That sort of stuff.'

'You know, if I have to resign, as I almost certainly will, we would have to sell this house.'

'No.'

'I think we would. We have over a million tied up in this house. We'll need to release some capital. It won't make any sense to live here, if I get the push. I'm not planning to stand for re-election after this. I'll stand down next time.'

'We can't sell this house Bill. People live here.'

'Yes, people live here. But without paying rent. If I have to go, or rather, when I go, I'd like to move away and start up again doing something else. We'd have money in the bank, we're just about young enough to start over. We always said we'd move out of the city eventually. I'm going to be finished in politics after this, Sally, and I can't expect to make a come-back. We won't be able to afford to live here, and it won't make any sense to hang on.'

'But we're a family here, Bill. A unit. We can't just turf them all out.'

'We should be encouraging them to move out and move on. It's not doing them any good to live here, economically. They're living in cloud-cuckoo-land here, really, aren't they? It's not viable. They're not making sensible plans for their future. They're just shelving those decisions because it's too easy here.

They're too comfortable. They're all just drifting. Honestly Sally, they need to get real and make some proper plans.'

'But, I really like having them around.'

'I know you do. I know. But we can't have them hanging around here just to keep us amused. You'll have to get them used to the idea that all this could come to an end. Will come to an end. Sooner rather than later, at this rate. We should be talking to them about their plans, and letting them know about our possible plans. We need to focus their minds a bit, so that they get the idea that they can't just hang around here forever, stuffing cats and drinking mayonnaise.'

We heard the front door open, then shut. Then we heard someone singing in that weird tuneless way people do when they are wearing headphones and can't hear the noise they're making. Sophie opened the kitchen door and saw us both at the table. She waved, and continued singing while she filled the kettle.

She switched the kettle on and turned around, and shouted above the noise in her ears, 'Do I sound like Adele?'

Before we could reply, Dan and Chrissy came in.

'Good rehearsal?' I asked them.

'Yeah,' said Dan. 'Scene three tonight. The one where I get to run on with a loaded gun and shoot someone.' He crouched down and shot from the hip. 'Bang!'

'Why?' said Sophie, pulling the plugs out of her ears. 'Why do you shoot them?'

'Because they want to sell the house we're living in. Me and Sonya. That's Chrissy, she plays Sonya. And we've got nowhere else to live.'

'Really?' I said. 'That's interesting.'

'So are you paying rent?' said Bill.

'Who?' said Dan. 'Is Vanya paying rent?'

'Yes. Is Vanya paying a market rent?'

'God Dad, I don't know. I think he's managing the estate, in return for living there.'

'So, he isn't paying any rent?'

'Well, I haven't asked to see his bank account.'

We heard another key in the lock. 'That's Ivor,' said Sophie.

Ivor appeared at the kitchen door. 'There's a weird lass at the front door calling herself Gentle Rain or something? Might have a screw loose? Ah told her just to hang about while I had a chat with youse.'

'Hi everyone,' said Gentle Rain, edging past Ivor. 'Hi. I'm so pleased to see you all.' She looked around. 'Everything looks just the same! I was so happy here. Listen, I've just fallen out with absolutely everybody I know. It's crazy! And I'm skint. And I don't know what to do. Can I stay here for a few days? I've got nowhere to go. If you don't mind, do you Dan?'

Dan was very casual, 'Why should I mind?' he said. 'I don't mind.'

'Thank you Dan. Thank you so much. You've no idea how good it is to see you all again. I'm desperate.'

'Eee petal,' said Ivor. 'That's reelly sad. But you've come to the right place here. These lot'll help you out. They look after everybody here.'

Gentle Rain looked up at him. 'Gosh,' she said, 'you're rather wonderful.' Then she turned to the rest of us. 'Everyone is wonderful here. This is such a wonderful place.'

'What?' said Bill. 'What's happening? What's going on here?'

'Hello, Gentle Rain,' I said. 'Or should we call you Victoria? Yes, of course we can put you up for a while. We have a spare room on the top floor. No problem. It's a small room, but it takes a single bed and a clothes rail.'

Victoria smiled at all of us. 'Perfect. That's so kind of you. I'm so grateful. You have no idea. Oh, and look! You have a gorgeous little bird!'

'Yes,' said Sophie. 'And if you're staying, you'll have to take your turn at emptying the dishwasher.'

'I don't mind, I'll empty it every time. Honestly, I don't want to make any demands on anybody here. I just want to hang out for a while until get my head together. I knew this would be the right place, and I love this little bird already.' She bent down to address Marra. 'Hello little bird. Aren't you just the sweetest thing? Look at your little feathery face! And your little beady black eyes! You're so fluffy and beaky and gorgeous, I love you to bits.' She stood up and looked at us all. 'It's so great to be back, honestly, you've no idea.'

'Well that's good isn't it? That's champion.' Ivor looked at Marra and back at Victoria. 'This here's me bord, Marra.'

'Fuck,' said Marra.

'He likes you,' said Ivor.

***

Gentle Rain had a long lie-in this morning. All the others had gone to work, and I was wondering whether to brave the BBC website when Jennifer rang me. She was at the Natural History Museum, waiting for Sam to turn up.

'You're early,' I said, you're not due to meet Sam until eleven.'

'I know, but I had to be out of the hotel, and there's no point in just wandering around.'

'You could have stayed here last night.'

'I know I could. Thanks Sally. But your place is so chaotic what with that crazy girl and the parrot and all those stuffed vermin. And there's so many people wanting the bathrooms in the morning and leaving hairs in the washbasins. I just wanted to be on my own to rehearse what I'm going to say to Sam, and spend three hours getting ready, and make sure I wasn't kept awake by carefree young people talking and, whatever, all night.'

'So, do you know what you're going to say? When Sam arrives?'

'Yes. I'm going to tell Sam that it's official now, I didn't kill my husband. I'll talk around it a bit, but that's the main thrust, obviously. And then I thought – and this is why I'm ringing really, to run this past you – then I thought I might propose to *him* this time, instead of waiting for him to re-propose to me. What do you think?'

I didn't know what I thought, but you can't just say nothing on the end of the phone. 'Well, that sounds interesting.'

'I've even got a ring.'

'For Sam?'

'Yes, obviously for Sam. I'm going to ask him to marry me and give him a ring. Not the same ring he would have had, obviously. I haven't got that one, and anyway, it's a bit cursed. A new ring.'

'Gosh.'

'Do you like the idea?'

'Well I like it, yes, of course.'

'The question is, will Sam like it?'

'Yes, that's the question. What can I say? Good luck. Give it your best shot.'

'I'm so nervous. And then I think, why? Why am I so nervous? After all, he wanted to marry me before he thought I'd murdered Frank. Once he knows I didn't murder Frank, what's to stop him wanting to marry me again? He can't be made of stone.'

I glanced at the kitchen clock. 'It's ten thirty,' I said. 'Good luck Jennifer. Ring me as soon as you can.'

'Just one more thing,' she said. 'If this goes well, obviously I'll be back with Sam and everything will be great. But if it doesn't, I don't think I could face just getting on the train straightaway. I'll need somewhere to hole up and cry and, you know, be really, really upset. I'll need some support. So can I come to yours for a while if I have to because this has all gone pear-shaped?'

'Oh.' God Almighty. 'Yes of course you can.'

'Thanks, Sally.'

'Listen, Jennifer,' I felt a sudden need to give her advice, 'before you go, don't push Sam too hard when you see him. Take things slowly. You might need to establish the old rapport before you go presenting him with that ring. He's going to need some time to come round. Don't rush at it headlong, he's more likely to back off if you do that.'

'Do you think?'

'I do, yes, definitely I do. If you go at this like a bull at a gate he'll take fright. Take it slowly. Just see if you can be friends again. Just have a nice time together first, before you start unveiling the wedding ring.'

'That wasn't how I was planning to play it.'

'Trust me Jennifer. If you corner him before he's ready you'll blow it.'

'I have to go. I need the loo. By the way, the Prime Minister and Foreign Secretary have both resigned.'

She rang off, and I might have uttered a cry of some sort. Whatever it was, it made Marra jump. After I had composed myself and prised Marra off the roof of his cage, I noticed there was a message from Bill on my phone. *'PM and FS both gone. Everything in flux here. Meetings all morning. Be prepared. Visiting eco-friendly housing estate this afternoon in Nether-Something-Thwaite. Can't remember where it is exactly but sounds northern. Late home. Xx'*

I left a key on the kitchen table and a note for Victoria, then I got my coat and bag, and went out to get in the car and drive up to school to see Lee.

***

Deborah in the main office at school told me that Lee was having a bad week. He hated everybody and everything, patience on the school's side was wafer-thin and goodwill was running out. There was talk of sending Lee to a neighbouring school to give him a fresh start somewhere else, and in that case obviously my mentoring role would come to an end. Deborah said she expected I would be heartbroken, and she asked how I would survive without seeing Lee again. I said I thought I would probably get over it in time, just about. We had a little chuckle, but then I picked up my lanyard and went off down the corridor to find Lee, and see what I could do to avert this disaster.

He was in truculent mood. I couldn't even persuade him to sit down at first.

'So, Lee, I gather you haven't had a good week?' I said.

'I ain't going to be a solicitor no more.'

'Oh, what made you change your mind?'

''Cos it was a fucking stupid idea in the first place.'

'So are you thinking about being a joiner, like your dad?'

'No, I'm thinking about being a politician, like your Bill.'

'Right.'

'Anyone can be a politician. You don't need qualifications. You just need people that'll vote for you. And you need to make arguments. I can make arguments. I made one this morning with Miss Simms. She wants me to come back and do art so I said I wasn't fucking going to do it and she couldn't make me.'

'That's not an argument Lee,' I said. 'If you're going to make an argument you have to give a reason for not doing art, and then you support that reason with a sensible argument.'

'Right. So I'm not doing it because it's crap and I fucking hate it.'

'I'm looking at your report card for this week Lee. It's pretty bad.'

He glanced at the card. 'It's a load of bollocks anyway.'

'Sit down Lee, and let's have a chat.' He sat down facing me astride a chair, Christine Keeler style.

'You know we don't have a Prime Minister at the moment?' he said.

'Yes, I knew that.'

'On account of she was fucking the Foreign Secretary?'

'According to some of the papers, yes.'

'According to your Bill.'

'So what's your point, Lee?'

'Well, there's a job for Bill. Innit?'

I laughed. 'I think you might be getting a bit carried away with this whole politics thing, Lee.'

'Why not? Why not Bill? And if Bill's Prime Minister, that's good for me.'

'How is that good for you?'

'Because if he's Prime Minister, he'll be able to help me get on. Dad says.'

'Lee, if you want to be a politician, you'll have to learn how to get on with people yourself. You have to able to make people like you, otherwise they won't vote for you. You can't just go around telling people to eff-off if you disagree about something. That's not going to persuade anyone to vote for you. Miss Simms won't vote for you if you talk to her like you did this morning.'

Lee registered this unpalatable fact. 'That's a bit shite,' he said. 'Everybody hates me.'

'Well we should work on that, and see if we can turn that around.'

'People just hate me. You can't do nothing about that. Miss Simms hates me.'

'She doesn't hate you, but she could like you more. Why don't you, this week, practise your social skills? You could start by smiling at people, instead of scowling at them in disgust as if they'd just eaten your pet hamster. See if you can start getting on with Miss Simms, so that when the time comes, she's more likely to vote for you.'

'But she's a moron.'

'She's a voter. That's what you have to remember.'

'Fuck it. I might just be a joiner.'

***

I texted Bill after I got home. I said, '*Thinking of going to history evening class. Won't go if you are likely to be home with news before ten. What's happening?*'

He texted back, '*No news yet. Have spent day in Muckle Wattle Bottom. It's beautiful up here. Stunning. Fantastic place. Amazing. I love it. You'd love it. See you after history.*'

So I went to the history class. I gave Judith a lift. When I left, there was a little crisis unfolding in our kitchen. Chrissy was advising Sophie on what to wear tomorrow for her interview. She suggested a plain black skirt and a white blouse. Sophie was disappointed, she had wanted to dress up. Chrissy managed to persuade her that a white blouse would be the best option, it would suggest purity and commitment and willingness to work hard. Sophie brought her white blouse downstairs to iron in readiness, and it turned out to be see-through. As I walked out, there was a lively debate in progress about the wisdom or otherwise of wearing see-through clothing at interviews. Ivor thought a nice little see-through number would be guaranteed to get Sophie the job, it would suggest fun, and romps, and willingness to compromise. Chrissy disagreed. I managed to get out before my opinion was required.

All the way up in the car to the history class Judith was speculating on Bill's political future. She said she thought Bill was very plausible when he was interviewed on TV, but he would have to resign because thanks to me, everyone now knows he knew about the whole parsnip carry-on between the PM and the FS, and he hadn't said anything. Although, she continued, Bill had said something confidentially to me of course, but that had backfired spectacularly when I had thought confidentially meant I could write to his mother and tell her all about it. Then she said she thought that the whole lot of them would have to resign, and there would have to be a general election. Obviously though, she said, they would have to appoint another leader to take them into the election so that they could get the good thrashing they deserved from the electorate. But the leader would have to be an expendable idiot, because of course they would lose big-time and the leader would have to go soon afterwards. She said fortunately that wouldn't be a problem, because there were plenty of expendable idiots to choose from in my husband's party. She said she hoped I wasn't taking any of this personally, but there was no point in beating about the bush. If you live by the sword, you expect to die by the sword, and that was just that. She said the final straw for her had been when the PM had tried to claim that her relationship with the FS had never been any sort of distraction from affairs of state, and she would have sacked him in less time than it takes to peel a parsnip if she'd needed to. Judith asked me what kind of idiot you would have to be to believe that? She said if you could believe that, you could be persuaded to insulate your house with Edam cheese. Then she said it must all be very distressing for me and she hoped I was holding up.

I said I was managing. Thanks for asking.

So I was more than ready to think about James I when I got to the history class. I wanted to step back a few centuries for a rest. Everyone in the group looked at me anxiously when I walked in, as if I had a smoking fuse sticking out of my jumper at the back. Arthur put his hand on my arm and told me not to worry, it would soon be over. Margaret said she thought I might come along tonight, and that's why she had made us all a tray bake of rocky road. It wasn't until Terry started telling us about James I that I was able to relax. James I's little skirmish with the Gunpowder Plot felt to me like a storm in a very small goblet. There was no reason why James should have felt particularly anxious about that plot. He couldn't have wished for a less competent gang of plotters against him. And as for Guy Fawkes and his fellow conspirators, any revolutionary who gives himself the alias of John Johnson and lights a fire to dry out a stash of damp gunpowder deserves to have his plot foiled.

I didn't go to The Executioner's for a drink after the class. But I did have a brief word with Max while Judith was in the loo when the class was over.

He edged over to me when he saw that Judith had left me unmarked, and said, 'Good to see you Sally. Really good to see you, I thought you might not come back to the group. Are you coming along to the pub for a drink?'

I said, 'Good to see you too, Max. I don't think I'll go to the pub tonight. I'm driving Judith, and I'd better get home. Maybe next time.'

'Of course. Yes of course. Must be difficult for you, for you both, for you and Bill, at the moment. I hope everything's okay, at home? With you and Bill? After what happened in...? You know. What happened in Stratford. Well. Poor bloke, he's got enough on his plate, I wouldn't like to think, you know, that I, that we—'

'I haven't said anything.'

'Oh good. Oh that's good. Best way I think. Don't want to, you know, upset things, for no good reason.'

'But I think I will have to say something. Soonish. Not now obviously. I just don't feel comfortable about not being completely honest about what happened.'

'Oh. Oh I see. That's a shame. Of course, that's just my view, and I'm not entitled to have any sort of view. It's up to you. Of course it is. Your call, entirely. Has to be. But... ' and then he came to an unhappy halt.

The toilet door swung open and there was Judith. 'Right,' she said. 'Ready when you are.'

***

It was nine thirty when I got home. I was looking forward to a cup of tea. I pushed my key in the lock, and as soon as the door opened I felt that the house was not at ease. I caught a whiff of something and I thought it was adrenalin.

I could hear muffled, emotionally-charged sounds from the kitchen. Sophie was coming towards me down the hallway saying, 'Oh great, you're home, thank god!', which was not relaxing. Marra was shouting 'Fuck! Fuck! Fuck!' in the way he does when he senses heightened emotion, and Dan appeared at the bottom of the stairs twirling his finger around next to his temple to indicate that someone had lost their mind.

Jennifer sat at the kitchen table with an almost empty glass of wine and a box of hankies in front of her. Ivor sat opposite her and they were holding hands across the table.

'Ah! Look petal,' said Ivor, 'here's your pal Sally. Tell her all about it, pet, and you'll feel better. I'll pour youse both a glass of wine. I'd have some myself, but this is shit stuff you're drinking, if you don't mind me saying.'

He stood up to get another wine glass, and I sat down.

'Sally.' Jennifer was very distressed. She had wads of paper hankies balled up in her fists and smudges of mascara everywhere but on her eyes. 'It was a disaster. Everything's gone tits-up with Sam. I can't believe it. I've spent all day trying to reason with him. He says he doesn't want to marry me. It's some sort of scruple he has about me and those stupid fucking pills I'm sick of thinking about. He doesn't care that I didn't actually kill Frank.' She blew her nose. 'Can you believe it? What the hell is his problem? Did he ever love me, Sally?'

'Er, sorry to interrupt,' said Sophie. 'But I think I'll go to bed now if you don't mind. I've got a really important interview tomorrow, and Chrissy says I need an early night. Chrissy's my interview coach.'

Jennifer looked at Sophie and then at me and said, 'Sorry? What the fuck? What's this?'

'That's fine Sophie,' I said. 'An early night is a good idea. See you in the morning.'

'Yeah,' said Sophie. 'And if it's okay, could you just, you know, keep the noise down? My room's just above here, and I can hear Marra clear as a bell when he gets going. In fact I can hear his actual bell, when he starts bashing it.'

'My heart is breaking here!' Jennifer was wailing now. 'Are you asking me to break it quietly?'

'Er, that would be good,' said Sophie. 'It's just, you know, with this interview... Anyway, see you in the morning! Wish me luck!'

'Good luck Sophie!' said Ivor.

'There's something the matter with that girl,' said Jen, after Sophie left the kitchen. 'Can't she see how upset I am? Keep the noise down? Did she really say that? I have to howl with pain until I feel as if I can bear this!'

'Oh shit,' said Marra, which saved me the bother.

'Mind,' said Ivor, who had managed to find himself a more acceptable glass of wine and sat down alongside Jen, 'there's always plenty more fish in the sea. A bonny lass like you shouldn't have much problem getting another fella. Why no.'

Jennifer turned to look at Ivor. 'Ivor, you're very nice. In fact,' she looked more closely, 'you're gorgeous. But the trouble is, you're so young. You're all so young here. That's the trouble. Your faces are too smooth, there's nothing written on them. You're walking round like blank pages. You're too young to understand anything. Or, to have any experience worth having. You're this far from being children. You're next door to being babies. Ivor, I was older than you when you were an embryo. I can't take someone that young seriously. Just wait, in another ten years you'll know what I'm talking about. How old are you now?'

'Twenty-one.'

'Twenty-one? Twenty-one! Oh shit.' She put her head in her hands. 'That's ridiculous.'

We heard the front door opening, and a light step in the hall. Victoria came into the kitchen with a halo of flowers in her hair. 'Hello everyone! I've had a wonderful day just walking and walking and greeting people and giving them flowers. It's been so cleansing and healing, I feel much, much happier than last night. And it was wonderful knowing I had all of you to come back to!'

'Well that's champion.' Ivor smiled at her with frank delight. 'Givin' folks flowers. That's just champion.' He turned to us and said, 'Isn't it?'

'Oh, shine a fucking light,' said Jen. 'I'm going to bed.'

I took her upstairs, and found her a room, and made up a bed and gave her a towel and told her to wait until nine in the morning before she tried to have a shower. We sat down on the bed together while she finished her wine.

'Sally,' she said, 'you were right – this honesty thing – it's a load of bollocks. It's ruined my life, I should have kept quiet. What was I thinking? What did I do it for? It was an indulgence. You were absolutely right. Just an indulgence. And it's cost me everything. It's too late for me to start again. I'm not twenty-one, I'm fifty-fucking-fifty. I'm not admitting to anything more than that, Sally. That's it as far as I'm concerned for the next ten years.' She waved her glass in my direction, 'Promise me you'll never confess to anything if you don't have to. Not your age, or who you might have murdered, or who you've slept with or what creams you're using and what you're using them for, just keep quiet about the lot. To hell with integrity. Believe me, it stinks. God, I hope the Flower Fairy and Little Miss Can-You-Keep-the-Noise-Down-Please are gone in the morning when I get up. I don't want to see a face under fifty for at least a week. I hate young people. They're so – new.'

I waited until she had stopped raging against fate and honesty and youth, and had calmed down enough to contemplate getting into bed. She was very tired. She'd been up since five thirty treating her hair with a deep nourishing conditioning masque to enhance shine, and applying make-up to her face which promised to fill tiny wrinkles in her skin and improve its elasticity. It had obviously worked because now she was able to stretch her face into any number of anguished grimaces, one after the other. I lent her a nightie and left her brushing her teeth, and said I would see her in the morning.

Everyone was in bed when Bill got home, including me. When he got into bed he said he'd had a fantastic afternoon looking at an eco-friendly housing estate in Cumbria. He said it had been wonderful to think about nothing else all afternoon but how to stuff cavity walls with sheep's wool, and grow vegetables on the roof, and re-cycle shit. He told me that these houses had triple-glazed windows which meant you could see three times as far when you looked out of them. They had solar panels on the roof which give you an all-over tan while you lie in the bath. The heating was powered by something called a heat pump, which was very energy efficient and fuelled by farts. He said the plumbing was very advanced. The toilets generate electricity with every flush and give you a bolt up the backside to stop you getting constipated. Householders would not need to own or run cars, because they would each be fitted with their own personal windmill helmet, enabling them to fly about like bumble bees and generate honey to feed directly into the National Grid.

Obviously I was half asleep so I may have got some of the detail wrong, but Bill's enthusiasm for the project was unmistakable. He said when he has to resign, or he gets the sack, we could relocate to the beautiful north and he would move into energy conservation and get some use out of his chemistry degree.

'Not chemistry, Bill. Your degree's the other one,' I said. 'Begins with an 'f'.'

'God yes,' he said. 'Physics.'

***

I was up at seven, to wish Sophie good luck for her interview, and check that she wasn't going out wearing a transparent blouse. Chrissy was already up making Sophie coffee and running through a few last-minute pointers.

'Now then Sophie,' she said, 'you should have a light breakfast. I'll make you a slice of toast, and you can have some jam to give your brain some sugar, and we'll just run over the replies we've practised to one or two of those potentially tricky questions.'

'Right,' said Sophie, who was now a zealous convert to the notion of interview training.

'If they ask you, *Why do you want this job Sophie*? What will you say?'

'I'll say because I'm committed to working in the care sector and it is the next step on the career progression ladder and I want to extend my skills set and meet new challenges.'

'Brilliant! And what will you say if they ask you how you dealt with a conflict in the workplace, and what skills you used to resolve it?'

'I'd say I helped to resolve a conflict over a work rota by writing out a new one that everybody said was amazing.'

'Great. And if they ask you if you can work under pressure in small spaces?'

'I'll say I love working under pressure in small spaces.'

'Excellent! Now, show me how you'll sit when you're being interviewed.'

Sophie turned her chair to face Chrissy and sat with her knees together, legs demurely crossed at the ankles, her hands folded and resting in her lap.

Chrissy smiled. 'Well done! Well done Sophie! You're ready I reckon. Just remember, keep calm, take deep breaths, don't be in a big rush to answer questions, take some time to think about your answers if you need to. I wish I could go in there with you. Let me know how it's gone as soon as you get out. Do you know where you are in the batting order?'

'What do you mean?'

'Well, are you in first? Or do you have to wait until last after all the others have gone in?'

'What others?'

'The others being interviewed.'

'Oh, there's just me. I'm the only one in for it. So I'll be first and last, I suppose.'

Chrissy stared at her. 'What?'

'Yes, there's just me. Nobody else wants the job. That's why I wasn't sure I needed the interview training at first. But I think it's been really useful. I'm bound to get the job now.'

'But—' said Chrissy.

'Anyway,' said Sophie, 'I have to go. Don't want to be late. See you later!' She crossed both fingers, and turned around on the spot. 'I've turned around for luck. Not that I'll need it with all the training I've had.' She picked up her bag. 'Bye!' And she left.

After the front door closed behind her, Chrissy said, 'Well, that was a waste of time. Did you know she was the only one in for it?'

I said no, I didn't, and because Chrissy seemed deflated, we had a chat. I managed to persuade her that her efforts hadn't been a waste of time, because even though we now knew the job was Sophie's from the beginning, Chrissy had discovered in herself a life-skills coaching ability which she probably didn't even know she had, and this might open up some opportunities for her in the future. Chrissy was mollified, and I was quite pleased too, knowing that when the occasion demands, I can still do a bit of bullshitting.

Got a strange phone call from school after Chrissy left, asking me if I can shed any light on Lee's behaviour. Deborah from the office said she is logging a lot of complaints from staff about Lee smirking and leering most unpleasantly at them, and did I have any idea what might be causing this latest horror?

I remembered my suggestion that Lee try to address the fact that people didn't seem to like him.

'Smirking?' I said. 'Deborah, he's not smiling, is he? Are you sure he's not smiling?'

'Smiling?' she said. 'God, I hope not. He's seriously unnerving some of the younger members of staff here. I hope he's not smiling. That would be pretty tragic.'

'I think he's smiling, Deborah. In fact, I'm sure he's smiling. Can you explain to people that actually Lee is simply smiling, because he wants people to like him better?'

'Sheesh,' said Deborah. 'That's a tough call. He's got people making the sign of the cross when they pass him in the corridor. I haven't seen this expression for myself, but I gather it's the stuff of nightmares.'

'He's just a kid, Deborah.'

'I know that. I understand that. But I'm picking up the pieces here, Sally. I had to make a cup of tea for the new English teacher in here yesterday and give her ten minutes counselling. Admittedly she's very new to teaching and she's still coming to terms with the fact that she hates the job, but then Lee smiled at her outside the office and she had some sort of collapse.'

'Right. That does sound serious.'

'It is serious. So if you could pop in sometime soonish?'

***

Jennifer came downstairs at ten. She looked around the kitchen sheepishly to see who else was at home, and was apologetic about last night. She said she hoped she hadn't upset anybody.

I told her everyone was at work, including Bill, who wasn't entirely sure whether he still has any work.

She said she would apologise to Sophie and Victoria when she saw them later, she hadn't meant to be rude, she was just so annoyed with them for being thirty years younger than her.

I said I was sure they wouldn't have taken any offence, they knew she was upset and they would have made allowances.

Jennifer said she hoped I was right. They were all good kids really and it wasn't fair of her to dislike them because they're all under twenty-five years old.

So to cheer Jennifer up, I said they were all good kids, she was right. And they were very young. However, in their favour, they were getting older all the time.

She said that made her feel better.

After her breakfast, Jennifer wondered if we should arrange to meet up with Judith at lunchtime this afternoon. She said it was years since she'd seen Judith, and it might make for a relaxing couple of hours. She wondered whether Judith might be able to cheer us up a bit.

I said expecting lunch with Judith to cheer you up a bit was like expecting to enjoy sharing a bath with a pit bull terrier. So we decided to go out for lunch just ourselves, and this gave Jennifer the opportunity to dissect her conversation with Sam the day before forensically, until she had exhausted every possible nuance, and even she grew tired of it. Then, fortified by hours of pointless speculation, she felt stronger and went off to shop for some retail therapy, and I went up to school, hoping to have a chat with Lee.

***

Deborah in the office was pleased to see me. 'Glad you could make it,' she said. 'He's in the library at the moment, he's due to serve a twenty-minute after-school detention for,' she squinted at the handwriting in the Staff Detentions Book, '*grimacing in a menacing fashion*, it looks like. I told him I thought you might pop in to see him.'

I made myself a quick coffee in the office and carried it across the yard to the library. I spotted Lee sitting on a table by himself snapping pencils. 'Lee,' I said, sitting down beside him, 'how're you doing? I hear you've been smiling at people?'

'Yeah,' he said. 'Like you said. To make people like me. Smiled at a whole bunch of people yesterday. And today. Made my face ache. Not used to smiling.'

'Lee, I'm worried you might be over-doing it. Wearing yourself out.'

'Wearing myself out smiling?'

'I think so. Like you say, you aren't used to it. You might have to build up to it gradually.'

'I might stop for a bit,' he said. 'People aren't smiling back anyway. Woman yesterday looked scared and fell over.'

'Really? That's odd. Just show me a smile, Lee, so I can see how you're doing it.'

He smiled.

'Right,' I said. 'Right. You can stop now, Lee. That's enough."

'You've spilt your coffee on my book.'

'Sorry. Sorry about that, Lee.'

'Right. I'm not smiling no more for a bit. Gotta rest.'

'I think so Lee. I think that's best. You have an intense smile. It must be tiring. Give yourself a rest for a while and just try to look relaxed, as if you don't hate people.'

'But I do hate people. I'm only smiling 'cos I want them to vote for me.'

'Try to relax, Lee. Give yourself a break. You've exhausted yourself smiling at people you hate. It must be very wearing. Can't you try to like people a bit more? It would be less of an effort then to smile at them. Less of a strain.'

'I can't like my teachers. I'd be a wuss.'

'You like me, don't you?'

He looked at me. 'Piss off,' he said.

'Okay, I'm going. I only popped in for five minutes.'

'See you next week,' he said.

'I won't see you next week, Lee. We break up next week. I won't see you until September.'

'Oh yeah.'

'Will you miss me?'

'Fuck, Miss,' he said. 'Piss off.' And then he smiled, very nicely.

***

Bill was at home when Jennifer and I arrived back within five minutes of each other. He said he was waiting for a phone call, and he wanted to be at home when it came. He looked oddly out of place, standing at the kitchen bench in a shirt and tie, not knowing quite what to do. Usually Bill always knows exactly what he has to do next. He never has nothing to do. His life is full and directed and purposeful. He isn't used to having nothing to do but wait for a phone call. Myself, I'd look entirely at home doing nothing but waiting for a phone call, it's my natural habitat, but Bill looked uneasy and uncomfortable.

By mutual unspoken agreement, Jennifer and I decided to galvanise Bill into some sort of activity. I think it must be an instinctive trait among women to want to give a job to any man who is standing around at a loose end. We want to occupy them with a task of our own choosing, rather than wait until they decide for themselves what they want to do. Jennifer suggested Bill put the kettle on, I suggested he might like to take his tie off and sit down, and tell us what this phone call he was waiting for was all about. But Bill said he'd rather not talk about work if we didn't mind, he'd been talking about it endlessly until he was deafened by the sound of hind legs falling off donkeys. He said he'd just like to do something mundane and useful, and listen to us chat.

I suggested he got changed and cleaned out Marra's cage, and he said that was a good idea, and he went upstairs to get out of his suit.

While Bill was upstairs Jennifer looked at me and shook her head and gave me a thumbs down. 'I think he's for the push, don't you? That must be the phone call he's waiting for.'

I shrugged. 'Looks like it. Poor Bill.'

But he was more cheerful when he came downstairs, the prospect of a job seemed to have energised him. 'Right then, Marra,' he said, rolling up his sleeves, 'let's be having you.' He manoeuvred Marra out of his cage and sat him on the back of one of the kitchen chairs, and then he spread the floor with newspaper, and set the cage down on that. Jen sat down at the table and said she had some texts to reply to. I stood at the table and started to assemble the ingredients for a hotpot I was making for dinner. Marra sat on the chair next to me, comfortably rearranging his feathers and watching me work.

We spent a pleasantly desultory forty minutes or so. Marra fell asleep on the back of the chair. Jennifer answered her texts and sent more. I prepared the hotpot and put it in the oven. Bill found a set of keys among the detritus at the bottom of the bird cage. He was cleaning it so thoroughly I wasn't sure Marra would recognise it as his home when he was put back into it. I didn't realise it was possible to disassemble his cage into so many component parts.

And then one by one, Chrissy, Dan, and Baz came in, followed by Ivor and Victoria, who had been out somewhere together and came in holding hands. They were surprised to see Bill sitting on the floor cleaning Marra's cage. Dan wanted to know if he had been sent home to spend more time with his parrot, and Bill said yes, he had.

We were all in the kitchen when Sophie arrived.

'So!' said Chrissy. 'How did the interview go?'

'Well. I didn't get the job.'

'What! You didn't get the job?'

'No. I didn't get it.'

'Fuck!' said Marra.

'Why?' said Chrissy, 'You were the only one in for it. Why didn't they give you the job, for Christ's sake?'

'Well it might have been my answer to one of the questions.'

'Which question?'

'Something about, what would I do if I went into someone's room at night and they had died. I don't think I got that one right. They said I needed more training.'

Dan was intrigued. 'What did you say you would do if you went into someone's room in the night and they had died?'

'I said I would just close the door and wait until morning, because everything seems better in the morning.'

Victoria nodded seriously as if she was considering this response.

Dan said, 'Sophie, how could that be any better in the morning? The dead person wouldn't be any less dead in the morning. They might even be more dead.'

'I think what Sophie means,' said Jennifer, 'is that if they were discovered to be dead at, say, midnight, they would be just as beyond help as they'd be if they weren't discovered until seven in the morning. Either way, there would be nothing you could do to help them, whether you find them at midnight or seven a.m. Although,' she hesitated and her voice wavered a little when she continued, 'I'm probably not the best person to have an opinion on this kind of thing. Considering my recent difficulties. Sorry Sophie, I shouldn't have put my oar in.'

'That's all right Jen,' said Sophie. 'When they asked me about it I didn't know what else to say. I just thought, most things seem better in the morning. I gave a truthful answer.'

Dan looked across at Chrissy. 'Didn't you tell her not to give any truthful answers? You never give truthful answers in job interviews, Soph.'

'And how would you know that?' said Bill. 'Have you had any job interviews?'

'Yeah I have,' said Dan. 'I had an interview for this gardening job, didn't I Baz? Baz was there. They asked me if I could shovel shit, and I said yes, and I got the job.'

'Well, that was telling the truth,' said Sophie.

'Look,' said Bill, standing up and brushing seed husks off his trousers, 'we need to have a truthful discussion now. All of us. Let's sit down.'

'Do you want me to go out?' said Jennifer. 'Is this a private round-table discussion? I can go out if you like?'

'Don't be daft,' I said.

We all shuffled around the table to make room for those still standing. We were short of a chair so Victoria sat on Ivor's knee.

Bill crossed his arms and leant on the table, looking around at us all. 'Guys, it can't have escaped your notice that my political career is coming to an end. Probably tonight. I'm waiting for a call, expecting to hear that I'm going to lose my ministerial position. There's going to be a general election very soon, and I'm not planning to stand for re-election. So I'll be looking for another job.'

'Chrissy's really good with interview training,' said Sophie. 'She'll teach you how to sit and everything.'

'That's good to know,' said Bill, 'thanks Sophie. And Chrissy. Anyway, the thing is, if I find myself out of a job – and I'm sure I will – Sally and I will have to consider selling this house.'

There was absolute silence. Then after a few long seconds we heard a splat. Marra had done a nervous poo. It fell to the floor and landed on a piece of newspaper.

'Sell this house?' said Sophie. 'Oh no. That would be terrible. But maybe it's one of these things that you worry about and it never happens?'

'I'm sorry guys, but I think it's very likely to happen. Almost certain. I'm afraid you would have to move out. We would all have to move out, and go our separate ways.'

'Shit,' said Baz. 'That's really bad news.'

Ivor shook his head, 'That's reely sad.'

'I can't believe it,' said Chrissy, 'I thought this would go on for ever.'

'I've only just found you all again,' said Victoria.

'Dad, are you being a bit pessimistic?' said Dan.

'Unfortunately not. I'm afraid my political career is pretty much over.'

'Some people were standing around outside the front door when I came in,' said Sophie. 'I meant to tell you, but we started talking about the job interview. They had microphones and stuff. I spoke to them when I came in. I've done the wrong thing again, haven't I?'

'Don't worry about it, Sophie, I don't think it matters any more,' said Bill. 'I'll go out and talk to them later. When I have something to tell them.'

Dan took out his phone. 'I bet you'll be on the box again, Soph.'

'Not again!' she said, weary of celebrity. 'Not again, surely. Why is everyone so interested in what I say? Honestly I don't care about being famous now, I'm sick of it. I just want to stay here like an ordinary person.'

'Shit,' said Dan. 'Here you are! Look at this,' he turned his phone around and we all watched Sophie, on our doorstep, just half an hour ago.

'Sophie! It's Sophie. Can we have a quick word?'

'I didn't get the job.'

'Oh? Well er, sorry to hear that Sophie. But actually, we were wondering what you thought of the problems Bill Forth is having at the moment. It's not looking good for him and his job this evening.'

'It's not my fault, is it?'

'Sorry? No, no. Nobody thinks it's your fault.'

'Because I shouldn't have said all those things last time, when I rang up the radio programme. You know, about people having nits. I felt really bad afterwards.'

'Did Bill Forth tell you you'd done the wrong thing?'

'No, no. He said don't worry about it Sophie, it's just politics. He said I should just say what I wanted to say. And he said if people have nits, it's up to them.'

'Would you be upset if he lost his job, Sophie?'

'With the houses? Yes I'd be really upset. If I thought it was my fault I might have to move out. But I don't know where I'd go now.'

'Would they want you to move out, the Forths?'

> *'No, no. They wouldn't want me to move out. They'd want me to stay. They'd say don't be daft Sophie you have to stay, we love you Sophie and we want you to stay. And that kind of thing. They'd try and persuade me to stay. And I'd stay because, you know, they need me. Anyway, if I didn't stay I'd have to give up my job.'*
>
> *'Oh yes. Where is it you work again, Sophie?'*
>
> *'In a nursing home. Merry Dale. I'm not bothered really about not getting that promotion. I really like the job I've got now, even if someone does die in the night. It's a good job. We play Bingo on Tuesdays. Anyway, I'll have to go in now. They'll be waiting to hear about my interview. And Baz is stuffing a cat. So,' she rolled her eyes, 'I'll have to tell him he's done a really good job. Don't want him going in a huff. Bye!'*

We took a few seconds to consider what Sophie had said, and to reconcile her faith in our love for her, and our need for her to live with us, with the fact that we had just given her notice.

Baz was first to speak 'Don't you like that cat I stuffed, Soph?' he asked her.

'No, I *do* like it,' said Sophie. 'It's really good. It looked great the last time I saw it. Much better than when you first brought it in.'

'I don't think I've seen the cat,' said Bill, ignoring the elephant in the room in favour of something smaller, 'where is it?'

'I'll get it.' Baz got up and went into the utility room, and brought out the cat, and put it down on the kitchen table. The cat was curled up comfortably with its head on its paws and its eyes closed. It looked very peaceful, and quite beautiful, but still, I made a mental note to scrub the table with bleach before we ate off it again.

Sophie explained, 'It didn't look like that when Baz first got it, after it was knocked down by the car. It looked more, how would you describe it Baz? It looked more spread out.'

'Does it have a message, this cat?' said Chrissy. 'Like the other stuff?'

But if it did have a message, we didn't hear what the message was, because Bill's phone rang. He got up and went into the living room to answer it. We heard him talking, but not what he was saying.

'Oh dear,' said Jennifer, 'sorry guys, but I don't think this is going to be good news.'

Sophie had her hands over her face, and Victoria started to stroke the cat.

Dan looked at Baz and asked him, 'Where will you go?'

'Dunno,' he said. He looked at Sophie. 'Maybe I could make a tree house and we could live in it Soph? Is there a law against that?'

'I don't think I'd want to live up a tree, Baz,' said Sophie. 'Not really.'

'I'll go back home, I suppose,' said Chrissy. 'You could stay at mine for a while, Dan.'

'Where will you and Bill go?' said Jennifer. 'When you sell up here?'

'We haven't decided yet, beyond a plan to down-size. Bill has a few ideas, he'd like to live further north,' I said.

'I'll have to go back to the north-east, me,' said Ivor. 'Don't get me wrong, the Toon's a great place. But I was loving it down here.'

'I don't know where I'll go,' said Victoria. 'I really don't. Maybe I'll go to the Toon.' She frowned gently. 'What is the Toon?' she said.

'It's Newcastle, pet. Newcastle's the best place to be if you can't be in London,' said Ivor. 'You'll need your coat, mind.'

'Do they like flowers in Newcastle, Ivor?'

'They love flowers in the Toon. If you start handing out flowers on the Quayside at weekends, they'll eat the lot.'

Bill came back and stood in the kitchen doorway. 'Change of plan,' he said. 'Looks like I'm the idiot who is going to lead the party to certain defeat in a general election. One of the perks of being expendable. And apparently, I'm popular among young people under twenty-five, and nobody else is popular with anybody. So, er, thanks Sophie.'

'Does that mean we're staying?' said Sophie.

'For a while. Until we get thrashed and they spend however long stabbing each other in the back over who'll replace me.'

'But you might win!' said Sophie.

'Oh yes,' said Bill, remembering how easily he could be quoted. 'So I might.'

He went to the front door to speak to the gathering out there. In the kitchen there was Prosecco and peanuts on the table before I had a chance to do anything with bleach. The cat slept on, unmoved, undisturbed by the sound of popping corks, and cries of 'Shit! That was close!'

Sophie couldn't resist making another appearance in front of the camera, and went out to speak to her public after Bill had come back inside.

We heard her being asked, 'Happy now, Sophie?'

'Yes,' she said.

'Do you think Mr Forth can win this election?'

'Yes, he'll win. He'll definitely win. He won't lose, or my name isn't Jack Robinson.'

***

Dear Ella,

I agree, it is odd the way Sophie keeps popping up on the radio and on television. We are almost used to it now. There does seem to be an appetite for her 'take' on things. Apparently, people don't always want the analysis of experts. Sometimes they just want to hear the thoughts of someone who is plainly bonkers.

Like you, I was puzzled by her affirmation that Bill wouldn't lose this election or her name wasn't Jack Robinson. I tried to work it out in bed last night, and failed. I think it means Jack Robinson will be our next Prime Minister. Anyway, Bill says he is certain to lose, and Jack Robinson agrees with him.

So yes, we're still here. Although probably not for that long. We are afloat, but there are rocks on the horizon. There was a general sense of celebration after the news last night. It's just a reprieve, but we have longer than we thought to prepare for the crunch.

To answer your question – no, it was never a goal of mine to run a hostel for disadvantaged young people, and anyway, I can't agree that they are at all disadvantaged. They're actually very talented. I've been trying to think of some way of combining their talents into one winning enterprise. Something that would provide a service people would pay for, and allow us all to stay together here. For anyone who has just lost their job, their house, their much-loved pet, their self-esteem, their sense of direction and their libido, we would be a one-stop shop. Chrissy would get them another job, Dan would build them a house, Baz would give their much loved pet new life, Victoria would make them feel appreciated, Sophie would give them something to care about, and Ivor would get their mojo back.

They are all very talented, and should all be successful. They want to put down roots here but the soil can't anchor them and is poorer for it. It's not looking too good at the moment, but Laura rang last night, to say she has an idea which she wants to discuss with us all. Apparently it's a winner, it just needs a bit of cash behind it to get it started. She's coming over tomorrow while little Harry is at Mini Mumblers.

I'm going to bed early tonight and will try that herbal sleeping remedy you recommended.

With love as always,

Sally Xx

Acknowledgements

Thank you so much again Kevin and Hetha Duffy at Bluemoose Books, for having the courage of my convictions.

Very many thanks to Lin Webb, who edited this book with a twinkle in her eye and a firm hand on the tiller. I could not wish for a more gimlet-eyed, sensitive and sympathetic editor.

And thank you again Lulu Allison, for another great cover design, I love it!

Many thanks to Cathy Rentzenbrink, for her warm and generous response to this book. Cathy's encouraging feedback is invaluable, and I love her cat.

And thank you Keith XX

If you haven't read
Domestic Bliss and Other Disasters,
Jane Ions' first Sally Forth chronicle,
here's a taster:

Chapter 1 – June

I have two very close friends who I've known for most of my life and I don't get on with either of them. Despite the long years during which we have remained friends, if they and I were stuck in a lift together for thirty-six hours, I am not confident that all three of us would emerge without wounds.

I'm comfortable with this, because a combative togetherness is what we have grown to expect from each other. We don't always see eye to eye, we are more likely to see eye to the back of the other's head, but up until now we have observed the three basic rules which determine whether a friendship will survive. We make an effort to meet up, we don't punish each other by being too successful and, very occasionally, we're honest with each other.

So when Jen told me what she was planning to do, I thought she was crazy, and said so. I said I didn't think she'd be daft enough to agree to it. I tried to make her reconsider, but now it's too late, she's done it.

She is leaving. She has sold the house she loves, and she has left her job at the doctor's surgery which has given us so many curious insights into human nature over the years. She has said goodbye to her treasured garden and her favourite coffee shop, and to me, her closest friend. Why? So that she can move three hundred miles north to be her daughter's child-minder.

When Jen first told me of this plan, I wanted to save her from this surge of self-annihilating maternal instinct. I felt that she was sacrificing herself on an altar to her grandchildren. The plan reminded me of a nature programme I watched years ago. It featured a spider who carried her eggs around on her back until they hatched, and then she lay down and allowed her infants to eat her alive to save them the trouble of looking for food elsewhere. I shouted at the television, 'Get up! Get up and shake them off!' But her infants were chewing at her ears, so she didn't hear me.

Obviously, I needed to be more subtle with Jen. I couldn't suggest to her that she shake her grandchildren off. So I just asked her whether she thought she was doing the right thing by giving everything up to become her grandchildren's child-minder. In my experience, *Are you sure you're doing the right thing?* is a very unsettling question. It engenders a sense of dread. I'm always quite happy with my decisions until someone asks me whether I've made the right ones. Then in an instant my resolve is shaken, I think I've made the wrong decisions, and I'm doomed if I don't change course.

So I asked Jen whether she thought she was making the right decision to move north to provide childcare for her grandchildren, and then I followed that up by saying it sounded like banishment into servitude to me. I said, far be it from me to interfere in a family decision, but I thought this family decision was completely wrong-headed. I said going into exile to be an unpaid child-minder was a terrible idea from her point of view, and she should be fighting it, not embracing it.

Jen understood that my reasons for wanting her to stay put were purely selfish. She knows as well as I do that a friendship built up over more than twenty years is not easily replaced, however dysfunctional it might have turned out to be. It takes years to know someone well enough to tell them they're an idiot. So instead of telling me to butt out and shut up and mind my own business, she said more tactfully that I might be putting a rather negative spin on things. She said it would be wonderful to see more of her grandchildren, of course it would. This could only be a good thing, surely?

I told her that the problem here is not that she will see more of her grandchildren, the problem is that she will see no-one *but* her grandchildren, and how could that possibly be a good thing? I reminded her that she is still young, only fifty. Her own youngest has only just left home. These should be her Prosecco years, not more years of baby formula and disposable nappies and whoops-never-mind-I-didn't-like-that-necklace-anyway. She should be letting her hair down, not tying her hair back to keep it out of the zinc ointment and whatever else might be going on close by.

Jen said she took my point, but she was in a difficult position. Her daughter Emily had suggested the move, telling her that the twins missed her and loved her so much and wanted her to look after them when their mummy and daddy were at work. Emily said she knew how devoted Jen was to her grandchildren, and it would be wonderful if she moved north and they could all be together. Jen didn't think she could then say to her daughter, 'Actually Emily, I think I'll pass on that one if you don't mind.' And so the plan has rolled on to fruition. And now she's gone.

Just before Jen left, but after she was committed to the move, she had a little panic about moving out of the city and living in the country, on the edge of a small town. She said it's probably irrational, but fields make her nervous. She was anxious because for the first time in her life she will not be able to hear the soothing background noise of a big city when she falls asleep at night. She'll miss the planes overhead, the thrum of traffic, car doors slamming shut, intermittent sirens, and voices calling to each other across the street. She said without her metropolitan lullaby it would be too quiet in the country, and too dark at night. She would find it impossible to sleep, tossing and turning in the peace and quiet, missing the orange glow of city lights and having to make do with moonlight. It was as if an umbilical cord she had relied on all her life would suddenly be cut, and she would be set adrift, diminished and diminishing. Uncorked. She would be so far away, with no friends and just her family for company, contemplating the severed end of her umbilical cord and losing substance.

I said I would visit her, and told her she could come back and stay with me whenever she liked. Her chin began to wobble, and it wobbled in a way that was not consistent with great anticipatory joy at being an on-tap grandma.

For her sake if not my own, I tried to think of some positives. I said I'd heard there were roads in the north you could drive on for over an hour without stopping, and there are hills up there with actual points on the top, and you can buy a nice little house and garden without mortgaging your DNA. There's space up there and clean air to breathe, and proper Yorkshire pudding. I said, no matter how far north, I'd come and see her, once she claimed some territory and secured her borders.

She said she would be on the wrong side of the country for proper Yorkshire pudding, but she was looking forward to getting her teeth into some Cumberland sausage. She is going to view a nice little house, perfectly adequate, a fraction of the price of her house down here, and after selling up she now has money in the bank which she plans to be very vague about when talking to her family. She quite liked the idea of living a more simple life, without clutter and surplus possessions to tie her down. I asked her where she would put her collection of thirty-eight china cruet sets. She said she has already sold them on eBay to someone who should have known better, and she hopes they like fannying around with a duster.

So, she left yesterday, we embraced on the pavement and she got into her little Polo and headed off towards the M25. I can hardly believe it, after all the confidences we have shared over the years during our more harmonious exchanges. I am the only other person in the world who knows what her husband used to shout during sex. You have to know someone really well before they tell you that kind of thing. It's not something you would share with a work colleague. If someone tells you that kind of detail about their life you know you are a trusted friend.

Anyway, it's academic now because the poor chap died of a heart attack during a surprise quickie before *Match of the Day*. He managed to shout out, apparently, but Jen said as last words go, his weren't very profound. She certainly couldn't put 'Goal!' on his tombstone.And now Jen has sold up and gone, and left me with her confidences and her pot plants. There's twenty of them in my front garden huddled together in pots of various sizes. They look as if they are hatching a plot to trot off after her.

It will be a while before I see Jen again, so I won't be sitting down with her to talk about Dan. Dan has come home from university with debts and no means to support himself. He is at a loose end. He is ranging about the house picking things up and putting them down again and staring out of the window and asking me what I do all day. It would be great to have him around the house again, if he wasn't giving every impression of having stumbled into the wrong life.

Dan told me last week that his latest plan is to make a living from performance art. I don't like to undermine him but, to be brutally honest, I can't work up any enthusiasm for this performance art career plan. Maybe I lack vision, or faith in miracles, but performance art seems to me to be a precarious career choice, compared to say, training as an accountant. I'm not saying Dan should abandon performance art and train as an accountant, but I had hoped that he might settle on something that would combine both strengths. Although I admit there aren't many performing accountants making a go of it out there.

If I had suspected for a while that he was planning to make a living as a performance artist I would have had time to get into the brace position. But he sprang this idea on me before I could think of a smooth and well-formed response, so my initial response leapt out, ill-formed and covered in verbal spikes. I used words like 'idiotic' and 'stupid' and 'completely mad', words that you should try to avoid in these situations. And now Dan's gone off in a huff. Thinking about it more calmly and with the benefit of hindsight, I should never have said that I have been putting on premenstrual performances for years and no-one has ever paid me a penny.

In truth though, your children should learn to give you warning when they intend to make sudden announcements about their future, then you would have time to buttress yourself against involuntary shrieking. If you had advance warning of them telling you 'I'm going to ride a unicycle around the equator to raise money for orphaned parrots', you might be able to say, 'That's an interesting idea, let's take a moment to consider it,' instead of saying, 'What? Like hell you are! Stuff the bloody parrots!'

It's being caught off guard that's the problem; it can make us sound so unsympathetic. It's the element of surprise we can't cope with, not just the idiotic proposal itself. Years ago, Laura came home from school and said to me, 'Mum, I've told Sarah we'll look after her pet rats when she's on holiday.' I think we were both surprised by my response.

Anyway, Dan has gone off to contemplate my lack of sympathy for his life, leaving me to think about my unsympathetic maternal responses to his plans. Maybe I wasn't very sympathetic but... a career in performance art? Give me strength. Better still, give me his university tuition fees back, if this is where it's got us.

Also, I could do with talking to Jen about Laura. There's something going seriously wrong there. We were so pleased, Jen and I, when Laura got married last year, but now she's had a baby and she keeps ringing me up and asking me why I didn't warn her about what a massive commitment it is to have a child. She says she didn't realise what she was taking on and I should have made it clear to her, warned her. I don't know how much clearer I could have made it, I've done my maternal best for her for twenty-six years – you would have thought she'd got the message that having children isn't exactly a rest cure. Apparently, I should have sat Laura down and explained to her that her life would never be the same again.

Jen and I used to have a bit of a rueful laugh about the belief entertained by most expectant parents that that they will be able to have children and carry on their lives unchanged afterwards. From our perspective, it seemed akin to thinking you could invite a rhinoceros into your home and hardly notice it. But now Jen's left, it doesn't seem quite so amusing.

***

Dan and I had a little heart to heart discussion this morning, or perhaps it was more of a spleen to spleen. He told me, *apropos* of my wake-up-and-smell-the-coffee career advice the other day, that I trample over his dreams. I told him I was having a few nightmares that he might be responsible for. He said the trouble with me was that I had lost my creative energy, my joie de vivre, my sense that anything is possible if you just have the passion to make it happen. He said his driving force was Carpe Diem.

I thanked Dan for pointing out what the trouble with me was, and at the same time I warned him that it was entirely possible to Carpe the wrong Diem. That's the trouble with all these little life-affirming slogans painted on wooden boards in gift shops. The last one of those I saw was in 'Coffee and Toffee' with Jen, and it said, 'All You Need is Love.' She looked at it and said to me, 'Well, that's a lie for a start.' And it is.

Anyway, I had the feeling this morning that Dan was building up to telling me something, so I was readying myself for another hare-brained scheme, but still, when it came it was a shock. He began by saying he needed some independent living space, and at first I thought, oh – he's going to move out, he has somewhere to go, maybe a friend with a spare room. He'd have to pay rent of course, so that would mean getting a proper job. We could be moving in the right direction here, I thought.

But that wasn't it. He wasn't planning to move out and get a proper job, he was planning to construct an extension to our house from recycled materials and live there independently, apart from meal times, which he would share with us. I said, after collecting my thoughts which were bouncing erratically around the room, 'But Dan, you have no experience of building anything. You can't build a shelter just like that, with no experience.'

Apparently, I'm wrong. More than half the world builds rooms and whole houses without any formal training at all. None. Dan explained to me that if mankind had needed an NVQ in Building and Construction to build a shelter, we would only just be moving out of caves. He said the Ancient Egyptians had built the pyramids without an NVQ between them.

I tried to be reasonable. I said I took my hat off to the Ancient Egyptians. I said credit where credit's due, the pyramids are stunning. They are all beautifully proportioned, and every single one of them is the right way up. But things were different then, there were no health and safety regulations, people didn't want windows, and the flat roof hadn't been invented. And then I changed tack because I thought I might be talking rubbish, and I reminded Dan that he always hated his Meccano set. He was always losing the little screws and wanting to use nails.

Dan said this would be nothing like building with Meccano, he would be using recycled materials, crates and plastic bottles and the kind of stuff you see at recycling banks. It would be intimately eco-friendly.

So I said – again too spontaneously – 'My God, Dan, you can't be serious! You might as well go down to the recycling bank and carve out some sort of burrow for yourself and live there like a derelict Hobbit. *Carpe diem*? You need to *carpe* some common sense.'

He said I was mocking his ambition, and I had no faith in his ability to make something beautiful out of rubbish. I told him a building made of rubbish would very likely look like rubbish. Sad, but true. He said it would be the best showcase for his performance art, and I said it would knock £50,000 off the value of our house. There was no meeting of minds. His mind was in the sky, my mind was on the ground. He didn't mind, and I did.

Jen texted me just after dinner, to say How r u doing?

I texted her back, Fine. I've fallen out with Dan over career plans.

But it's good to spork, she texted. She had obviously had a tiring day. Glad you're ok. I'm feeling low. Grandchildren wonderful but v young. Maybe I need a man? Think I do. Lonely here.

Chapter 2 – July

I spoke to Bill last night about Dan's rubbish extension. Bill is Dan's father, and I like him to be fully briefed on all his son's eccentricities. I don't believe in shielding him from his children's bizarre decisions just because he's a very busy man. I tell him as soon as I see him if either of his children plan to do something particularly stupid. So I outlined Dan's plan to build a one-bed studio out of waste products to the side of our house, and Bill said, 'Why not let him do it? If he's adding an annexe made of plastic milk bottles to the side of our house, he won't have time to hang around the pub hoping someone will buy him a drink. Much better to have him working out how to construct a bachelor pad out of the contents of our recycling bins. If it falls down around him, at least it's not likely to be very heavy; he should survive it.'

I thought about it and decided there might be something in that argument. If Dan is building a rubbish annexe, then he's not doing anything worse, and this should be a cause for celebration.

So, I have given Dan the go-ahead to throw rubbish at our house, and he and I are friends again. He asked me this lunchtime if I would collect all our used plastic bottles because he will need them for his window installations. His construction will be called 'Aspire'. It will speak to his generation and say, *Re-Cycle and Build your Life!* Unfortunately though, when it speaks to my generation it will say, *There's a Pile of Crap Stuck to the Side of your House!*

I got my hair done this afternoon. Highlights and a trim. Abbi usually does it, but she was off today because she has accidentally poked herself in the eye with her contact lens, so Denise did it. She looked about the same age as Dan, and we got chatting while she was wasting yards of tin foil putting highlights in my hair.

I asked her if she was living at home still, or if she had a place of her own. She said she was living at home with her parents. I said that's nice, but apparently it's not. She said her parents complain about her all the time. Oh dear, I said, why is that? Thing is, she said, she has to put her earphones in as soon as she gets home from work, so she doesn't have to listen to her mum and dad talking, and she spends as much time as she can in her bedroom on Facebook and Instagram. Well, I said, clutching at straws in what seemed to be a pretty bleak landscape, I expect you all watch a bit of telly together in the evenings? No, she said, she doesn't watch telly hardly at all. Sometimes she takes her dinner upstairs into her room and eats it there.

I looked at her in the mirror and thought she must be a little ray of absolute sunshine to live with, and I felt better about Dan at least talking to me about his plan to live in a pile of rubbish at the side of the house.

When Denise was finished with my hair she asked me if I would like tea or coffee, so sweetly that her mother would have swooned to hear it. I declined politely, because I wasn't quite sure what she might do to it, given that I was the same generation as her parents. So off she went for half an hour, leaving me with my hair all packed away in neat parcels of tin foil, reading a copy of *Hello!* like an extra-terrestrial searching for some meaning to life on Earth.

I rushed off to meet my friend Judith in Marks and Spencer's café after my hair. Judith and I were at school together, I've known her longer than Jen, but we have just started meeting up more regularly again. Judith has three adult children, and they are all, every one, doing extremely well. I try not to let her talk about her children if possible. There's one at Oxford University and one at Cambridge University and another one shitting gold bars somewhere in America. You'd think she'd have the decency not to mention them, but no, as soon as the toasted tea cakes arrived she told me that the one at Cambridge is going to do a PhD in something very clever, Neurofuckingology I think she said, and then she waited for me to be very impressed. She wanted me to say, 'Wow! Neurofuckingology? How amazing! That's so clever! Wow!' But instead I said, 'Shall I pick up a pot of jam to go with these teacakes?'

Judith doesn't give up easily. She ignored the jam query and told me that when her daughter gets this PhD, she'll have a very lucrative future in plastic polymers. I told her to try not to get upset about it, it would probably turn out all right in the end.

Honestly, it does me no good to meet up with Judith. I'm a nice person when we sit down together but, by the time we leave, I'm not. I don't bear her any ill-will, I just wish she didn't exist. We're meeting up again in a fortnight.

Bill's mother is coming to us tomorrow for lunch, so there will be conversation then of a different kind. My mother-in-law usually comes with an agenda of topics she'd like to talk about, and once she's gone through the list she starts again at the beginning. Last time she came, Bill excused himself when she'd gone full circle and begun again, saying this was where he came in.

***

Bill's mother, Ella, comes to us most Sundays for lunch. When she came in today she said that we seemed to have a small shanty town springing up to the side of our house, and what was the problem exactly? I said not to worry, it was a project Dan was involved in. She said good, she was glad he was making himself useful, and the sooner he got the whole lot cleared away, the better.

Dan opened his mouth to say something, but I caught his eye and gave him a look which meant, 'Don't stir this pot Daniel, your grandmother will never approve of any plan to build with recycled packaging materials, however eco-friendly you tell her this is.' It was necessarily a complex look, but Dan understood my meaning, and he didn't say anything. Instead we covered the usual topics over lunch, including all the old favourites. We discussed how difficult it is to get good help in the garden, how lucky you are to have good help in the house, how there is no-one around to help you in the bank, and so on and so forth.

Problems with her high street bank are exercising Ella particularly at the moment. She said she used to go in there and have a chat with the bank tellers, and they all knew her name, and they helped her out if she made a mistake when she had to fill in forms. Her visits were a pleasant experience. But now when she goes to the bank and is confronted with all those machines lining the walls, the atmosphere is hostile. She says she may as well be in an episode of Dr Who. She daren't interact with the machines in case they start flashing and shouting 'Exterminate!' and waving little stalks at her. Dan loved the idea and said if the cash machines did that he would look for a job in a bank.

After lunch Ella likes to reminisce. She asked us if we could remember Lily Cooper, originally from Bolton, who used to keep a horse in the field behind her house in the country. Ella had urgent news concerning Lily, so she pressed us to remember her. We did our best. We racked our brains to remember Lily Cooper. You must remember her, said Ella, you were so fond of her horse. We tried to remember her horse, we tried to recall our fondness for the horse, we tried to visualise the field, the horse, the woman, the horse in the field, the woman on the horse, Bolton, women in general – but we drew a blank.

We confessed, and said we just couldn't remember Lily Cooper, or her horse, or our love for her horse. But tell us about her anyway, we said, it might jog our memory.

‘Well,’ said Ella, ‘she’s dead. Died last Tuesday of a stroke.’

Oh. We looked at each other. That’s that then. We can’t remember her – and now she’s dead. There was a general sense of relief. ‘How’s the horse?’ said Daniel.

I got up to make the coffee, and when I brought it in on a tray, Daniel had gone out somewhere, to see someone about something. Bill thought he would take his coffee upstairs because he had to do some preparation for a meeting tomorrow, if we two ladies didn’t mind. Go ahead, I said, your mum and I will chat over coffee. No problem.

So Ella and I drank our coffee, and I heard about her dizzy spells and her constipation and all the kind of stuff that men can’t be trusted with. We puzzled over that little rash that won’t go away. Ella said it was a shame the rash was on her bottom, because she thought it would benefit from being exposed to some fresh air. After about half an hour Ella asked me if I remembered Jill Robertson. I said – is she dead? She said no, she’s having the outside of her house painted buttermilk yellow.

Oh good. Better news for Jill.

Daniel rang me when Bill was taking his mother home. He doesn’t usually ring when he’s out so I was expecting trouble. ‘Mum,’ he said, ‘I’m bringing a friend round. She’s going to help me with Aspire, but she hasn’t eaten for a few days so I’ve asked her round for the rest of that roast.’

‘Why hasn’t she eaten for a few days?’ I asked him. He said he didn’t know, he hadn’t asked her, and anyway, it was none of our business. I said I thought it was our business if she was going to turn up and eat the rest of our roast.

Anyway, Daniel arrived with Gentle Rain at about ten o’clock, just as Bill and I were going to watch the News.

***

Yes, Dan’s friend is called Gentle Rain. She has long blonde hair and a sweet smile and she came in and said softly, ‘Hello

Daniel's mum, I'm Gentle Rain.' I'd had a glass or so of wine by then and I said, 'Hello Gentle Rain, pleased to meet you. I'm Big Roast Dinner.' Bill laughed but Daniel didn't.

Anyway, both Dan and Gentle Rain tucked in to what was left of the roast, despite Gentle Rain having qualms about eating meat. I had to reassure her that the lamb had been organically farmed and ethically reared and had frolicked all summer long among buttercups and daisies and died of an excess of happiness and a longing to swim in gravy and mint sauce. I don't know whether I convinced her, but her appetite did. She ate everything on her plate.

They slept out under the stars last night in sleeping bags at the side of the house. I said I didn't think that was a very good idea, but Dan said it was.

***

Jen rang me this morning. She said she had caught a stomach bug from Tiffany, one of the twins, but she was looking after Sammy, the other twin, because he was sickening for it now and he couldn't go to Tumble Tots.

I said, 'For heaven's sake Jen, you can't be expected to look after Sammy if you're not well yourself. They're asking too much of you.'

But she changed the subject in that rather annoying way she sometimes does, and said, 'How's Dan?'

So I told her we were letting him build an extension made of rubbish on the side of the house and he was planning to live in it. I said we weren't happy about it but we were hoping it would stop him spending his time in the pub.

I think after that we both reckoned we were quits in the stupidly indulgent stakes, so I asked her whether she still thought she might need a man.

Jen said she did. She said she was lonely, to be honest, despite settling into the bosom of her family. Her family's bosom was lumpy and uncomfortable, it was incompatible with rest and lacking in a civilised wine o'clock routine. Her daughter and son-in-law were frantically busy all the time, her grandchildren were too young to be any use to her. She needed an adult to hang out with in a middle-aged sort of, seen-it-all-before sort of, more-wine-don't-mind-if-I-do sort of way. Preferably a man, of course, preferably rich, well groomed, good fun, short finger nails – and please, no stock of boring stories he simply has to tell. Not that. She has done her stint on that front with her last husband. She has served her time, and these are new days. So, Jen asked me, what could I suggest?

I said join a class. She said what sort of class? I said anything but embroidery or knitting woollen animals – what about art? She said she couldn't draw for toffee. I said perfect, she needs the tuition. She said what if the art class is full of women of a certain age looking for rich men with short fingernails? I said join a French class, there are far more men than women in French classes. She said, really? Is that so? I said yes, everyone knows that, it's something to do with the effect of testosterone on the vocal cords.

Anyway, I think she's got the message. And what is absolutely certain is that she's not going to find a man when she's wiping her grandchildren's bottoms. Jen has wiped her fair share of bottoms, she has had three children of her own. She needs to live a little.

And speaking of going out and living a little, I have a smear test this week.

***

Smear test. You'd think they could give it a better name than that. They weren't trying very hard, when they named that test. Smear test, for goodness sake. It doesn't even sound respectable. It might as well be a grot test or a blot test. Or a smudge test, or a smut test or a scum test. Personally, I'd draw the line at being told I had to turn up at the GPs' surgery for a scum test. If someone offered me a scum test I'd reject it on principle, so why am I trotting along meekly for a smear test? We should rearrange the letters a bit, and see if we can come up with something better. I had a go this morning. If we left out the 'm' and rearranged the letters it would be an arse test, but in terms of aesthetics we're no further forward.

Anyway, the GP was lovely, just a young girl. Not a great sense of humour. She got down to business briskly and efficiently, snapping on her rubber gloves and inserting the vagitron where it needs to be, cranking it open to have a good look around. It's difficult to say anything sensible when you're lying flat on your back while someone peers up your vagina, but you do feel that a little bit of light conversation might help dispel the awkwardness. So, in a desperate bid for levity, I asked her if she ever worried about being pulled in. She looked up and said, 'I'm sorry?'

Obviously, she's not the frivolous type. God knows what she's written in my notes.

I had a bit of shopping to do afterwards, as Dan and Gentle Rain would be wanting something to eat this evening, after a hard day on the rubbish tip. She's a sweet girl, but I don't think Gentle Rain is her real name. I don't think that's the name on her birth certificate. She must have given herself that name. Difficult for me to understand, after the years I have struggled with my own daft name, why anyone would deliberately choose to give themselves such a curious name.

For twenty-two years I was very happy to be Sally Bailey. It was a nice bouncy name, I liked it. Then I married William Forth and from one day to the next I became Sally Forth and sounded like a call to arms. I'm used to it now, of course, but it took a few years. If I'm honest, I think it might have altered my personality slightly. You can't hang back with a name like Sally Forth, that would make you an oxymoron.

On my way back to the car with my shopping a young woman wearing a tabard and carrying a clipboard leapt out at me from a doorway next to H&M and asked me if I'd like to sponsor a cat. I thought I'd misheard her at first, I had to ask, 'Did you say sponsor a cat?' 'Yes,' she said, so I asked her – 'Sponsor a cat to do what?' 'Nothing,' she said, 'you wouldn't be sponsoring it to do anything.'

I couldn't quite get my head around it at first. I told her that when I was a girl, cats just got on with being cats, they didn't require sponsorship. I don't mind sponsoring a cat to climb Everest or swim the Channel, but sponsoring a cat to be a cat seems a bit ridiculous.

The young woman put her hand on my arm. She said if I had five minutes she would tell me about the work they were doing with traumatised cats, and she began by asking me if I had ever had a cat. I suddenly felt very weary, so I gave her fifty pence and told her I had six cats at home and I had to go because they would be missing me terribly. No-one deserves a lecture on traumatised cats after a smear test.

When I got home Laura's car was parked across the drive, so I had to park on the road. Oh dear, unannounced visits from Laura never bode well. She must have something to tell me, and it's unlikely to be something I want to hear.

I've had a bit of a session with Laura. She's a young mother. Her baby, Harry, is only four months old and she's struggling with it a bit. I didn't like to tell her that I'm an older mother with children in their twenties and I'm struggling with it a bit too. So we discussed her struggles as if I didn't have any.

It turns out that it's the commitment of motherhood that is continuing to bother her. Her baby is ruling every aspect of her life. When she wakes up, when she sleeps, when she eats, when she goes to the toilet, when she goes out, when she goes home, when she sees her friends – if she sees her friends.

She asked me if I knew how long it had taken her to get ready to drive the ten miles from her house to mine this afternoon? I said I could imagine it took a bit of organising. She said it did, and it was so difficult now for her just to leave the house. There was so much kit to assemble first – bottles, nappies, creams, wipes, carry cot, change of clothes, favourite toys, (all for the baby, none for her), endless straps to tighten and adjust, fasten and unfasten.

I sympathised. I said I could remember how difficult it was to leave the house with a baby in tow.

But it's so much worse now, said Laura, than it was for me. There's much more equipment now, and more stuff to assemble and take with you when you go out. Most of it hadn't been invented back then, when I squatted down behind a bush to give birth to Laura.

I said yes, that's probably true. Back in the day when I was a young mum and wet nurses were two a penny, we just wrapped the baby in a rabbit skin, threw a firkin of ale into the cart, and hitched it up to the oxen. We were ready to set off for the nearest witch-burning in no time. It was a breeze.

Anyway, sadly, that observation didn't help, so I tried to cheer Laura up by telling her that in fact, for most of the time you have children, they're adults, and then you can leave the house no problem. In fact, coming back to the house is more likely to be a problem, because that's when you have to deal with what they've done to it while you've been away. And on that subject, I suggested she might like to cast her eye over the rubbish metropolis clinging to the side of our house that her brother was responsible for.

At least this took her mind off her own concerns. She said what on earth was I thinking of letting Dan make such a mess? Why didn't I tell him to clear it all away? The neighbours must hate me. She couldn't believe Dan was actually thinking he could live in a pile of rubbish. She would never, ever, allow little Harry to do anything like that to her house. I had to take a firm stand.

I promised her I would. I said I would definitely stand firm. I was trying to calm her down. She was overwrought, poor thing, a combination of not enough sleep and too many hormones and the discovery that her whole life had been hijacked by someone who hadn't even learned to sit up yet. I gave her a soothing cup of tea, but she continued to fret.

What did I mean, she asked me, when I said that most of the time you have children, they're adults? Surely, once a child reaches the age of eighteen, they are responsible for themselves and your responsibility as a parent ends? She certainly wasn't planning to fuss over little Harry once he reached his eighteenth birthday. Once he reached eighteen years old, her job would be finished, and she would be her own woman again, and he would be responsible for himself. Then she asked me if I could make her a couple of chocolate cakes and bring them over next week, and look after Harry for a few hours while she had her hair cut.

I love her more than life itself, but it was such a relief when she packed up little Harry and all his accessories, and went home.

Jen texted me this evening. She said – Trying out tart class tomorrow night. Inside info --Apparently there are men! Some unattached!! Some young enough to have own feet!! How u?

I texted her back – Session with Laura. Motherhood getting her down a bit.

Jen texted – After 4 months?

Me – Just a wobble. Art class? Men with teeth?! Keep me posted. Wear red dress, Scoop neck. Gives you lots of sex apple xx

Such a strange dream last night. I was running up and down a beach next to the sea. I had the children with me. They were growing at the rate of about ten years a minute. Seconds after making sand castles they were teenagers, and then they were looking at a glass boat on the shore. They started shouting against the wind, 'Mum! Dad! We're going to sea in this boat!' 'No!' I said, trying to make myself heard, 'No! It's made of glass!' 'That's okay', they shouted back. 'It'll be fine.' 'It won't!' I was yelling now but they couldn't hear me, 'It won't! It's made of glass! It'll break!' But they jumped in, and paddled out to sea.

Then I saw the oars lying on the sand. They were at sea in a glass boat without oars. 'You've left your oars!' I called after them, frantic. 'You can't steer the boat!' They cupped their hands to their mouths and shouted across the waves to me, 'Don't worry Mum! We don't need oars!' I picked up the oars and crashed into the sea after them, and the water woke me up.

I sat up in bed. My heart was pounding, and I was too hot. Bill woke up, 'Bad dream?' he said.

'Yes,' I said, 'I dreamt Dan and Laura went to sea in a glass boat.'

'Glass boat?' Bill said. 'God. Isn't that bloody typical?' And he turned over and went back to sleep.

I went to sleep too. But it took me a little while.

So I was tired going into school today to help with the lunchtime clubs and do my teaching assistant stint in the afternoon. It's the end of term in less than a week, and the kids are going bonkers. Fortunately, lots of them have decided to take the day off. I saw Tom Jenner, Head of English, and he said he had a full-time supply slot in the English department next term if I was interested.

No fear, I said, I was having time out. Almost twenty years of new initiatives at the beginning of each term was quite enough for the moment, thank you, and if I had to spend another five minutes discussing *To Kill a Mockingbird* I would catch the wretched bird and wring its neck and eat it with chips.

Tom knows I love schools and I can't keep away altogether, but I told him last year I'm not coming back to full-time teaching any time soon, supply or otherwise. There's no other job which requires you to argue with someone about whether or not they need to go to the toilet, and it takes its toll.

So, I went along to the maths department just to help Lee with his sums and generally keep him out of the teacher's hair.

Today we were given what the teacher assured us was a game to play. We were matching numbers with shapes, and it was billed as loads of fun. I got started, and tried to interest Lee in some triangles, but he regarded them with frank loathing. I tried to convince him that this was actually just a game, a bit of fun, and not really maths at all. But Lee pitied me for being the gullible fool that I was. Work which disguises itself as fun is an abomination in Lee's view, he has no respect for it. He said I could play with triangles if I wanted, but personally, he thought triangles were shite.

When I got home, Dan came in from the recycling emporium and said he'd cook dinner. I said, great, and asked him if he would wash his hands first. He said we would be eating in the south wing of Aspire, which was now finished, and I should wear something nice. Gentle Rain was dressing up.

'Right,' I said. 'So how formal is this?'

Dan said it wasn't 'formal', obviously, but a lot of effort was going in to building Aspire, so I should make a corresponding effort on this inaugural social occasion, and wear something appropriate. I said I thought a boiler suit would probably be about right, but Dan said I could do better than that.

I asked Dan what he was planning to wear, and he said he would wear his best jeans, and his 'Fuck Me Sideways' T-shirt. So I knew I'd have to make an effort.

Dan made a vegetable and lentil stew which was approved of by GR. No ingredient ever had legs or a beating heart, so nothing had suffered to provide our meal. It was absolutely safe to eat, if you ignored the fact that the lentils had taken a pounding.

Bill wondered if we should put some ham to it, we had some in the fridge.

I said no, if you're invited out for a meal you don't go trying to improve your hosts' efforts with left-overs you've brought from your fridge at home. He reminded me that we were just stepping outside to eat in a lean-to rubbish burrow resting against the side of our house. I said yes, but even so... Anyway, we took some wine, because we didn't think we'd get through the evening without it.

Aspire seems to be made mainly of crates, plastic sheeting lined with cardboard, and plastic drinks bottles. I didn't look too closely.

I wore my pink acrylic jumper which washes like a rag, and a pair of black jeans. Gentle Rain wore a green silky dress which had one or two tiny holes in it, apparently they were cigarette ash burns. I asked her if she smoked, and she said no, not since her Conversion. I didn't ask, Conversion to What? No sense in looking for trouble.

We ate our stew and Bill made a few enquiries about the prospect of Dan looking for gainful employment, which Dan didn't seem to understand. Gentle Rain talked to me about fulfilment through artistic expression and I offered to sew up the holes in her dress. Dan talked to Bill about the dangers of being consumed by a consumer society. Bill replied with details of Marks and Spencer's retail management graduate programme. We were at a summit meeting in a bunker with no interpreters. We couldn't understand each other, and then it got dark and we couldn't see each other. So we called it a day, and went back into the house carrying our plates and put them in the dishwasher. Dan and GR went off to the pub to meet some friends.

I poured myself the last of the red wine and said to Bill, 'Hang on, why are we letting Dan throw rubbish at our house to keep him out of the pub, if he's going to the pub anyway?'

'Ah yes,' said Bill, 'but he's going at ten o'clock, not six o'clock. And he's living at home, instead of in some sort of squat drinking cheap lager and smoking weed with people who never brush their teeth. The rubbish is worth it,' he said. 'It's a small price to pay. It would be different if Dan was old enough to be a proper adult.'

I said, 'Dan's reached his twenties – how old does he have to be before he's a proper adult?'

Bill said that he saw Dan as somewhere between a child and an adult, still halfway between a boy and a man. An emerging adult. He thought there should be a name for people in this transitional stage, people who won't grow any taller, but who still expect that life will be fair, and that you should always just be yourself, and that Christmas will be fun, and that one day you will win the lottery. 'Daft' would fit the bill.

***

I was beginning to feel quite relaxed about the rubbish annexe, until Susan Forster from next door started banging on my front door late this afternoon to tell me about the rat. She said she'd seen a rat running out of the pile of crates and towards her house. I said – 'A rat Susan? Are you sure it wasn't a squirrel?'

'Of course I'm sure it wasn't a squirrel!' she said. 'Since when did squirrels have long, pencil-thin tails?'

I couldn't remember when squirrels had long pencil-thin tails, so I had to concede that it could have been a rat. Anyway, Susan needed calming down a bit so I asked her in for coffee and a chat to see if I could defuse things. She sat down at my kitchen table and described the rat in some detail, its pointy nose, its whiskers, its long tail. By about five-thirty I was sick of hearing about it, so I gave her a glass of red wine, and miraculously she started to think it might have been a small cat.

I said – 'Funnily enough Susan, I've seen a small brownish cat running about recently which I thought at first was a rat.' That cheered Susan up so much I began to feel bad about it being a bare-faced lie. We got quite merry together in the kitchen once I produced the wine. Susan is much better company after a unit or two of alcohol, or maybe I expect less, but the chemistry works in the right direction. Susan said she hadn't had such a nice glass of red wine since the night after the Brexit vote, and

I said I hadn't had such a nice glass of red wine since squirrels had long pencil-thin tails. We did laugh.

After Susan left, I decided to give Dan and GR a public health lecture on rat infestations the next time I see them.

I thought about Jen when I was filling the dishwasher after dinner. I should have heard from her about the art class. I started to worry about suggesting she wore her red scoop-necked dress for her first art class outing. Maybe I should have advised against it? Jen has a very generous bosom and there might be a lot of bending over at an art class. She might have felt a bit uncomfortable with such a low neckline. I imagined her sitting at her easel, all in red with her magnificent cleavage on display. Oh well – too late now. She'd have looked wonderful, and she would have somewhere to put her paintbrush when she wasn't using it.

***

Jen rang this morning. Very upset. Her art class has been a big disappointment. There were only two men – one was there with his wife, and the other was a train spotter who only painted steam trains and said 'Choo choo' instead of hello and goodbye and told her that his marriage had gone off the rails and hit the buffers.

I hadn't heard Jen so upset for a long time. I think the trauma of the move must have caught up with her, and the whole 'Choo choo' business had unnerved her. She said her marriage hadn't been any great shakes, but she was an optimist. She wanted to have another crack at a relationship before her face melted and her bum slipped all the way down her legs to the back of her knees.

'Look Jen,' I said, 'the answer is staring us in the face here – you have to join an online dating agency.'

She said she didn't know how to do that, and she would feel embarrassed to ask her family, it was just impossible, she wasn't that good on the computer, and her lap top was rubbish. She was close to tears.

I told her I'd help. I said I would find out about it and get her started on a dating website.

She said 'How? How will you find out? You're not that good on the computer either.' She reminded me of the time when I did an online shop and bought six kilos of mushrooms.

I told her to forget the mushrooms. Everyone is allowed one online shopping fiasco and it usually involves mushrooms. Anyway, I said, I would get some advice. I have two young adults hanging around the house, and I could ask them for help. They have to be good for something, and they're bound to know about dating websites. I told her they might even help to write her dating profile.

Jen said she would write her own dating profile, if it came to it, thank you very much. But in the meantime, maybe I could make a few discreet enquiries about dating websites, without giving too much away? Of course, I said. I promised her I'd make some sensitive enquiries and let her know what I managed to suss out.

So, when Dan and GR turned up this evening I told them that Jen was desperate for a man and her only chance of finding one was a dating agency, and I had promised to help because I thought she was going mad with frustration looking after her grandchildren. I said I would need some assistance from them.

Yeah, they said, no problem, they could help with that. Probably tomorrow, because they had to go out soon to see a man about some more crates and possibly some small bales of hay.

I told them about Susan Forster seeing the rat. Gentle Rain got very excited and wanted to put food down for it. She said she'd heard that rats were very intelligent and made excellent pets. A friend of hers doing psychology at university had trained a rat to play *God Save the Queen* on a primitive keyboard. I had to stop her there and say I don't care whether you can train rats to play *Swan Lake* on a primitive nose flute, you must not encourage them onto the premises with food.

GR looked at bit puzzled at my anti-rodent rhetoric, and Dan made the mistake of accusing me of being hysterical. It was a mistake, because nothing is more designed to make me hysterical than someone accusing me of being hysterical. I told Dan that in all the circumstances I was nowhere near hysterical enough. I said if he wanted to see me in proper hysterics he should entice performing rats into my garden and then stick around because he wouldn't be disappointed. Then I told them both that they must not keep food in Aspire, or whatever they were choosing to call it, unless the food was sealed in an air tight container inaccessible to a rat, with or without training in picking locks.

They looked aggrieved, and said they kept Aspire practically as clean as an operating theatre. They wondered if Susan might have been mistaken about the rat sighting. I told them it had taken a very nice glass of red to have any effect on Susan's eyesight, and I didn't want to have to make a habit of it.

They got the message, and they promised they would have loads of advice on dating agencies for Jen in a day or two, if she could just hang on that long.